INTENDED

H. L. Macfarlane

COPYRIGHT

This one is definitely for me.

I'm in love with a fairytale
Even though it hurts.
'Cause I don't care if
I lose my mind,
I'm already cursed.
Fairytale (Alexander Rybak; 2009)

Map of Erath

EQAN
LOPOX
OHUS
ESHIJAN
Eshijan broke off during Great Shift
ATRALIA
IKKOR
APIAS
U THESH FAULT LINE
= forest
ATRALIA
ESHIJAN
Duega mountain (4,000ft before shift, now 1000ft)
volcanoes, formed during shift
Mt. Duega (Mr Silver residence on outskirts)

The Magic of Erath

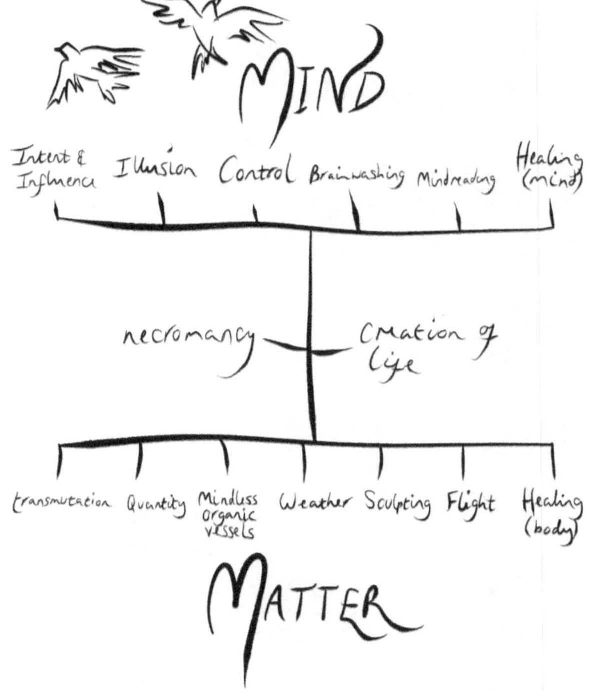

CHAPTER ONE

HE FOUND HER IN THE WOODS.

He always found her in the woods. It was late February, and bitterly cold, but that didn't matter. Whenever Edward Hope could not find his daughter within the boundaries of Mt. Duega, Charlie was invariably in the woods.

"As if she doesn't know she's late," Edward grumbled, knowing that the Alliance would be deeply unhappy with the two of them being late to another meeting. But it was difficult to be angry with Charlie. She never deliberately ran off to annoy her father, after all. She loved the forest which marked the border between Atralia and Eshijan more than anything, and that was all there was to it.

Eshijan hadn't always been their neighbour: fifteen years ago their home country hadn't shared its eastern border with anyone. Where the woods ended the steep coast dropped off into the ocean, stretching on unimpeded for thousands of miles.

But after the Great Shift everything changed.

Eshijan came crashing into the Atralian coast, resulting in a line of dormant volcanoes sprouting north of Duega Mountain. The mountain itself had sunk into the mantle in the process, too, and was now barely more than a hill. Everyone still called it Duega Mountain, anyway.

The meeting Charlie – and, by extension, Edward – was currently late for concerned the lengthy, difficult peace negotiations taking place between both countries on either side of the new border, and the continent of Lopox as a whole. It was not the kind of meeting one was late for.

They were going to be late, anyway.

The sky was grey and overcast; very little light reached beneath the bows of the dark pine trees covering the path Edward carved through the forest. But he knew exactly where Charlie would be so, though he struggled to see in the permanent twilight, his footsteps were steady and sure.

When he was younger Edward had adored the woods that almost completely encircled the town of Mt. Duega. He'd spent his summers fishing and swimming in crystal-clear ponds nestled in amongst the trees. He'd spent winters huddled around bonfire after bonfire in any number of its tiny, hidden clearings, inventing ghost stories with his friends and drinking stolen wine.

He'd met his wife because of the woods and, by extension, gained a daughter because of it. Edward so loved the area that he'd even become the mayor of Mt. Duega at twenty-one after his father passed away.

But Edward was no longer besotted with the woods. It had lost its charm during the Great Shift. Now the trees and everything living beneath them made him uneasy: every sight, every sound, every smell. He was anxious to escape its shadow.

Charlie, however, was a different story entirely. She wandered through the forest every day without fail, eager to discover new nooks and streams and fallen trees she'd had no knowledge of before. Yet no matter how long she spent in there she always ended up in the same clearing at one point or another.

Birch and oak trees surrounded her favourite moss-covered

meadow, marking a drastic change from the evergreens that made up the bulk of the forest. Their bare-boned branches indicated precisely where the Uthesh fault line ran between Atralia and Eshijan but – though being this close to the border during such political unrest would make anyone else uneasy – Charlie did not care.

When Edward finally found his daughter she was singing to the trees, as usual. Winter still firmly had the woods in its grip: the wind bit and stung at Edward's cheeks the moment he set foot in the clearing, and when he inhaled through his nose the air was thick with the scent of deep, unrelenting cold.

But with Charlie's vocal encouragement the meadow was beginning to *grow*. Even now, as Edward watched, Charlie whispered a melody to the mound of dirt she was perched upon, causing fern fronds, blades of grass and the beginnings of bluebells to shoot up all around her. Bluebells, which were not due for another month.

The feeling of Charlie's magic all around softened Edward's heart. She was talented well beyond her years, though nobody could ever know the full extent of what she could do. So father and daughter kept the limits of her magic close to their chests, for if anyone found out...

Charlie's magic would no longer be hers and hers alone, but a commodity for others to control.

"I swear to Uthesh, Charlie," Edward said, announcing his presence to his daughter in the process, "if you're deliberately causing me trouble by being late..."

Charlie turned and stood at the sound of her father's voice, the ghost of a smile on her lips. It was the same smile he himself wore whenever he was trying not to foolishly grin at the wrong time. Her eyes matched his, too: hazel, gold and green all melded together like the glass marbles Edward collected as a child. The colour combination looked astounding when the sun crossed her face; in the dim February light, however, and at the very mention of the Lopox Alliance meeting, Charlie's eyes grew dull and flat.

With an exaggerated sigh Charlie stood up and placed her hands on her hips. "Must we really have another meeting?" she moaned. "This feels like the seventeenth this week."

"It's the fourth," Edward corrected, closing the distance between them to inspect his daughter's dress. It was covered in dirt, torn at the sleeves and made of a fabric which was far too insubstantial for the time of year. But Charlie did not seem to care that she was shivering beneath the cotton and gauze.

One of her mother's old Midsummer dresses, of course, Edward concluded. *As usual.* He tutted aloud. "Could you not have even *tried* to keep yourself clean? We'll have to head back to the house for you to change."

"Why do that when we could simply skip the meeting?"

He snorted before he could stop himself. "Hardly likely. They'll be discussing the watchtower again today."

Charlie sighed again as she cast her gaze over the meadow. "Like every other meeting." For a moment she lingered on the bluebells she'd been working on. They just barely peeked out from the earth, furled buds quivering in the cold February air.

Then, giving her father no warning whatsoever, Charlie thundered through the trees in the direction of Mt. Duega. Edward wasted no time in following her. "Why is it not enough that you don't want the watchtower constructed here?" she complained, not for the first time. "You run the place!"

"Yes, well...if I had the authority to ignore the *entire Lopox Alliance* then that would solve all of our problems. But alas—"

"But alas," Charlie parroted back, visibly frustrated. "What is it you want me to do today?"

Edward knew she wouldn't like his answer. "The usual. Delay construction for a few months."

"Delay it?" Charlie rolled her eyes. "Da, that's what you have me do every time. Why can't I blast the thought from their minds once and for all? Wouldn't that—"

"Doing that would draw too much attention to us. To *you*. If the watchtower were to disappear from the Alliance's plans out of nowhere then the wrong people would grow suspicious. And if they grow suspicious..."

Charlie sighed for the third time. She'd been sighing a lot recently, something which Edward didn't like one bit. Twenty-four long years of experience had taught him that a restless Charlie was the worst Charlie.

"Then they'll realise something – *someone* – is Influencing their decisions," she relented. "Yes, yes, I know."

It was a debate Charlie and her father had circled around on several occasions. Her ability to Influence people's very thoughts and decisions was far more dangerous than her ability to sing growth into living, organic matter. All Charlie had to do was speak a word or two in a particular direction or push her own feelings on a person and the outcome of a vital war meeting or an election for a new head of state would be decided.

Of course Edward had used Charlie's magic to Mt. Duega's advantage over the last fifteen years: she was responsible for preventing further conflicts between Atralia and Eshijan along their new-found border. But the precious years of peace Edward and his daughter had worked so hard for were coming to an end.

War was on the horizon, and they both knew it.

By the time they reached the town hall Edward was out of breath whilst Charlie was markedly unperturbed by their rushed journey. Glumly she picked at the silk shirt and stiff, smoke-coloured trousers her father had forced her to wear for the meeting.

"What's so wrong with me wearing a dress?" she grumbled. "You know I hate trousers. They're so restrictive."

"If you had one made of something more substantial than gauze," Edward muttered, taking a moment to compose himself before easing open the ancient, gnarled oak door that led to the meeting room, "that contained precisely zero holes – and was *clean* – then we could talk about you wearing a dress to official meetings. Jonathan, I'm so sorry we're late!"

Charlie knew better than to continue complaining to her father like a petulant child in front of the Lopox Alliance officials. She didn't want to be in the meeting – never mind the fact she hated her magic being used for politics – but Charlie ultimately knew her father meant well. And, besides, a watchtower being erected in Mt. Duega was not something Charlie personally wanted.

If only her father would allow her to destroy the notion of creating the watchtower once and for all.

Jonathan Crank was clearly irritated by their late arrival. He turned a scowl to Charlie, for it was obvious she was the reason for the delay. She always was. "I do not have time to be sitting around for half an hour waiting for you, Hope," he said. "You know I'm expected back in the Capital this evening."

"I thought that's why you hired that overpaid transport magician as your assistant?" Edward countered, in no mood to hear the man make up false complaints.

Crank did not respond.

The meeting room was largely taken up by a circular table with space enough to seat ten people. Six chairs were currently taken so Edward claimed one of the four vacant ones, with Charlie on his left whilst Crank sat on his right. Just one seat at the table remained unoccupied.

There were eight Alliance officials in total, all representing different magical factions across the continent of Lopox. One representative hailed from Atralia – the southernmost country on the continent – and was the only man not currently present at the table. Charlie hardly bothered to remember his name:

whenever a meeting with the Alliance was centred specifically around Mt. Duega, the responsibility of representing the place fell onto the shoulders of Edward Hope.

And me, Charlie thought, disgruntled. She hated working in politics and was already counting down the minutes until she could return to the woods, but she nonetheless resisted the urge to look out of the window towards the trees. It would take all her effort to concentrate on the meeting in order to work out when to Influence the handful of people who had the power to decide what to do about Eshijan.

"They keep rejecting every draft Charter we give them," one of the representatives complained. "They don't like any of the terms set out for non-magicians."

"But that's their culture," Edward countered, patient in a way Charlie knew very well was carefully practised. "There isn't as much prestige associated with magic as there is in Lopox. Magic is very much for the benefit of everyone in Eshijan."

"Are you suggesting we don't care about those born without magical talent?"

Charlie watched as her father barely avoided bristling at the comment. They both knew fine well that, across most of the continent, non-magical folk were considered expendable – especially in times of war. The magicians made all the weapons, yes, and drafted spells of death and destruction to utilise against opposing forces. But it was the common people who took on the brunt of the labour and almost all the consequences associated with war.

Injury. Disease. Famine. Death.

It was one of many reasons Charlie was desperate to leave the meeting and return to her beloved forest.

"It doesn't seem as if we'll ever get them to agree to join the Alliance as it currently is," Jonathan said. He coughed to clear his throat before continuing. "And we can't change our entire

Charter just to suit a foreign country that, for all intents and purposes, appeared out of nowhere. For all we know another Great Shift will occur and then we'll be rid of them. The best thing we can do is observe our – hopefully temporary – neighbours to see what they do."

And there it was. The watchtower. It was Charlie's time to step in.

"Surely the watchtower would be deemed a first act of war," she said, plastering a disarming smile on her face. She touched her father's arm, and he in turn squeezed her hand. They were a united family front: something the archaic Lopox Alliance very much respected and approved of. Charlie and her father were good, old-fashioned magicians, with a well-known family name behind them who had always served the Alliance well. If Charlie had risen to such a position from a no-name family then her magic would have cast suspicion upon herself long ago.

It amazed Charlie, sometimes, how much thought her father must have put into how best to utilise his daughter's abilities within such parameters.

Another member of the Alliance narrowed his eyes at her. Charlie thought he might have been from Laskey, way up in the north of Lopox, but she didn't care enough to confirm this. "What do you suggest?" he asked, clearly not expecting a plausible solution from her. "That we don't protect our borders? That we don't keep track of what they're doing and merely *hope* that they're doing the same?"

"Mount Duega has been trading with the towns on the Eshijani border for years now without incident," Charlie said, ensuring her words were inflected with the same relaxed and trusting feeling as the smile on her face. "We talk to the traders and they talk back. Eshijan has no intention of starting a war with us. The border is quiet. Whilst I understand the importance of knowing what our neighbours are doing, constructing a watchtower right now could be interpreted in a negative fashion. Why not try another, more *compromising* Charter negotiation before considering the tower again?"

Delay, delay, delay. That was all Charlie had been doing for years now. Delay the tower. Delay cutting back the woods. Delay closing trade routes.

Delay inevitable conflict.

She never truly prevented anything. A flash of anger crossed her mind, though Charlie was quick to contain it before it Influenced the men around her. The last thing she needed was for them to be angry.

It was clear from the faces of the representatives that Charlie had them convinced. Her words on their own would never have held such sway with them, but with magic wound into every syllable they were helpless to contradict her. Collectively they nodded their heads in agreement, murmuring amongst themselves about how sensible the idea was. As if they had come up with it themselves.

It was how they always were.

Charlie allowed her mind to wander as the rest of the meeting pushed forward, no longer interested in what was being said. It would have been easy to redirect their conversations about bullet stockpiling or redistribution of magicians or even Crank's plans for his sixtieth birthday, but Charlie knew her father would never have allowed that.

Eventually her eyes found the window and she gazed into the woods behind the glass, feet itching to escape the oppressive air of the meeting room. Seconds ticked by like hours, and Charlie's eyelids began to droop. It was only when the representatives stood from their seats to shake hands, bow and exchange pleasantries that Charlie finally forced her attention back from the promise of the forest.

One by one the men left, until all who remained in the room were Charlie and her father. Edward smiled, a glint of pride in his eyes. "Good job today, Charlie. It seemed as if you barely had to Influence them at all to get them to listen today. Has your magic truly grown that much in the past year?"

Charlie shrugged. She didn't care.

But it was clear Edward was not satisfied by her response. "You're so talented," he said. Charlie headed out of the meeting room before he could continue, for she felt a very familiar lecture fast approaching. Her father shadowed her every footstep. "You've done a lot for Mt. Duega already. But you could do so much more for Lopox as a whole if you put your mind to it. You—"

"Do we really have to have this discussion again, Da?" Charlie cut in, scowling as she exited the town hall and began traversing the cobbled streets of Mt. Duega towards the woods. "I have no interest in politics. I don't want to be shipped off to the Capital or some country on the other side of Lopox to serve people I don't like for a cause I don't care for. I'm happy where I am."

"But if you just—"

"And where would you be without me in your meetings? What would you do with me on the opposite side of the continent?" She barked out a laugh at the thought. "You'd be hopeless! I'd like to see you do half as well running the town without me."

Edward's temple twitched. "I was doing just fine running the town before you started helping me, you know. But you and I *both* know things are getting worse between the Alliance and Eshijan, and you're not a teenager anymore." He paused for a moment, which Charlie didn't like one bit. A pause always meant her father was about to ask something big of her. Something far bigger than she was ever willing to give.

"Charlie," he said, choosing his words carefully, "when I was your age I had a six-year-old daughter and I'd been running Mt. Duega for three years already. What have you achieved in that same time frame? I'm not asking you to give your whole life over to this conflict. Just a few years, until the issues with Eshijan are sorted out. Jonathan mentioned to me that—"

"Don't you *dare* talk about my future with men like him," Charlie fired back. "My life is my own. I will do with it what I please."

There were only two hours of light left before sunset – when Charlie knew even she would have to give in to the shiver currently coursing through her body and return home – so she was too impatient to finish the conversation with her father properly. Charlie quickened her gait, all but running towards the woods in her haste to reach the trees.

But Edward was not done. Charlie had pushed off her responsibilities one time too many, and he'd had enough. "We're not finished!" he hollered after her, though Charlie resolutely ignored him. "If you would just consider—"

"I'm not moving to the Capital!" Charlie screamed back, not caring that the folk who lived on the outskirts of Mt. Duega had popped their heads out of their doors and windows to see what the commotion was all about. They were used to Edward and his daughter arguing, for it was a regular, often public occurrence. Normally both of them could see the humour in this; today was another matter. "I'm not moving anywhere!"

It was in that moment, when Edward caught up to Charlie beneath the first score of pine trees, that her own words struck an idea in his brain. For Charlie *didn't* need to move halfway across the continent or even to the Capital to have greater Influence than she did now.

The eighth member of the Lopox Alliance lived and worked from his estate on the very edge of Mt. Duega. He spent so much time working on bigger issues that he had entrusted Edward over the years to take over all meetings that specifically involved their shared home, which had worked out perfectly so far.

Now, having taken on the man's responsibilities at the border for twenty years, Daniel Silver owed Edward a favour.

He knew exactly what that favour would be.

"What if you didn't have to leave Mt. Duega?" Edward asked Charlie, voice very quiet.

She crossed her arms, peering at her father in obvious suspicion. "What do you mean I wouldn't have to leave? Just what are you scheming?"

"Mister Silver is looking for a new member to join his central team on his estate," Edward said. "Go and work for him."

It took Charlie a moment to recognise the name. "...the eighth member of the Alliance?"

Her father nodded. "And by far the most distinguished of them all. Charlie, you should see his magic in action. Even *you* would be impressed. There's so much you can learn from him – not just about politics. I swear, you wouldn't regret—"

"I'm not interested."

"Charlotte Hope, this is not a negotiation!" Edward exploded, having finally run out of patience. "You will take the position with Mr Silver whether you like it or not."

Charlie's nonplussed attitude faltered in the face of her father shouting at her. He *never* shouted at her. He never pressured her to do something she didn't want to do – not really. "But—"

"*No,*" Edward cut in, extending to his full height to tower over his daughter. "This is the only deal you're getting. If you refuse then you're no longer welcome under my roof *or* in Mt. Duega. Find someone and somewhere else to burden with your intense desire to do absolutely nothing."

It took Charlie several long, painful seconds to process what her father had just said. And then she panicked. "You can't – you can't mean that!" she cried, though Charlie knew he did. If he'd been lying then Charlie would have been able to sense the Intent behind his words. Yet still she fought her father's decision. "You can't possibly mean that. You can't kick me out. Where else would I go?" She motioned around herself with flailing arms. "This is my *home.*"

Edward could only laugh at his daughter's protests. He'd finally found the leverage he needed to spark a fire in her to work towards a goal that wasn't completely selfish; he wasn't about to give in to her complaints now. "You and I both know I can," he said. "I'm the damn mayor of the town, Charlie. And you should know that I'm not lying. So what will it be? At least try and work for Mr Silver - with my promise that you can do whatever you want after a year—"

"A *year?* Da!"

"One year, yes, and you'll be thankful it isn't longer," Edward warned. "Do this and I'll get off your back about your career. Or you can completely cut yourself off from me, the people of Mt. Duega and your beloved woods. It's your choice."

Charlie wanted to argue. She wanted to run away. She wanted to scream at her father. Then, for the briefest of moments, Charlie felt the weight of her Intent subconsciously reaching towards Edward, urging him to reconsider his threat.

She pulled the magic back immediately, horrified. It was an unspoken rule between father and daughter that Charlie never Influenced him. It was one of her fiercest, most important principles.

And so it was that Charlie gritted her teeth, held back a roar of discontent, and slumped her shoulders in defeat.

Edward grinned. It wasn't often he won against his daughter - almost never, in fact - and this victory was huge.

"Mister Silver it is, then."

Chapter Two

THAT CHARLIE HAD BEEN FORCED AWAKE at the crack of dawn for purposes other than escaping to the woods was almost impossible for her to grasp.

That she was riding in a carriage with her father to start a real job was even more unfathomable.

"I'm not going to clean."

"Of course not."

"And I'm not working in the kitchens, either."

"Naturally."

"And I'm not—"

"Charlie," her father interrupted, voice stern and exasperated in equal measure. "You know perfectly well Mr Silver's central magic team do not perform household tasks."

"But do I really know that, Da? What if they do? And I'm just a *trainee*," Charlie spat out, as if the word disgusted her. "Who knows what he gets his trainees to do to impress him?"

"Daniel Silver is not a monster, Charlie."

Charlie did not look convinced, though Edward reasoned

that the sour curl of her upper lip could just as easily have been the result of a lack of sleep. Upon discovering that she was expected to show up at Mr Silver's estate at nine o'clock sharp Charlie had rebelliously stayed in the woods until the early hours of the morning, despite the bitter cold.

When Edward woke her up at six so she could shower and make herself presentable for her new job, Charlie's rebelliousness had quickly turned to dismay and defeat.

A quick survey of his dour-faced daughter caused Edward to sigh. He had managed to get her into a white blouse, black pencil skirt and smart leather shoes. But Charlie had resolutely refused to don her traditional magician's robes over her clothes – in the Hope family colours of sage green and russet gold – even though she was supposed to wear them for all formal meetings.

That's never stopped her from ignoring protocol before, Edward mused. *It's unlikely I'll ever be able to change her mind about them.*

Still, even without the robes Charlie certainly looked much smarter than she usually did. Whilst her father was an imposing man, broad-shouldered and built like a tank, Charlie Hope was willowy and tall; she suited the clothes Edward had picked out for her well.

She was the very image of her mother, especially with her wild, walnut-coloured hair curling uncontrollably around her shoulders. Charlie's hair was not naturally this way – it was honey-coloured and fell in soft waves, like Edward's – but she had been glamouring it to look like her mother's ever since the Great Shift brought Atralia and Eshijan together.

The day her mother disappeared.

"Could you really not have tied your hair back, Charlie?" Edward complained, when Charlie made no attempt to respond to his previous statement. "Or, even better, braided it?"

Charlie huffed out her chest. "If *not a monster* Daniel Silver fires me for my hair then that's his problem, isn't it? And besides," she muttered, curling a lock of hair around her forefinger, a wistful expression on her face, "you know I like it this way."

Edward was uncomfortable with Charlie so keenly wanting to look like her mother. He wished for her to be her own person, but who was he to tell her to stop? Charlie had been just nine years old when her mother was lost to her. He did not have it in him to ask her to get rid of the glamour.

It was also just about the only Matter magic Charlie was at all capable of doing: Edward knew he'd be a fool to discourage her from practising it.

A sleepy silence lulled between them, Charlie's eyes focused on the view of the woods outside the carriage window whilst Edward observed his daughter. It didn't take him long to notice Charlie wringing her hands in her lap and intermittently crossing her legs before uncrossing them once more.

"You're nervous," Edward said, surprised. "You're never nervous about anything."

Charlie clucked her tongue. "You know I don't like working with other people. And I have to *live* with them, too? I'm worried I'll—"

"We both know you're far too in control of your powers to Influence them by accident," Edward scolded before Charlie could finish complaining. "You've been working with the Alliance officials for years now without incident; Uthesh knows there have been times *I* wished I could Influence them to be quiet. And you've spent just as many nights sleeping in the forest as you have done your own bed – I hardly think living in Silver's estate for a year will be that difficult for you. So what are you actually nervous about?"

A pause. Charlie disliked getting caught in a lie by her father; he was the only one who could see right through her. It meant there was ultimately no point in her disguising how she felt.

"I've never met an immortal human before," Charlie finally admitted, hating the flutter in her stomach that came with saying such a thing aloud.

"Ahh," Edward said, finally understanding. "Daniel Silver the monster, you mean?" He chuckled before he could stop himself, garnering a glare from his daughter. "You've met Immortal Folk in the forest before. So what's bothering you about an immortal human?"

"They're different!" Charlie pointed towards the woods through the window. The sun had properly risen now, basking the tips of thousands of conifers in a pale golden glow. "*They* were born that way. Created immortal - plucked from the very energy of the planet to exist in the shapes granted to them."

"That's very poetic."

"Immortal humans, on the other hand," she continued, ignoring her father's jibe, "have to work to ascend their mortality, and even then they must choose between the life they knew and an entirely alien one that stretches on forever. That must change a person, right? Make them more...detached...from the rest of humanity."

"I don't imagine it *must*," Edward said, wishing to soothe his daughter now he knew her concerns were valid and not, in fact, all that trivial. "It certainly isn't true of Daniel Silver, at least. I've known Silver all my life. He's a good man. He cares about people. *All* people, not just magicians."

"But if it doesn't change you then why haven't *you* ascended, Da? I know you could if you wanted to."

Charlie had brought this up before - usually after a jaunt in the forest spent socialising with the Immortal Folk. He reached out for her hands, squeezing them when Charlie dutifully gave them to him. "You know why. I'd rather live my life in the span of a few decades - make every moment count - than to have it stretch on forever until—"

"Until life has lost all meaning and the mere mortals existing around you no longer matter?"

Edward had to give Charlie that. He couldn't even refute it. "Point taken. But Silver isn't like that. You'll...like him."

"That pause makes me feel like you're not so sure about that."

"I guess that's up to you to find out." A rumbling beneath the carriage and the slowing of wheels alerted both Edward and Charlie to the fact they'd reached their destination. He let go of his daughter's hands and stood up, stooping low to avoid the ceiling of the carriage. "Come on," he said. "Up and out. That's us here."

But Charlie made no move to get up, even when the carriage came to a halt and Edward opened the door for her. She merely stared at her father, hazel eyes uncharacteristically troubled. "...you didn't tell him what I can do, did you?"

Edward softened at the question. He gave Charlie a reassuring smile. "That's your secret to tell, not mine."

"Good. That's good." She was visibly relieved by her father's confirmation. "I don't want anyone to know, not even him."

This impressed Edward. It was clear his daughter was precisely aware of how dangerous her magic was – of how risky it was for anyone to merely *know* of its existence within her – even if she constantly pretended like she didn't care about her skills in the slightest.

"Then nobody will know," he said. And then, his smile turning to a doubtful smirk: "You'll just have to impress them all some other way."

"Oh, great. Can't we turn around and leave, Da? I promise I will never take my role in the annoying Alliance meetings lightly ever—"

"Not a chance. Out."

And so it was that Edward Hope and his daughter exited their magic-drawn carriage upon the extensive, paved courtyard in front of Daniel Silver's estate. Charlie stared at the building she was faced with, constructed entirely from smooth, spotless, pale grey stones, and was momentarily stunned to silence.

For though the building was only two storeys high – with a sloping, tiled roof and pewter windowsills – and lacked the turrets or towers Charlie had expected to see for a man of Daniel Silver's stature and wealth, the house was nonetheless impressive due to its sheer size.

The only grand features were the wrought-iron double doors that led into the place, inlaid with illustrations and scroll work which glinted silver in the morning light. Charlie could not discern from her position in the courtyard what the drawings depicted and consigned herself to check them out as soon as she had a chance.

Charlie turned on the spot to make sure that she was, in fact, still right on the border of the Mt. Duega section of the woods, convinced that the carriage had taken them through some kind of magic portal to another place entirely.

"How have I never come upon this place before?" Charlie wondered aloud, all nervousness forgotten in the face of curiosity. She walked towards the enormous building then ran along its façade, stopping when she reached the right-hand corner to peek around it. "It goes so far back! This place is gigantic!"

"It's built in the shape of a squared-off horseshoe," Edward explained, amused by Charlie's excitement. "There's a courtyard in the middle which extends into the rest of the grounds and, then, the woods. It's really quite a beautiful estate. You'll love the gardens."

Charlie stared at her father, mouth hanging open as she walked back to his side. "Do the woods *surround* this place?"

He nodded. "Why is that such a surprise?"

"Because I thought I knew every inch of the forest!"

"I would be more surprised if you'd come upon this place before, Miss Hope, given that my estate is cast entirely in protective magic."

Charlie froze at the unfamiliar voice, all previous frivolity and wonder quashed in a second. For there, standing in the middle of the now-open scroll work doors, stood a man who could only be Daniel Silver.

The man was tall – taller even than Charlie's father – and had a manner to him which Charlie could only describe as aloof. When he walked down the front steps of his estate to greet them Charlie noted his appearance first and foremost before risking digging beneath the surface.

Dark, fitted trousers were paired with pointed-toe shoes. An immaculate magician's coat as silver as his surname was buttoned all the way up to the column of his throat. His blonde hair was tied back at the nape of his neck with a few artful strands framing his face. And...

Glasses? Charlie was taken aback by the presence of wire-framed, circular lenses perched upon the man's nose. *Magicians never wear glasses. Poor sight is so easily fixed. Which means that him wearing them is deliberate. Do they even have a prescription? Is it pure vanity?*

Such unimportant thoughts filled Charlie's head, distracting her from probing into the man's mind and Intent. But her faraway gaze went unnoticed; Daniel Silver had already transferred his bemused attentions to her father.

"Edward," he said. "You owe me enormously for this."

"Then consider me glad I had such a big favour due of you in the first place." The two of them shook hands and, when her father smiled, there was no falseness behind it. This was shocking to Charlie – there was always a practised falseness when

Edward smiled for the rest of the Alliance.

He actually likes this man, Charlie realised. Ordinarily that would be enough for her to let her guard down around a person.

But not today.

"Unfortunately I can't dawdle," Edward said, which was the first time Charlie was hearing about it. "I have a town meeting to prepare for. Charlie's – ah, someone's already taken her belongings in."

It was true; a servant dressed in white had appeared out of nowhere and was now taking Charlie's two suitcases inside.

She turned to her father, stomach sick with unease. "Da! You can't—"

"You're a big girl, Charlie," he scolded. "You know how busy I am these days. And I'll be back in two weeks! You'll hardly have time to miss me." He looked at Daniel Silver. "We're still meeting then, yes?"

Silver nodded in affirmation.

"Then I best be off." Edward pulled his daughter in for a tight embrace, though she was too numb by his sudden departure to reciprocate. "Be good and *behave yourself,*" he whispered into Charlie's ear.

"If he deserves it," Charlie muttered, which earned her a scornful look from her father when he broke their hug.

"Charlie—"

"I know, I know. I love you, Da."

"I love you too. See you in two weeks."

And with that Edward Hope stepped back into the magic-drawn carriage, waving to Charlie through the window until he reached the end of the road and she could no longer discern his figure.

A long silence stretched out, then, save for the twittering of a handful of morning birds which remained in Mt. Duega for the winter. Charlie tuned into the sound, breathing in the crisp air in an effort to reassure herself that she was not all that far from home – not really. She was still surrounded by her beloved woods. It *sounded* like her woods. It *smelled* like her woods.

Daniel Silver was staring straight at her.

Charlie flinched, then hated herself for doing so. The last thing she needed was for the man to think she was intimidated by him, though in truth she was. So when he beckoned with a finger for her to come closer Charlie bit back her nerves and walked towards him.

I feel like he's trying to work me out in one fell swoop, she mused, when Silver's gaze swept from her feet to her head, back down again, then settled on her eyes. For a moment Charlie genuinely believed that he *could* get her measure so quickly, and pushed out her Influence on instinct in order to direct him elsewhere.

But before the tendril of magic could reach Silver, Charlie coiled it back in. Her father would hate it if she Influenced her new employer – and she agreed with him. *It will only make my life harder,* she concluded. *I'd have to keep my magic active at all times to stop him from realising someone is working it upon him in the first place.*

For Charlie had no doubts left in her mind about just how powerful Daniel Silver was now that she was finally in close proximity to him. Her father hadn't lied; the raw magic emanating off him was staggering. The urge to Influence him returned, just for a moment, when Charlie's curiosity over how much of her own magic she'd have to use to break through Silver's defences overwhelmed her.

Once more Charlie had to reign herself in. *Focus on something else. Like his glasses. They're definitely prescription,* she thought, tilting her head to see the slight distortion the lenses caused to Silver's face.

"Just what is it that you're thinking, Miss Hope?" the man asked, noting where Charlie's attention was with passive interest.

"That a magician as strong as you shouldn't be wearing glasses."

"Coming from a young woman who didn't deem it necessary to brush her hair nor tuck in her shirt for her first day at a new job?"

Both quips left their respective tongues in close succession of each other, leaving Charlie in no doubt what the man's first impression of her was. *So he's obsessed with image,* she concluded, glancing down to see that her shirt was indeed untucked. She made no attempt to fix it nor to tidy her hair, which was always unkempt when Charlie left it unbound.

Her decision not to tidy herself up was clearly noted by Silver. His nose wrinkled in distaste, causing his glasses to slide downwards. When he pushed then back up Charlie couldn't help but say, "That wouldn't happen if you fixed your eyesight."

"My personal preferences aren't of your concern. Are you always this rude upon meeting people for the first time?"

"Rude?" Charlie blinked her eyes innocently. "I'm merely making an observation."

"Yes, with the intent of being rude."

Oh, you have no idea, she thought, resisting the urge to say something else that would most definitely be construed as such. Instead, Charlie crossed her arms over her chest and attempted to stare down her new employer. When he remained silent she asked, "So where am I staying, anyway? Or are we going to stand out here all day?"

In lieu of answering her question Silver took a step towards her and mirrored Charlie's crossed arms. Another frown furrowed his brow, causing his glasses to slip once more.

Behind the lenses Charlie noted his eyes were very, very blue.

"Are you a Mind or Matter magician?" Silver demanded, clearly discomfited by the fact he hadn't been able to work it out yet.

Charlie resisted the urge to smile at this invisible victory, then replied honestly, "I'm useless with Matter."

"Mind, then. Any specific strengths?"

"I don't know. I guess you'll have to find out for your—"

"Miss Hope, I'm warning you. I don't have the patience to deal with this attitude of yours."

"I guess you'll have to fire me, then."

For the briefest of moments Charlie was certain that Silver was about to explode. His temple twitched, and his hands gripped his forearms with tense, barely-constrained irritation. She prepared herself for a shout. A curse. An immediate dismissal.

Instead Silver closed his eyes, exhaled, then turned back towards his expansive house. "Uthesh give me strength, I understand exactly what you're doing. Follow me, Miss Hope."

Well that didn't work out the way I wanted it to, Charlie sulked, nonetheless dutifully following Mr Silver into his abode. *I suppose Da would never forgive me if I deliberately got myself fired.*

The man strode far too quickly through his house for Charlie to make out much of her surroundings, but since the morning sunlight hadn't reached the corridors yet she knew it was pointless to try and memorise the layout, anyway. When a tawny cat leapt from a shadowy windowsill into Silver's arms moments later Charlie jumped in fright.

But then Mr Silver smiled, and all she could focus on was him.

Gone was his detached demeanour and barely-contained temper. Faint lines creased the sides of his eyes, which lit up at the mere sight of the animal. He looked happy. Normal.

Like a mortal human being, not a man who was going to live forever.

"Kit," Silver said to the cat, scratching its chin before bopping its forehead with his own. "Just where have you been hiding all these weeks?"

The cat – Kit – mewed in response before turning its impossibly green eyes on Charlie. She took a small step back in shock.

It's from the woods. Daniel Silver is friends with an animal kin of the Immortal Folk?

Charlie supposed she shouldn't be surprised. Silver's estate was right on the boundary of Duega woods and he was immortal himself. It *shouldn't* have been a surprise.

Except that it was.

Never in all her twenty-four years had Charlie known another soul who fraternised with creatures from the woods.

When Kit meowed at her Charlie was brought starkly back into the present. Silver was staring at her staring at his cat, who jumped from his arms to slink down the corridor. Charlie turned her head to watch Kit leave until he disappeared around a corner.

"Miss Hope."

"Yes?" she murmured, attention still on the tawny forest cat.

"In here," Silver said, opening a door on his left and indicating inside when Charlie finally focused on him once more. All signs of his previous easy smile were gone.

Numbly Charlie entered the room, careful to give Mr Silver a wide berth as she did so. Her Influence magic was exacerbated by close contact; for years now she had barely touched another soul, save her father.

Inside the room was sparsely furnished with high-quality, oak-carved pieces: a high-backed bed, a wardrobe, a chest of drawers, a desk, a full-length mirror and a chair.

"My Chief-of-Staff will deal with you shortly," Silver said when Charlie perched upon the bed, testing the spring of the mattress with splayed fingers. "Don't treat her with the same disrespect you have thus far shown me."

Charlie clucked her tongue, keeping her eyes averted as she muttered, "I wouldn't dream of it."

The shudder of the door not-quite-slamming closed was all the reply Charlie got. But when she strained her ears she just barely heard Silver lament, "Just what have I agreed to?"

She threw herself onto her back with a smile. Silver may have worked out that she was trying to get fired but that didn't mean he *wouldn't* fire her.

After all, if Charlie was the most incompetent employee Daniel Silver had ever taken on then he'd have no choice but to dismiss her...or risk the wrath of his political sponsors who had all so desperately wished to have their children taken under the man's wing.

A small, mischievous laugh left Charlie's lips. "I give him a week."

CHAPTER THREE

CHARLIE HOPED TO AVOID CRIMSON CATCHING her sneaking into the gardens but, as with the previous seven mornings, no such hope was to be found.

She had not, in fact, been fired one week into the job.

"How many times must I tell you this, Miss Hope?" the Chief-of-Staff admonished, seemingly appearing out of thin air to stand sentry by the servant's door out of Daniel Silver's estate. "If you're up at dawn then you're working from dawn. So don't even think about gallivanting into the gardens."

Charlie made no attempt to hide the scowl that darkened her face. Silver's Eshijani-born Chief-of-Staff seemed intent on working Charlie every hour of the day so that she had no choice but to fall into bed, exhausted, straight after dinner. Perhaps this was to stop her from trying to run out to the woods so early every morning. Perhaps it was to stop her from attempting to run out to the woods in the *evening*, instead.

Whatever the reason, for the last week all Charlie had been doing was working under the direct supervision of Crimson.

And she was terrible at it.

"Why can't I have just one morning to myself?" Charlie

grumbled as she followed Crimson towards the room she'd spent most of her working hours in thus far. It was surrounded by glass on three sides and looked out onto the as-yet unexplored courtyard and the woods beyond.

Taunting Charlie. Waving her lack of freedom in her face.

She fell into a chair and resisted the urge to curse when the Chief-of-Staff pushed a stack of paper towards her.

"Because then you'll cause trouble," Crimson said simply, answering her question whilst taking another stack of paper for herself. She held up the top sheet for Charlie to see. It was a single-page flyer detailing temporary restrictions on trade along the length of the Atralia-Eshijan border. "Duplicate the information from this flyer onto every blank sheet of paper."

Charlie wanted to complain, not least because she hated the message she had to duplicate. For coming to work for Daniel Silver had made one thing clear above all else: her work Influencing the Lopox Alliance officials didn't do all that much in the grand scheme of things.

This must be why Da wanted me to set my sights higher, Charlie thought, glumly taking the flyer in hand to review its contents. She didn't want to admit that her father was right. She didn't *want* to work in politics, even if it was for a cause she cared about.

But at least Silver and his team were against the impending war. Charlie wouldn't have lasted a single week if that were not the case. *Da wouldn't have made me work for him if Silver was pro-war, either. He—*

"Pay attention!"

"*Ack!*" Charlie cried, deep blue ink leeching slowly but surely into her fingertips even as she watched. The sheet of paper below her hands was dripping with the stuff.

With a flick of her wrist Crimson magicked the ink away. "Try it again," she instructed. "Stop letting your mind drift and *concentrate.*"

"That's easy for you to say," Charlie couldn't help but retort. "Your speciality is duplication magic."

"And?" Crimson raised a sharp eyebrow. "Do you think that's the only magic I'm capable of?"

"...no?"

"Exactly. Just because it isn't *your* speciality doesn't mean you can't do with improving upon it. Try again."

"But—"

"No 'buts', Miss Hope. Try again."

With a sigh Charlie attempted to force her attention back onto the flyer in her hands. She knew how to duplicate physical matter...in principle. Her father could do it. Hell, half the people in Mt. Duega could do it if they were even vaguely magically-inclined.

But Charlie Hope could not. For her it was like trying to speak a language she had only ever heard uttered aloud once.

Invariably her attention began to wander once more after a minute or so of unsuccessful duplication attempts, eyes focusing on Crimson's hair as she got to work on her own flyers. It flashed in the artificial light emitted from a crystal lamp set in the ceiling, as fiery and imposing as her name.

Her hair was, in fact, how she came to be called Crimson. Back in Eshijan before her powers manifested the woman had been called Wei, and her hair had been as black as night. But when she first created fire Wei's hair transformed: body parts sometimes changed when powerful magicians came into their abilities.

In another world Wei might have been an elemental magician. She was incredibly gifted with Matter magic, after all. But her grandfather was a prominent politician so, when the Great Shift brought Eshijan and Atralia together, Wei was sent to the border to act as diplomat between the two countries.

Two years later she began working for Daniel Silver, and had been acting as his Chief-of-Staff for the last seven.

Charlie learnt all of this in the course of a single day. After that Crimson refused to answer her questions when it became apparent Charlie talked and talked and talked in order to avoid doing any work whatsoever.

So now Charlie's days were filled with criticisms, cold shoulders and absolutely no joy to speak of.

Once the sun was fully up the door to the glass room opened, alerting Crimson and Charlie to the fact they were no longer alone. *Imagine if I had simply stayed in bed instead of trying to leave for the woods again,* Charlie glowered as she watched the other two members of Daniel Silver's central team walk in, fresh-faced and eager to get on with the day's work.

But then Mr Silver himself followed them through, and Charlie was quick to pull her anger back in.

The man had appeared in front of her only twice during the past week, for he had been away on a business trip for several days. Though he spoke not a word to her on both occasions Charlie had felt the weight of his judgemental stare crushing her down right in front of him.

He knew she was useless.

It was clear he was waiting for more.

Don't wait for more, Charlie thought, averting her eyes when Mr Silver's gaze fell on her before taking a seat beside Jean, his personal relations magician. *Give up looking for something in me. Deem me useless and send me home.*

It was with some relief that Mr Silver didn't linger his attentions for very long on Charlie. He and Jean had a month of visits across Atralia – and the continent of Lopox as a whole – to organise.

Charlie was shocked when she first discovered that Silver did not, in fact, go to every conference and meeting he was expected to attend in person. More than half of them he attended via controlled illusions, which were maintained by Jean.

I suppose he couldn't possibly attend all of them and still manage to get some sleep, Charlie mused, trying and failing once more to focus on her own work. *Crank is cantankerous enough and he has a travel magician transporting him from location to location!*

Though Mr Silver himself had been absent for much of the week Charlie had been working non-stop with the other two members of his central magic team. It had taken her less than one morning to get both of their measures.

She sneaked a glance at Jean when he produced a palm-sized illusion of Mr Silver, a frown of concentration furrowing his brow as he made the illusion move its arms. The man was perhaps three or four years older than Charlie herself, with expertly slicked-back silver hair, silver eyes and flashy clothes to match. It was clear he sought to emulate his boss' name with all of his fashion decisions.

Jean had not said all that much to Charlie so far, though she sensed his physical attraction to her within seconds of meeting him. But he had been quick to dismiss both his attraction and Charlie as a whole when her magical ineptitude became apparent.

The other member of the team, Luca, was a young woman of an age with Charlie. Short and stocky, with green eyes and long, lovely auburn hair, Luca had no doubt been gifted a boy's name for being the first-born child in her family, just like Charlie.

Not that Luca had told her this herself. She had made her dislike of Charlie obvious from day one, quashing her hopes that, perhaps in Luca, she might have made some kind of friend.

Between Luca's quiet dislike, Jean's quiet apathy and Crimson's quiet disappointment, Charlie was beginning to discover that being terrible at her job was absolutely no fun at all.

Charlie was bored. Charlie was lonely. Charlie wanted to be in the woods.

She almost missed Daniel Silver's barbed comments, which he had seemed incapable of suppressing the moment he met her. She almost—

"What are you doing, Miss Hope?!" Silver cried, startling Charlie back to the present.

"Huh?" She stared at Silver as if it were obvious. "Trying to duplicate the flyers."

"Trying, perhaps, but all you're succeeding in doing is wasting time and magic. How in the name of Uthesh did you manage to destroy the message from the flyer so completely?"

Looking down at the paper in her hands Charlie realised he was right. She had managed to duplicate something – which was better than the mess she had created earlier, to be sure – but it wasn't the entire message from the original flyer.

No, it was merely the first line, over and over and over again.

"Crimson, I told you Miss Hope had no capacity for Matter magic," Silver said, directing his irritation at his Chief-of-Staff. "So how is that she's been put in charge of quantitative tasks?"

Crimson waved a dismissive hand and a stack of perfectly replicated flyers appeared in front of her boss. "Not in charge. I was simply keeping her out of trouble."

This only served to further frustrate Silver. "I did not hire Miss Hope for you to have her work on pointless tasks!"

"What else would you have me do with her? She's useless at everything."

Wow, she certainly doesn't soften her words, Charlie mused, more impressed than annoyed at Crimson's criticism. She was correct, after all.

But the woman's explanation simply would not do for Daniel

Silver. Abandoning the illusion he was helping Jean construct he moved over to Charlie's side and magicked her useless flyers into oblivion. Only by flinching away at the last moment did Charlie avoid the man's hand touching her own.

"It's only paper," she grumbled. "It's not as if I ruined something valuable. Like *bullets.*" Charlie spat the last word out; it hadn't taken her long to figure out why Crimson had been encouraged to develop her duplication magic. For though Silver was against a war with Eshijan that didn't prevent him from having to listen to majority rulings from the Alliance, which included creating, duplicating and stockpiling ammunition. Charlie would know.

She'd listened to Jonathan Crank discuss the matter at length on numerous occasions.

Silver chuckled humourlessly. "Uthesh forbid we let you close to a bullet, Miss Hope. And you know how I feel about using magic for such reasons; there's no need to take that dour tone with me."

But then he frowned. When *had* Silver told Charlie how he felt regarding using magic to duplicate ammunition?

With a start Charlie realised she was Influencing him, and in a flustered panic dragged her Intent back. *This is bad, bad, bad,* she thought, helpless to do nothing but watch the man puzzle over his confusion.

Then the moment passed, Silver's expression smoothed out, and he said, "If you're set on improving your abysmal Matter magic then watch Crimson until you get your duplications *correct.* Otherwise assist Luca."

The glare Luca sent Charlie's way told her very much not to bother her.

"I'll work with Crimson," Charlie said, eyes downcast.

Only after Silver returned to his work with Jean – whom Charlie could sense was infuriated with her for having taken

Silver's attention away from him – did Charlie dare to thank her lucky stars that her Influence had not been identified.

If Silver wasn't so against the war then he might have realised my feelings didn't belong to him once my magic wore off...which wouldn't be long, since it's him.

The fact the man had noticed something wasn't quite right when Charlie's magic was in the process of working deeply unnerved her. She wasn't used to it being detected. But since it wasn't intentional the Influence she exerted hadn't been especially strong; had Charlie deliberately used her magic she was sure even Daniel Silver wouldn't have had a clue what was going on.

That her exerting her Influence *wasn't intentional* unnerved Charlie even more than almost getting caught.

The day dragged on and on with no end in sight; by the time Crimson gave Charlie permission to finish up for the day she was tense and tired and desperate to run off from everyone. So she bolted from the group without a single word of good-bye, disgusted with herself when her eyes began to sting with tears.

"Why am I *upset?*" Charlie sniffed, making a beeline for her room with the intention of hiding under her duvet and not showing up for dinner that night.

When she reached her destination Charlie threw her bedroom door open with all the delicacy of an elephant. But when she noticed a tawny cat sitting on her bed, waiting for her, Charlie closed the door behind her as gently as she possibly could.

"What are you doing in here?" she asked the cat, sitting down beside the animal and allowing it to paw her leg. "It's Kit, right? Kit the cat? Did Silver name you?" She chuckled softly. "It's so unoriginal it's almost funny."

Kit mewed in response, then nudged Charlie's hand until she stroked his head. She was only too eager for the affection –

and the contact – after a week of nothing but admonishments and silence. It helped settle Charlie's heart; after a mere minute of attention from the cat she felt her unshed tears disappear completely.

When Charlie curled up on the bed Kit settled in the crook of her elbow, content to doze alongside her. But after an hour or two a gnawing hunger in Charlie's stomach prevented her from doing much else but think about food.

She roused the cat from his slumber; he let out a gargantuan yawn and stretched his spine before sitting up to look at her expectantly. Charlie noted he had a long scar crawling across the length of his shoulder blades to his tail, and for a moment wondered how in the world a cat managed to injure itself in such a way.

Her stomach grumbling pushed the thought aside.

"Want to sneak into the kitchen with me?" Charlie asked Kit. He merely stared unblinkingly up at her, then in one swift movement jumped down to the floor.

Happy that she had a partner-in-crime, Charlie slowly opened her bedroom door and padded down the corridor once she was sure nobody was around. She hadn't yet been given the opportunity to explore Mr Silver's expansive house but she did, at least, know how to reach the kitchen in the servant's quarters.

When Kit leapt up to the windowsill directly outside the kitchen and tapped his nose against the glass Charlie slumped her shoulders in disappointment. "Is this where we say good-bye? I guess you need me to open that, right?"

It was silly of me to think Silver's cat would keep me company all night, Charlie mused as she carefully unlatched the large, double-paned window. *How pathetic of me to crave a cat's company, anyway!*

But though Kit jumped through the open window onto the shadowy grass of the courtyard outside, he made no effort to go anywhere. He mewed at Charlie, turned his gaze towards the direction of the woods, then looked at her once more. His vivid green eyes flashed impossibly bright against the darkness all around him.

Charlie cottoned onto his meaning immediately. Glancing behind her to ensure nobody had been following them, she nimbly manoeuvred over the windowsill and closed it shut behind her without locking it.

A giddy feeling in her stomach that had entirely nothing to do with missing dinner caused her lips to slide into a smile. The air outside was cold, and there was a breeze that caused Charlie to shiver even as she stood there, but it was a dry night with clear skies.

Perfect for an evening beneath the trees.

"What trouble do you think we can get up to tonight, Kit?" she asked the cat, eagerly breaking into a run when he began bounding away towards the woods.

For the first time since moving into Daniel Silver's estate Charlie felt like herself once more. *I am not made for politics,* she thought when she reached the first line of trees. She breathed in the scent of pine needles, winter earth and the vague promise of spring upon the air, relishing every ounce of it. *I belong here.*

If she could spend her evenings beneath her beloved trees, Charlie thought that maybe – just maybe – she could struggle through a torturous year working for Mr Silver and prove to her father that she simply wasn't fit for such a job.

She pushed the niggling feeling that he would be disappointed in her deep, deep down; by the time Charlie lost sight of Mr Silver's estate she forgot the notion entirely.

CHAPTER FOUR

CHARLIE HOPE HAD CREPT BACK INTO Daniel's house just before
the crack of dawn four days in a row. The protection spells he'd
cast on his entire estate alerted him to her sneaking through a
window near the kitchen each and every time, rousing him from
sleep and putting him in a foul mood for the rest of the day.

Today, on the fifth morning, Daniel was ready and waiting to
interrogate the young woman about her odd routine.

It wasn't that he was interested in what Charlie was doing. Or,
at least, that wasn't his primary reason for confronting her. No,
all Daniel wanted was to warn Charlie to cease her nightly
activities so he could get some blessed peace and quiet...or face
the consequences.

Even so, Daniel felt inordinately foolish waiting, hidden, in
the shadows of the kitchen for the tell-tale alert that Charlie was
making her way back into his abode.

He closed his eyes, shifting his glasses so he could rub at his
brow. *For all I know,* Daniel mused, stifling a yawn as he did so,
*Charlie will interpret me telling her to stop as some kind of
challenge to keep disappearing. She definitely seems the type.*

Daniel did not manage to swallow back a second yawn, and

he considered giving up on his fool's errand in order to grab another hour or two of sleep. A moment later, however, the smallest magical disturbance in the air alerted him to the fact that something was not quite as it had been.

Opening his eyes Daniel confirmed that Charlie was nowhere to be seen yet; someone or something else had caused the disturbance.

"So you're following the mayor of Mt. Duega's daughter around? Interesting indeed."

"Unusual for you to be so bold as to revert forms where someone might see you, Kit," Daniel murmured. "And no, it is not interesting. It's *inconvenient* at best." He cast a sidelong glance through slitted eyes at the source of the voice, unsurprised to see the true form of his cat.

Kit sat with his lithe, willowy frame extended carelessly across the windowsill above the kitchen sink, though the dawn-dark glass behind him was not open to have let him in. His russet hair seemed to gently blow in an imaginary breeze, his gaze carefully tracking Daniel's expression as the two of them sized each other up.

Kit's eyes were the same impossible, vibrant green that they were in his cat form, only now they matched his strangely inhuman face. It was the slant of Kit's ears and those flashing eyes of his that were a dead giveaway for what he really was: one of the Immortal Folk of the forest. A Drus.

That he was also Daniel Silver's cat was a secret known to nobody but Daniel himself.

"It's amusing to see you so rattled," Kit said, eyes glinting at the thought. "This is certainly a significant development in your life, Daniel. Things have been boring around here lately."

"Oh, so impending war is boring to you?"

"Between humans, yes." Kit ran a hand through his tousled hair to sweep it from his face. He yawned, then stretched out his spine in an absurdly feline way. "Oh, what I wouldn't give for it to be summer already! Or spring, even. I'd settle for spring. Anything but this cold, grey *nothingness.*"

"Is that what you were doing in the woods before Miss Hope began working for me, then? Waiting for spring?" Daniel was genuinely curious as to what his friend had been up to. "I hadn't seen you in almost two months. It isn't like you to be away from the comfort of my fireplace for so long."

"...something like that."

Daniel knew Kit was not going to elaborate on what *something like that* meant, and he wasn't in the mood to figure it out. So he asked: "Do you truly think taking on Edward Hope's daughter was the right thing for me to do? Or was it a horrible mistake?"

Kit did not respond. Instead, he looked out of the darkened window with the smallest of smiles on his face. A person who did not know him might have described his expression as wistful. Daniel, on the other hand, was well-versed in every one of the Drus' expressions.

"I know that look."

A singular glance from Kit. "What look?"

"That satisfied smirk on your face. You're happy I took on Hope's daughter – and that I'm currently awake waiting to scold her – which can only mean one thing."

"Which is?"

"She's going to continue to be nothing but trouble, and you're going to enjoy watching me try and deal with her."

Kit's smirk widened into a sharp-canined grin. "Oh, you know me so well, Daniel. And on that matter..." His feral, unnatural eyes narrowed, focusing on something through the darkness past the window that Daniel could never hope to see without the aid of magic. "There she is now. I shall bid you good-bye."

"Wait!" Daniel cried out after his friend as he magicked himself scarce, remembering too late that he wanted to know why Kit had been spotted disappearing into the woods in his cat form along with Charlie most nights. He was reasonably certain Kit was doing it to amuse himself – and infuriate Daniel in the process – but when an Immortal Folk was involved, one could never know for sure their motives.

Now alone once more, Daniel readjusted his glasses, tightened the sash of his silver robe, shook out his shoulders and prepared for the confrontation to come. He could sense Charlie nearby, which meant she had gone through the protection magic across the grounds of his estate and was close to the building.

A ringing in his ears a few seconds later told him she was coming through the window. Gritting his teeth against an inevitable fight he moved through the shadows of the kitchen to stop her in her tracks just as she landed in the corridor in front of him.

"Morning, Miss Hope."

It was with some satisfaction that Daniel watched Charlie Hope yelp in fright away from him. The young woman was a mess: slender twigs poked out of her wild hair; dirt darkened her face, hands and bare feet; tiny cuts littered her skin, and there were more than a few ragged tears in her clothing.

Daniel couldn't believe how filthy she was.

"I-I thought you were in the Capital!" Charlie stammered, quickly backing away from Daniel. He merely followed her every footstep down the corridor.

"I had Jean send an illusion since I haven't been getting much sleep as of late. I wonder why that is?"

"I don't – this is the first time I've stayed out all night, I swear." But Daniel merely stared Charlie down, challenging her to elaborate on her lie. When it became clear to her that she was caught Charlie's shame and fright abruptly melted away. She straightened her posture, fixing Daniel with a defensive glare as she said, "What I do in my own time doesn't concern you."

He was somewhat satisfied by Charlie deciding there was no use in lying or prostrating herself at his feet. The young woman's behaviour over the last few days – during daylight hours – had been so completely at odds with how fiery she'd been when Daniel first met her. From all he had observed and been told by Crimson, Jean and Luca, Charlie was constantly deferring to them and apologising profusely for her magical failures yet seemed entirely resistant to trying to improve.

Daniel did not believe the version they'd been working with was the true Charlie Hope at all.

He had no patience for her wasting his time.

"No," he conceded, though the look on his face told Charlie his agreement with her statement was in no way a victory for her, "but your appearance and manners whilst you work here do. If you're going to spend all night doing Uthesh knows what—"

"All I'm doing is going to the woods," Charlie grumbled, averting her eyes. "It's not as if I'm wasting time in a tavern or sleeping my way through every willing person in Mt. Duega."

It took Daniel every inch of willpower he possessed not to snort out a laugh at Charlie's brazen answer. "And I suppose you think I should be thankful for that?"

"For not making a scandal of myself? I should think so."

"You're *already* a scandal, Miss Hope. Your very existence as my employee is an affront to my sponsors."

To Daniel's surprise, Charlie took a step towards him with a venomous expression contorting her features. "Oh, so the daughter of Edward Hope, mayor of Mt. Duega and the man who does *your* job for you regarding the border isn't good enough for them? Are they looking down on my father? Are you?"

"If I felt that way about Edward I'd never have hired you,"

Daniel replied, surprise turning to understanding and perhaps the smallest iota of respect for Charlie. It was clear she couldn't care less about working for him - she tried to get herself fired the very moment they met, after all - but she didn't want people bad-mouthing her father.

He's important to her. Likely more than anyone else; I should have realised that from the way she didn't want Edward to leave her here without him. And it's clear Charlie isn't friendly with anyone on my estate...except my cat.

It was in that moment that Daniel realised Charlie Hope was lonely.

"I won't stop you going into the woods," he sighed, somewhat regretting the words the moment they left his lips. But Daniel knew it was the right thing to do all the same.

Charlie's anger deflated all at once. "You...won't?" she asked, uncertainty and mistrust plain as day on her face.

"No. But if you don't want people looking down on you - or your father - they you have to at least take care of your outward appearance."

"I do try, I swear," Charlie replied, twisting a curl of dark hair around a finger until a twig fell out. But the ghost of a smile was on her lips, suggesting to Daniel that she didn't try very hard in the slightest.

"Unfortunately for you, trying isn't good enough around here if you don't put your full effort in, which it's apparent you're loathe to do. So until such a time that your attitude changes..."

Daniel crossed his arms and cocked his head, regarding Charlie from her head of tangled curls all the way down to her mud-soaked toes.

"S-stop looking at me like that," she muttered, genuinely concerned about his concentrated gaze. "Just what are you - *ah!* No! Don't do that!"

But it was too late. Between one moment and the next

Daniel worked a cleaning spell upon Charlie, eliminating all hints of dirt and cuts and stray twigs and torn clothes from her person.

Then her hair changed.

Before Daniel's very eyes Charlie's wild head of dark curls were transformed into soft, blonde waves that tumbled down her back past her shoulders. Even in the dim light of the corridor it shone, golden and lustrous.

It was lovely. *Charlie* was lovely, in her newly clean and tidy state with her hazel eyes wide with surprise, all traces of her previous defensiveness gone in the abrupt wake of Daniel's magic.

"You...had a glamour up?" he said, pushing all such inappropriate thoughts to the side. "I thought you said you weren't great with Matter magic?"

"Take your spell away!" Charlie cried. She pulled at her hair, aghast at the destruction of her own magic. "Let me put the glamour back up. Let me—"

"Answer the question."

"It's the only Matter magic I've ever been able to cast. It's—"

"It's a very *good* glamour," Daniel interrupted, walking around Charlie to check that his spell had destroyed it completely. His curiosity was well and truly piqued. "I didn't even sense you had one up."

"And?"

"And nothing. Except that you've been lying to my face from the moment we met."

"Not intentionally."

"I don't believe that."

Daniel stopped circling Charlie to stand in front of her, searching her face for...something. A sign of what she was hiding, perhaps. But though her expression was still one of indignation she nonetheless gave absolutely nothing away about her magic, her lies, or herself.

"I'm not removing the cleaning spell," Daniel finally said when Charlie did not rebuke his previous statement. She made to complain but he held up a hand to stop her. "The magic will prevent any and all imperfections from landing on you – be it dirt, tangled hair, bruises or anything else you might otherwise stumble across. But it will also prevent you from putting up your glamour."

"That's just unfair!" Charlie exclaimed, entirely appalled.

"What's unfair is you taking this job from somebody who actually wanted it, Miss Hope." Daniel gave Charlie a moment to respond to his critique. But she said nothing, keeping her gaze resolutely on her feet, so he continued: "Since it's clear to me that we both regard your father well the least you can do is *allow* my spell to remain until such a time that I can trust you to maintain your own appearance."

"Which is?"

He paused for a moment to consider. "Potentially never."

"Mister Silver!"

It shocked Daniel to hear his name uttered by Charlie, for in doing so he realised she had refused – whether deliberately or otherwise – to address him directly thus far. His stomach squirmed uncomfortably at the thought, though Daniel had no idea why.

The young woman's expression was genuinely pleading when she locked her eyes on his. "Don't do this to me. Please. I don't feel like myself without the glamour."

"You should have thought about that before acting like this. It isn't as if you weren't given any warnings to keep yourself tidy, Miss Hope. You have only yourself to blame."

For a moment it looked like Charlie wished for nothing more than to retort. But then she bit back whatever she'd planned to say and turned on her heel to leave.

Daniel grabbed her hand without thinking.

"What are you—" Charlie gasped, eyes wide and *fearful*, Daniel realised, as they took in the sight of his hand clasped around hers.

"The magic for the security system," he said, too quickly, feeling ashamed for grabbing Charlie without permission but not letting go regardless. He sent out a pulse of magic through his skin into hers. "Do you understand it?"

Several seconds of tense silence passed between them. Charlie puzzled over the magic, never once relaxing her posture or leaving herself unguarded. It was only after she slowly nodded her head that Daniel let her go.

"Good," he said, very quietly. "Now you won't wake me up at an ungodly hour every morning. I might finally get some sleep."

Charlie brought her wrist to her chest, massaging it as if Daniel had burned or bruised her instead of merely touched her. "So you trust me with the security spell to your estate but not to keep myself tidy?" she muttered, more to herself than to him.

At the ridiculousness of her question Daniel couldn't help but laugh. "Yes."

"That doesn't make any sense."

"I know. But neither do you."

"Can I go now?" Charlie asked, ignoring Daniel's last comment. "I'd like to get some sleep before Crimson realises I'm already up."

Daniel was tempted to say no simply to punish Charlie for forcing him awake to deal with her. But he knew that wasn't fair nor appropriate behaviour for him to exhibit as both her employer and as a man. "Go," he said, turning from Charlie to retire to his own bed for all the good it would do.

There was no doubt in Daniel's mind that he'd spend the rest of the morning puzzling over what Charlie Hope was capable of...and what exactly she was hiding from him.

CHAPTER FIVE

THOUGH IT HAD BEEN BARELY TWO weeks since Edward sent his daughter off to work for Mr Silver he felt as if months had gone by. Charlie was chaotic, messy, disorganised and never around when Edward was looking for her but, in spite of those things, he missed her terribly. Perhaps he missed her *because* of them.

Worrying about his daughter so much had left Edward haggard and sleep-deprived, which the residents of Mt. Duega found to be entirely endearing. *At least they don't see my fatigue as a sign of incompetence,* he thought, grateful that his rapport with the town was so strong.

And so it was that there was a spring in Edward's step as he approached Mr Silver's estate, eager to see Charlie before or after his impending meeting with the man himself. His mood wasn't dampened even when a wild sheet of rain blasted him in the face the moment he got out of his carriage.

Edward could have protected himself with magic; instead, he allowed himself to act exactly as his daughter would have and let himself feel every last drop of it.

Charlie would be proud, Edward thought, wiping rain from his face as he stepped up to the intricately detailed scroll work doors and knocked upon their iron surface, patiently waiting for a servant to see him in.

The inscriptions upon the doors were written in a very old version of the Atralian mother tongue. So old, in fact, that Edward could barely understand a word of it. But the drawings were easier to comprehend, illustrating an old myth about Atralia and Eshijan being neighbours many thousands of years ago.

Charlie's mother had often recounted this nonsensical myth to their daughter before bed many years ago – when the young family were still together and happy. It was therefore Charlie's favourite, though she had never asked Edward to recount it even after the loss of her mother.

He was glad when a servant appeared, stopping Edward's uncomfortable thoughts about the past – and of the myth carved in iron – before they could destroy his good mood.

"Mister Hope, it's so good to see you again!" Crimson, Daniel's Chief-of-Staff, announced after he'd been brought into the expansive house.

He gave her a warm smile. "It's been too long, Wei. How have you been?"

"You know fine well it's Crimson when I'm working," she scolded, though going by the happy expression on her face it evidently didn't matter to her in the slightest. Crimson was always happy to see him; if Edward spared her affection half a second of thought he'd have easily realised the woman was attracted to him.

She led Edward through the central hallway. "I've been busy looking after your daughter," she said. "She can't seem to stay still for longer than a minute, did you know that?"

"Oh, achingly so."

"Mayor Hope!"

Edward glanced behind Crimson to see Jean waving at him from the glass-walled meeting room Daniel Silver had painstakingly built himself so he could look out onto the courtyard of his estate whilst he worked. On several occasions Edward had coordinated with Jean for Atralian events, so he knew the man quite well.

The auburn-haired Luca sat beside Jean. Edward wasn't that familiar with her, though he had high hopes that the young, hard-working woman would prove to become a friend for Charlie.

"It's good to see you both," Edward said, inclining his head towards Jean. "I hope you've been looking after Charlie, however troublesome she may be."

At this a flash of confusion crossed Jean's face, followed shortly afterwards by a horrified epiphany. "She's...Uthesh be good, she's an *Edward Hope* Hope?"

"And that makes a difference?"

Edward turned; he wasn't the one who had spoken. And there stood Charlie, a familiar, confrontational expression on her face that almost caused him to laugh out loud. But then Edward realised something was very, very different about his daughter.

"Your hair," he murmured, closing the distance between them to run a golden curl between his fingers. "You dropped your glamour." It made his heart happy to see Charlie look like herself once more, though going by the scowl contorting her lips she didn't share the same sentiment.

"I didn't *drop* it."

"Mister Silver put a spell on her to keep her clean," Luca piped up from the meeting room. Edward didn't enjoy how pleased she sounded about it. When Charlie fired a glare at the young woman he resisted the urge to sigh.

"Things are going just about as well as I could have hoped," Edward told his daughter, fondly rapping his knuckles over her head when she stuck out her tongue. "How have you been?"

"Awful," Charlie replied. Edward knew she wasn't lying. "I hate it here. I've learnt my lesson. Can you take me home?"

"She's learned nothing so far – not through lack of trying on my part," Crimson said, but not unkindly. Edward noted that Charlie didn't look at Daniel's Chief-of-Staff with dislike...which was just about the most positive response he'd seen from her thus far. Crimson nodded at Edward. "I'll let Daniel know you're here."

"Thank you."

Barely a second passed before Jean abandoned Luca to rush to Charlie's side. "You should have said you're the daughter of Mayor Hope," he eagerly insisted. "I've worked with your father in the past, Charlie. It would have given us something to talk about."

Charlie stared at him in silence until Jean held up his hands in surrender and slowly backed away, but there was a gleam in his eye which told her the damage of her parentage had been done. Jean would no longer be disinterested in Charlie now he knew who her father was.

It was the last thing she needed.

"Come on, you," Edward said, placing a hand on the back of Charlie's spine to career her away from an inevitable fight. "Must you cause trouble everywhere you go?"

She clucked her tongue, thoroughly disgruntled. "It's not *my* fault they don't like me."

"Jean didn't seem to dislike you."

"Only after he realised I'm your daughter. Honestly, what an idiot."

"That's not very fair of you, Charlie. There are more than a few Hope families in Lopox. My great-grandfather—"

"Was a whore. I remember."

"Charlotte!"

"Well what else would you call him?" she challenged. Edward realised, in that minute, just how much he missed each and every combative conversation he'd ever had with his daughter. But he couldn't tell her that – nor could he regret sending her to work for Daniel Silver. If Edward did that then Charlie would know, and she'd immediately run home safe in the knowledge her father truly wanted her there.

He'd never be able to get her to do more with her miraculous talents again.

"A whore, then," Edward finally conceded, laughing softly. "So tell me, Charlie: what's so awful about being here?"

She shrugged. "Pretty much everything. My first day off in *two weeks* is tomorrow. How insane is that? It's slave labour, I swear."

"And?"

"And nobody likes me."

"Have you made an effort with them?"

"What's the point? They think they have my measure already." Charlie swung her arms back and forth as they walked down the corridor together, seemingly completely fine with nobody liking her, and paused only when they reached one of the many windows that punctuated the corridor walls. Edward knew without looking that her sights were set firmly on the woods.

"You can't just rely on the Immortal Folk for company," he said. "When was the last time you saw one of them, anyway?"

A troubled shadow fell across Charlie's eyes. "Last autumn." And then, quieter: "Where are they all, Da?"

"I don't think they like the impending threat of war."

"Neither do I. Neither do you. But we're still here anyway, defending our home."

"Is that what you're doing here, not making friends or putting any effort into your job?"

Charlie threw her father a filthy look. "Don't make me shut you up."

"As if you'd dare."

"Not if anyone was within range. If we went outside, however..."

He merely bopped her on the head in retaliation. They both knew Charlie would never Influence him despite her many threats to do exactly that throughout the years.

"It's not funny, Da," Charlie insisted, though her features had softened and there was the hint of a smile on her lips. "I hate it here. I feel...trapped."

Edward leaned against the windowsill, not entirely sure what to tell her, then inclined his hand for his daughter to follow suit. Charlie did so with a huff of resigned breath. Behind the glass the bitter late-winter rain pelted the courtyard. It almost sounded like hail.

He touched Charlie's hair again. "Did Mr Silver really cast magic on you to keep you clean?"

"...yes." She drooped her head. "He said it was my own fault."

"I'm sure it was."

"Da!"

"What do you want me to say? I've been harping on at you about keeping tidy and presentable for years now."

"Yes, but..."

"But what?"

"But what if I don't want to?" Charlie shook away her sadness in favour of indignation. "Why is *he* allowed to wear glasses wilfully but I'm not allowed to be anything less than perfect? Why can't I just look the way I want to? It's discrimination, I tell you!"

Edward ruffled his daughter's hair. "Looking like you've run through a briar and wearing glasses are not the same, and you know it." And then, to remind Charlie about what she was doing on Daniel Silver's estate in the first place: "I know you can put up with his cleaning spell. I have the utmost faith in you. You've already made it through two weeks of your employment here, after all!"

"Yes, just another fifty to go..."

"I wasn't aware there was a clock upon your employment with me, Miss Hope," Daniel remarked, sarcasm dripping from his tongue as he made his presence known. In truth he'd heard the duo's last few comments regarding appearances, and had been puzzling over whether he truly *was* discriminating against Charlie until the time frame of her employment was brought up.

Seeing father and daughter together with their golden, wavy hair, leaning against the window in the exact same casual fashion, took Daniel starkly aback. The family resemblance was so much more obvious now; before Charlie's glamour had been stripped he'd hardly been able to identify her as Edward's daughter going by appearance alone.

The look Charlie gave him was full of daggers. "Yes, because it was so obvious I wanted to be here of my own free will."

"Clearly."

Edward looked from his daughter to Daniel, surprised at the way they spoke to each other. He'd never heard of anyone daring to speak to the man in such a way – and getting away with it.

Charlie had gotten under Daniel's skin in the precise fashion Edward knew she would.

"Should we head into your office?" Edward asked, inclining towards the door situated behind Daniel. He lightly touched Charlie's hand when Daniel nodded. "I'll talk to you when I'm done, all right?"

"It's not as if I have anywhere else to go," Charlie bit out, though her eyes on the woods told Edward another story entirely. But he wasn't here to talk with his daughter so, though he was loathe to leave Charlie alone, Edward followed Daniel into his office.

The man quickly ushered for Edward to take a seat in front of his desk, offering him a glass of water before pouring one for himself and returning to his chair.

"Well done on the watchtower delay, by the way," Daniel said, getting straight to business. "How you continue to convince Crank and the rest of the Alliance to hold off on it baffles me." He meant it: for years now Daniel had been mystified as to how Edward Hope gracefully handled the situation along the Atralian border with little to no push-back. It reassured him that his home town had such a competent man in charge of it. *Too competent,* he mused. *It's high time Edward rose above his current station.*

Edward chuckled softly at the compliment. "Let's just say I have my ways."

"You aren't bribing them, are you? Not that I wouldn't whole-heartedly commend you on such a thing. Though I'd have to distance myself from you if such a scandal broke out for the sake of my own image, of course."

Another laugh. "No. Nothing as...unsavoury as that." The look on Edward's face as he took a sip of water suggested otherwise.

Daniel peered at the mayor for a long moment, taking in the shadows beneath his eyes and the decidedly dishevelled state of his hair. It seemed in need of a cut. "You look like you've seen better days."

"You don't look too great, either, if we're insulting each other," Edward countered. "Why is that?"

"I'm exhausted. Your daughter is to blame."

A raised eyebrow. "Oh?"

"Not like that," Daniel bit back, clucking his tongue at the suggestive look on Edward's face. *Who would tell a father they were sleeping with their daughter, anyway?*

"Then like what?"

He considered if it was wise to sell Charlie out to her father then immediately hated that he was wondering how it would affect her if he did so. *She holds zero regard for how her actions affect anyone else, after all.* Daniel settled on saying, "Tell me more about why you had me take on your daughter."

"I don't think there's anything to say that I haven't already said."

"You said nothing save for practically blackmailing me," Daniel countered. "Edward, you knew I couldn't just hand out the job. I had dozens of applications from across the country. There were influential families who had been vying to secure that position for their sons and daughters for months."

"I know. But she's worth it, I swear." When Daniel did not reply Edward continued with his plea. "She can be a bit flighty and difficult to handle," he admitted, "but you can trust my word that it's worth fighting with her to have her on your side."

Daniel's temple twitched at the mere mention of *fighting* with Charlie. "What makes her so special, then?" he asked, keen to get a straight answer from Edward as to why his daughter avoided any and all questions pertaining to her magic. "Which areas of magic does she excel in? Is she Matter or Mind-oriented?"

"Mind for sure. She's useless with Matter magic."

"But she can perform an excellent glamour."

"That's true."

"So what exactly are her magical strengths?" Daniel asked

again.

"That's not up to me to tell you."

"Can't tell me? Or *won't?*"

"The latter, I'm afraid," Edward said. He was pleased with the man's interest in Charlie...though he knew she would kill him if he said as much out loud. "It's up to Charlie to tell you. If she ever trusts you enough, that is. Have you given her any reason to?"

"No, but—"

"Please respect both myself and my daughter enough to stop asking me to elaborate."

Of course Daniel didn't want to let the issue go. He was desperate to know exactly what it was Charlie Hope could do. But it was obvious he would get no further information from her father today.

"Fine," he sighed, sinking into his chair. "Fine. Let's talk about the trees being felled in the woods."

Edward perked up at the change in topic; this was exactly what he'd come here to discuss. "I was hoping you'd bring that up. It's completely unsanctioned. A strip fifty meters wide right by the border was razed to the ground mere days ago! Just who —"

A blast of bitter, freezing wind smelling of woodsmoke and pine needles blew from the large window situated behind Daniel's chair, interrupting Edward's question and causing both men to flinch.

"I thought I closed that," Daniel muttered, getting to his feet to redo the latch. Once it was sealed a mewing alerted him to the presence of his cat; Daniel peered at the animal suspiciously. "I was wondering where you'd gone, Kit."

The cat leapt deftly into his lap when Daniel sat down once more, Edward's eyes following its every movement. "Your cat can open windows?"

"This surprises you?"

"I suppose not," he chuckled. "A cat that's lived as long as you have isn't a mere cat, after all. How long has it been since you achieved immortality now? Eighty years? Ninety?"

"It's rude to inquire about one's age."

"I think that only applies to people who live a natural lifespan, Daniel, not someone who ceased ageing decades ago."

Daniel's lips quirked into a smile at the comment. He stroked his cat, who purred luxuriously when his fingers crossed the long scar that trailed the creature's spine. "Eighty-seven years since I 'ascended', as the Eshijani would put it. I was thirty-five when I chose to commit to it."

"You don't regret it?"

"Are you thinking of doing the same thing?"

"Ah – no, I don't think it's for me," Edward murmured. Though his words were soft his expression was set in such a way that Daniel knew the man was not likely to change his mind.

A shame, he thought. *He has been a reliable presence in my life.* But this was not the first time the people Daniel held in high regard would age and pass on without him, and it certainly wasn't going to be the last.

"So what are we going to do about the woods?" Edward asked, bringing their conversation back onto the actual topic at hand. "We can't possibly allow the unsanctioned cuts to continue. Do you have any idea who's responsible for them?"

"I'd hazard a guess that Jonah knows about them and is simply letting them happen. You know how Laskians are; their country is so far from us they simply don't care about maintaining Atralian woodland."

"Not to mention Ritten's been applying for extra magicians lately to deal with the crop shortage up there," Edward agreed, troubled by the thought. "Eshijan is incredibly fertile land. He likely wants war to break out so Lopox can take hold of all their resources and distribute them up north."

Daniel nodded approvingly. "Sounds like you've thought about this before."

"Do you think Crank knows?"

"Almost definitely."

"Which means *sanctioned* forest culls are only a matter of weeks away," Edward grumbled. "And—"

Edward paused, then frowned, then smothered a laugh. Daniel was only momentarily confused before he reached out his magic and realised somebody was standing outside his office door, listening to them.

It wasn't difficult to make an educated guess at who it was.

"Won't you come in, Miss Hope?" he said, raising his voice so there could be no doubt in her mind that he knew she was there.

"Charlotte Hope, get in here," Edward added on, clearly amused by his daughter's antics.

Daniel raised an eyebrow. "Charlotte?"

"Only when she's in trouble."

"Which is often."

"I can hear you both, you know," Charlie scowled. The moment she opened the door Kit gracefully slid off Daniel's lap to curl himself around Charlie's ankles, rubbing his chin and tail against her leg. Daniel knew Kit was doing it to distract him – or annoy him – so he ignored it.

"Yes," he told Charlie. "I'm evidently aware of that. Why were you eavesdropping?"

It was Edward who answered on her behalf. "Because even if she pretends not to care, my daughter naturally wishes to know exactly what's going on at the border. Charlie has been integral to my meetings with the Alliance for close to ten years now; it's only natural she wants to know what they're doing to the woods."

That piqued Daniel's interest. Of course it did. If Edward's daughter was so important to his success in maintaining peace along the border then obviously Daniel wanted to know more about it. "You never told me this when you forced me to hire her," he said, attention torn between Edward and his daughter.

Charlie kept her attention firmly on Kit.

"I'd have told you if you refused to take her on otherwise," Edward said, not at all joking. "And on that note…" He got to his feet and pulled a surprised Charlie in for a quick hug. "I must be on my way. I'm needed at a last-minute meeting regarding the new Saturday market restrictions."

Her face fell at his abrupt good-bye, especially because she knew it for exactly what it was: a lie. "Da—"

"I'll see you tomorrow," Edward promised his daughter. "It's your day off, isn't it? Unless you no longer wish to spend it with your old man?"

"It'd break your heart if I didn't spend it with you."

"Which is why I know you're secretly a doting, loving daughter." He kissed Charlie on the forehead, squeezed her hand, then opened the door. "So tomorrow?"

A genuine smile Daniel had never seen before crossed Charlie's face. "Tomorrow."

A nod from Edward towards Daniel. "I'll look into the woods issue further and get back to you."

The door swung closed behind Edward when he left and a heavy, awkward silence fell between Charlie and Daniel. She squirmed on the spot, eyes focusing first on the window and then on the door. It was obvious to Daniel that she wished to be anywhere but in his office.

"Why did you never tell me you attended Alliance meetings with your father?" he finally asked her, breaking the unbearable quiet.

"It didn't seem—"

"If you say it didn't seem relevant then I swear to Uthesh, Miss Hope—"

"Fine." She bent down and picked up Kit, who was still curled around her ankles – he mewed in delight and cuddled against her chest in response – before giving Daniel an answer. "I didn't want the responsibility of going to more meetings. Happy?"

"No. Just what exactly are you doing here?"

"Da forced me to work for you. I thought you would realise at least that much by now."

"Oh, trust me, I know," Daniel agreed. He stood up, curiosity causing him to leave the barrier of his desk to get closer to Charlie. *As if a closer inspection will tell me anything about her.* "But why do you continue to stay here?" he asked. "Why not simply leave?"

Charlie did not take a step back when Daniel drew near, instead choosing to hold her ground. But she clung to the cat in her arms a little tighter, all the same. "...because he said he'd ban me from living in Mt. Duega, including the woods," she admitted.

"And you...believed him?" Daniel was incredulous. It was obvious the man adored his daughter. Under no circumstances would Edward Hope have given such an ultimatum to his only—

"He was being serious," Charlie said.

"How could you know that it wasn't an empty threat?"

"Because I know my father. He meant it."

Daniel considered this for a moment. It was clear that, at least, Charlie believed her father's stern stance to be true.

Taking into account how angry she had been two days before at the idea of Daniel's sponsors bad-mouthing Edward, Daniel reached the only conclusion Charlie's testimony pointed to.

"So you genuinely love and respect your father and – above that – Mt. Duega. And the woods, of course," Daniel added on, when he caught Charlie stealing a glance at the trees through the rainy window behind him. "You're even willing to put up with an evidently unpleasant situation in order to keep your place there. Although you could certainly make your situation less unpleasant if you only—"

"What's your point?" Charlie cut in, steely-eyed. "If you have one, that is. I'm beginning to think you merely enjoy listening to the sound of your own voice."

Daniel almost laughed at her bold insult.

Almost.

"My point being that," he began, "now that I know this, I know how to push you to actually try with your job."

Charlie didn't like the sound of that at all. She gripped Kit so tightly that he dug his teeth into her hand, though Charlie didn't seem to care nor notice. "...and what does that mean?"

"I have a meeting with a couple of Eshijani representatives a week from now," Daniel said. "You'll attend it with me."

She barked out an incredulous laugh. "I think you'll find I won't."

"I think you'll find you don't have a choice. Unless you want me to tell your father you're deliberately sabotaging your job in the hopes of getting fired?"

The retort Charlie had prepared caught in her throat. She cast her gaze anywhere but at Daniel, so obviously anguished at the prospect that he almost thought he felt her despair himself. "...fine," Charlie eventually muttered. "Fine. What's another meeting on top of the thousands I've already been part of?"

Daniel resisted the urge to grin or punch a victorious fist through the air. Instead he slid his glasses back up his nose to hide his glee. "Excellent. Make sure to dress well."

"As if I could do anything else with your damn magic on me."

"Ah yes, I forgot."

"No you didn't," Charlie said, rolling her eyes. In her arms Kit almost seemed to roll his, too. Daniel made a mental note to admonish him later.

He turned from Charlie to hide the small smile that was curling his lips. He couldn't stop it. The young woman was, in fact, far easier to deal with that Daniel had originally thought. "You can go now, Miss Hope."

"Gladly!" she cried, slamming the door on her way out – taking Kit with her – but Daniel didn't care.

He was one step closer to working out what Charlie Hope was truly capable of.

Chapter Six

Charlie slammed her hands back to her sides in frustration. It did not matter how she tried to push and pull at the magic Silver had wrought on her: it wouldn't budge.

"I don't understand," she told her reflection, frowning until her furrowed brows cast shadows over her eyes. "I can't even find the edges of his magic..."

Behind her Kit lazed on the bed, content to exist in a liminal space between sleep and wakefulness. Charlie had thought Silver would be annoyed at his cat's preference for spending all his time with her; instead, it seemed as if the man was decidedly unbothered by his pet abandoning him.

"Just how does this spell work, Kit? Hmm? You must know how your master's magic operates. No? Nothing?"

The cat remained resolutely silent.

Charlie could only laugh at her question. Her father had told her how impressive Silver's magic was. She'd felt it herself, emanating off the man as if he simply couldn't contain it all. Of course she couldn't dismantle his cleaning spell, nor overwrite it with a variation of her original glamour. Charlie had worked hard enough just to perfect that one aspect of Matter magic – it had taken her the best part of her teenage years to get the hang of it – so the thought of creating another glamour that would work over Silver's ridiculous cleaning spell was an impossible notion.

Charlie Hope was stuck in her own skin, oppressively protected from anything which might dirty, dishevel or harm her.

She hated it. And yet...

The memory of Daniel Silver's magic sinking into her very being was not a sensation Charlie could admit to hating. She could still feel it even now, tingling at her nerves until she was aware of nothing else but the magic. It coursed through her veins, changing her, protecting her.

After one final attempt at pulling the wretched, wonderful spell apart Charlie flung her hands up in surrender and turned from the mirror. Kit was still solidly half-asleep, and when she opened the door of her bedroom he made no attempt to move.

"Are you coming?" she asked the motionless cat. "I have that meeting this afternoon. I won't be back for hours."

The only response she got was a yawn and the twitch of Kit's tail so Charlie left her bedroom quite certain that, after she returned from the meeting with the Eshijani, the tawny cat would still in all likelihood be lying there, waiting for her.

So they could go to the woods.

Charlie was already counting down the hours.

In truth Charlie was too early for the meeting, though she figured she should eat something before it started. From experience she knew there was little more embarrassing than being hungry and having her stomach growl in front of political officials. It made Charlie look like a child. With only her father as witness this didn't matter, as she would invariably be Influencing everyone else in the meeting to bend to her will.

If she appeared immature yet managed to affect the meeting in some way *now,* Silver would be aware that something was awry.

No, Charlie thought, shaking her head. *Don't use your Influence in the meeting whatsoever, no matter what happens. Do nothing. Call Silver's bluff. Make him realise it was a mistake to demand you attend.*

It seemed all Charlie's thoughts these days circled back to Daniel Silver.

It wasn't that Charlie wanted to think about him, of course, but it was hard not to when she was working for him, and he was critical of all she did, and his magic weighed heavy and curse-like upon her skin.

But though Charlie wanted to despise the man, she simply couldn't.

The way Silver had looked at her once his magic had taken effect lingered in the back of Charlie's mind. She had felt what he felt, of course, which only made things worse.

He hadn't expected Charlie to clean up so well. It had shaken him up for some reason.

He isn't a teenage boy, she grumbled. *And it's not as if I'm completely different when my glamour is dropped. I'm still the same person.*

But even Charlie couldn't convince herself with such a lie. Her glamour was her armour, giving her an excuse to remain distant from all the people and issues that surrounded her. It gave Charlie the freedom to happily spend all her time in the woods, never addressing the fact that it was her own magic, not the way she acted, that distanced her from other people.

Charlie could do nothing about her magic – nor her fear of losing control of it in the heat of the moment. She *could* do something about her appearance.

But Daniel Silver had taken that away from her.

It took Charlie an embarrassingly long time to realise that she had taken a wrong turn towards the kitchen. Since she was still getting used to her surroundings – she hadn't even found the time or energy to explore the courtyard yet, given that whenever she was free she ran off to the woods – Charlie had to admit that she wasn't entirely sure how to get to the kitchen from where she was.

So she closed her eyes, focusing her efforts on trying to gauge the space around her. Charlie had never been very good at spatial awareness magic even though her father was excellent at it but, even so, centring herself for a moment allowed her to at least catch the sound of a voice to her left. It was low yet enthusiastic, melodic in the way a voice could only be when it was in the full swing of discussing something of interest.

It was Daniel Silver's voice.

Charlie followed it.

A minute later she came across a door held slightly ajar; on silent feet she padded towards it, peering through the gap to see what was going on inside.

It appeared to be some kind of lecture hall. Luca and Jean sat at two separate tables, their attention directed entirely towards Silver, who stood at the front of the room. The air beside him had been hardened into an invisible screen upon which scrolling text simultaneously appeared as he spoke.

Just what is going on? Charlie wondered, curious despite herself. The meeting with the Eshijani was not for another hour. Since Charlie had not been tasked with doing anything else beforehand she had assumed everyone else had free time. So what was Silver lecturing Jean and Luca about? Was this something she was supposed to have known about? Or had she been deliberately excluded?

Charlie's heart beat faster at the thought, feeling somewhat sick even if she didn't want to admit to it. *I haven't given them any cause to tell me about such things. If they don't ask me to attend lectures or anything additional to the minimum work expected of me then that's my own fault. But even so...*

It felt awful to be on the other side of the door. It was a familiar feeling; usually, however, Charlie deliberately instigated her own exclusion.

Not this time. Not today.

Such negative feelings were beginning to spiral out of control in Charlie's mind. It wouldn't do to Influence the people in the room because she couldn't control her emotions – not least whilst she was spying on them – but Charlie didn't want to leave before finding out what Silver was teaching Jean and Luca, either. So Charlie wrapped herself in a little magic to make herself as unnoticeable as possible and breathed slowly and deeply until her sadness, frustration and self-directed anger washed away.

Then she focused once more on Daniel Silver's voice.

"The key to creating something from nothing – a real thing, a tangible thing – is to master illusions first and foremost," Silver said, creating a dappled grey stallion the size of a dog right in front of him to prove his point. It galloped across the room and straight through Luca, who held her hands over her face and cried out in fright.

Charlie had seen good illusions before but Silver's magic was nonetheless impressive to behold: if she hadn't known any better she would have genuinely believed the horse was real, despite its size.

With a clenching of his fist the miniature horse disappeared. "This is where people ultimately fail when it comes to creation magic," Silver continued, when Luca had gotten over her scare. "Transmutation is Matter magic, whereas illusions are Mind. But creating something from nothing...that takes both branches of magic." He nodded towards Luca. "Since you're ultimately training to be a magical healer, being able to create organic matter from nothing is a vital skill. People need not worry about injuries if you're on-site with them, able to create organs and blood from thin air."

She is training to be a healer? Charlie thought, impressed despite herself. It was an incredibly difficult branch of magic; Charlie couldn't imagine ever having the mental fortitude to master it.

Sparing a glance at Jean, Charlie saw that his attention was on his hands. He had created a tiny imitation of Silver's stallion upon the palm of his hand but even from Charlie's vantage point she could see something was off about it. The overhead lighting didn't seem to hit its flanks quite right.

Silver laughed softly when he realised what Jean was doing. "It's the texture of the hair, Jean," he explained, walking towards the man and added his own magic to the illusion. It immediately improved it. "You've perfected humans already – which is commendable on its own – as well as inanimate objects, so unless you intend to move into film-making or theatre I highly doubt you need to worry about such attention to detail on an animal."

"But even so," Jean muttered, holding the illusion for another few seconds before letting it go, "illusions are an art form. I'd rather like to master all aspects of it for my own satisfaction."

"A noble pursuit, for sure. Mastering a skill for the sake of the skill alone is something rarely witnessed in people these days."

"You sound like an old man," Luca joked.

"I suppose I am. With every passing decade my back aches more and more." Silver bent double, feigning injury, then promptly straightened just in time to avoid his glasses falling off his nose to the floor.

All three of them chuckled at the exaggerated comic display. *And that's my cue to go,* Charlie thought, her stomach twisting uncomfortably at the sign of Daniel Silver laughing so easily with

Jean and Luca when all she got from the man were sighs and scornful remarks. *I am not meant to be here. I should—*

"Do you make a habit of lingering in doorways, Miss Hope, or do you intend to join us?" Silver called out without looking in Charlie's direction. He did not sound angry; rather, he seemed almost happy to invite her in.

Charlie backed away from the door, instead. "I didn't mean to intrude. I'm just going to—"

"Come in," he said, this time an unmistakeable order.

Charlie was compelled to obey.

Luca glared at her when Charlie tried to figure out where to sit. Jean, on the other hand, eagerly pulled out the vacant chair beside him. Charlie resisted the urge to roll her eyes, for ever since he'd found out who her father was Jean had practically fallen over himself to be more accommodating of Charlie.

But she remembered what her father told her: she needed friends. She hardly ever came across the Immortal Folk nowadays, and Charlie knew fine well she couldn't rely on a cat for all her social needs.

Just because the reason Jean changed his tune about me was superficial doesn't mean we can't become friends, Charlie mused. And she was lonely. Truly, she was.

She sat down beside him.

Once Charlie settled down Silver spared her a singular glance through his glasses, blue eyes unreadable even to her, before pulling a small green pouch out of the pocket of his robes. When he upended the contents into his hand Charlie saw that it contained sand the golden colour of her hair.

"Whilst mastering illusions is important for learning how to make something from nothing," Silver said, as if Charlie had never interrupted him in the first place, "learning transmutation is just as important. You need to understand the properties of your original material – in this case, sand," he allowed the grains of sand to fall from his left fist to the open palm of his right hand, "as well as the properties of your intended material – in this case, silver..."

When the man returned the sand to his left hand it was no longer dark blonde but glittering, shimmering silver.

Charlie gasped despite herself: transmutation was a rare skill, especially performed so seamlessly. The expression on Silver's face had not changed once during the process – nor had his internal magic or feelings.

He was in complete and perfect control of the process. It was effortless.

Daniel Silver's lips quirked at the reaction he elicited from Charlie. "I did not consider you so easily impressed, Miss Hope," he said. "It is a well-known fact that I've been able to transmute almost anything into silver since I was a child. It is making silver from *nothing* which is the far more difficult skill."

With a flourish he poured the transmuted sand back into the green pouch, returned it to his pocket, then inhaled deeply. This time Charlie *did* feel a fluctuation in Silver's magic, but it was fleeting and inconsequential.

The man splayed his fingertips together and then pulled them apart a split second later. At first Charlie could see nothing between them, but then the finest strand of silver just barely glinted between his forefingers, then another and another.

By the time Silver's hands were as wide apart as his shoulders dozens of threads of his signature metal connected his fingertips. With a careful turn of his right wrist and then his left Silver twisted the stands into a perfect helix.

It was beautiful. Dangerously delicate and ready to break at any given moment, but Silver held the helix so tenderly between his hands it remained steady and solid. As if it were a baby rather than a metal structure.

Charlie wanted to touch it – to possess it. She just barely

managed to stop herself from reaching out as if to steal the magical helix though there was no hiding the fact she was leaning forward in her chair, entirely rapt with the demonstration.

She didn't possess the inclination to care about her obvious display of interest.

But Silver was too focused on his own creation to notice Charlie's enthusiasm. "I have an affinity for silver," he murmured, stating the obvious, "which is why I can do this so easily. If I tried to magic – say, gold – into creation it would be much more difficult for me."

"What about organic matter?" Luca asked, in-between taking furious, scrawled notes entirely by hand. "Flowers, for example?"

At this Silver smiled grimly. In the blink of an eye his metal helix disappeared, then he directed his magic between his palms. The level of effort he exerted this time was far more palpable and, for a moment, Charlie thought the man might actually fail.

But then a bouquet of lilies appeared in his hands, white and pure and—

"Dead," Silver said sadly, tossing the flowers almost carelessly to Charlie so she could inspect them. She jolted in surprise when he did so, instinctively pulling away from him when she caught the flowers.

Jean poked his head over Charlie's shoulder to investigate the blooms alongside her; sure enough, there was no life to be found in their stems or petals. The lilies were perfect – the scent emanating off them gentle and intoxicating – but they would imminently wilt, unable to absorb water and keep themselves alive because they never *were* alive.

"Can you make them, you know, less dead?" Jean asked, reaching over Charlie's shoulder to rub a petal between his fingertips. "It doesn't seem that much harder to go from these to a plant with roots and a functioning biological system."

"That's where you would be wrong," Silver said, taking the bouquet from Charlie before she was quite ready for him to in order to pass them over to Luca. "Breathing life into organic matter – whether it was already alive or, more dangerously, if it was not, is a different subject entirely. It's the most complex of Mind and Matter magic combined. Very few magicians have ever been documented capable of such a skill. Alas, I am not one of them." A low, self-deprecating chuckle. "Luckily for us, so long as the body being operated on is still alive, constructing 'dead' organic organs and limbs is almost all we humans really require from this form of magic. It's..."

But Charlie was no longer listening. This was the first time she had ever listened to someone talk about the skills she herself possessed: skills she took for granted. Charlie had been using her Intent magic for years, honing it under the careful eye of her father. It had remained secret, yes, but Charlie actively used it. Her ability to breathe life into Matter, however...

Unless she was in the woods Charlie did not use it. Her father had asked her not to. Begged her, in fact. Charlie had been content to keep her creation magic to herself – and to the woods – and so had never questioned him.

Until now.

A moment later Silver vanished the dead flowers he had created and clapped his hands together. "Well, that's all for today," he announced, before directing his attention at Charlie. "It was very magnanimous of you to join us this time, Miss Hope."

"I...didn't know about your lectures," she admitted, feeling very small in the face of such a comment.

"Crimson informed you of them the day you arrived."

"I didn't listen to anything she said."

"*Clearly.*"

At this admonition her temper flared. Charlie couldn't help it; it was her default reaction to the man. "Excuse me," she muttered, bolting from the lecture hall without warning. Her face flushed with shame as she fled, for it really *had* been her own fault that she didn't know about Silver's magic lectures.

If Da could only see me now, Charlie thought, willing away a humiliating wave of tears. *I'm learning just how useless I truly am, and I don't like it.*

Charlie didn't make it far before Silver came rushing after her. "Don't just run off!" he demanded, reaching out for her shoulder the moment before Charlie wheeled around to face him.

"What do you *want* from me?" she spat out, all bared teeth and raised hackles in order to hide her own insecurities. The man was too close; his attempt to grab her brought him mere inches from Charlie's face. She could have reached up and wrenched off his glasses if she wanted to.

And Charlie *wanted* to, just to see what he would do.

Instead she did nothing.

From the way Silver hesitated it was evident he hadn't expected Charlie to react in such a way nor intended to end up in her personal space. He took a step back to place a more respectable distance between them. "I won't tolerate you not attending this meeting," he said, voice softer than it had been mere seconds before.

"No need to insult me further, Mr Silver," Charlie replied, tone clipped and dripping with practised politeness her father would have been proud of. "Of course I'm not missing the meeting you're forcing me to attend."

"Then where are you running off to? Crimson and I need to brief you on the agenda."

At this Charlie barked out a humourless laugh. "I do not need to prepare for a meeting with the Eshijani and the Alliance.

I know exactly what I'm doing."

Despite the fact Charlie Hope had come to work for Daniel Silver with every intention of being as useless as possible she had to admit that she'd had enough. Having people belittle and dismiss her grated on Charlie far more than she could have ever expected.

This meeting will go well, she thought, relishing Silver's confounded expression at her statement. *Better than well. I'll progress relations with the Eshijani further than in any meeting I've ever attended before, Da's warnings be damned.*

She would make certain of it.

CHAPTER SEVEN

The meeting with Eshijan was imminent, and Daniel was beginning to seriously regret his rash decision to demand Charlie Hope attend.

"What do you mean you *know* what you're doing?" he asked, deeply suspicious of Charlie's barbed reassurance that she would be fine.

She shrugged dismissively. "Exactly that. So if you care to show the way then please do so, Mr Silver."

The false politeness in Charlie's voice thoroughly irked Daniel. He was already struggling to deal with the conflicting feelings he had about her finally appearing at one of his lectures – only to discover that she had not, in fact, listened when Crimson told her about them in the first place, which was the reason she'd never come to them.

Charlie had shown genuine interest in his lecture. She demonstrated that she actually liked magic and would happily learn more about it. *So why does she never try to improve her skills? Why does she act so apathetic in her work when she can clearly perform excellent glamour magic?*

Why, why, why. There were so many unanswered questions

about Charlie Hope that Daniel wanted an explanation for, but what he *didn't* need was Charlie messing with his mind directly before an important meeting.

He suppressed a resigned sigh. "This way," he said, before marching down the corridor. Charlie's footsteps behind him reassured Daniel that she was actually following him rather than running away.

He kept expecting her to run away.

When they reached a modestly sized wood-panelled meeting room frequently used for Alliance meetings – Crank disliked being in direct sunlight so preferred the sheltered nature of the room to Daniel's glass-walled one – he was surprised to find Crimson still standing in front of the doors.

"The Eshijani insisted on a view of the garden," she said, a small smile on her face. "As you predicted."

"I bet Crank was happy with that," Charlie muttered, just as Daniel himself was about to say the same thing. He gaped at her, instead.

Crimson chuckled. "It seems you know the man well, Miss Hope. I trust Daniel has briefed you on what to expect today?"

"Apparently our young protégé here doesn't need such instruction," Daniel answered on Charlie's behalf. The young woman avoided his gaze. "Given that this information came straight after discovering Miss Hope deliberately had no idea of the lectures I hold, it doesn't exactly bode well."

"I *did* tell her about them. On numerous occasions, in fact."

"Evidently I didn't think Mr Silver would have anything of note to say," Charlie blithely replied, a wan smile on her face as all three of them made their way to the glass meeting room.

Crimson could only shake her head in dismay, though Daniel could tell perfectly well that she was smothering a laugh at the comment. This wasn't the first time he'd seen proof that his Chief-of-Staff liked Charlie Hope, despite the young woman's bullish insistence on being less than mediocre at her job.

"Last chance for you to decide Miss Hope shouldn't join us," Crimson pointed out when they reached the meeting room, hand on the door handle waiting only for Daniel's instruction to open it.

Daniel watched Charlie's determined expression carefully as he straightened his collar and glasses. He had expected her to complain further, or panic, or deliberately misbehave to get out of the meeting, but she had done none of those things.

He wanted to see exactly how prepared she was to feel so confident in herself.

And so it was that Daniel shook his head at Crimson, resisted the urge to remind Charlie that he'd inform her father about her numerous attempts to get fired if she didn't behave, and ordered the door open.

Inside the meeting room were two Eshijani officials – Daniel identified the taller man as Lee and the shorter as Arjun, both of whom he had met before – as well as Jonathan Crank and Jonah Ritten, the Laskey representative from the Alliance.

The man Edward Hope was currently investigating regarding the woods being cut down.

At once the Eshijani stood to bow to Daniel. He returned the favour. "I appreciate you coming all the way here to talk with us," he said.

Arjun inclined his head. "It is only fair we do so given that you came to us last time. Ah, Crimson, your grandfather sends his apologies. He is unfortunately stuck attending to another matter."

Crimson bowed beside Daniel, allowing her to hide the flash of disappointment that crossed her face until it disappeared entirely. "He is a busy man," she said. "I shall be sure to contact him later."

In truth Daniel – and, going by their faces, Crank and Ritten – was disappointed, too. Grandmaster Feng was a prominent Eshijani figure and had been the Alliance's main point of contact thus far. Without him present Daniel doubted today's meeting would come to all that much.

To his surprise and horror Charlie rushed past Daniel in order to bow to the Eshijani, too. He couldn't tell her off in front of everyone else without seeming unprofessional so had no choice but to hope she really did know what she was doing.

When Charlie summoned a perfect, miniature laurel tree behind her back without once breaking her genial smile Daniel hardly managed to suppress his shock. The leaves on the tree's tiny branches were lush and vibrant, as if the tree had been potted in Midsummer instead of early March.

It was beautiful in its simplicity. Charlie Hope was not going to embarrass Daniel but, it seemed, overshadow him.

She held the tree out to the Eshijani with both hands; they gasped in delight. "It is good to see you again, Lee," Charlie said, not in Atralian or even the common tongue of Lopox but in Eshijani. "And you, too, Arjun. Much luck and success to you both as always."

Daniel could only stare at her. *Just who is this woman?* he wondered, thoroughly bewildered. It was almost impossible for him to associate the Charlie Hope who crept back into his house at dawn, covered head to toe in dirt, with twigs in her tangled hair and bruises on her legs, with the version who currently stood before him. A polished, immaculately dressed, *professional* individual, who had prepared for the meeting well in advance by sourcing the perfect gift for the Eshijani.

"Miss Hope," Lee said, beaming at her, "we did not expect to find you here. How is your father?"

"Well, I think." She cast an entirely staged mischievous glance at Daniel. "Alas, I do not get to see my father much ever since coming to work for Mr Silver. He keeps me busy all day!"

The men laughed. "He must be missing you, then."

"And me him," she replied. "But we are not here to discuss my father. Won't you take a seat?"

It was only after everyone was seated – Charlie easily slotting herself between the Eshijani and Crimson – that Daniel took proper notice of the other Alliance members present. Jonathan Crank did not at all seem surprised to see Charlie at the meeting, suggesting that Edward had already told him about her new employer. Jonah Ritten, on the other hand, seemed deeply unhappy with her presence.

He must think Edward sent her to spy on the rest of the Alliance on his behalf, Daniel thought, feeling stupid that he was only wondering *now* if that had been Edward's intention all along.

"This room gets warm so early in the year, Silver," Crank complained quietly from his right-hand side. He patted at his lined forehead with a silk, embroidered handkerchief. "It's barely March and I'm already sweating!"

"We'll use my other meeting room next time," Daniel promised, though it amused him to see the older man – though 'old' was a relative term whenever he was around – sweating in the weak March sunshine spilling over the courtyard and through the glass walls.

Besides, Daniel far preferred this room. Looking out onto the greenery outside calmed his soul and reminded him about what he was working to protect. If it wasn't entirely impractical to do so he'd have built his entire house from glass when he had the layout drawn up.

The meeting began as they always did, with pleasantries exchanged and the agenda discussed. Out of the corner of his eye Daniel spotted Charlie listening attentively, back stock straight, not a single hair out of place.

She was so unlike herself Daniel could scarcely believe it.

"We had hoped to discuss the woods being felled at the border," Arjun said after some time had passed. "We heard no mention of sanctioned culls; a witness even reported that some of the trees were on the Eshijani side of the border."

Daniel was not at all surprised that this was being brought up – he only wished Edward had been able to address the issue properly beforehand so he had more to say on the matter.

"Perhaps Jonathan can shed light on this," he told Arjun, pre-empting the man from pushing the responsibility onto Daniel himself. "I must admit to being curious about this, too."

"Ah, unfortunately the cull was performed by an entirely unsanctioned, privately-operating group," Crank explained hastily. "It shall not happen again."

"Make sure it doesn't." Lee's eyes were sharp and unamused; it was clear he didn't believe a word Crank said.

Jonah Ritten coughed to bring attention to himself. "Perhaps if we could agree on a more favourable trade agreement then we might be able to avoid more *unsanctioned* timber felling."

"Is that a threat?"

"Of course not," Ritten reassured, though everybody knew it was. "But we have witnessed such events across much of Lopox lately. We have a shortage of natural resources in many of our northern countries and not enough magicians talented in transmutation to make up for this shortage. It is no surprise the common folk have taken to stealing."

"And you expect us to fix that problem for you by accepting your sub-par trade agreement?" Lee said, visibly angry. "You have made not one single change to the agreement, nor the Charter, since the last time Grandmaster Feng spoke to the Alliance."

This was true.

"We have delayed building a watchtower at the border as a sign of our continued trust in Eshijan," Jonathan chimed in.

"Surely that must count as a sign of progress? We want this relationship to work – but all good relationships take time. You cannot expect the member states of the Alliance to agree to all of the changes you have proposed we include."

"You have agreed to none of them!"

Oh, Uthesh be good, Daniel thought, watching and listening in dismay as the room devolved into bitter arguments. This was why he preferred Feng to attend meetings, for he knew how to keep his calm in the face of the Alliance. But Daniel felt bad about this; the Eshijani were rightfully angry with Lopox. The existing Charter *wasn't* fair for them, just as it wasn't fair for non-magicians across the continent.

The Alliance as it currently stood was too conservative to result in any change to the Charter. Daniel had convinced himself that all he had to do was patiently wait a generation – maybe two – before affecting change himself within a far more liberal set of colleagues. The people around him hadn't always been so set in their ways, after all.

"Perhaps it might be sensible to trial a trade agreement based on places where a word-of-mouth one has already worked," Charlie said, her soft voice cutting through the cacophony of the room as if she had shouted.

Daniel opened his mouth, a knee-jerk rebuttal on the tip of his tongue, before he realised that Charlie's suggestion was a good one. *Very good, in fact,* he thought, impressed. He glanced at Crank and Ritten. *But they will never agree to it. They'll—*

"Such as the agreement Mt. Duega has with Ramas?" Arjun asked.

"That might work," Crank mused, deep in thought. "Miss Hope, might your father be willing to take charge with this?"

Wait, what?

"With input from ourselves, of course," Lee cut in.

Charlie beamed. "But of course."

"Then we'd be happy to plan such a thing. How long do we intend to run it?"

Jonathan Crank looked to Daniel for a suggestion. It took him a painfully long time to get to grips with what was going on and form a reply.

"Two months?" he finally said, when Crimson surreptitiously kicked his shin. And then, when his brain caught up with his mouth: "I am hosting a gala in May on my estate. Perhaps the two of you – and Grandmaster Feng, of course – would like to attend, and we can discuss how the trial fared then?"

The Eshijani officials murmured their approval, clearly content with this turn of events.

For the rest of the meeting Daniel kept expecting Crank to come to his senses or for Ritten to vocally protest to the temporary trade agreement; neither of the men had ever been in favour of improving the Eshijani side of the agreement in all their years on the Alliance.

But the meeting went smoothly. Smoother than any meeting regarding the border had gone in a long, long time.

After everyone nodded their thanks for a pleasant afternoon Daniel made a beeline for Charlie, intending to congratulate her on her excellent idea – and ask where it came from. *Has she been sitting on it for a while? Was it Edward's suggestion? Or something else entirely?*

But the entire group had barely made their way out of the meeting room before Charlie disappeared as if she had never been present in the first place.

"Just where—" Daniel began, before spotting Charlie through a window heading towards the woods. His right hand clenched into a fist at his side, incensed that she had, in fact, done exactly as he expected her to do and run away.

"Ah, Miss Hope likes to recentre herself in the woods after work," Crimson explained to the Eshijani, who watched Charlie through the glass with curious expressions on their faces.

Arjun laughed. "Not unlike your grandfather, then! That is a shame. I had hoped she would join us for a drink or two to celebrate a fruitful meeting."

"Mister Silver and I can drink enough for three," Crimson said, directing the entire group towards the parlour room. "Or, at least, I can. It's something *I* share with my grandfather."

More laughter from Arjun and Lee.

After a servant had poured drinks for everyone and Crank had engaged the Eshijani in a rather banal conversation about fishing, Daniel pulled Crimson to the side to talk to her privately.

"That was a good lie you told the Eshijani," he said, careful not to be overheard. "About Miss Hope, I mean."

At this Crimson seemed to take offence. "What I said wasn't a lie, Daniel. Why would you believe that it was?"

"Because...well, she goes there to goof off, does she not? To avoid being asked to do anything."

"What is *goofing off* if not taking yourself out of a stressful situation in order to take a breath and recentre yourself? What is different between what Miss Hope does in her spare time and what *you* do in your spare time, reading by the window in your study or talking to your cat?"

"I—"

"Charlie likes being in the woods," Crimson cut in, abruptly changing to the young woman's first name. "You like *looking* at it from the safety of your house. One is not superior to the other."

Daniel held his hands up in defeat. "All right, all right. I get it. I didn't realise you were her biggest supporter."

A quirked eyebrow. "I'm not; that would be her father. But I see potential in Charlie that could be better coaxed out with acceptance and encouragement instead of shouting at her and controlling her."

Daniel felt like tearing his hair out. "I see potential in her, too, else I would have fired her already. But there's only so much patience a man can have."

"Best find some more, then," Crimson said, dismissing Daniel with a flick of her ruby hair on her way back to rejoin the Eshijani and Alliance officials. Jonathan Crank, who two hours earlier had been complaining about the sun on his face being too hot, was now requesting a servant light up the fire in the hearth.

With a sigh barely hidden beneath a hand Daniel rejoined the group, too, though his thoughts were on Charlie in the woods.

Patience, indeed. If I wasn't already immortal I'd be an old man by the time Charlie did something without anyone pushing her to do it.

Edward Hope had told Daniel it was worth fighting with his daughter to have her on his side. Kit told him that the young woman would make his life interesting. Now his Chief-of-Staff was telling Daniel that he needed to be patient with Charlie Hope.

"She better be worth it," he muttered in an undertone, drinking from a glass of whisky when it was handed to him.

The fire Daniel felt as the liquid ran down his throat reminded him of her.

CHAPTER EIGHT

It was Charlie's precious day off and spring was all around. Though it was only early March – too early by all accounts for many of the plants in Silver's garden to begin sprouting and growing and blooming – the mild weather over the past week or so had encouraged growth where mere days ago there had been none.

There was another factor nobody but Charlie knew was at play, too: Charlie herself.

Her behaving well for the meeting with the Eshijani seemed to, finally, have given her an inch of freedom with which to be alone during daylight hours. Naturally, this meant Charlie was exploring the expansive courtyard of Daniel Silver's estate, happy to escape the watchful gaze of Crimson. She could not have picked a better day to do so: the sun was shining, the air was fresh with the scent of cut grass, and her employer was blessedly away to the Capital for a few days.

Of course Charlie was going to use her small window of hard-earned independence to convince the plants all around her that they could grow just a *little* more than they already had.

Her current focus was a large bank of wildflowers which marked the border between the immaculately presented courtyard and the woods. Afterwards, if time allowed, Charlie would whisper sweet encouragement to the rose bushes which lined the building into letting loose a few early spring blooms.

Silver will be so surprised when he returns from the Capital, Charlie thought, voice hitching in excitement as she sang to the daisies and the bluebells and the snowdrops and the clover. There were tulips, too, but given their size Charlie knew she had to breathe a little more life into them than the others.

So her singing grew just a little louder. Brighter. Frenetic.

When purple petals so dark they were almost black began unfurling Charlie gasped in delight. She'd never seen tulips in such a shade before – night incarnate in broad daylight, so stark a contrast to her eyes that Charlie loosed an accidental burst of magic out of sheer excitement.

The magic sent a shudder through the reeds which circulated a glass-smooth pond off in the distance to Charlie's left. A wooden viewing platform was built into the northern bank of the pond, allowing one to view the entire courtyard – and the woods – in all their splendour.

Charlie imagined diving off the platform into the pond in summer, a giggle flushing her skin. This was her element, not a stuffy meeting room: sunshine above her, plants all around her, the very earth beneath her teeming with life.

"The meeting was not so bad," she told the new tulips, glancing around her before bounding on impulse towards the lake instead of the rose bushes, looking for ducks hidden in the reeds protecting new clutches of eggs.

In truth the meeting had been excellent. Charlie knew it, Crimson knew it and Daniel Silver knew it, too. She had managed to avoid suspicion over tampering with the thoughts of both the Alliance members and the Eshijani, leaving Mr Silver and his Chief-of-Staff believing that Charlie's idea had been enough on its own to bridge a gap between both sides of the conflict.

Let them believe I am somehow that convincing, Charlie thought, bending low to chirrup out a little song for a pair of nesting ducks. They ruffled their feathers in response. *So long as they don't know how I am doing it.*

Deciding that she did indeed want to tackle the rose bushes, Charlie made her way along the gravelled pathways of gleaming white which sectioned the lush lawn of the courtyard into perfect squares, a smile on her face and a skip in her step. So long as she could keep everyone's suspicions at bay – as she had been doing her entire life – then the rest of Charlie's employment was likely to fly by in a flurry of successful meetings.

Her father had been right: she could do so much more working for Mr Silver than she could only working on behalf of Mt. Duega with him. Charlie Hope was going to settle things between Lopox and Eshijan once and for all...then return home content to while away the rest of her days doing exactly what she was doing now.

Making things grow.

"I wonder what colour you'll be," Charlie crooned when she reached the first glossy-leaved rose bush. It was far too perfectly pruned for her taste, not a single thorn nor branch nor leaf out of place. If Charlie had her way it would crawl halfway up the side of Daniel Silver's house, wild and uneven.

When the smallest of rose buds began to unfurl Charlie knew in her heart that she should stop. It really was far too early for roses; any further growth would be too obvious that something was afoot.

She couldn't stop herself, anyway.

"You...can make flowers grow?"

All at once Charlie shut up at the sound of the feminine voice, frozen in place with her eyes firmly on the rose still growing in front of her. It was the palest of pinks – barely a blush upon a young woman's face.

"You can, can't you?" Luca pressed, sweeping in front of Charlie to inspect the baby rose. She glanced at her, frowning when Charlie didn't respond, then returned her attention to the flower. Luca's auburn hair was too bright against the pale rose, jarring and somehow unnatural and entirely out of place.

"This is amazing," Luca continued, touching the petals and then, carefully, the thorns of the rose. "I was watching you from the kitchen when you were over by the wildflowers. I couldn't believe what I was seeing; I knew I had to come closer to confirm it. You can really make—"

"I can't do anything," Charlie bit out, the words tumbling from her mouth. All at once she remembered where she was and what she had to do. Pushing out her Influence she urged Luca to forget what she saw. "All I was doing was admiring the flowers. They're out so early. Aren't they beautiful?"

One second passed. Two. Three.

"They're...yes, they are," Luca agreed, going at once from glassy-eyed and confused to lucid and content. "They smell amazing. Were you trying to hide from everyone again?"

Charlie flinched for an entirely different reason. "I didn't realise you'd noticed," she said, averting her gaze.

To her surprise Luca snorted. "As if anyone *couldn't*. It's almost impossible to find you outside of work hours. Do you eat in your room? Or in the woods with Mr Silver's cat?"

A beat too late Charlie realised she'd Influenced Luca to be too relaxed and far too quick to trust her – to converse with her when Luca had made it abundantly clear she disliked Charlie. Guilt washed over her at using her Influence in a situation when it had been entirely Charlie's fault she got caught making the flowers grow in the first place.

She at least owed Luca some answers in retribution for what she'd done.

"I...find it difficult to cope with new surroundings – and new people," Charlie said, following Luca when she inclined her head towards the pond. "And you know I didn't want to work here in the first place. I find it much easier to run off to the woods than make an effort with everyone."

"So why work for Mr Silver at all?"

"Da forced me to. He wants me to 'make something of myself', as it were."

"Ha!" Luca said, appearing vindicated. When they reached the pond she picked up a promisingly smooth stone and attempted to skim it across the water. But she failed miserably, and they both watched as it sunk beneath the jewel green surface. "Are you an only child, too, then?" she asked.

This surprised Charlie. "How'd you know?"

"You have a boy's name, like me. Atralian tradition to give your first-born a boy's name alongside parental pressure to do well usually means that someone is an only child."

"That's...awfully astute of you," Charlie murmured, taking her time in choosing a smooth-faced stone for skimming. "Though it's actually Charlotte, not Charlie. But I hate being called Charlotte, so please forget I even told you that."

When Charlie threw the stone across the pond she murmured words of encouragement to the water to facilitate its journey – something that went entirely unnoticed by Luca in her Influenced, trusting, oblivious state.

The young woman let out a noise of disbelief at how far the stone skimmed. Charlie counted thirteen steps before it finally succumbed to sinking. "How are you so good at that?" Luca complained.

"Practice," Charlie lied. "I'm useless at everything else. You have to let me have this one skill."

"You can't be that useless, otherwise why would Mr Silver have invited you to that meeting between Eshijan and the Alliance?"

"Because of my father."

Luca frowned. "I don't believe that."

"It's the truth, I swear it!" It wasn't entirely false: Silver had only ordered Charlie to attend based on her father's testimony. She sighed when she saw the frustrated expression on Luca's face. "But I'll try harder to justify working here. I really will. I'm honestly not all that impressive with magic, though. You've already seen me try and fail at basically everything!"

"As long as you mean that. I fought so hard to get this job...it stings that you swanned in when you don't even want to be here."

Charlie did not respond, for she didn't know what to say. It hadn't ever occurred to her just how frustrated Luca had been. *I thought she simply disliked me because I wasn't trying. I didn't think about how my attitude undermined everything she'd worked so hard for.*

The two of them leaned against the wooden railing of the viewing deck for a while after that, Luca shivering slightly in the March air whilst Charlie revelled in the chill on her face. Eventually Charlie was reasonably sure the lingering effects of her Influence had dissipated, leaving Luca safe to leave her company without risk of her acting out of character.

"I better go," Luca said, as if reading Charlie's mind, stretching her arms above her head in the process. "I have some notes I want to go over."

Charlie was shocked to discover she was disappointed to see her leave. *Without my Influence she has no interest in talking to me. Of course.* "Oh," was all she said, throat too tight to form a coherent sentence.

"But I'll see you at dinner?" Luca smiled mischievously. "If you don't run off to the woods beforehand, that is."

The surprised smile Charlie gave in return was far too happy. Obnoxiously so. "I'll see if I can manage that," she said, still grinning even when Luca waved good-bye and disappeared through the courtyard and into Silver's estate.

Her good mood lingered even two hours later, when finally Charlie dragged herself from the courtyard to clean up for dinner – only to remember that she didn't *need* to clean up. Because of Silver's magic Charlie didn't even need to bathe; the water sloughed off her skin and hair leaving her completely untouched and bone dry.

Don't let that spoil a good day, she thought, urging the man out of her mind with a scowl as she approached her bedroom. But when Charlie opened the door she was shocked to discover the room was not empty, nor was the intruder Kit.

It was Crimson, sitting cross-legged on Charlie's bed.

"You've been hiding something from us all," the woman said the moment Charlie closed her door.

"No I'm not," Charlie said, instinct pulling the words from her mouth so quickly that it was obvious it was a lie. She was about to push her Influence towards Crimson when she paused. *If she's found something out then I need to know what that is so I can avoid tripping myself up in the future.*

"...how did you come to that conclusion?" Charlie mumbled, falling onto the bed beside Crimson.

The Chief-of-Staff raised an eyebrow. "You're not going to deny it?"

"What's the point? You're not going to let me off the hook if I deny it."

"True." Crimson regarded Charlie through critical eyes, as if attempting to see why the young woman was being so obedient. "After Daniel said you didn't need to prepare for the Eshijani meeting I knew I had to watch you – and only you – whilst it went on. And I discovered something very, very interesting."

Charlie squirmed uncomfortably. "And what do you think you saw?"

"I know exactly what I saw, Charlie Hope: there is no *think* about it. You moved the thoughts and decisions of everyone in that room like pieces on a chess board – with but one well-placed idea. You've really been holding out on us all this time, haven't you? Daniel will go ballistic when he realises he's had an Intent user under his employ that he had no idea about!"

Oh, Uthesh be good.

"You can't tell him," Charlie insisted, readying her magic to wipe Crimson's thoughts clean. "You can't tell anyone."

Crimson folded her arms across her chest in an expectant manner, not sympathetic in the slightest to Charlie's pleading. "Care to elaborate?"

She tried to find the words to explain how she felt, then decided on an altogether more dangerous tactic. "How do you feel about a war with the Eshijani, Crimson?"

"Naturally I'm opposed to such a thing. Why do you ask?"

"Are you really sure that's how you feel about it?" Charlie pressed, throwing out one hook of magic and then another and another, prying away at Crimson's own thoughts until they were replaced by notions planted there by her.

A pause. And then, so confidently anyone would have believed Crimson believed every sword she spoke: "If I've adapted to Atralian culture then so can the rest of Eshijan. The Lopox Alliance would be right to organise an invasion into the country to bring it under its control."

For a minute or two Charlie simply allowed Crimson's statement to hang in the air. Then she pulled her Influence back, little by little, until Crimson's thoughts were her own once more. Going by the confusion and subsequent horror that flashed across the woman's face Charlie knew her point had been made.

"I know you can't feel the difference between your own thoughts and the ones I pushed on you," she said, "but since they're such opposing ideals I hope you can understand how dangerous it would be for other people to know what I can do."

"Silver is...a good man," Charlie continued. "Regardless of how I act towards him even I can see that. But he is also a politician, and an influential one. If he knew what I could do – if anyone knew – my abilities would end up being used for situations I won't even pretend to be able to understand. So please, Crimson – Wei – don't tell anyone."

To Charlie's great surprise, the Eshijani woman smiled. "A sensible answer, and the one I would have given myself. I guess you are not so lost a cause as you make yourself out to be. I agree that we cannot risk anyone knowing of your abilities. I'm assuming your father knows?"

"Of course."

"Anyone else?"

Charlie shook her head.

"Do you plan to Influence me into believing this conversation never happened?"

"Absolutely."

Crimson laughed whole-heartedly. "I do enjoy how honest you always are, Miss Hope, even when you know that means people will not like your answer. But I have an alternative proposition for you: I'll help you cover your tracks – including keeping Daniel out of the loop – providing you don't use your Influence magic on me."

"You...would really do that?" Charlie asked, comforted and taken aback in equal measure by the fact she knew it wasn't a lie.

"I wouldn't offer to do so if I didn't mean it. But keep in mind: Daniel won't remain oblivious forever. He's onto you already. So if you want to shake him off for a little longer – until your year with us is up – I'm afraid you'll have to make yourself a little more impressive in other areas to distract him."

"...which means?"

Crimson's eyes lit up with glee. "Which means you have to step up to the plate and be the best damn employee he's ever had. No more slacking off, Charlie Hope."

CHAPTER NINE

KIT BEGAN EVERY MORNING AS HE always did: waking in the boughs of his favourite birch tree not far from the edge of the woods by Daniel Silver's estate.

He stretched his arms above his head, using the tree's rough bark to scratch an itch on his shoulder as he basked in the deliciously warm morning sunshine. It promised a hot, settled day, and reminded Kit that it was May already.

Immortal Folk felt the passage of time differently than humans; it seemed as if it were only yesterday when Charlie Hope came to work for Daniel Silver and Kit returned from his winter hibernation.

It had not been Kit's intention to leave Daniel for so long over winter, considering the two of them had never been apart for longer than three weeks prior to this year. But the forest was so empty of his kin nowadays that Kit found himself wishing to sleep longer and longer whenever the months grew cold and dreary.

Even now, though he could sense a sparse handful of his kin nearby, Kit could not spot a single one of them with his keen eyes. A sadness washed over him. Once upon a time he would wake up and be surrounded by Dryads and Nymphs and Satyrs, gentle music meandering on the breeze, each and every one of them entirely unafraid of anything.

But Erath was very much in the age of mortal men. It had been for a long time now. Many of the Immortal Folk had chosen to float through the energies of the planet, in wait for a kinder time, instead of retaking corporeal form.

It had happened before, after all. It would happen again.

Jumping from the birch tree Kit followed the sound of running water until he found a burn snaking through the bustling late spring undergrowth. He caught flashes of his reflection in the gurgling water: messy, tawny hair; the venomous green eyes and long, pointed ears all of his kind possessed; sharp features and suntanned skin.

The Immortal Folk weren't keen on mirrors and reflections so Kit often went weeks and weeks with no idea what he looked like. He had seen himself through the eyes of a cat many a time in Daniel Silver's house, of course, but rarely in his real form.

Though even this form is temporary, Kit mused, cocking his head to the side simply to watch his broken reflection do the same. After all, his current body was merely a vessel for Kit to exist in until such a time that he, too, gave himself back to the planet, waiting to be reincarnated in another time – another age.

Kit splashed his face then cleaned his ears and the back of his neck, relishing in the bitter sting of the burn's water. The sun and the air and the trees may well have been in the late stages of spring but the water still held a whisper of winter to it. The whisper would not truly disappear until June.

Satisfied with his preening Kit stood back up, took his time stretching out each and every one of his muscles, then lazily padded through the woods until he reached the border of Daniel Silver's estate. Between one blink and the next he shook himself into the form of a cat, then bounded past the obscurity of the trees towards the expansive, grey-stoned building.

Most of his kind laughed at Kit's fondness for the man – as well as the form he took to be with him – but Daniel was Kit's best friend. He had been for several generations now. Kit could not imagine spending his days with anyone else but him... especially now.

The best way for him to keep abreast of what was going on between Lopox and Eshijan at the Atralian border was to remain right by Daniel's side.

Things had been weird in the woods ever since the foreign country came to be Atralia's neighbour once more. Kit had not been around when the two countries last shared a border, thousands of years ago; the very few creatures who were did not like to talk of those dark days.

But something was different now. Something urgent and dangerous.

Kit didn't need to know what it was to fully and utterly believe it: he could feel it in his bones.

The Immortal Folk had therefore been keeping tabs on humans more often than usual ever since the Great Shift fifteen years ago, so whilst his kin used to laugh at Kit spending all his time with Daniel, the man's position within the Lopox Alliance – and his trust in Kit to divulge all that was going on between the continent and Eshijan – had grown increasingly important.

The quietest of singing filled Kit's sensitive ears as he entered the pristine courtyard of Daniel's estate. He knew it was Charlie; with the sun rising so early now Crimson could not possibly set her to work at dawn any more.

Though Charlie had admitted to Kit that Luca caught her in the act of singing life into flowers two months ago, she simply couldn't resist the pull of new springtime growth. It was inevitable that Charlie ended up once more singing nonsense words and lullabies to the primroses and the hyacinths and the creeping ivy, eyes shining with the strength of her own power as she watched everything around her bloom.

Kit enjoyed this version of Charlie Hope most of all.

A small family of rabbits bounded past Kit, not at all threatened by his cat form. They knew, instinctively, what he really was. Attracted by the magic-imbued singing they eagerly hopped towards Charlie.

In the morning sunlight Charlie's hair shone golden and bright, almost as dazzling as the smile on her face when she knelt down to stroke the boldest rabbit. "Good morning to you," she crooned. The grey rabbit twitched its nose, chinning her hand to mark Charlie as its family. "I see you're all doing well today. Should I sing you a song?"

When Kit playfully stalked towards her Charlie spied him out of the corner of her eye. Her grin only grew wider when he bounded the last few metres between them to beat the rabbit for a place on her lap.

"Good morning to you, too, Kit," she laughed when he nuzzled his face against her cheek. "I cannot stay here much longer. Perhaps only another song or two and then I must head back inside."

Charlie did not sound as sad about work as she used to. Kit had witnessed her throwing herself into her job over the past two months, using every ounce of cleverness she possessed to get over her lack of skill in most areas of magic – all to impress Daniel Silver and the rest of his political team.

He should have been proud of Charlie. For her entire life she had been separated by other mortals bar her father, her magic almost a physical wall that prevented her from reaching anyone else. But Charlie's progress resulted in her becoming more and more distant from the woods.

From Kit.

No longer did she come to the woods every night, choosing instead to visit only twice a week in order to rest properly. It had been a very long time since she had visited the forest so infrequently.

Of course Kit had known Charlie before she was forced to work for Daniel. She knew him, too, though not the cat form he took around her, nor his name. Kit didn't like keeping such a secret from her but, for the sake of gathering information on the political unrest between Lopox and Eshijan – and ensuring Daniel continued to confide in him – Kit had to maintain his guise around Charlie.

He had absolutely no doubt his best friend was fascinated by and, more importantly, completely besotted with, the young woman. Daniel being Daniel of course had no idea how he felt: with every passing decade Kit had watched him create a wider gap between himself and the rest of his kind.

It was no coincidence Daniel had shut off his heart immediately after his wife chose not to cross over to Immortality with him, decades and decades ago.

But Daniel would work out his feelings eventually, Kit was sure. His best friend's heart was not quite as impossible to reach as the man himself believed it to be.

It would therefore do Daniel Silver absolutely no good to discover Kit had loved Charlie Hope for years before Daniel had ever met her.

Eventually Charlie unfolded her legs and got back to her feet, letting out a yawn that scattered the rabbits as she did so. "Perhaps I should sleep in tomorrow morning, Kit," she said, Kit following close at her heels as they made their way through the courtyard. "All these early mornings and late weekend nights in the woods will be the death of me!"

They both knew she would never do such a thing: Charlie happily ran on three hours of sleep every night if it meant she could surround herself with nature every morning. Which meant she often napped before dinner, which suited Kit just fine. He loved napping on Charlie's bed, curled up in her arms in peace and quiet for two blessed hours every day.

Charlie bent down to scratch his ears. "Come on, then," she said, leading the way back towards the servant's entrance to Daniel's house. "We might be able to steal some fresh bread from the kitchen if we're quick. Or...you could leave. See you later, Kit!" Charlie called after him when Kit skipped off down the corridor towards Daniel's office.

Though Daniel would never say it out loud, he became jealous if Kit spent too much time with Charlie instead of him.

Kit thought his jealousy was adorable.

When he slunk into the office Daniel was standing by the open window, fanning himself against the balmy morning air. The day would be a hot one, Kit knew, especially if his friend insisted on wearing his thick-woven silver robe. Daniel was a stickler for appearances and rules; he would never take his formal magician's uniform off within work hours unless the situation called for it.

Which means he will suffer in the heat all day. What a fool.

Daniel glanced at Kit without turning to face him, unsurprised by his silent approach. "You're later than usual. Spending time with Charlie, I assume?"

"Perhaps," Kit said, leaping onto the man's desk to make a nest out of the papers neatly stacked on top of it. Daniel's shoulders flinched at the obvious attempt to annoy him.

"Just what is your obsession with her?" Daniel asked, moving from the heady flower-scented air to collapse onto his chair, apparently already exhausted with the day.

Kit almost parroted the question back at his best friend. Instead he squirrelled his head beneath Daniel's hand until he scratched his ears. He purred luxuriously when the man relieved Kit of an itch that had developed when he was in the garden. "Perhaps you should find out for yourself."

"...and what is that supposed to mean?"

When he looked up at his best friend Kit found that

Daniel's face was contorted by a frown that was equal parts impatience and confusion. Kit would never grow tired of seeing – or creating – such an expression.

"You always ask me about Charlie instead of talking to her yourself," Kit said, flicking his tail this way and that. "Maybe, if you took even the smallest of chances and spoke to her about something other than work, you might discover for yourself why I am *obsessed*, as you put it."

Daniel did not reply. He knew Kit was right. He knew it, but that didn't make the Drus' advice any easier to follow.

There was nothing more enjoyable to Kit than watching the man struggle to do something that should have been easy for him. That *had* been easy, decades ago.

"You're hopeless, Daniel," Kit murmured, closing his eyes to settle in for a morning nap when it was clear Daniel had no response to his challenge. "Just remember that Charlie is a person rather than a puzzle and you'll do just fine."

Daniel clucked his tongue. "She's both."

"Guess that means she's perfectly matched to you."

"Shut up and go to sleep."

There were many other things the two of them had to discuss – about how the temporary trade agreement was going, about how more trees in the forest had been felled, about the inevitability of war – but Kit decided these topics could wait for another day.

After all, he and Daniel had all the time in the world to talk.

Kit did as he was told and fell asleep.

CHAPTER TEN

Before Charlie knew it her Crimson-enforced impeccable employee act had thrown her into May.

Silver had moved his lecture to the courtyard; it was an unbearably hot evening meaning it had been all but impossible to maintain the attention of his team for much longer than a minute or two. Luca had suggested using cooling magic to make the lecture hall bearable but, when Charlie instead suggested they hold the lecture outside, Silver – much to her surprise – eagerly agreed with her.

So there they all were, sitting on comfortable garden chairs in a small circle, Charlie revelling in the sunshine warming her scalp. For the first time since Silver placed his cleaning spell on her Charlie was glad for its protection – it meant she could not get sunburnt.

Even Crimson had joined them for the lecture once she saw it was being held outside, for which Charlie was grateful. Ever since the older woman discovered her Intent magic the two of them had grown much closer. Charlie always felt more comfortable when she was around, especially when she had to deal with Silver.

At first Charlie didn't bother properly listening to what the man was saying. She was too happy to be in the garden, the scent of honeysuckle sweetening the air all around her. Between acting as much like a model student as she could muster, sitting in on Alliance meetings and liaising with her father regarding the temporary Eshijani trade agreement, Charlie hadn't had much time to simply *exist*.

When a jewel-blue damselfly flew past Charlie whistled at it, infusing the sound with magic to encourage it to land on her nose.

Luca giggled when the creature settled on Charlie, which in turn garnered the attention of Silver.

He raised a judgemental eyebrow. "If the garden is too distracting for you, Miss Hope," he said, "we could go back inside."

"Oh, don't mind me," she replied, wriggling her nose until the damselfly became airborne once more. It fluttered past her eyelashes, lingering for a moment before heading back to the pond. "I'm listening."

"I'm sure."

"Perhaps we should all stay hydrated," Jean cut in, deftly summoning a large jug of ice water and a platter of glasses. "Thirst is terrible for your mood. Otherwise Charlie might incite us all to begin screaming at each other." By *all* he meant Silver and by *each other* he meant Charlie, of course, but nobody corrected him.

He handed a glass first to Charlie, brushing his fingertips against hers as he did so. "Best not to bother him when it's this hot," he told her in an undertone, artificially silver eyes glinting mischievously. "He doesn't do well in the heat when he's in his formal wear."

Charlie was careful to maintain a polite demeanour as she took the water from Jean, and did not respond to his jibe. His interest in her had only grown with every day that Charlie tried harder with her job and proved her worth, and it wasn't something she was equipped to deal with.

Influencing Jean away was out of the question. Charlie already felt bad enough about using her Intent magic on Luca, back when she caught her making the flowers grow. *And that situation resulted in us becoming friends,* Charlie mused, as Jean handed out glasses of water to the rest of the grateful circle of people. *It's unlikely I would be so lucky a second time around. If I Influence Jean into leaving me alone and something goes wrong...*

Charlie would have to deal with the after-effects of such a disaster for another nine months, and Jean may well end up permanently altered by her magic.

No, she couldn't risk it. Charlie had to deal with Jean's interest in her like every other human being on the planet.

By ignoring it in the hopes he would eventually move on.

"I would never rile anyone up whilst in the garden," Charlie said, putting on a carefree air that she didn't entirely feel. Jean's choice of words made her skin itch, for she *could* incite everyone into a screaming match with a single, magically-inflected word.

Or with no words at all, Charlie thought, glancing at Crimson. The woman's expression was bland but she could tell that, beneath the surface, Crimson knew exactly what Charlie was likely thinking right now.

There was another layer to what she could sense from Crimson: namely, the woman urging Charlie *not* to be so combative with Daniel Silver.

Charlie truly meant to behave – the man was discussing old stories about magic, something which she was actually interested in – but she couldn't resist locking her eyes firmly on his and saying, entirely off-handedly, "You were talking about myths, Daniel?"

The choice of words had the precise effect Charlie had intended, no magic required. Silver was so taken aback by his most rowdy employee referring to him by his first name that he coughed and spluttered around a mouthful of water.

She hardly even uses 'Mr Silver' to address me, he thought, trying his best to ignore the sniggers from the group at his rare moment of foolishness, *and now she jumps straight to using my first name? She is clearly trying to rile me up, despite her assurances that she isn't!*

It was with some effort that Daniel managed to grasp onto his original train of thought, mentally prepared what he was going to say, then continued his lecture.

"There's a lot to learn about magic from Atralian myths," he said. "And, of course, from further afield across Lopox and the rest of the world. There are myths which teach us of magic we have long since forgotten how to perform. Stories about a time when magic we now know how to perform would have solved a problem in the past and thus prevented catastrophe. Legends which deal with magic being abused, or magic implemented to the benefit of the people, or any other number of things. So I ask you all: what is your favourite myth?"

There was a pause as people considered their answer. Crimson was the first to respond. "In Eshijan it is often told that, when the sun is red, it is bleeding new magic upon Erath. It's common practice for expectant mothers to pray when such a sun appears in the sky, hoping that their unborn child shall be blessed with some of this new magic."

"Ah, I've heard that one," Silver replied, nodding his head in approval. "There is an Atralian equivalent, I'm sure. Wishing for the best for one's children is a common theme in stories passed down from generation to generation. Anyone else?"

"There's the one about the man who turned himself into a woman in order to seduce the king of Laskey, whom he hated," Luca piped up, scrunching her brow as she tried to remember the tale. "He broke the king's heart by revealing who he really was just as a major war between the northern countries of Lopox broke out."

"Yes, but didn't the king tell the man he loved him no matter how he looked on the outside?" Jean added on. "And then the man was confused, because he had developed feelings for the king during his time as a woman?"

"That tale is more about being true to oneself and to not deceive others than it is about actual magic," Daniel said. "Though it's certainly one of the more entertaining stories folk pass on to their children."

"What's *your* favourite myth, then?" Charlie demanded, admittedly curious to hear the man's answer but also not wishing to give her own answer, either. For Charlie's favourite myth was far too tied into her memories of her mother – memories that she did not want to have to share with other people.

They were hers and hers alone.

Silver cocked his head to the side and met Charlie's challenging stare; on his brow she spied several beads of sweat practically begging to run down his face. Then Silver looked to the west where the sun was slowly descending in the sky, and let out a low breath.

"It really is too warm for my robe," he murmured, unbuttoning the article of clothing before sloughing it from his skin. It left the man in a thin cotton shirt, which he also unbuttoned to his clavicle before rolling up the sleeves to his elbows.

Then Silver let his thick hair loose to fall just above his shoulders, sighing in contentment when he ran his fingers through it to ease several strands away from his face.

Lastly, Silver removed his glasses. "Since I'm not reading anything there's no need for them," he said, as if that somehow explained the fact that he was taking them off now when he rarely ever did so.

Charlie watched his every movement as if she'd never seen the man before in her life; the version of Daniel Silver who now sat opposite her was wildly different than the way he'd always presented himself to Charlie before.

Did he hear what Jean told me? Charlie thought, too stunned to stop herself from staring at the man. *He must have. This feels too...deliberate. It's so unlike him. It's so...*

Charlie didn't really know what it was. All she knew was that she couldn't stop looking at Daniel Silver, face softened by his pale hair blowing in the wind in stark contrast to the lean, muscled forearms his rolled-up shirt sleeves revealed.

If Silver noticed Charlie gawking he didn't show it on his face nor react in any other way she could sense. "You wanted to know my favourite myth, Miss Hope?"

You'd think I'd never seen an attractive man before, Charlie thought, deaf to Silver's question. *But it isn't fair that he's handsome. He can't be handsome* and *powerful* and *immortal. That's too many things. Uthesh be good, Charlie, get it together. People are staring. People—*

"Miss Hope?" Silver inquired politely. "Are you—"

"Yes!" Charlie cried out, feeling foolish and far too hot. She squirmed uncomfortably in her seat, trying her best not to flush in embarrassment when Luca sniggered at her.

A flash of amusement crossed Silver's face but he otherwise, blessedly, did not react to Charlie's obviously flustered state.

He turned slightly in his chair to address the entire group. "My favourite myth is a very, very old one, indeed," Silver began, his voice taking on a sing-song quality that hadn't been present before. "Many thousands of years ago, Atralia and Eshijan were one country, and made up a large portion of the eastern continent of Ohus."

Between his hands he magicked liquid silver into existence,

shaping and forming it into two land masses before moulding them into one. It was then that Charlie realised which story Silver was recounting: *her* myth. Her mother's myth.

The one Charlie insisted on listening to every night as a child, though it gave her nightmares just as often as it filled her head with wonderful dreams.

"One day," Silver continued, "because it always happens one day in the stories, an immortal magician gone drunk on his own power created an army of wicked creatures with which to scour the earth and bring it under his control."

The silver in his hands morphed into all manner of twisted monsters: one with a gaping maw and teeth like knives; another with a dozen spindly, elongated legs and pincer-like arms, and another with an almost catlike head bearing a singular bulbous, watchful eye.

Charlie was struck by how beautiful the creatures were as they ebbed and flowed before her in a terrible, fairy tale sort of way, though she supposed that was only because they were made of liquid metal, the size of her index finger, and a fictitious work of Silver's mind.

"Noben, the monsters were called, or at least that's the translation in modern Atralian," Silver said, eyes finding Charlie's silently demanding she get locked in his tale – as if she wasn't already. "It took all the magicians of Ohus and the Immortal Folk who made their home in the expansive woods combined to stop him. The Noben were slain, one by one, and their remains buried deep underground. But the magician merely laughed at them all when they thought themselves victorious."

A shiver ran down Charlie's spine despite the heat of the day as she watched the metal monsters break into a hundred tiny pieces. Around her everyone else was just as engrossed in Silver's magnetic retelling of the Noben myth, but there was something different about the way he directed the story at

Charlie.

She desperately wanted to be the only one present in the garden with him. She didn't want anyone else to hear Silver – the way his voice ran low and melodic as water over stone – recount her darkest, most favourite tale.

"For the man was, of all things, a necromancer," Silver continued, all at once bringing his shards of metal together to reform the tiny army of monsters, "and he could bring the Noben back whenever he liked. To prevent this the Immortal Folk rent the country in two, sending the part which would become Atralia halfway across the ocean – along with half of all the Noben body parts. Without the full bodies upon which to work his forbidden magic, and having drained himself of too much Matter magic to create new life from scratch once more, the magician could do no further damage."

The next part of the myth was the part Charlie most feared. But, even so, she leaned towards Silver, urging him to continue with her Intent before she could stop herself.

When Silver spoke again his words almost tumbled out, though he did not know why. His heart was pounding where before it had been settled; he was excited and enthralled by his own story, though of course he knew the ending.

"But even then the magician was still dangerous. An immortal magician cannot be killed, as their spirit is simply given back to nature and is eventually brought back into a corporeal form. To combat this, what is now the country of Eshijan buried the magician in a sealed tomb underground, deep within the woods. Some say that, now Atralia and Eshijan are back together once more, the two halves of the magician's monstrous abominations have been brought back together. If a necromancer were to sing them back to life then one could reasonably assume they would possess the power to rule the world."

Too suddenly Silver reached the end of the tale, the liquid metal between his hands dissipating into nothing, and Charlie was not prepared for his silence. Her Intent still hung in the air like a hook upon which Silver was caught, though the man did not know it.

When Silver's expression flickered between confusion and clarity Charlie realised what she was doing and pulled her magic back in as quickly as she dared, hating herself for having used it in the first place. It was too dangerous for her to use her Intent magic directly on Silver, especially after Crimson had helped Charlie keep the truth of her abilities secret from him for the last two months.

"Do you believe it?" Jean asked what felt like an eternity later, breaking the taut and tense atmosphere which had fallen over the group. "The myth, I mean. Do you think it's all true?"

Silver considered this for the briefest of moments before replying, simply, "No."

"That's a lie," Charlie immediately refuted.

They all stared at her – Silver most of all. He frowned. "What makes you say that?"

"Because it's a lie. You believe every word that came out of your mouth."

Perhaps it was the way Charlie had framed her answer. Perhaps it was the startled look on Daniel Silver's face at being called a liar. Perhaps it was because Charlie had pulled her Intent magic away and Silver's intoxicating story was over.

Either way, Luca, Jean and Crimson stood up, sensing an argument between Charlie and Silver imminently brewing.

"We are so late for dinner!" Luca said. "I didn't realise the lecture ran over as much as it did. If you don't mind, Mr Silver..."

"Not at all," he replied tersely, all attention firmly on Charlie. "My apologies for running late."

For a moment it looked as if Jean was going to pull Charlie

along with them but a warning look from Crimson told him to leave her be.

Charlie wanted nothing more than to run away.

She knew she couldn't.

The air was abuzz with insects and birds and the gentle hum of the wind, but to the two people left in the garden it may as well have been silent.

"Miss Ho—Charlotte," Silver said, quietly, as if he feared breaking that invisible silence.

She made a face at the name. "Charlie, or nothing."

"Charlie, then." Her stomach squirmed at the sound of her name on Silver's lips. It was uncomfortable only because it *wasn't* uncomfortable, which worried Charlie immensely.

What concerned her more was that she was annoyed Daniel Silver had not seemed to react to her using *his* first name with anything but irritation.

"You never told us your favourite myth," Silver – Daniel – pressed, when Charlie did not say another word.

"I didn't need to."

"And why is that?"

"You already spoke it so well."

The words in all their sickening sincerity fell out of her before Charlie could stop herself, but their effect on Daniel Silver was profound.

Without his glasses on she had an unblocked view of his eyes. They had gone wide at her statement. He ruffled his loose hair as if he wasn't used to receiving a compliment.

Even bathed in the early evening sunshine Charlie could tell that he was blushing.

"I – excuse me!" she cried, unsure what to do with the visual information she had just received. Her only option was to run away.

"Charlie, wait!" Daniel called out from behind her, but Charlie didn't stop.

Couldn't stop.

She had just been sincere and honest with the man, which were two things Charlie Hope had sworn she would never be towards Daniel. The effect they'd had on him made her happier – and more terrified – that she could have possibly anticipated.

It was a long time before Charlie herself stopped blushing; she blamed it on the unseasonably hot day.

CHAPTER ELEVEN

DANIEL WAS MAKING HIS WAY ON FOOT to Mt. Duega. The journey took over an hour without a carriage but he had woken early that morning, unable to sleep even though the air was quiet and still. But it was hot – too hot for May – and Daniel's day off, to boot. He wanted to *do* something, not linger in his bedroom trying to get back to sleep.

So Daniel dressed in a linen shirt and trousers to combat the heat – it was his day off, after all, so he deemed his oppressive work robes unnecessary – tied his hair away from his face far more casually than usual, then headed out of his estate just as the servants were rising from bed.

The fresh air would do him good, and it had been too long since Daniel had visited his home town. And if he happened to stop by Edward Hope's house whilst he was there who would think to question him?

Daniel should not have been surprised when Kit bounded out of the woods in his true form when he reached the road. "Off to see the mayor?" the Drus asked, guessing the intention of Daniel's trip immediately. "Mind if I join you for the walk?"

"I'd be happy for the company," Daniel said, meaning it. It had been months and months since they had gone for a stroll as two men instead of one man and his cat. Well, as close as the both of them were to men, given that Kit was not at all human and Daniel was immortal.

With a flourish Daniel summoned a pastry from the kitchen, tossing it at Kit when he matched his stride. "It was baked yesterday, so it might be stale, but I know how much you like the apricot ones."

Kit's eyes shone with a delighted fervour as he took in the sight of apricot jam and sticky, sugared pastry in his hands. Then, without warning, he stuffed the entire thing into his mouth.

"I take it Miss Hope wasn't in the forest last night, then?" Daniel asked before he could stop himself. Ever since he'd given Charlie the means to bypass his security magic she no longer woke him up with her dawn returns, though sometimes Daniel roused from sleep in time to hear her creep through the corridors on her way to her bedroom, anyway.

He hadn't heard her this morning, so he knew what Kit's answer would be, yet still Daniel wanted to know if the two of them had spent the evening together.

He didn't know why it irked him so much.

"Too tired from work," Kit said. Or, at least, attempted to say around a mouthful of pastry. "You're working her too hard."

"You only say that because you miss your plaything."

"Maybe." He swallowed down the last of the baked good Daniel had gifted him, eyes tracking the long, curved road that ran into Mt Duega. "Why are you going to meet Edward Hope so early in the morning, and on foot no less? Is he not meant to come to your estate on Monday?"

"I thought it might do me good to stretch my legs." The truth. "And besides...I've put so much work on Edward's shoulders with this temporary trade agreement. The least I can do is save him the trouble of coming by my house every time we need to meet." Also the truth.

But it wasn't the real reason Daniel wished to visit him.

"You're robbing him of the chance to see his daughter, you know. Nowadays Mayor Hope usually only gets to see Charlie when he has a meeting arranged with you."

At this Daniel flinched, for he hadn't thought about that at all. His estate was only getting further and further away as he continued walking down the road. *I could simply transport myself back,* Daniel reasoned, glancing behind him, though transportation magic made him feel sick.

Kit laughed raucously at his hesitation, and slapped Daniel on the back. "You worry too much, my friend. Of course you should go to the mayor's house. After all, how do you expect to spy on Charlie if you miss this opportunity to visit her home?"

"I am not – of course I'm not – there is no *spying* going on!" Daniel spluttered, his reaction giving him away entirely. He shot Kit a glare when the Drus laughed even harder at his expense.

"Lie to yourself all you want, Daniel," Kit said, wiping tears of mirth from his eyes, "but I know the truth. You have an ulterior motive in visiting Edward Hope at home; the least you can do is be truthful about it."

Daniel said nothing. He hated how well Kit knew him. What he surmised *was* true, at least partially: every time Daniel had tried to speak to Charlie over the last few days it seemed as if she simply spirited away. After he recounted the myth of the Noben in his lecture it was clear she had been trying especially hard to avoid him.

He didn't know what else to do. So here he was, walking to Mt. Duega, hoping that the house Charlie grew up in might shed some light as to how Daniel might be able to broach a proper conversation with her.

To his relief Kit dropped the issue when Daniel did not reply, and the two of them fell into an easy, companionable silence for much of the walk. Throughout the decades Daniel had spent many a day like this with his best friend, both of them content to tune into the world and its magic without uttering a single word.

The woods on Daniel's right were teeming with life. Behind the forest, on the horizon, were the peaks of a dozen volcanoes, which erupted once or twice after the Great Shift but had remained dormant since then. Thankfully none of the eruptions had been major events, the lava spilling from the volcanoes doing nothing but providing fertile new land for the trees to expand and grow.

He still found it odd to look towards his home town and not see the towering Duega Mountain overlooking the place from above the clouds. Ever since it had partially shrunk into the mantle the overgrown hill had become a popular tourist spot for those venturing down to the most southern tip of Lopox, but Daniel missed the grand mountain the way it used to be.

An unforgiving, gruelling climb. A dangerous ascent in dull weather. A hike not for the faint-hearted. But the reward was worth it: the most breathtaking views across the ocean to the right, and Atralia to the left, one could ever hope to witness.

Now even the view had changed.

"We're here, Daniel."

With a start Daniel realised he had walked several paces further than Kit, who had stopped in his tracks right on the border of Mt. Duega.

"Come visit the market with me?" Daniel asked, knowing Kit would say no but wishing his answer would be otherwise. Once upon a time Kit had no issue with appearing in the town. As with the mountain and the view over the ocean, this had also changed in recent years.

Kit smiled grimly, shaking his tawny head as he did so. "Perhaps in another lifetime. Besides, I have something I wish to investigate."

"You? Investigate?" Daniel chuckled in disbelief. "Well I never."

"Even I am not so lazy when the woods are being cut down," Kit replied.

It was a serious end to an otherwise very pleasant walk.

Above them a swallow dipped low, narrowly avoiding Daniel's head on its way to its nest beneath the roof of a thatched house nearby. "Well..." he murmured, trying to work out what to tell his friend, "hopefully Edward will have more information regarding who's responsible so I can relay it to you."

"Maybe. Or maybe I'll find out first."

"Would you tell me if you *did* find out who was responsible?"

The softest of smiles. "Of course," Kit said, turning towards the wood. "We're best friends, aren't we?"

"If that's the case then tell me what you know about Charlie Hope!" Daniel called out after him, though the words echoed on the air and the only response Daniel got was Kit laughing as he disappeared beneath the trees.

Sighing, Daniel took one final, sweeping glance of the forest before walking into Mt. Duega proper.

The town was a mishmash of different housing styles; back when Daniel was a child the place could have been barely called a village. It had since grown in haphazard stops and starts, magical and non-magical folk alike building their houses with whatever materials they could get their hands on. Eventually that became the 'style' of the town, and ever since then whenever new houses were built it became something of a competition to see how different they could look compared to existing residences.

White-washed stone with thatched roofing. Red brick with grey slate. Rough slabs of rock with slanted timber. Dark-washed wood with neat rows of tiles. The town hall, in the centre, was a grand yet austere building made of smoke-coloured stone, two floors high with a spire tower. It had undergone magical remodelling after the Great Shift collapsed the tower but nobody looking at it now would ever realise it had been broken.

When Daniel arrived at the morning market he snaked through it at a glacial pace, taking his time in case Edward Hope decided to sleep in. It was Saturday, after all. So he browsed a selection of Eshijani liquor – taking note of the prices, which were far fairer to the foreign merchants than the prices the Alliance had originally wanted to set – procuring three bottles of apricot-flavoured spirits for his team.

Apricot. Should I get some for Kit?

Daniel bought four, just in case.

When he came upon Edward Hope's house he first took note of the erratic selection of flowers, trees and bushes growing all around it. There were vibrant orange roses creeping up a wall; a lilac tree so overgrown its leaves pushed against a windowpane; broad-leaved ivy snaking up the chimney, and so many wildflowers in the grass that the dizzying assortment of colour threatened to give anyone looking upon them a headache. Bees swarmed over everything, the very air abuzz with them.

For the most fleeting of moments Daniel felt an overwhelming urge to prune everything into tidiness and order, but then the urge passed and a slow smile spread across his face, instead. He breathed in the heady, perfumed air of the garden until his lungs were full of it.

The entire place *screamed* Charlie Hope. It had her mark all over it.

After allowing himself to simply stand there and bask in the sheer liveliness all around him, Daniel walked up to the front door – also covered in ivy – and used a well-hidden brass knocker to announce his presence.

A stumbling behind the door informed Daniel that Edward

had likely tripped in fright at the sound of the knocker. He stifled a laugh.

"Just who is – Daniel?" the man said when he opened the door, surprise plain as day on his face. "To what do I owe the pleasure?"

Edward had finally cut his hair; it no longer curled around his ears or swept across his forehead, and revealed that a sparse number of silver hairs had grown in amongst the gold. It made him look altogether older.

Or, rather, Daniel mused, fiddling with his glasses, taking them off to clean them on his shirt before replacing them on his nose, *it makes him look his age. I always forget how young Edward was when he began working as mayor.*

"I...went for a morning stroll and thought I'd stop by," Daniel replied, feeling awkward now that he was standing in Edward's doorway. "It feels like I've been getting lazy in my old age."

"Old, indeed," Edward huffed, waving at him. "You're in the prime of your life and always will be. Well, come in, then. Have you had breakfast?"

"Yes," he lied, for Daniel did not want to impose upon the man. He was led into what he assumed was the living room and cajoled into sitting upon a green velvet-upholstered easy chair.

"Nonsense," Edward replied, seeing through Daniel's lie with terrifying efficiency. "You never eat so early in the morning – I've learnt that much throughout the years. Do you like bacon?"

"I'd never turn it down, especially if you have any bread from Lydia Bowen's bakery."

"Ah, it's her son who runs it now," Edward said, a sad smile on his face. "Lydia passed away almost ten years ago."

"Oh."

Daniel wasn't often struck by such specific instances where his immortality worked against him. For some reason the knowledge of the baker's not-so-recent death hit him differently today than it might have a few months ago.

"As it happens, John is just as talented as his mother was, and I have a half-dozen rolls in the kitchen," Edward said to cut through the awkward silence Daniel had accidentally wrought upon them. "Sit tight and give me ten minutes."

The moment Daniel was left alone, of course, he got up from his seat to investigate his surroundings. All around the living room were photos littering the walls. Some were in wooden frames, some gilded metal, some merely glass, but each and every one of them detailed Edward Hope's life throughout the years.

Edward as a boy, fishing with his friends. Edward as a teenager, drinking what looked suspiciously like wine with a young, red-haired woman who might have been his first girlfriend. Edward's parents laughing together at a wedding.

His own wedding? Daniel mused, moving from photo to photo for a sign of Edward's late wife. He had met her once, Daniel was sure. *What was her name? Sonia? Sarah?*

He simply couldn't remember.

Even when an infant – then toddler, then child – Charlie began appearing in the images there was no sign of the woman, but by then the thought altogether left Daniel's mind in favour of focusing on Charlie.

Her childhood photos all showed a bright, happy little girl with hair so blonde it was almost white, laughing with her father or playing in their overgrown garden or swimming in one of the many ponds within the woods.

But then Daniel frowned. There were no photos of Charlie with anyone but her father. There were no friends – no boys or girls or anything in-between – to be found within the snapshots of her life.

When Daniel reached the photos of Charlie as a teenager he

spotted the exact moment she began glamouring her appearance. *She must be around seventeen here,* he mused, spotting a tell-tale defiant pout on her lips that Daniel had grown very familiar with.

And though Charlie still smiled for the camera, and still laughed with her father, her previous childlike happiness had been entirely lost from her expression.

"Alone," Daniel murmured, tracing a hand across the glass protecting a photo that was clearly far more recent. Charlie lying in the garden, a flouncy white dress exposing her shoulders, purple flowers in her wild hair, eyes closed to the sun. A faun rested on her stomach.

It was the most peaceful Daniel had ever seen Charlie. The most at ease.

Yet still she was alone.

"Was sitting for ten minutes too difficult for you?" Edward teased, reappearing in the living room with two rolls overfilled with bacon in his hand.

"Apparently so," Daniel chuckled. He waved a hand around the room at large. "You have so many photos. I was intrigued."

"By my daughter?"

He always hits the proverbial nail on the head, he thought, suppressing a grimace. "By your entire family, rather. I'm surprised there don't seem to be any photos of your late wife. What was her name?"

To Daniel's surprise Edward flinched. The man carefully placed the two plates of food on a wooden table littered with reams of notepaper before responding to his question. "Serena."

Ah, Serena. That was it. Serena Hope.

"So why no photos, if you don't mind me asking?"

"I...don't like to dwell on the past."

"But surely your daughter would like to have photos on

display of her mother? To remember her by?"

"Charlie's version of her mother is in her head," Edward murmured, avoiding Daniel's gaze. "She wouldn't find her in any photos. Better it remains that way. Oh, would you look at the time! I suddenly remembered I have a town meeting to attend!"

"But it's eight in the morning, and a Saturday," Daniel complained, allowing himself to be ushered back to the front door nonetheless. "And what about breakfast?"

Edward summoned a paper bag, placed the bacon roll in it and thrust it at Daniel. "Here you go," he said, a forced smile on his face. "We can talk at the gala next week. Until then!"

He slammed the door in Daniel's face.

"What just...happened?" Daniel asked aloud, dazed and confused by his forced whirlwind exit from the Hope residence. "Did I say something wrong?"

As he slowly headed down the garden path Daniel could only conclude that Edward did not wish to discuss his late wife. *I suppose people all have their own way of dealing with grief,* he mused. *Only...*

Daniel tore off a chunk of the piping-hot bacon roll the man had prepared for him and took his time chewing it, savouring the salty tang of it on his tongue.

Only it didn't feel like grief.

Now genuinely curious about the Hope family as a whole, Daniel decided that he wasn't quite ready to return home just yet, and could do with stretching his legs a while longer.

The walk back would help him process all he had – and *hadn't* learnt – from within the mysterious family's home.

Chapter Twelve

"Any of that apricot stuff left that Silver gave us, Jean?"

Jean lifted the bottle of sweetened Eshijani spirits up for Charlie to see, swirling around the dregs of what was left to demonstrate that the answer was no. But then two more bottles of the stuff appeared out of nowhere; to Charlie's right Luca gasped in delight, and Jean grinned. "I meant to keep these back for another night but I guess drinking them now wouldn't hurt."

"My hero," Charlie said, grabbing one of the bottles, pulling out the cork and pouring the liquid straight into her mouth before Jean could protest.

Luca grimaced at Charlie. "Don't be disgusting. We have to drink from that, too, so use a cup like a normal person."

"Don't feel like it."

"*Charlie—*"

"Fine, fine," Charlie said, relenting. She picked up the delicate silver cup she'd abandoned on the floor beside her – wondering if Daniel had willed it into existence from nothing – and filled it to the brim with alcohol. "Uthesh be good, Luca, you sound like my da."

"Then he has far more sense than you, and I am glad to be compared to him."

"Are we really going to spend tonight bickering?" Jean complained, when Charlie stuck her tongue out at Luca. "I'm far too tired for that. Aren't you, too?"

"Yes," both women replied, clinking their glasses against Jean's. It was late, and the three of them had collapsed in a heap in the glass meeting room for a drink that had quickly turned into two, then four, then seven. But the alcohol was well-deserved; even Charlie had worked herself into exhaustion over the last two weeks.

Preparations for the gala tomorrow evening had taken up every waking moment of their time. With the Eshijani attending, alongside all eight Lopox Alliance members, the garden party had become a vital political event which nobody on Silver's team could afford to mess up.

The rain that had battered down on the estate all day threatened to ruin things, anyway.

"Do you really think Crimson will be able to dry everything out in the morning?" Charlie asked around a mouthful of liquor. "I know she's supposed to be good with fire magic, but..." She pointed through the glass walls towards the torrent currently crashing down upon the eerily dark courtyard.

"She's dealt with worse than this," Jean reassured her. "So long as it *stops* raining tomorrow then everything will be fine."

I'll check on all the flowers before the gala if I can, Charlie decided, knowing that the rain had likely destroyed more than a few of them.

Kit, who was curled on Charlie's lap, startled in his sleep when a roll of thunder crossed the sky. A twinge of guilt twisted her stomach; Charlie hadn't had much time for the cat recently, nor for the woods. Her feet itched for an adventure.

After the gala, she promised herself – and the cat – scratching

Kit's his ears until he purred. When Jean offered to top up her glass Charlie dutifully held it out for him.

"As I was saying before the need for more alcohol interrupted us," Luca said, a gentle hiccup causing her to giggle softly, "how did you know I have a fiancé, Charlie? It's not as if I wear any engagement jewellery or have ever mentioned him."

She shrugged. "I could just tell. I'm good with these things."

"I call bullshit."

"It's true, I swear!" she laughed. Then Charlie leaned in towards Jean and Luca, curling a finger to draw them closer. "Let's play a game and I'll show you how good I am."

Jean grinned, eagerly coming closer than Charlie had intended, but in her tipsy state she didn't mind when his shoulder brushed hers. "I like games. What do you propose?"

"Tell me four statements about yourself," she said, "only one of which is the truth, and I'll tell you which one it is on my first guess."

"Oh, I used to play this with my school friends!" Luca exclaimed, recognition bright in her eyes. "All right, I'll go first." She thought about her statements for a few moments. "Number one: I was engaged to be married to another man before I met my fiancé. Two: when I was seventeen my parents kicked me out of the house for a week when I said I didn't want to study healing magic. Three: my application to work for Mr Silver was rejected twice before I was accepted. And four: I think Crimson has had the hots for your dad for at least a year."

Charlie winced at the last statement, though secretly she was pleased by the notion. Then she focused on Luca's Intent, and frowned.

"Not fair, Luca," she said. "You're only supposed to give me *one* truth, not four."

Luca let out a low whistle, clearly impressed. "Damn, you're good. She's good," she aimed at Jean. "You next."

That Charlie had correctly deduced Luca's truths seemed to incite a competitive flame in Jean's heart. He nudged Charlie's shoulder. "I'm not gonna make this easy on you, Hope."

"I'll be the one to decide that."

Jean took longer to decide on his statements – clearly because he was actually making three of them up, unlike Luca – then said: "First...my real eye colour is blue. I didn't mean to permanently turn them silver when I tried out a glamour spell a few years ago but now I'm too ashamed to ask anyone to help me turn them back. Second: last year I went to a conference in the Capital and ended up sleeping with a man. Third—"

"That one was the truth," Charlie cut in, a smile curling her lips at the look of surprise on Jean's face and Luca's delighted laughter. "How was he?"

To his benefit, Jean recovered from his shock immediately. "Very good, from what I remember. Not an experience I wish to repeat but certainly not the worst thing to have ever happened to me at a conference. Should we try and guess *your* truth, Charlie?"

"I mean, you could try," she said, stroking the long scar down Kit's spine when he nudged her hand for attention. Both the alcohol and the rain thundered in her ears, tearing down her internal walls and emboldening her to share more about her life with Jean and Luca.

Is this what having friends feels like? Charlie wondered, knowing she was pathetic for thinking such a thing. She was so woefully underdeveloped as a human being.

"Try us, then," Luca said. "Let's see what ridiculous things you try to pass off as the truth."

"My glamour magic is the one spell I've ever been good at," Charlie began, the lie smooth as silk on her tongue. "I was born in the woods. I've only slept with one person before. I've never left Mt. Duega in my entire life."

"Did you have those prepared from the beginning or something?" Jean asked, eyebrow raised at the speed with which Charlie came up with her lies.

"I just have a very active imagination. So which one was the truth?"

It was amusing to watch the two of them puzzle over her answers. Charlie imagined they'd pick her fourth statement, or perhaps her first. They were certainly the most plausible options given what Jean and Luca knew about her.

"There's absolutely no way you were born in the woods no matter how much you love it there," Luca murmured, chewing over her answer. "Um...you've never left Mt. Duega?"

"But she worked with Mayor Hope for years so that's unlikely," Jean correctly pointed out. "I'm sure you at least visited the Capital once or twice."

"I actually visited every country in Lopox the summer I turned twenty-one," Charlie told them. "It was supposed to be a 'birthday present' but I knew Da had business to do up north. I was in such a mood when we got back that I didn't speak to him for two weeks."

"You're such a *brat!*" Luca gasped, outraged on Edward Hope's behalf.

"Oh, don't I know it. I felt so bad afterwards but I didn't have it in me to apologise."

"So if that's a lie," Jean said, bringing the conversation back around to its original point, "and there's absolutely no bloody way you were born in the woods...wait. Number three is true, isn't it? You've only slept with *one* person?"

"That would be accurate." Both Jean and Luca frowned at Charlie, deeply suspicious. Somehow that made her embarrassed by her own answer. "It's true, I swear," she insisted, blushing furiously. "I wasn't interested in any of the boys I grew up with in Mt. Duega."

That part was a lie.

"But still," Jean said in complete disbelief. He watched Charlie's expression carefully, as if he might somehow read the truth for himself on her face. "You have only, in all your twenty-four years of existing on Erath, had sex with *one person*? You, the wildest, most impulsive girl I've ever met?"

He meant it as a compliment, which ordinarily Charlie would have found funny. That Jean genuinely liked the parts of her that had caused him to dismiss her in the beginning was the kind of irony Charlie enjoyed.

But someone else other than the three of them heard what Jean had just said.

Daniel Silver was standing in the doorway, magician's robe unbuttoned, a glass of whisky in his hand and a fiery flush across his face to match.

His gaze on Charlie was just as hot.

"Mister Silver!" Luca cried the moment she saw what had distracted Charlie. "We didn't hear you open the door."

"Did you overhear what we were talking about?" Jean asked, not at all bothered by their employer's presence.

At first Daniel didn't reply; he was too busy watching Charlie watch him. Then: "It wasn't so much *overheard* as it was the lot of you screaming. Whatever happened to telling secrets in a whisper?"

Jean shrugged, then elbowed Charlie with a conspiratorial gleam in his eye. "There's no secrets between us, right? We were simply letting off some steam; apologies if we interrupted your solo drinking. Won't you join us?"

Charlie was shocked by Jean's open invitation to their boss, but then she reasoned that he'd worked for Daniel so long now that the two of them probably drank together fairly often. Still, when Daniel closed the door behind him and sat down on the floor, directly opposite Charlie, she flinched away an inch or two.

This was not something I was prepared for, she thought, momentarily stroking Kit so hard he let out a low growl of warning.

Daniel smiled wanly at his cat. "All evening I was wondering where you were when, all this time, you were in the company of my employees? You no-good *pet.*"

Kit flicked his tail, then settled into Charlie's arms once more.

"Do you want some of this, Mr Silver?" Luca asked, indicating towards the Eshijani liquor. "It's so good!"

But Daniel shook his head. "That was a gift for the three of you...which I can see lasted all of about two hours."

"You can't divulge secrets sober," Jean laughed. "Speaking of which, you were saying, Hope?"

"I was saying nothing. We were done."

"Oh come off it! If you've really only slept with one person in your *whole life* then you're obligated to tell us about it. How was it? How'd it happen?"

Charlie wanted nothing more than for Daniel to say the topic of conversation was inappropriate, or that it was late, or that they all needed to be up early in the morning, but the man said nothing. He merely sipped his whisky and watched her, waiting to see what Charlie would do.

Of course she wanted to run away. It was mortifying to be put on the spot like this – especially about such an intimate part of her life. But Charlie had already revealed more about her personal life tonight than she had to anyone else aside from her father.

And the person she slept with.

The alcohol – and perhaps something else, too – drove Charlie to speak.

"I was nineteen," she began. "And it wasn't...ah, how do I put this?" Charlie pondered her words carefully. "It was a Drus, not a human."

"That has *got* to be a lie," Luca bit out, incredulous. "Come on, Charlie. I know you love the woods but *come on*."

"It's not a lie." Charlie kept her eyes downcast, counting the stripes in Kit's tawny fur, a soft smile curling her lips as she recounted the memory. "Five years ago there were more Immortal Folk in the forest not afraid to show themselves to humans. I met him – the Drus – when I was swimming close to the Uthesh fault line one afternoon. We spent all weekend together. Da was so angry that I disappeared for three days without warning him first." She laughed. "Yeah, he was furious. I thought I might see the Drus again but I never did. The end."

Of course it wasn't the end. Charlie made no comment on how the reason she never slept with any of the young men from Mt. Duega but instead one of the Immortal Folk was that they weren't affected by human Mind magic. They were built too differently. Having sex with the Drus was the one and only time Charlie had been certain her own feelings weren't Influencing the other party and in so doing removing their ability to properly consent to such a thing.

Charlie's magic was a blessing, her father often said throughout the years.

All too often it felt like a curse.

When nobody spoke Charlie lifted her head, confused about why there wasn't a bigger reaction to her cutting her story off so abruptly. But then she saw the reason why: all three people around her were flushed beyond the mere scope of alcohol, their eyes glazed over with obvious lust.

The air was full of Charlie's Influence.

She had gotten so lost in her memory she hadn't realised she was using magic at all.

Luca's gaze was faraway – she was thinking of her fiancé, Charlie concluded. But Jean was leaning against Charlie's shoulder, all attention on her, all feelings and impulses directed at her. By making skin contact he'd become overwhelmed by Charlie's magic. If she didn't move away he would likely *act* on those impulses.

Charlie shifted on the spot, creating enough space to break their contact, just as Daniel Silver reached out a hand to touch her.

The look on his face was even worse than Jean's. Charlie, in her drunken state, knew she was happy to witness it.

He was looking at her as if she was all he'd ever longed for.

But it isn't real, Charlie reminded herself, though her own magic dulled the thought. She looked at Daniel's hand outstretched towards her, ignoring the trance-like state of everyone in the room, and reached out her fingertips to meet his.

If we touch now, she thought, heart thumping in her chest as Daniel's blue eyes fixed on hers, *then what happens next? What—*

Kit meowed loudly, stood up in Charlie's lap, and licked her chin. All at once Charlie came back to her senses...along with everyone else.

She scrabbled to her feet; Kit jumped from her arms to wander over to Daniel. "I-I'm tired! And drunk! I need to—"

"Charlie?" Luca said questioningly, shaking her head as if that would allow her to make sense of the last five minutes. "What just – did you finish your story?"

"I'm going to bed," Charlie insisted, ignoring her. She glanced at Jean, who was still looking at her with obvious desire, but couldn't bear to look at Daniel.

If Charlie looked at him and all she saw was her own magic – or, worse, that with her magic gone he held no real feelings or attraction towards her whatsoever – then Charlie thought she might burst into tears.

She fled.

I like him, Charlie could only conclude, a horrified blush spreading across her cheeks at the realisation. *I honest-to-goodness like Daniel Silver.*

She couldn't imagine anything worse happening to her than this.

Chapter Thirteen

It was all Daniel could do to wait until he and Kit were away from prying ears within the protected walls of his chambers before he rounded on his friend.

"Just what in the name of Uthesh was that?"

The cat merely stared at him. "Was what?"

"Was you interrupting...well, whatever was going on."

"And what, exactly, was going on?"

Daniel felt like tearing his hair out at Kit's evasive answers, though it wasn't the first time the Drus had avoided topics of conversation he had no intention of being honest about.

So Daniel changed his line of questioning. "Charlie wasn't lying about the Drus she met in the woods, was she?" he asked, pouring himself a glass of amber whisky from a bottle summoned from his study. "Do you know who it was?"

Kit sat in front of the empty fireplace, licked a paw then cleaned his ears, in no mood to even change form to converse properly. "I hardly think that's an appropriate thing to ask me, Daniel. On Charlie's behalf I'm declining to answer."

"So you *do* know."

A hiss escaped Kit's teeth. "Why do you care? What has that got to do with you trying to figure out her magic? Or is this to do with something else entirely?"

"I don't – I don't know!" Daniel roared, so obviously conflicted and infuriated that Kit couldn't help a pang of sympathy twisting his heart. Then, just as quickly as it flared up, Daniel's anger extinguished.

He sagged against the enormous bay window which had been installed in his room to wash his bed in sunlight every morning. But it was now black as ink – an almost perfect mirror. Daniel carefully avoided Kit's pointed stare reflected at him in the glass.

In one belated swallow he downed his whisky and sighed. "I just...don't know."

When Kit shook into his real body and placed a hand on his shoulder Daniel startled at the suddenness of the cat's transformation, as well as his touch.

"I think you need to sift through everything that's confusing you on your *own*," Kit said, not unkindly. He squeezed Daniel's shoulder. "It isn't my job to do it for you. Or have you been immortal so long already that you've forgotten what it is to be human?"

"It isn't – that has nothing to do with it."

"No? So you haven't forgotten what nervousness feels like? The moment you get within ten feet of Charlie it's as if you've forgotten how to be your regular, charming self. It's very amusing."

Daniel sputtered in indignation, which made Kit laugh despite himself. The man had become far too frustrated and pent-up over the decades.

Then Daniel drooped his head. "She avoids me on purpose, and even more so recently. I can tell."

"You're her boss. Call her into your office to talk."

More outrage from Daniel. "I'm not using my position of authority to force her to speak to me!"

"Your morals shall be the death of you, then."

"A far nobler way to live and die than to take advantage of a young woman," Daniel muttered, all at once hating his own reflection. He turned from the window, removed his robe and began unbuttoning his shirt to get ready for bed.

"True." Then, with clear mischievous intent, Kit said, "I guess you better find a situation in which Charlie might naturally – and willingly – loosen her tongue, as it were. Imagine if such a situation were already planned..."

Daniel clucked his tongue at his friend's obvious suggestion. But as he changed into his bedclothes he couldn't help but mull over Kit's words. "The gala tomorrow evening," he murmured, more to himself than to Kit. "With everyone drinking and celebrating – and being outside – Charlie might..."

"The gala it is, then." Kit grinned, feral and inhuman, then promptly shook himself back into the form of a cat. On deft paws he leapt onto Daniel's bed to curl up at the foot of it before the man himself slid beneath the cotton covers. "And Daniel..."

"Yes?"

"If you mess up this time I'm never listening to you complain about Charlie again."

Daniel let out a low chuckle. "That's only fair. Deal."

Hours later, when Kit was fast asleep and sprawled across what felt like half the bed, Daniel lay wide awake, mulling over the evening's events and what they meant.

He couldn't believe what his own feelings were telling him, even now.

I like Charlie Hope, Daniel thought, not at all pleased by this problematic conclusion. *I genuinely like her. I want her to look at me, and not flinch from my touch, and—*

And like him back.

Daniel had no doubt things were going to end very, very badly for him.

Chapter Fourteen

It was one hour until the gala began and Charlie was completely and utterly spent.

She had lain awake in bed until almost dawn agonising over everything that had happened under the influence of alcohol the night before. But despite having been drinking copiously Charlie wasn't hungover and, even if she had been, there was no time for her to indulge in such a feeling between the dearth of last-minute gala preparations everyone had thrown themselves into.

It was in this way that Charlie managed to push all of the previous night's uncomfortable revelations to the side whilst she focused on her work.

Now, with just sixty minutes left to go until the guests were due to arrive, Charlie was finishing her fifth and final trip sneaking around the courtyard to bolster the flowers that had been damaged by the torrential downpour.

The late afternoon sky was thankfully clear and bright, the air fresh and sun hot on Charlie's skin as she whispered to the ivy and the roses which grew on the right-hand wall of the grey building. Since these plants couldn't be seen from the courtyard Charlie in truth didn't need to mend them until tomorrow, but once she was done...

She had to don her dress and a smile and begin avoiding Daniel Silver in earnest for an entire evening.

Everything that had been said and done the night before came crashing back down upon her in one fell swoop.

I can't believe how out of control my magic was last night, Charlie thought, vowing to never drink in the company of other people again. Gently she stroked the velvet petals of a pale, creamy rose, simply to have the feeling of something solid beneath her skin. Something real.

Unlike the feelings she had forced upon not just Daniel but Jean, too. Charlie reasoned that at least she had known Jean already liked her. He flirted with her. He saw no reason to hide the fact he was attracted to her.

So long as Charlie gave him a wide enough berth until she could be sure her Influence had dissipated from his mind then she was sure no harm would come from Charlie having woven her magic on Jean in the first place.

Daniel, however...

Charlie wanted him to like her. Wanted him to look at her the way he had under her Influence.

It's not a big deal, Charlie tried to reassure herself, pulling her hand away from the rose with a gasp when she nicked her forefinger on a hidden thorn. She sucked the blood clean from her finger – though Charlie knew Daniel's protection spell would prevent it from drying on or otherwise marring her skin – tasting salt and iron on her tongue. *You've liked people before. All you have to do is wait your feelings out until they go away.*

So why did it feel like Charlie's feelings weren't going to go away?

"I was wondering where you were," came a voice from Charlie's left, startling her out of her miserable reverie. It was Jean, resplendent in a midnight blue suit that complimented the artificial silver of his hair and eyes remarkably well. "Why are you out here instead of getting ready for the gala?"

Why can't I just be attracted to him, instead? Charlie mused, forcing as genuine a smile as she could muster to her face. *He already likes me. That makes things so much easier.* Yet Charlie knew her feelings for Jean would never be anything other than platonic.

"All I have to do is change my clothes and put my hair up," Charlie said, answering Jean's question. "Mister Silver's cleaning spell takes care of the rest."

She never thought she'd be grateful for the man's accursed spell, but there was a first time for everything.

"I suppose you wouldn't be you if you didn't leave everything to the last minute," Jean chuckled, taking a few steps forward to close the gap between them. He frowned when he spied a flash of red across Charlie's right hand, and grabbed it before she could pull away. "You're bleeding. What happened?"

"I was admiring the roses," Charlie explained, which wasn't a lie. When she felt the buzz of magic cross from Jean's hand to her own she resisted the urge to pull away, letting the man instead finish his spell and release her when he was done.

The cut on Charlie's hand had disappeared.

"There you go," Jean said, smiling in satisfaction. "I may be disgraceful at healing magic when compared to Luca but I can at least handle something this small."

"...thank you, Jean," Charlie said, somewhat uselessly. She didn't know what else to say – what else she *could* say – without risking Jean misconstruing her kindness or gratitude for something more. She had been avoiding Jean all day just as much as Daniel Silver. More, in fact, for in truth Charlie hadn't seen her employer once.

Currently Jean was looking at her far more intensely than he had prior to Charlie accidentally weaving her Intent magic the night before, his attraction to her doubled because he felt the pull of her own feelings.

It didn't matter that those feelings had been directed towards the memory Charlie possessed of the tawny-haired Drus she met five years ago; in her drunkenness the subject of her Intent magic had not been at all specific.

And of all the people on the planet who could have witnessed it, why did Daniel Silver *have to be there when I lost control?*

"Do you mind if you give me a few moments alone, Jean?" Charlie eventually asked, no longer able to maintain her disingenuous smile. "I'm a bit nervous about tonight."

"Of course." He grazed his hand against Charlie's where the cut from the rose had been, then leaned in towards her ear to murmur, "I'll see you at the gala. First drink on me?"

"...they're all paid for by Mr Silver."

"Oh, how convenient. Either way, I'm not taking no for an answer." With that Jean laughed and waved himself off, and Charlie was left once more alone.

Hopefully my Influence will wear off soon, Charlie thought sadly, rubbing at her ear as she watched Jean walk away so spiritedly it was clear he didn't imagine she might turn his offer of a drink – or anything else – down.

It wasn't fair on him. It was wrong.

That Charlie hadn't been in control of her Intent magic made her wish for nothing more than to sob against her father's chest – like she had done the first time Charlie realised she'd *made* the boy she liked like her back. Since then Charlie had grown entirely detached from any and all romantic entanglements.

Last night was a stark reminder of why she maintained such a solid distance between herself and the rest of the world.

A thump against a window several feet away starkly caught Charlie's attention. Curious, she wandered over to investigate.

"Oh, no," she gasped, when she spied the body of a bird beneath the window. A swallow, barely old enough to leave its mother's nest, with broken wings and a chest breathing far too heavily from the shock of hitting the glass.

With utmost care Charlie bent down and picked up the bird in her hands to inspect the damage. Its beady eyes were bright and shining, but then...

One last fluttering breath and the life the swallow had only just been clinging onto was gone. A deep, lamenting sadness filled Charlie.

She could not help the creature if it was dead.

But something felt different about the bird; about Charlie; about that very moment. Instinctively she knew she could do something about the swallow's fate, though by anyone's measure that was impossible.

Charlie took a breath, opened her mouth and sang the impossible, anyway.

Chapter Fifteen

"Accursed...shoes!" Daniel glowered, marching back to the carriage he'd used to pick up said shoes from a cobbler in Mt. Duega with obvious impatience. He hadn't meant to leave them in the carriage upon his return – of course he hadn't – but he'd been so scatter-brained all day it ultimately came as no surprise to Daniel that he'd forgotten to bring them in.

If the damn carriage wasn't protected from external magic I could have just summoned them, he thought when he reached its gilded doors, fumbling with the handle before finally managing to slam the door open with far too much force. It reverberated off the carriage, filling the air with a metallic echo that caused Daniel to wince away from his own mistake.

His nerves were shot. He hadn't felt this way in a very, very long time, and it made Daniel wildly uncomfortable. But then he remembered what Kit told him: he had grown too used to keeping his feelings at arm's length throughout the years. It was Daniel's responsibility, and Daniel's responsibility alone, to reconnect with the things that made him human.

That included his nerves regarding his feelings for Charlie, and the fact she would in all likelihood reject him.

After Daniel retrieved his shoes he felt thoroughly ruffled, so before heading back inside to finish getting dressed he allowed himself to close his eyes and breathe deeply for a minute or two. It was in doing this that he caught the whisper of a voice upon the air.

Daniel followed it without thinking.

Just what is going on? he wondered, suspicious, stalking towards the voice as quietly as possible. It was coming from the right-hand wall of his house – as far away from the courtyard and the impending gala as could possibly be. There shouldn't have been anybody lurking there.

When he turned the corner Daniel altogether forgot about his suspicions. For there, in front of him, stood Charlie, an injured swallow clutched between her hands. She was singing to it.

No, Daniel realised, as the meaning of what he was witnessing finally dawned on him. *Not just singing to it.*

Before his very eyes the swallow's broken wings not only straightened themselves out but the bird itself *grew,* out of its juvenile state and into a full-fledged adult. When it was entirely recovered it chirruped a thank-you at Charlie, then swatted her face with its wings in its excitement to be airborne once more.

A giggle escaped Charlie's lips that Daniel had never heard before. It matched the girl from all of Edward Hope's photos – the girl who was as happy to be alive as the swallow was, before something took that joy away from her.

Only then did Daniel realise the rose bushes lining the wall had grown far more blooms than there had been a mere two days ago, and the green-and-yellow ivy crept over a foot higher towards the roof.

Charlie Hope could sing life into organic matter.

She could make things grow. Daniel had witnessed it with his own two eyes; there could be no doubt about it.

Daniel took a step towards Charlie before abruptly stopping

himself, rushing around the corner and flattening his back to the wall to avoid the risk that Charlie might catch him spying on her.

There had been a reason Charlie didn't want Daniel to know about her magic, but there was little reason he could think of for Charlie to hide such a miraculous ability. It was a rare and wonderful gift to find in the realm of humans; a form of magic meant only for good.

Which means she's hiding something else. Something not so good. Something...

He couldn't work out what that something was.

So Daniel went back inside to finish getting ready for the gala, though he wished for nothing more than to continue watching Charlie sing to the plants and the birds and the insects until they took over Daniel's entire estate.

But tonight was his best, and perhaps only, opportunity to connect with the young woman who had – as Kit so aptly predicted – made Daniel's life a whole lot more interesting from the very moment she was thrust into it.

Tonight Daniel would bare all to Charlie, and hope she did the same in return.

CHAPTER SIXTEEN

 ready and emerged outside the gala had already begun. A flutter of nerves disturbed her stomach as she surveyed the slew of people in the courtyard from the top of the dining hall stairs leading out onto it. Some faces were familiar from her time working with her father, some complete strangers, but all of them were resplendent in finely-tailored suits, stylish dresses or magnificent robes.

Yet it was the appearance of the gala itself which stole the show.

Daniel and Jean had truly outdone themselves with the design of the event. Charlie knew they'd worked endless sleepless nights to create the look they wanted, and it had paid off.

A dance floor of polished birch wood had been constructed in the centre of the courtyard, whilst globes of warm light floated overhead. The sun was dipping closer to the horizon, basking the entire garden in late evening sunshine, so for now the globe lights seemed ethereal and difficult to spot. But Charlie knew once night fell they would illuminate the gala like a thousand fireflies.

A four piece band played from a silver pergola artfully

overgrown with ivy. Their gentle, sweeping music carried on the breeze until Charlie almost believed the wind itself was singing.

In the distance, above the pond, soft spirals of sand came up from the water and were transmuted into sparkling red and gold, then blue and bronze, then green and silver, then back again. Several plush seats had been added to the decking overlooking the pond, a servant dutifully on hand to provide guests with refreshments whilst they rested.

And then there were the flowers. Everywhere Charlie looked there were flowers, saved from drowning in the previous day's rain by Crimson's fire magic and – though nobody else knew it – Charlie's magic.

There were velvet roses and tricolour violets and huge, impressive sunflowers; clematis blossoms and frothy wisterias and pale, pretty lilacs; a sweeping lawn of daisies, poppies, clover and sky blue cornflowers that surrounded the entire courtyard and then, of course, there was the woods in the background.

There were all those flowers and a dozen more Charlie knew the name of, then several even she could not recognise. Yet she had helped each and every one of them grow all the same.

Charlie was glad she'd spread out her singing from the early morning until right before the gala so nobody became suspicious about the garden suddenly improving all at once. But, now that she could see her work for herself, Charlie realised it would have been worth being caught just for the view she had now.

The air was thick with floral perfume, heady and euphoric. It was like a drug to Charlie when she breathed it in, calming her nerves and telling her everything would be fine.

The gala was simply a party, even if it was an important one. Charlie had been to parties before. She could handle it just fine.

"Charlie!"

At the sound of her own name called out in her father's voice Charlie rushed down the final few steps to the courtyard, delighted to see that the man had already arrived.

"Da!" she cried, wasting no time in embracing him despite the audience they had. Edward rested his chin on his daughter's head and squeezed her tight, only letting Charlie go when she pushed on his chest and mumbled that people were watching.

They both knew she didn't care.

"I see you got your dress in time," Edward said, appraising his daughter's appearance. "I was worried it wouldn't arrive from the Capital until tomorrow. You look wonderful."

The dress in question had been constructed based on a design Charlie had spied in one of Luca's fashion magazines. Covered in a springtime floral pattern, the tightly-laced bodice gave way to a loose, flouncy skirt falling just below Charlie's knees. Short, delicately frilled sleeves slipped off her shoulders; paired with her hair pulled into an almost careless twist held together with the barest hint of magic, they served to expose Charlie's delicate collarbone.

Charlie was even wearing gold heels at Luca's insistence, and though she disliked wearing them Charlie had to admit they complemented the dress well.

She turned on the spot in order to make her dress swish around her legs, grinning at her father. "I love it. Thanks for buying it, Da."

"Call it an early birthday present," he said, making to ruffle Charlie's hair before remembering that doing so would ruin all the work she'd put into it. In truth Edward had already bought many other gifts for Charlie in preparation for her twenty-fifth birthday the following month, and intended to buy several more.

She was all the family he had in the world, after all.

"So this would be your daughter, Mayor Hope?" an aged Eshijani man who was standing a short distance away said. If his shocking violet formal robes hadn't given away his identity then the presence of Crimson by his side certainly did, leaving

Charlie in no uncertainty as to who he was.

Edward beamed at the man. "Indeed it is. Grandmaster Feng, it's a pleasure to introduce my daughter, Charlie, to you. Charlie —"

"I've heard so much about you from Wei and Mr Silver," Charlie cut in eagerly, bowing her head at Feng before she forgot her manners entirely. She reasoned it was correct to use Crimson's real name when talking to her grandfather; going by the woman's look of approval Charlie had guessed correctly. "I have been looking forward to meeting you for some time."

"And I you," Feng said, inclining his head in turn. "I hear I have you to thank for bringing the temporary trade agreement into existence!"

A resigned, good-natured sigh came from behind Charlie, and her heart skipped a beat. "Must we really start talking about work so early?" the source of the sigh complained. "The evening has only just begun."

When she turned on the spot Charlie found Daniel Silver standing there.

"Ah, the host of the evening!" Edward exclaimed, motioning for Daniel to join them. "I was wondering where you were. I'm..."

But Charlie was no longer listening to her father. The pull of her Intent was so strong as she watched Daniel seamlessly join the conversation that Charlie barely managed to control it.

He looked disgustingly, intimidatingly good; a shiver ran down her spine merely looking at him.

Daniel had removed his glasses for the evening, and expertly slicked his pale hair back instead of tying it at the nape of his neck. Rather than robes, which Charlie had expected him to wear, Daniel had opted to don a dark tailcoat and trousers paired with a silver, embroidered waistcoat, matching cravat and white shirt.

It was like seeing Daniel as he must have looked ninety years ago, before he became immortal and was merely a man living in another time.

If Charlie hadn't been so fixated on what she thought of Daniel she might have realised he was looking at her the same way she was looking at him.

By the time Charlie paid attention to her surroundings again she realised she'd lost track of the topic of conversation going on around her several times.

It was only when Feng said, "Surely it is time you found a new wife, Mayor Hope," that she truly reinserted herself back into reality.

Her father laughed nervously as he always did when someone brought up the prospect of him marrying once more. "Oh, I am not so old yet as to have to worry about that! And I'm far too busy with work to find a wife, in any case."

"One can only afford to dedicate so much time to work if one is immortal," Feng replied. "Otherwise what a waste of your life! Have you ever considered ascending? My grand-daughter here insists on breaking my heart by refusing to even try."

Feng had reached immortality in his early seventies, and insisted on feeling younger with every passing year of this new part of his life than he'd ever done as a mortal human.

But Crimson did not feel the same way about the subject as her grandfather did. "I would prefer to make every moment count within my natural lifespan," she said, glancing at Edward so quickly that only Charlie caught her doing so, "than to live forever."

"Oh?" Charlie quirked an eyebrow at her father, elbowing him in the chest in the process. "That sounds familiar."

Edward winced away from her elbow when Charlie made to jab him a second time. "You be quiet," he muttered, though he didn't look entirely unhappy by what she had insinuated.

"At this rate I shall have nobody left to listen to my old stories!" Feng continued lamenting, clearly enjoying having an audience to listen to his complaints. "Like the origins of the Immortal Folk, or the creation of the Kiroji, or—"

"Kiroji?" Daniel inquired politely.

"Ah, in your tongue it would be...Noben? Undead monsters?"

"Noben, yes," he replied, satisfied. "That's what I thought. I - Miss Hope?"

For Charlie had ducked out of the conversation without excusing herself, though she knew it was rude to do so. But Jean had locked his gaze on hers through the crowd at that exact moment; Charlie, desperate to avoid him for as long as humanly possible, wound through the gala in an attempt to lose him.

"A drink, Miss Hope?" one of the servants asked her when she made to hide behind them. She accepted one simply so they would linger by her for a few moments, giving Charlie enough cover to scope out if Jean had lost sight of her.

But she couldn't see him anywhere. He—

"There you are!"

I have zero luck.

"Hi, Jean," Charlie said, turning to face him with a smile she hoped wasn't too much of a grimace. Jean took a drink from the servant before they moved on to another group, then looped his arm through Charlie's to lead her towards the pond like it was the most natural thing in the word.

"You took your time talking with Grandmaster Feng," he said, voice animated in such a way that Charlie knew he'd had several glasses of champagne already. "The old man sure can talk. I thought you'd never be able to escape!"

"Good thing I managed to, then," Charlie replied, realising glumly that staying with her father - and ogling Daniel Silver -

would have, in fact, allowed her to escape Jean. "You...look like you've been having a good time."

He gave her a dazzling, drunk smile. "But of course! The head of public relations must drink with every guest! I'm made for this kind of thing."

"You're going to sleep for a week after this!"

Charlie wished he would...if only to remove any and all traces of her Intent.

When he bent in against her head and tucked an errant curl of hair behind her ear Charlie couldn't help but flinch. "I can think of something far more preferable than sleep happening in my bed tonight," Jean murmured. His breath was hot and tickled her skin; Charlie held up a hand to protect herself from it.

Jean merely kissed her hand.

"Jean," Charlie panicked, trying her best to move away despite their interlocked arms, "I—"

"If you haven't worked out that Miss Hope isn't interested in you yet, Jean, then you're far more hopeless than I ever imagined," Daniel – *where did he come from?* Charlie wondered, shocked by his sudden, decidedly irritated appearance – told the man. He fired a warning glare at Jean's arm entangled through Charlie's until he stepped away from her.

She breathed a sigh of relief when he did.

"Ah, I didn't mean any offence," Jean said, eyes darting from Daniel to Charlie and then back again. His expression was unabashedly confused by both his boss' interruption and the knowledge that Charlie wasn't interested in him. "If you'll... please excuse me."

An empty pit expanded in Charlie's stomach as she watched him all but run away. It was her own fault Jean felt like this – had acted this way towards her. Charlie drank the glass of champagne in her hand to fill the pit before her guilt could consume her, breaking her earlier promise that she would never consume alcohol in the company of other people again.

A long minute of silence passed between Charlie and Daniel. She didn't know what to say or do or how to act. She couldn't even look at him. "...I could have handled that," Charlie eventually muttered, knowing full well that she had no idea how she was actually supposed to have done so.

"I know," Daniel replied. "But I couldn't help it. Champagne?"

Charlie's previously empty glass filled back up before her very eyes, though she had been about to refuse. She tilted her head towards Daniel, a frown on her face as she made to complain that he hadn't even let her respond, when his previous sentence replayed in her head.

I couldn't help it, he said. Couldn't help what, exactly?

"Will you take a walk with me, Charlie?"

The question took her starkly aback, especially the bold, eager tone with which Daniel asked it. "You...want to take a walk with me?" she parroted back, unsure how to answer his request.

In the evening sunlight Daniel's pale hair shone like starlight, looking every inch an unreachable immortal rather than a mere man. Charlie found herself almost unable to look at him as he nodded his assent. "Very much so," Daniel said, offering Charlie a careful smile. "If you'll suffer my company for a while."

"I—" Charlie didn't know what to say. She cast her gaze around the gala. Everyone was talking and dancing and laughing, doing exactly as they pleased.

And even though Charlie should have said no – especially after what happened with Jean – all she could think of was why *shouldn't* she? Everything was so difficult and overwhelming for her nowadays. Just once Charlie wanted to follow her own urges without feeling bad about it.

She returned Daniel's careful smile; his broadened into a grin that lit up his features so painfully it was all Charlie could do to restrain her Intent.

"I suppose I could *suffer* for a few minutes," she said, knowing that she definitely would.

But not for the reasons Daniel Silver was insinuating.

Chapter Seventeen

As the two of them made their way past the pond Daniel found he had no interest in the beautiful scenery around him.

He only had eyes for Charlie.

It was as if, now he had finally come to terms with the fact he was interested in more than whatever it was she was hiding, Daniel could do nothing but appreciate how lovely the young woman was.

"What do you think of the gala?" he asked when they paused for Charlie to admire the glittering sand spiralling up from the pond.

She glanced at him out of the corner of her eye. "You asked me that five minutes ago."

"I did?"

"Definitely."

"What was your answer?"

"I said it was very pretty."

"So you did."

When Charlie blushed Daniel realised his own face was hot,

too. *Uthesh be good, why am I so nervous? I'm acting like an idiot.*

But he couldn't help it. In the light of the brilliant sunset Charlie Hope in her floral dress was a literal spring goddess. A faint breeze lifted wispy curls of hair around her face like they were dancing, and when Charlie brushed them away Daniel became aware of how delicate her wrists were. He had grabbed her wrist when he confronted her about sneaking off to the woods every night – how hadn't he hurt her? Or *had* he, and Charlie merely didn't say anything?

But Daniel couldn't dwell on such a thing when he found his gaze, for the umpteenth time that evening, casting itself over Charlie's entire figure. Her dress was cut low, exposing her neck and shoulders and collarbone and filling Daniel with the unbearable urge to unlace the bodice and remove the garment entirely.

So much for a spring goddess; Daniel was mentally defiling her and couldn't even find it within himself to feel bad about it any longer.

When a couple of politicians from the Capital vacated the lookout deck over the pond Daniel was quick to take their place. He leaned over the wooden railing, heaved out a breath to steady himself, then lifted sand from beneath the water to transmute it into a horde of silver, mechanical fireflies. When he set them free across the pond Charlie watched them depart with hungry eyes.

"They're beautiful," she murmured, copying Daniel leaning on the wooden railing as she did so. Then she let out a low whistle, and a smile curled her lips. "They're not as beautiful as the real thing, though."

When the air filled with the golden glow of genuine fireflies Daniel could do nothing but stare at the sight of them intermingling with his artificial ones. Now that he knew Charlie's affinity for life magic he only grew more and more impressed by her. *Does the mere existence of her magic draw out life?* Daniel wondered, glancing at her. *Just where did the fireflies come from?*

"Convenient that they showed up just to prove your point," he said, testing Charlie to see what she would say.

But Charlie merely shrugged. "Hardly. It's sunset, over a pond, in May."

"That's...fair."

"Do you actually *do* anything else apart from turn things into silver or make silver from nothing?" Charlie teased, when Daniel sent one of his own fireflies to land on her fingertip. Her eyes narrowed as she took in the intricate details of the artificial creature. "Not that these aren't impressive. They're gorgeous, actually. Like the Noben you made last time."

"I'm not sure if that was an insult or a compliment."

"A bit of both. I hardly see you work with any other kind of magic."

At this Daniel let out a heavy sigh. His silver creations fluttered in the air, a moment away from falling apart, so with the clenching of a fist Daniel broke them back down to sand.

"Why did you do that?" Charlie asked, disappointment plain as day on her face when the firefly on her finger dissolved in front of her very eyes.

"Because you're correct that I haven't been working with any other kind of magic lately. It's exhausting."

"That's...care to complain further?" Charlie smothered a laugh with her hand. "It might make a change from *me* complaining."

"Oh, what I wouldn't give for a break from that!" Daniel agreed, taking a long draught of champagne before shifting his position slightly so he was turned towards Charlie.

When she mirrored his body language, eyes bright and intent

on his, a painful thump in his chest suggested Daniel would not be able to be this close to Charlie for very long before doing something he would probably regret.

"Do you remember what you said to me after you'd been working here for...about a week, I believe?"

"I say a lot of things," Charlie remarked, though a small furrow creased her brow as she tried to recall the specific moment to which Daniel was referring.

"You say a lot with the purpose of saying nothing at all," Daniel couldn't help but point out, though before Charlie could retort he added on, "but this time you meant exactly what you said."

Then a flash of understanding crossed Charlie's face. "Do you mean when I criticised you for making bullets?"

"Yes."

"What about it?"

"You were correct," he said. "The Alliance has had me making countless silver weapons and ammunition for months now. Crimson helps duplicate them, of course, but it's stifling to make them all. Never mind what they're being stockpiled for, the work itself is so...regimented."

"I thought you *liked* order," Charlie replied. She pointed to herself. "I mean, look at the magic you put on me simply because you couldn't keep me tidy."

"You wouldn't *listen*. That's different."

"No it isn't."

"Yes it—"

Daniel stopped with the childish argument when he realised Charlie was laughing at him. He risked moving a little closer to her. "What's so funny?"

"*You* are." Charlie's eyelashes fluttered over her cheekbone when she closed her eyes for a moment. "You take everything so seriously. What do you even do to relax? Lock yourself up in your office, drink, and do more work?"

"Now that isn't very fair," Daniel said, though he couldn't help himself from smiling at her flawed observation. "I do a lot of things in my spare time – when I used to have it, that is."

"I don't believe you. Give me an example."

He waved towards the glittering sand coming from the pond. "I like designing things. I like making things. Not bullets and weapons," Daniel added on, when it was clear Charlie was about to bring them up. "Like the fireflies or...yes, like the *Noben.* Come with me."

Daniel grabbed Charlie's hand before he could fully process what he was doing; if he mulled over anything he might or might not do for too long then he knew he'd get absolutely nowhere.

"Just where – where are we going, Mister – Daniel?" Charlie asked him, breathless from surprise. But she didn't try to pull away nor stop him, so Daniel merely held her hand tighter, revelling in the feeling of her skin beneath his own, and quickened his pace away from the pond and the courtyard.

"You'll see when we get there," was all the response Daniel gave Charlie, though he threw a grin over his shoulder that did not in any way reassure Charlie about what he was doing.

He led her along the narrow path which led past the rose bushes, pausing for a second to appreciate the magic Charlie had used to make them bloom so well, then finally stopped when they reached the front doors into his house.

When Charlie took her hand away from his Daniel felt its absence keenly. She crossed her arms over her chest. "What are we doing here?" she asked, suspicious.

In answer Daniel walked right up to the scroll work doors and slapped a hand against them.

"I designed and made these doors," he said, waving for Charlie to stand beside him to more closely inspect them. "The rest of the house I had a team of far more proficient architectural magicians construct, but the doors...those are mine and mine alone."

"You're not kidding, are you?" Charlie asked, taking uncertain steps up to the doors until she could feel the cool iron of them beneath her fingertips. She scanned the Old Atralian tongue upon it. "I kept meaning to look at these properly – ever since I got here, if I'm being honest – but I never got round to it. *Ah!* You really did make these!"

Daniel found he could do nothing but stand and smile as Charlie excitedly took in the illustrations upon the door, recognition flooding her face when she realised they matched the Noben models he'd crafted from liquid silver.

Not caring about her dress Charlie knelt to investigate the door from the ground-up. "Uthesh be good, I can't believe I didn't make the connection...look, there's the insane magician himself! And there are the Immortal Folk – heh, that Satyr looks funny – and there's..."

"You know," Daniel said, more to himself than to Charlie, "when you told me the myth of the Noben was your favourite story I wasn't sure if you were mocking me. I can see now you were being sincere."

Charlie clucked her tongue as she got back to her feet, eyes still scanning the details of the iron door. The sun had set now, quickly casting their surroundings in deep shadows, but a few errant globes of light had made their way around the building from the courtyard. Daniel motioned one over with a whip of magic to allow Charlie to continue investigating the door.

"And that's..." she muttered. "Ugh, my Old Atralian is awful. What does it say up here, Daniel?"

It still made him shocked and inordinately happy to hear his name upon Charlie's tongue. He looked to where she was pointing, well above her own eye level.

"It says..." he squinted, then brought the globe light closer to help him out. "Uthesh be good, this is hard without my glasses. Read it out to me."

Charlie let out a low chuckle. "Ironic that you don't have them on the one time you need them."

"Shut up. What does it say?"

"I can't see it from down here. I – wait, what are you doing?!" Charlie cried, when Daniel bodily picked her up by the waist and lifted her to the text.

"Can you see it now?" he asked, trying his best to ignore the blood rushing past his ears at the fact he successfully pulled off such a bold move. Daniel hadn't been this close to a woman in decades, let alone a woman he was hopelessly interested in.

But nobody was around to see him make a fool of himself. There was only Charlie, and if Daniel didn't take Kit's advice and open up to everything he felt about her then he was doomed.

Bold was the least he could be.

When Charlie squirmed and planted a hand on the top of Daniel's head for balance he tightened his grip around her waist until she felt more secure.

"Um..." Charlie began, after a very long, awkward silence passed between them. "It says—"

She spoke Old Atralian in a stunted accent, though Daniel was impressed she could still pronounce many of the words at all. The language had evolved a lot over the last few hundred years; Daniel only chose the older tongue for his inscriptions because the original manuscripts detailing the myth of the Noben had been written in it.

When Charlie was finished reciting the text Daniel translated it in his head, then said aloud, "*Those who do not learn from the past are doomed to repeat the same mistakes.* Unless you're immortal and were around to witness the original mistakes, in which case you're either stupid or cruel."

"*That's* what it says?" Charlie called down, peering at Daniel over her shoulder in disbelief.

He could only laugh. "Just the first part. Though I feel like my amendment is rather apt. Clearly I didn't think in such terms back when I was twenty-five."

"Wait, you were only twenty-five when you created these?! It wasn't, like, ten years ago or—"

"More like a hundred. Though the decades start to meld together after the first fifty or so of immortality. Truth be told I hadn't realised it had been so long since I made the doors..."

A pause. "That's...kind of sad, isn't it?" Charlie ventured from above him. "That's what my father is so afraid of when it comes to immortality. That he'll lose his humanity."

"I'm not – there are things I've done so I don't forget who I was, back when I was mortal," Daniel bit out, desperate to defend both himself and the humanity Kit had already pointed out that he was losing. "Like my glasses. I could have fixed my eyesight but I thought it would serve as a good reminder of the body I was born with. I know you believe my glasses to be mindless vanity – and perhaps there's an element of that, too – but still. It *does* remind me of the fact I'm only human, immortal or not."

When Daniel loosened his grip Charlie slowly slid back down to the ground, though he didn't let her go. He merely kept her in the circle of his arms, Charlie facing the door in front of him, as if waiting to see if she would object.

Don't object, Daniel begged, eyes boring a hole into the top of Charlie's golden hair. He had managed to make it this far into the evening talking to her simply as a man talking to a woman he liked; if she turned him away now Daniel didn't know what he would do about it.

In his arms, it took every ounce of Charlie's willpower not to tremble. It was as if Daniel was toying with her – seeing how long it would take until she lost control of her Intent and allowed it to overwhelm them.

But Daniel Silver didn't know about Charlie's magic. He didn't know that, if Charlie had looser morals, she could easily use her magic to indulge the longing she held for Daniel to look at her as if he might go insane if he didn't touch her immediately.

Equally, however, Charlie knew perfectly well that the way Daniel was acting was not at all how a boss and employee were supposed to act. She had witnessed him joke around with Jean and Luca and Crimson – saw that he was, in fact, capable of relaxing and even had a sense of humour that wasn't grounded entirely in sarcasm and dry, acerbic wit – but this was the first time *Charlie* was dealing with this version of Daniel.

He was charming. He was funny. He was honest. He was—

"Charlie?"

Her heart stuttered to a stop when she felt Daniel's breath on her ear. It was entirely unlike her reaction when Jean had done the same thing, when all Charlie wanted to do was flinch away.

Charlie's face was blazing hot. No, her entire body was; from her head down to her toes all she could feel was a deep, roiling heat.

It was impossible to keep her Intent under control.

"Charlie, turn around," Daniel said, when she chewed her lip and didn't respond to him saying her name the first time.

"I can't," she bit out, terse and on edge. "I can't. I—"

"You can," he insisted, voice low and heavy. Daniel's hands were still on her hips; with the barest of pushes he coaxed Charlie into turning to face him. "See? That wasn't nearly so hard as, say, ruining five hundred flyers or sneaking out to the woods every night, was it?"

Even in heels Charlie was still several inches shorter than Daniel – she hadn't really acknowledged how tall he was until he'd lifted her off the ground. And so it was that Charlie had to tilt her chin up to respond to Daniel's joke directly to his face, and in so doing realised that there was absolutely no humour to be found in his expression.

His blue eyes were burning into Charlie's own, lips pursed together in barely contained restraint. The vein in Daniel's temple was twitching – as were his hands on Charlie's waist. The barest hint of sandalwood and salt emanated from the soft sheen of sweat on his skin.

When Charlie delved further she found Daniel's heart was pounding harder than her own.

My Intent has taken over already, Charlie realised, horrified at the thought that perhaps it had been working on Daniel Silver from the very first moment she saw him that evening. *None of this is real. It's all fake. It's—*

"Charlie, talk to me," Daniel begged. His voice was so rough – so unsteady, like his fingertips separated from Charlie's skin by bare millimetres of fabric – that it physically pained her to hear it.

She didn't know what to say. All Charlie knew was what she wanted to *do.*

So she did it.

Charlie grabbed Daniel's collar and crushed his lips against her own, hating herself for giving into her impulses. She hated herself, but couldn't hate the way Daniel's eyes grew wide as he realised what was happening.

Before she lost herself completely Charlie pulled away, though her hands still gripped so tightly onto Daniel's collar she knew the material beneath her fingers would surely be creased forever. She was allowed this one moment, she decided. Just one second to store in her memory.

"You..." Daniel breathed, staring at Charlie in utter disbelief. "You actually – you feel the same way."

It wasn't a question.

Then he slammed Charlie against the door and kissed her properly.

Daniel's hands roved up Charlie's body to her hair, running through it to pull her closer and unravelling the delicate magic which held it up in the process.

She was helpless beneath his insistent tongue, coaxing her lips open until Charlie's own tongue found its way into Daniel's mouth, too. They both tasted of champagne, simultaneously light and complex but perfectly, achingly balanced.

When Daniel groaned in longing the sound did alarming things to Charlie's body. She bucked against him, a leg curling around his thigh until Daniel removed his hands from Charlie's hair and hoisted her up to lock her legs around his waist, instead.

"Uthesh be good," he growled against her lips, kissing the edge of Charlie's mouth before trailing down to her neck. Charlie's breathing came in stops and starts, overwhelmed by how quickly the situation had moved into senseless, impulsive oblivion.

Except it *wasn't* senseless.

All at once Charlie froze in Daniel's arms, pushing him away when he didn't immediately let her go.

The frown of confusion that contorted Daniel's features was heart-wrenching. "Charlie?" he asked, chest heaving. His eyes were glazed over with desire; it was clear that, unless Charlie herself said anything to the contrary, Daniel wouldn't stop.

And neither would she.

"I'm sorry," Charlie mouthed, ducking under Daniel's arm to untangle herself from his embrace. "I'm so, so sorry."

She fled.

CHAPTER EIGHTEEN

By the time Daniel came to his senses Charlie was nowhere to be seen. He was standing there, the space between his arms entirely empty, as if Charlie had not been there at all.

As if she hadn't kissed him. As if Daniel hadn't seen desire written plain as day on Charlie's face, so exquisitely hidden that right until that moment Daniel himself had no clue about her feelings until Charlie chose to make them known.

And now she was gone.

"Charlie!" Daniel called out, trying to kick his brain back into gear and failing miserably. He ran around the building to the rose bushes in the vain hope that she had hidden herself there.

No luck.

Daniel had wanted to talk to Charlie tonight about the fact he knew she could breathe life into matter. That she could make things grow.

Going by the horror on her face as she pushed him away, Daniel doubted she would ever let him go near her again.

It was only after searching fruitlessly for ten minutes that Daniel realised exactly where Charlie had run off to.

The woods.

He turned his gaze to the dark, silent trees. It felt wrong to follow her in there. An invasion of her privacy, somehow, though of course Charlie did not own the forest.

Daniel wished for nothing more than to follow her, but he didn't.

"She said sorry," he muttered, finally returning to the gala feeling thoroughly dejected and full of a frustration that had everything to do with experiencing Charlie's legs wrapped around his waist for a single, agonising moment before she bolted away. "What does she have to be sorry for?"

If anything Daniel was the one who should have been sorry. Even if Charlie was attracted to him – and this evening proved once and for all that she was – Daniel was her employer. Her boss. If he had been in his right mind he should have waited until Charlie's year of working for him was up before pursuing anything.

But Daniel *hadn't* been in his right mind. *Just why wasn't I in my right mind?*

How Kit would laugh at him now. Daniel felt completely and utterly useless.

"Ah, Daniel, there you are!" Crimson said, seemingly appearing out of nowhere, though Daniel knew he had likely been too stuck in his own head to notice her appearance. "My grandfather was looking for you. Something to do with the trade agreement."

"Of–of course," Daniel said, wincing at the roughness still present in his voice. "Sorry for my absence. Lead the way."

He barely noticed where he was going as Crimson led him to Grandmaster Feng. But when he saw the wan, guarded smile on the aged man's face Daniel knew the conversation they were about to have was a serious one.

He didn't have time to worry over Charlie and how royally he had screwed things up with her right now. Daniel had a job to do.

"It seems you are a difficult man to find, at your own party, no less!" Feng said. "Might there be somewhere – *ah* – quieter, that we might discuss things?"

Daniel nodded. "I know just the place, if you do not mind walking for a few minutes."

"My favourite pastime, as it transpires."

After throwing a surreptitious glance around him to ensure nobody was paying them much undue attention, Daniel led Feng – Crimson remained behind to keep watch over the guests – towards the rose bushes Charlie had sung into excessive bloom mere hours ago. Where she had coaxed a baby swallow into adulthood with a gentle, quiet voice Daniel had never heard from her before, healing the bird's broken bones in the process.

It felt like he'd witnessed her perform the miracle in another lifetime. One where Daniel held onto the childish hope that Charlie might not yet reject him.

Stop thinking about her.

The Eshijani magician took in the fat, luxurious roses with appraising eyes. "You have an excellent gardener, Daniel."

It was all he could do to laugh instead of scream. "...you could say that. But what is it you wish to discuss? Wei mentioned something to do with the trade agreement?"

"Then I shan't mince words with you," Feng said. The smile he'd kept on display until now dropped entirely. "I have it on good authority that the final report regarding the temporary trade agreement has been tampered with."

Daniel frowned. "Tampered *how*, exactly?"

"The report that the Lopox Alliance will be given next week will contain falsified records dictating that sales of Eshijani products are down across all of Atralia. Because of the high prices, it will say. But you and I both know better, Daniel."

Of course he knew better. Business had been booming on this side of the border: Eshijani merchants had eagerly brought more goods to local Atralian markets now that a fairer trade agreement had been put in place. Their products were sold just as quickly as they were put on display.

"I will handle it," Daniel assured Feng. "I'll find out who's been tampering with the official records."

"I suspect it to be a member – or members – of the Alliance itself."

His mind crossed immediately to Jonah Ritten. "I suspect that, too."

"So how will you deal with it, if the perpetrator is one of your own?"

Daniel did not know, but he couldn't exactly say that to Grandmaster Feng. "I have my ways," he said, even though – other than asking Edward Hope to investigate the matter – he didn't. With a heavy sigh Daniel glanced back towards the twinkling lights of the gala. "We better return before anyone becomes suspicious."

"Then I shall count on you to handle this matter," Feng said as they made their way back to the courtyard. "I do not wish to see all our progress thus far destroyed so easily."

"Neither do I."

After the Eshijani magician left his side to converse with his grand-daughter Daniel forced himself to weave through the gala, talking to this official then that socialite and then a host of people he could in all honesty not recognise in the slightest. A numbness spread through his body as hour after endless hour merged into one.

Daniel had been foolish to think only of Charlie all evening – and for so long leading up to the gala, too. Stupidly, recklessly foolish. He had a job to do, after all. It was important, and time sensitive, and bigger than himself and Charlie.

And besides, he thought, looking to the woods again, *Charlie ran away. Like she knew kissing me was a mistake.*

Though it certainly hadn't looked that way from where Daniel had been standing.

But the last thing Daniel wanted was to ruin things for either of them. If she would only pursue it seriously then he was certain Charlie had a promising career ahead of her.

The next time he saw her Daniel swore that *he* would apologise to Charlie, and promise that he would not seek to break their professional relationship again. It was the least he could do; his feelings should not have been placed on her shoulders to bear in the first place.

Until then...Daniel could do nothing but throw himself back into his work, as he had done for decades and decades already.

It was clear that romance had long since been taken off the cards for him.

CHAPTER NINETEEN

By the time Charlie collapsed in the woods near the Uthesh fault line she had been running for almost an hour and was close to hyperventilating.

"What have I done what have I done what have I done?" she moaned, writhing in the dirt as if it might take pity on Charlie and swallow her up. But the loose earth didn't even discolour her dress or stick to her skin thanks to Daniel's magic.

Charlie sourced a stone beneath her fingertips and flung it at the closest tree. The forest undergrowth was so soft that the rock didn't even make a satisfying noise as it fell back to the ground.

"Damn him," Charlie whispered, tears falling hot and heavy before she could stop them. Even grinding the palms of her hands against her eyes did nothing to quell the tears.

It wasn't Daniel's fault Charlie felt this way. It was her own fault. She'd pushed her Intent onto him and given into her own feelings when she should have kept them locked up. Daniel Silver was the victim, not the perpetrator.

Yet if I had never met him...

The entire gala with Daniel had been a fairytale that quickly and inevitably devolved into a nightmare. Charlie had long since come to terms with the fact she would likely never meet someone she loved who, in turn, loved her, without her Influence first affecting their feelings.

Yet she had fallen for the intoxicating fairytale all the same.

When it became clear she wasn't going to stop crying, Charlie removed her hands from her eyes and burrowed her fingers deep into the earth. She had always come to the woods when she didn't know what to do; wouldn't it give her the solution to her problems now?

But all she got from the trees around her was quiet.

"Quiet is the last thing I need," Charlie told the dirt. "I need loud. I need life. I need so many impulses I can't hear myself think."

The answer she received to her plea was the mewing of a cat.

She choked on a sob. "Hey, Kit," she said, locating the cat's vivid green eyes by following the tell-tale rustle of ferns to her left. He leapt deftly between them, landing directly in front of Charlie in order to stare at her, on her hands and knees, uselessly clutching at dirt. The thought forced a laugh from behind her teeth before she could stop it. "I know how pathetic I must look right now. No judgement, all right?"

Kit did not make a sound. He merely sat there, a black shape against a black forest, and kept Charlie company.

But somehow that was enough.

There was a darkness the woods afforded Charlie which she had never experienced anywhere else. It was rich and all-consuming, preventing her from seeing the ends of her fingertips nor Kit's tawny fur nor the trees that encircled her. In truth Charlie did not know how she managed to reach her favourite clearing in the forest under such conditions in the first place.

Charlie lay down, dirt cool and calming on her cheek, and closed her eyes.

Breathed in. Breathed out. Breathed in. Breathed out.

She did not open her eyes again until the quiet all around her was broken. Except, Charlie realised, when she surveyed her surroundings and listened closely, that nothing had interrupted the quiet. There was no rustling in the ferns. No birds shuffling in the sky or in the trees. No water gurgling along a riverbed or falling into a pond.

There was nothing.

But still, the forest was not quiet.

"Strange," Charlie murmured, ear to the earth as she tried to work out what was going on. "Kit, can you—"

The cat was gone.

Mere minutes ago Charlie would have been upset by Kit leaving her but for some reason she no longer felt alone. There was something in the soil, Charlie realised, the more she focused on it.

A thrumming. A buzz.

A life.

A dull memory skirted around the edges of Charlie's mind, informing her that the woods had felt like this once – and only once – in her entire life.

The day Charlie's mother died.

And then, out of nowhere, the sound of a pan flute resonated on the air. It circled around the trees, whispering between leaves and vines and stones, before it reached Charlie's ears. By the time she heard it she realised that the woods no longer felt so sleepy.

The smallest of lights caught Charlie's attention. Then another, then another. *Fireflies*, she concluded, thinking briefly of the one's she'd summoned for Daniel before rising into a sitting position. The light the insects emitted revealed the silhouettes of horns and antlers and pointed ears and sharp green eyes.

The Immortal Folk.

The music of the pan flute paused. "Sing for us, Charlie Hope," a voice from the trees urged, both oddly familiar and strange, before they continued to play. But when Charlie peered through the foliage to try and discern the musician a host of creatures appeared in the meadow, joyous grins upon their strange, inhuman faces as they pulled Charlie to her feet.

A Nymph with iridescent skin and thick, blue hair put a garland of flowers on her head; another, identical Nymph put her hand in Charlie's and squeezed it tight.

"Dance with us," they said.

"What are you celebrating?" she asked, puzzled but nonetheless delighted by the appearance of so many Immortal Folk.

"You," the voice from the trees said between notes on the pan flute. "So sing, and dance, and forget your troubles."

Charlie had a lot of troubles she wished to forget.

She did as she was told.

Chapter Twenty

Never had Charlie so viciously and desperately wished to avoid someone like she hoped to avoid Daniel Silver the day after the gala.

It didn't help that she crawled into bed long after the event was finished, all her energy expended in the woods with the Immortal Folk. Charlie was inclined to believe she'd imagined her time with them; lying on a comfortable bed within the solid confines of her room made her jaunt into the woods seem impossible.

Except that it wasn't impossible. It had happened – from the life she felt in the very earth beneath her fingertips to the sound of the pan flute upon the wind to the Nymph sisters urging Charlie to dance with them.

And sing.

It was with some relief that Charlie remembered everyone had the day off to recover from the gala. If she'd had her way she would have remained in the safety of her bed all day, protected from any possible encounters with Daniel.

Charlie's stomach, however, had other ideas.

So Charlie crept from her room, a blanket clutched around

her shoulders a poor attempt at anonymity as she scurried to the kitchen...and bounded right into the one man she would rather like to never see again, even though that was a lie and Charlie knew it.

Daniel stared at her bizarre, blanketed appearance in obvious surprise. "Miss Hope," he said. "You're...here."

Charlie's heart sank at his reversal to her surname.

"I'm here," she mumbled, eyes firmly on her feet.

A moment of silence. Then Daniel coughed rather uselessly. "I wanted to apologise for yesterday. What happened - the position I put you in—"

"You don't have to apologise," Charlie cut in, horrified by the prospect. "You did nothing wrong. I—"

"I will not have you believe you have to be sorry when you don't," Daniel said, firm and resolute. "And I don't want things to be awkward between us, either. You have grown into a rather fine member of my team; it would be a blow to us all to lose you now."

The compliment should have made Charlie happy. Instead, Daniel reverting to a more formal relationship between them - setting up walls to protect himself from her - stabbed Charlie right through the heart.

It hurt so badly she couldn't stand it.

"Of course," Charlie forced out of her mouth, tearing her gaze from the floor to make eye contact. It was in this way she realised that Daniel was averting his gaze, and that his cheeks still held some of the flush Charlie had witnessed when they'd kissed the night before.

Is my Intent still affecting him? Charlie thought, stricken. *I was sure I couldn't feel it any more. I was sure I—*

"Um," Daniel said, fiddling with his glasses and very clearly uncomfortable with Charlie openly staring at him. "If you'll excuse me, I have some work to attend to. Enjoy the rest of your day off."

Charlie could only stand there, mouth agape and eyes wide at the spot where Daniel had been standing long after he left. For if her Intent was no longer affecting him and he still reacted in such a way merely speaking to her, then...

Then not everything I felt last night came from me. Right? Right?

Charlie simply couldn't tell. With the number of times her Influence had spiralled out of control around Daniel over the past few days Charlie realised she could no longer tell the difference between real and fabricated feelings anymore.

It worried her to no end.

"Well...that's definitely one way to advance, Hope."

Charlie turned and abruptly remembered the Jean-shaped problem she still had to solve; in the drama and excitement of her time with Daniel and, then, the woods, she had entirely forgotten about it.

Now that was coming back to bite her.

"It – it wasn't like that," she stammered, noting that Jean looked haggard and hungover. *And no longer affected by my Intent,* Charlie realised with relief. "Nothing—"

"I saw the two of you by the front doors last night. I didn't mean to – I was looking for you so I could apologise for being an arse." Jean let out a self-deprecating chuckle. "Who knew that, all this time, you had the hots for our boss?"

"It's nothing," Charlie insisted once more, hating that things had to be nothing. "Last night...I was drunk. Mister Silver was drunk. It was stupid. It—"

"That so-called apology between the two of you right now didn't look like nothing to me," he pointed out, annoyingly astute for a hungover, exhausted mess of a person. A scowl shadowed his brow. "And now all of us will have to ignore the two of you failing to ignore one another."

Panic rose in Charlie's throat; she took a few steps towards Jean, almost tempted to crumple his shirt in her hands as she begged him to stay quiet. "You haven't told anyone else, have you? You can't tell anyone!"

"I don't need to. If I can see what's going on then, trust me, Crimson has already known for a while. Luca and the rest of the staff won't be far behind."

Charlie had no response. Jean was right and they both knew it. Charlie had been so absorbed in her own head lately that she hadn't tried in the slightest to hide her emotions from her face. Everyone knew how combative she was with Daniel – it wouldn't take much of a stretch for any of them to believe that Charlie arguing with him had been one big flirtation.

She wondered if it truly had been, all along.

"Don't ruin your career by taking this too far," Jean said, a surprisingly concerned expression on his face. "If word gets out that Mr Silver is sleeping with a member of staff whom he hired as a favour then, trust me, that will *not* look good for either of you. He'll be able to recover from it – that's the way these things go, after all – but you won't, Charlie. I don't want that for you. I really don't."

It was clear every word out of Jean's mouth was genuine.

"Thanks for your candour," Charlie said. She forced a smile to her face. "And you don't have to worry about anything. I'm not going to make the same mistake again. All things considered having you see what happened last night is a blessing in disguise. I needed the wake-up call."

When Jean chuckled softly Charlie felt herself relax a little. "Just don't come crying back to me when you realise what a catch I really am."

"As if. Was the apology you were going to give me all lip

service?"

"Of course not." Jean swished his hair out of his face in an entirely exaggerated manner. "I'm nothing if not a gentleman. I have no interest in pursuing women who don't have an interest in me, no matter how beautiful they are. Sorry, Hope. You're too much trouble."

She could only laugh. She *was* too much trouble, after all. Charlie had made peace with that a long time ago.

Or, at least, she thought she had.

It was only after Charlie lay once more in bed, beyond exhausted yet unable to sleep, that she pondered everything Jean had said.

She didn't care about her own career, so the idea of sullying it was of no consequence to Charlie. But her *father* cared about it and, clearly, so did Daniel Silver. She didn't want to cause more trouble for the man than she already had.

Tumbling onto her back Charlie stared out of the window, not quite focusing on anything. Her feet itched with the urge to go back to the woods – the Immortal Folk had made it clear she was invited to join them whenever she liked – though Charlie knew she would regret it given how tired she was.

And besides, there were far more important things for Charlie to be troubling herself over. She might not have cared about her career but the more time she spent actively preventing war between Atralia and Eshijan the more it mattered to her that she saw the conflict through to its eventual resolution.

She had nine months left of her employment with Daniel Silver. Nine months left within which to negotiate peace between Lopox and Eshijan...

Without thinking of Daniel as anything but her employer. It was going to be a very, very long nine months. Too long to think about now.

Charlie rolled out of bed and escaped to the woods for one

more night of dancing.

CHAPTER TWENTY-ONE

SEVEN AGONISING DAYS HAD PASSED SINCE the gala. Daniel did not find that time had made it any less awkward – nor less frustrating – to avoid Charlie.

It didn't help that he had been working with her more closely over the past few days in preparation for the end of the temporary trade agreement. Sitting across from Charlie day in, day out, both of them poring over notes and laws and past treaties – pausing only to ask the other a question about something they might have come across in their research – was almost unbearable.

Daniel found himself watching Charlie work almost as often as *he* did any actual work, his mind entirely focused on her every movement. It was as if the physical contact between the two of them at the gala had awoken something in Daniel that had previously lain dormant for decades. Something which entirely ignored the fact Daniel had sworn to leave Charlie alone.

Charlie chewed on the end of a pencil and Daniel wanted to kiss her.

Charlie ran a hand through her hair and Daniel wished it was his hand, instead.

Charlie readjusted the sleeve of her dress when it swept off her shoulder and Daniel wished he could rip the material off her entirely.

He wanted her. Daniel wanted Charlie Hope so badly he could scream.

He wished he could say he no longer cared about finding out exactly what the young woman could do with her magic. Truly, he wished he could, but that mysterious part of her that Charlie kept secret was part of her appeal and Daniel knew it. He was getting closer to figuring out the truth, for sure, yet he was also afraid of what he'd find.

Having analysed past events over and over and over again Daniel was now certain that Charlie could tell when someone was lying or telling the truth. But that wasn't everything she was hiding – not even when combined with her creation magic.

So Daniel was scared.

Perhaps it was the strength of his own feelings towards Charlie that frightened him.

"You're not even trying to hide the fact you like her now, are you, Daniel?" Crimson said, startling Daniel so severely that he jumped from his seat by the window in his office.

He had been watching Charlie try to work on some kind of magic in the garden, not realising until looking at his clock that he'd wasted half an hour doing so. Daniel wasn't sure what Charlie was actually attempting; going by her scrunched up features she was clearly failing miserably.

"I didn't hear you come in," Daniel admitted, sitting back down again and attempting to locate some semblance of calm within himself.

There was none to be found.

Crimson raised an eyebrow. "I *did* knock, you know. Interesting that you didn't even deny what I said."

"Is there a point in denying it to you?"

"Absolutely not."

"Then do you disapprove?"

"On the contrary," Crimson said, joining him by the window to unceremoniously spy on Charlie, "I believe she's the only one who can match you."

Daniel was so surprised by this answer that he could do nothing but gawk at his Chief-of-Staff. Then the cogs in his brain began turning, and he wondered why in the world she would believe something like that.

"You know something about Miss Hope that I don't," Daniel said, eyes narrowing at Crimson as he realised he was speaking the truth. "What is it that you know?"

Crimson could barely suppress the grin that threatened to break across her face. "If her father never told you, and Charlie herself hasn't told you, and you haven't worked it out for yourself, then it definitely isn't my place to tell you."

"As my Chief-of-Staff it is literally your job to tell me things about my employees."

"Then I guess you'll have to fire me."

Daniel felt like tearing his hair out just as he watched Charlie attempt to do exactly the same thing through the window. But then he drooped his head in defeat. "How did you work out... whatever you worked out?"

"Pure chance," Crimson said off-handedly. She tapped the windowpane in Charlie's direction. "It helps that I've been watching her like a hawk to make sure she behaves. You learn a lot about a person from watching them constantly."

"If that were the case I'd know what she's hiding by now, too."

Crimson was abruptly taken aback by how easily Daniel admitted to watching Charlie. It was entirely unlike him to be so honest. But it wasn't just Daniel's feelings and well-being that were on the line here; Crimson genuinely cared about Charlie, and she didn't want to see her hurt during Daniel's journey to seek the truth about her.

"Do not pursue anything with Charlie if you aren't serious about her – if you're merely curious about her powers," she warned, her expression brooking no argument.

Daniel barked out a laugh. "Given her nature I'd say she's the one who'd never be serious or who'd drop someone once they've satisfied her curiosity. She's young, after all."

Even as he said it Daniel knew fine well it was a lie.

"Ah, you damn immortals," Crimson lamented, seeing right through Daniel's lie. "Between the two of you it is not Charlie who is detached from her emotions. Does it make you uncomfortable, knowing she could get bored of you and reject you?"

"...it terrifies me."

"As it should. That means you're serious. So stop being a coward and *do* something about it. Everyone around here is sick of watching you act like a lovelorn puppy whenever you spy on Charlie Hope."

Before Daniel could form a rebuttal Crimson swept out of his office, closing the door with an air of finality behind her. For a long moment he did nothing but stare into space, before guiltily returning to watching Charlie through the window.

She had collapsed onto the grass now, seemingly having given up on whatever impossible task she had given herself. But Charlie held a lock of golden hair out in front of her, which finally allowed Daniel to work out what she had been doing.

Charlie was trying to remove his cleaning magic.

Not for the first time – especially after what Charlie had said at the gala – a wave of guilt washed over Daniel at the fact he'd imposed such a restrictive, invasive spell upon her.

And, even worse, *enjoyed* the fact his own magic was circulating through her body.

Daniel resolved to permanently remove the spell as soon as it became possible for him to touch Charlie without filthy motives taking over his brain, which right now seemed like never. Daniel didn't want to be rid of such thoughts, after all. Acting professional around Charlie had only made his urges and impulses worse.

Why did she say sorry after we kissed?

Right now all that separated Daniel from Charlie was a pane of glass. A stupid, insubstantial pane of glass. Daniel could open the window and jump over the ledge, or take the long way around to the courtyard doors, or simply transport himself to Charlie's side using magic. It would literally be that easy to talk to her.

To be honest with her – and himself – once and for all.

Avoiding Charlie was getting Daniel nowhere.

When a cat-shaped Kit prowled across the courtyard and deftly settled on Charlie's stomach Daniel found himself pausing with his hand on the window latch. Something told him that having Kit around when he tried to speak to Charlie was a terrible, terrible idea.

Which meant Daniel had to ensure he could speak to Charlie when he knew for certain Kit was in the woods, unable to interrupt them. For he was sure Kit *would* interrupt them, just as surely as Daniel knew Charlie would continue avoiding him if he didn't make the first move.

She had apologised for making the first move at the gala, after all.

Kit had never explained his behaviour after interfering with whatever connection Daniel and Charlie had forged the night the team had been drinking. It was unlikely the Drus would do so now even if Daniel demanded it of him.

Daniel's memory of the entire conversation he'd had with his staff that night was hazy from whisky, and once or twice he'd thought for sure he'd imagined the fact Charlie reached out for him the way he'd reached out for her, unable to resist his own impulses. But the more he analysed his memory, along with what had occurred at the actual gala, the more he was sure nothing had been imagined between himself and Charlie at all.

Which meant Daniel had to speak to Charlie alone so they could work things out once and for all. No fancy galas or glasses of champagne or best friends masquerading as cats or employees around to potentially alter the interaction.

He would try one final time to connect with Charlie Hope. And then, for her sake, Daniel would have no choice but to give up on his obsession.

CHAPTER TWENTY-TWO

IT HAD TAKEN HER WEEKS AND weeks of trying whenever she was sure nobody was watching, but finally she managed it: Charlie successfully threw off Daniel Silver's cleaning spell.

Water had never felt so good.

She thought it ironic that, upon removing his cleaning magic, the first thing Charlie did was take a bath. But Daniel's spell had prevented her skin and hair from soaking in steaming, fragrant water just as it had protected her from soil and twigs and blood and bruises.

A bath was exactly what she craved.

Daniel's estate held an expansive bathhouse within it. The bath itself was more like a swimming pool, capable of accommodating ten people sitting around its edge on low seats built beneath the water. But it was after nine on a Tuesday evening; Charlie had the entire place all to herself.

It was divine.

Around her the bathhouse was sculpted from marble, quartz and precious metals. The seamless curvature of the walls, low ceiling and the bath itself made Charlie inclined to believe the room had likely been moulded first in clay and then transmuted into tougher, more beautiful but altogether harder to work with materials.

Either way, the resultant effect was that of an ethereal, echoing cave. It didn't feel like the bathhouse was part of a house but, rather, a fixture in a fairy tale. Magic was seeped into every crevice.

It almost felt like the woods.

If Charlie hadn't been magically protected from the elements she'd have had cause to appreciate the bathhouse well before now. As it stood, this was the first time she had ever looked at the place and properly taken note of how much care went into the architecture.

Charlie arched her neck against the edge of the bath, allowing her body to float in the large expanse of bubbling, soapy water. The scent of lavender and honey floated on the steam, filling her nostrils and sending Charlie into a deep, all-consuming state of relaxation.

This was bliss. Being in her own skin – being able to *feel* things on her own skin – was something Charlie had taken for granted before Daniel worked his magic upon her.

She would make certain never to allow such a thing to happen again.

Around her shoulders Charlie's hair ebbed and flowed, the water turning it a dark, glimmering gold. She hadn't put her glamour back up yet, though was looking forward to working the magic upon herself before she went to sleep so she could look at her reflection and see the shadow of her mother once more.

But something had stopped Charlie from changing her appearance for now. Perhaps it was the idea of bathing in her *own* skin that stayed her hand. For after all, Charlie's hair was blonde like her father's, soft and wavy and generally well-behaved. The wild, dark curls she'd worn for years now did not really belong to her.

A low sigh escaped her lips. Charlie had been dead on her feet all day, long nights spent dancing in the forest finally catching up to her. But if she didn't celebrate with the small band of Immortal Folk she had come to consider her friends then all Charlie did was think about Daniel, which was the last thing she wanted.

So dancing it was. Dancing and laughing and singing, singing, singing, watching with delight as trees, vines, ferns, flowers and all manner of wildlife hung onto every word that fell from Charlie's lips.

The life beneath her feet lapped up her magic with an unslakeable thirst.

Charlie began to sing now, her voice whisper-quiet but echoing around the bathhouse louder and louder with each passing second. There was no life around her to benefit from her magic; instead, Charlie inflected the words with her own relaxed Intent simply for herself.

Charlie closed her eyes, breathed out and released all the tension in her muscles that she'd held since the gala, and everything around her was still and peaceful and quiet.

There was nobody in the world but Charlie.

Until Daniel Silver walked in.

He had not known Charlie was bathing. Coming across her like this was an entirely fortuitous accident. At first he didn't even spot Charlie through the steam coming off the bath, but he could hear her sing and felt her magic.

A shiver ran down his spine as his entire body relaxed. *Odd,* Daniel thought, surreptitiously ensuring the door to the bathhouse was locked so nobody could walk in on either of them. *I haven't even set foot in the water and I already feel so at ease. Just what is...is this Charlie's doing?*

He hung his towel on a silver rack on the wall, entering the pool-like bath as far from Charlie as he could possibly manage.

The last thing he wanted to do was frighten her, after all. She hadn't yet noticed his presence.

But frighten her was precisely what he did. All at once Charlie stopped singing and ducked beneath the surface of the bath, finally sensing another person nearby.

Not just another person: Daniel, specifically.

This isn't happening, she thought, panic surging like vomit up her throat. This isn't—

"Miss Hope!"

Daniel's shout was mostly absorbed by the water, but it boomed off the walls and ensured Charlie had no doubt her name had been called.

Slowly – though she didn't want to – Charlie popped her head out of the bath, twists of hair dripping soapy water down her face as she located Daniel through the haze.

Charlie noted that he was sitting about as far away from her as he could get within the confines of the bath. His head was cocked to the side, regarding her curiously. "I wasn't aware you could breathe underwater."

It took Charlie far too long to find her voice. "I can't."

"Then what were you doing down there?"

"Nothing."

"It wasn't exactly the best place to hide, all things considered."

"...I'll leave you in peace," Charlie mumbled, making to get up even though she was mortified by the prospect of Daniel seeing her naked after everything that had happened between them so far.

"No, don't," Daniel called out, too loudly and too quickly. "Don't," he said again, quieter, when it was clear he had startled her. "You were here first. I'll keep to myself, so...so..." Something caught his attention that Charlie couldn't see. He narrowed his eyes in her direction. "Wait."

On instinct Charlie sank further into the water until barely the top half of her face was visible. But this only caused Daniel to wade through the bath towards her, decidedly *not* keeping to himself. He peered down at Charlie, quizzical and calculating, whilst she did everything in her power to avert her eyes from the very obvious nakedness of the man.

"You removed my cleaning magic," Daniel said, either oblivious to the fact he had no clothes on or so completely comfortable in his own skin that he didn't care. At this point Charlie genuinely had no clue which was the right answer.

Either way, he'd caught her with his spell deactivated.

Charlie turned from Daniel to rest her arms on the side of the bath so she could answer him without having to look at him – and so Daniel couldn't see her, either.

"Only in my own time," she muttered, too flustered to form a proper defence. "Please don't force another permanent spell on me."

An awkward pause. "You can keep it off if you want."

"I...can?"

"I never meant for it to remain on you so long," Daniel admitted. "It was wrong of me to subject you to such a cruel punishment."

"So why didn't you remove it?"

"...the answer is shameful."

He wanted Charlie to ask what that meant.

She remained infuriatingly silent.

Not wishing to end the conversation there Daniel sat back against the bath, arms outstretched along the ledge behind him, and waited for Charlie to realise he was no longer standing so close to her before speaking again.

"You haven't put your glamour back up," Daniel said, genuinely curious as to why. "Since you removed the cleaning spell I assumed that would be the first thing you'd do."

At first it seemed like Charlie wouldn't respond. She glanced at him, then down at the water as if double-checking it was still opaque with soap and bubbles.

She turned around.

"I guess having to spend the last four months or so looking at myself in the mirror made me a little more comfortable with what I actually look like," Charlie sighed, twisting a lock of hair around her finger as she did so. "It's not as if I used a glamour to hide from other people in the first place, anyway. I've always been fine with looking like *me* around others."

Daniel had long since suspected this. He watched Charlie continue to twist her hair and longed to touch it himself, though of course he resisted. "What was the purpose of the glamour, then, if not to change how others perceived you? To distance yourself from them? To feel close to your mother?"

When Charlie flinched he knew he was correct. "...how did you know?" she whispered, staring at Daniel as if terrified he could read her mind.

He wished he could. Everything would be so much easier if he knew exactly what Charlie was thinking. What she was feeling.

"The week before the gala I stopped by your house to speak to your father," Daniel said. "I was looking at the photos in the living room—"

"Oh, Uthesh be good," she cut in, mortified, "tell me you're lying."

He couldn't help but smile. "You were an adorable child. Whatever happened to you?"

Charlie merely glowered at him.

"Anyway," he continued, fighting not to laugh at the

scandalised expression on Charlie's face, "I noticed there were no photos of your mother. I met her once, actually, years and years ago, but for the life of me I can't remember what she looked like. It was only in thinking such a thing that I realised she probably looked something like you when you have your glamour up."

Charlie didn't reply. But it was clear she was mulling over Daniel's observation, her previous scowl replaced with a blank look of concentration.

Then her eyes grew far too bright, and Daniel realised Charlie was close to tears.

Uthesh be good, what did I do? Daniel thought, shocked by how vulnerable she looked. He dithered over trying to comfort her but ultimately didn't: he had no idea what to say.

"I can barely remember what she looked like," Charlie admitted, rubbing a soapy palm over her eyes. "What she sounded like. What she smelled like. But her hair...I could never forget how wild her hair was. When I managed to glamour mine for the first time Da looked at me like he'd seen a ghost." A soft, sad chuckle. "That's how I knew I must look like her. Da doesn't like talking about her – it hurts him too much. But the way he reacted when he saw my hair...that was all I needed to keep my own memory alive."

I'm an awful person, Daniel realised, as he watched Charlie blink away her unshed tears until she looked as if she had never been upset in the first place. *I severed an important connection for her without once thinking about what I was doing. I was so selfish.*

He reached out a hand towards Charlie before pulling it away at the last minute. "I'm sorry, Charlie," Daniel said, using her first name before he could stop himself. "It's useless to say that now, but I am."

To his surprise, Charlie laughed. "You didn't know. How could you know? And you were right that I didn't care enough about my appearance in professional settings. It was a lesson I needed to learn."

"But not the way I forced you to learn it."

Charlie didn't reply; they both knew Daniel was correct. But the silence that fell between them afterwards didn't feel quite so awkward as it had done before.

Counting that as progress, Daniel rested against the edge of the bath and closed his eyes, content to simply be in Charlie's company. He had never intended to cross paths with her today – certainly not within the confines of the bathhouse. But he had learnt something new about her. Perhaps tomorrow, or the day after that, or the day after that, he could discuss the way he felt about her to her face, honestly and properly.

Daniel knew when Charlie finally relaxed without witnessing it, which was strange. He could feel it.

Down to his very core he could feel it.

What is this? Daniel wondered, his mind full of hazy, welcoming fog. *I felt this when I entered the bathhouse, too. Just what is it that Charlie can do? She isn't singing any more. Is this all in my head?*

But then the relaxed atmosphere around him changed. The feeling of the *air* changed.

Daniel just barely opened his eyes, watching Charlie without her noticing through the steam. She was rosy-cheeked, gaze deliberately looking anywhere but at Daniel. The water around her seemed unsettled as if she were squirming beneath it.

The mere idea of Charlie, naked beneath the bath's soapy surface, eliminated all such thoughts of relaxation from Daniel's mind, and he became painfully aware of the situation he was in.

How did I think this would go well? Daniel internally screamed, shifting uncomfortably as his body began to react to the rapidly escalating thoughts circling his head. *I should never have come in here once I realised Charlie was present. I should have—*

A wave of overwhelming desire hit Daniel like a ton of bricks.

He couldn't escape it. It clouded his mind, his eyes, his nerves, his nose, until it was all Daniel could focus on. Like a man possessed he surged towards Charlie to trap her between the wall of the bath and himself.

"Mister Sil-Daniel, let go!" Charlie cried, wide-eyed and flailing when Daniel locked her wrists within his hands, holding them hostage as she struggled against his grasp.

He leant his forehead against Charlie's, barely able to contain himself. "What are you doing to me?" Daniel gasped, chest heaving. "What is this wicked game you're playing? Why can't I —"

"I'm not doing anything!"

"Stop *lying* to me!"

Daniel wrenched his left hand from Charlie's wrist and place it against the artery in her neck. Her pulse was painfully fast – faster than his own. It reminded Daniel of how Charlie had looked at him after she kissed him.

After *she* kissed *him.*

"When I realised you were alone in here I only hoped to talk to you," Daniel murmured against her ear. The scent of Charlie's skin overwhelmed his senses, floral and delicate and cutting right through the swirling steam of the bathwater.

Before he knew it Daniel's fingers left Charlie's pulse to travels downwards – across her collarbone, her breasts, her waist – before settling between her legs.

Charlie bit out a moan so alluring in response to his touch that what little remained of Daniel's self-control threatened to evaporate entirely. "Truly, I did," he growled, when his fingers moved faster and Charlie squeezed her thighs around them, eyes glazed over and breathing so accelerated that Daniel's own breath hitched to match her rhythm. "But it's as if...as if... something is pulling all the thoughts from my head and making me act upon them. I've never acted on my impulses like this before – never, in a hundred years – so why? It's like something is influencing—"

Suddenly everything clicked into place. He was being *Influenced.*

He stared at Charlie in new-found wonder. "You can...use Intent magic?"

"That isn't—" Charlie began, gasping against Daniel's fingers still firmly between her thighs. "You have it all wr—"

"Why are you lying to me?" he demanded, dragging his lips from Charlie's ear to the column of her throat. "Tell me the truth. You're an Intent user. You—"

"It's usually under control!" Charlie shuddered beneath Daniel's touch. "No, it's *always* under control. But lately, w-when you've been around, I just can't...stop it."

"And why is that?"

When Charlie shoved against Daniel's chest to put some distance between them it wasn't just the physical movement he felt. No, her Intent receded alongside it, and Daniel regained some semblance of self-control.

Only to discover there was none left.

"No," he said, pushing his body against Charlie until nothing could come between them. "No, I can feel you pulling away. Don't." He stroked her face and kissed her eyelids, her nose, her mouth. "You've been Influencing the Alliance meetings, haven't you? Right from the very start and I didn't even know. I'm such a fool. Don't pull away, Charlie. Don't."

Then Daniel kissed her neck, hands freely roaming over Charlie's body getting more urgent with every beat of her throbbing heart.

"S-stop," Charlie gasped, not knowing for how much longer she could contain her Intent before losing control entirely. She was afraid; what would Daniel think, in the morning, when his senses returned to him and he realised he'd done something with her he'd invariably regret?

But Daniel's onslaught was insistent. "Why?" His breath was hot and desperate on Charlie's lips. "You *want* this, don't you? That's why this is happening, isn't it?"

"But that's the reason!" she cried. "How can I ever know something is happening without my Influence if I can feel it directly affecting a situation? If I – if I can't control my own desires?"

"You underestimate my defences, Charlie. I wouldn't be doing this if I didn't want to...and you're too decent to let it happen if that were so."

All at once Charlie froze. What Daniel was saying – what he was insinuating – was that her magic wasn't the only force at play here. Which meant...

Daniel Silver likes me? He actually...

"...how can you be so sure?" Charlie asked, too overwhelmed and excited and downright terrified by Daniel's fingertips trailing back down between her thighs to say much else.

But his answer fell from his tongue easily. Like he never doubted it for a moment.

Like he'd never doubted *Charlie* for a moment.

"A woman who saves broken birds and makes the flowers grow cannot be a bad person," Daniel said, all at once admitting to Charlie that he had worked out the full extent of her magic without her knowing.

She stared at him. Gaped at him.

"You weren't – this isn't just because *I'm* making you feel this way?"

After all the trouble and grief and frustration Daniel had gone through on behalf of Charlie Hope, her question was a cruel joke.

"Are you testing me, Charlie?" he asked, breath ragged against her lips. "After the gala – after everything – how could you *possibly* be this blind to how I feel towards you?"

It was only then that Daniel realised Charlie's trembling was just as much to do with nerves as it was to do with where he was touching, and he starkly remembered what she'd admitted to Jean and Luca – and, unwittingly, Daniel himself.

"You weren't lying when you said you'd only slept with one person before, were you?" he murmured. Charlie tried to look away but Daniel tilted her chin to face him. "Just be honest with me."

"Would you rather I was experienced at the expense of having manipulated the feelings of other men?" Charlie retorted, fiery and defensive. But her supposed anger didn't mean all that much in the face of how she whimpered when Daniel slid his fingers inside her, nor how Charlie was shaking in her attempt to resist touching him back.

"No," Daniel said, "though I wouldn't judge you if you had. I simply want to understand you. I don't want to ruin this before it's even started."

It was this reassurance that finally calmed Charlie down. Slowly, carefully, she nuzzled against Daniel's hand when he stroked her cheek. "This is all so unfamiliar to me," she whispered. "I don't know what I'm doing."

"I don't think I do, either."

Charlie quirked an eyebrow despite herself. "Says the man with over a century of experience."

"If you think I've whiled away the decades sleeping around with every person who catches my eye then I'm sorry to disappoint you." Daniel brushed the barest of kisses against

Charlie's lips. "A friend recently pointed out – several times – that I've been rather detached for a long time now. So it's...been a while for me, since I've felt like this."

The mere thought of Kit brought something else to the forefront of Daniel's mind. "The Drus," he bit out before he could stop himself. Charlie frowned, confused at why Daniel was bringing them up. "The one you...met...five years ago. Immortal Folk aren't affected by human Mind magic."

"Yes?"

"So you knew you couldn't accidentally Influence him."

"Yes," Charlie said again.

"So it was the safest choice you could make."

For the third time: "...yes."

Charlie made no mention of the fact she had truly, genuinely liked the inhuman Drus; she hadn't slept with him simply because he was 'safe'. But she didn't tell Daniel.

That was a secret for Charlie and Charlie alone.

"You don't need to play it safe with me," Daniel insisted, slinging an arm around Charlie's waist in the process. Every inch of his skin was against her own. Taunting her. Teasing her. "I can handle it. I can handle you."

"Can you?"

Charlie didn't want the answer to be no. She didn't want the answer to be anything but Daniel's blue eyes watching her with an intensity she'd never experienced before. To have his lips on hers, and her legs wrapped around his waist, and all words lost in favour of moans and cries and gasps for air.

"I'm more than willing to find out," Daniel said, the full length of his body strained and torturous against Charlie's. "So don't...don't hold anything back, and I won't, either."

All at once Daniel was no longer close enough to Charlie. She wanted more.

Needed more.

Charlie nodded her head.

In an instant Daniel entered her in a shock of nerves and barely restrained impulses, his mouth claiming hers as if it belonged to him. The sensation knocked the very air out of Charlie's lungs and filled her up with something else entirely; something solid and present and demanding all of her attention.

Demanding all of *her.*

Most importantly: Daniel's desperate, shaking hands as they seized Charlie's hips and thrust against them were driven by *his* feelings, just as Charlie's starved reaction to him doing so was driven by hers.

Finally, as if she had been waiting for it all her life, Charlie slung her arms around Daniel's neck and lost herself entirely.

CHAPTER TWENTY-THREE

"...DON'T THINK IT'S WISE TO EASE up on weapons preparations despite this. What do you think, Mr Silver? Mister Silver?"

"Daniel," Crimson not-so-subtly coughed, bringing him starkly back to reality.

"Yes, I'm listening," Daniel said, though in truth he absolutely wasn't. He was too busy going over everything that had happened the day before. Charlie was also present at the meeting; when she caught Daniel's gaze and blushed faintly he had no doubt she was thinking about the same thing he was.

And yet...

"Surely Mr Silver and Crimson have produced more than enough ammunition for now," Charlie said easily, demonstrating that, unlike Daniel, she had in fact been listening. "Since all the stockpiling is supposed to be a precaution and we're not actually *wanting* to go to war with Eshijan any additional preparation seems excessive."

Charlie was right, of course, but Daniel had said the same thing many times before without gaining much traction.

But he wasn't Charlie.

He didn't have Intent magic.

"That's...true," Jonathan Crank relented. "Since we're already dealing with someone having tampered with the temporary trade agreement report it would probably be best for us to suspend the rest of the stockpiling. Yes, yes, that's what we should do."

It was that easy. It was literally that easy for Charlie Hope to turn a situation to her advantage. It didn't matter who was on the end of her magic: if she willed it, it happened.

Daniel couldn't believe he hadn't noticed it before now.

As the rest of the meeting progressed Daniel felt himself going through the motions of responding to questions and providing ideas, safe in the knowledge that everything would go in his team's favour so long as Charlie continued Influencing the Alliance.

Allowing his thoughts to wander again, Daniel found himself stealing glances at Charlie more and more often until he simply accepted the fact he was no longer paying attention to the meeting whatsoever.

Daniel had slept with Charlie Hope. He worked out the full extent of her magic and was honest about his feelings and he had slept with Charlie Hope.

After their encounter in the bathhouse Charlie had run off to her room, thoroughly embarrassed, and in his idiocy Daniel had let her. He vowed not to be so stupid today.

Nothing was going to interfere with his good mood nor his plan to invite Charlie to spend the night with him.

It was clear Charlie was well aware of the tension between herself and Daniel, and for the majority of the meeting she pledged to ignore it. But it grew increasingly difficult for her to do so and, eventually, Charlie felt it was entirely unfair that she should be subjected to the weight of what Daniel was thinking without messing with him in return.

She pushed out a hook of her Influence to ensnare Daniel

and Daniel alone, overwhelming his mind with entirely unprofessional, distracting, filthy images.

Well this is different, he mused, resting his head on a hand to indulge his unexpected, intense daydream. Daniel didn't usually have such thoughts during official meetings, though he never normally spent the evening before said meetings touching every inch of a beautiful woman he was utterly bewitched by, either.

It took Daniel far too long to realise Charlie had implanted the thoughts in his head rather than them having appeared organically.

If Charlie was amused by what she'd done it certainly didn't show on her face.

It wasn't long before it grew difficult for Daniel to resist the impulses Charlie was forcing upon him. He tapped his foot repeatedly, tensed the muscles in his stomach and adjusted his posture as if doing so might somehow ease the growing strain he felt against his trousers.

Charlie could have done this to me from the very beginning, Daniel realised, cheeks growing far too hot. *But she didn't. How does she have so much self-control?*

If Daniel had felt like this back in February he wouldn't have been able to keep his hands off her.

He supposed that was the point of Charlie keeping her magic to herself: it was dangerous and easily twisted towards nefarious means. But right now he didn't have it in him to care about such things.

Every wicked idea Charlie was implanting in his head, Daniel was desperate to indulge.

When the meeting finally, agonisingly, came to an end it was all Daniel could do to say good-bye to his colleagues, politely and silently sweep Charlie down the corridor and open the door to his office before his impulse control crumbled entirely.

Daniel pressed Charlie against the door before she could speak a word.

She eagerly reciprocated his advances.

"You're a cruel woman," Daniel growled against the hollow of her throat, revelling in the feeling of Charlie beneath his hands once more. "I can't believe you could so easily do that to me in such a *professional* situation."

Charlie let out an unsteady chuckle. "You were asking for it. You do realise I can sense what you're thinking, right? It made it difficult for me to focus."

"Then I guess we're both to blame."

When Charlie flung her arms around Daniel's neck and pulled him closer he eagerly kissed her. For several minutes that was as far as they went, but when Daniel's hands roved beneath the hem of Charlie's shirt she stiffened.

Daniel paused immediately. "What's wrong?"

"Jean," Charlie replied, looking troubled.

"*Jean?*" Daniel echoed back, not at all expecting that to be Charlie's answer.

"He saw us at the gala," she sighed. "And...warned me afterwards, about what a tryst between us would look like to your followers and sponsors. And he's right, you know. If we're going to keep whatever this is going then we need to keep it quiet."

"And do you want *whatever this is* to keep going?" Daniel asked, knowing it was the only part of what Charlie said that he currently cared about.

A delicious blush cross Charlie's cheeks. She nodded. "Yes. Yes, I'd like that very much."

And though he didn't want to – his body was aching, burning, begging him not to – Daniel took a step back from Charlie and allowed herself to tidy her ruffled clothes.

"Then it's best not to do such things in my office," he said, twisting his body away slightly to hide his obvious desire from her. "But I'll...see you later? After dinner?"

"If you don't work until after dark like you always do." It made Daniel absurdly happy to think Charlie was so aware of his usual routine.

"I think I deserve an early night for once, don't you?" he ventured.

Charlie cocked her head to the side and very pointedly cast her gaze from Daniel's face to his groin. "I suppose it depends on what you mean to do with it."

A filthy retort was on the tip of Daniel's tongue but Charlie opened the door and vacated his office too quickly for him to say it. So Daniel let out a little chuckle, instead, and settled into the embrace of his desk chair.

He had several solid hours of work left to do that he knew fine well he'd never be able to concentrate on.

He felt like a hormonal teenager.

"I'd rather you didn't kick me, Daniel," Kit's muffled voice said from beneath the desk.

Daniel leapt out of his chair in fright. "Don't just appear out of nowhere!" he bit out, heart thumping at the presence of the green-eyed cat at his feet.

"Nowhere?" Kit parroted back at him, stretching out from beneath the desk before trotting over to the middle of Daniel's office. Once there he shook into his true form, rolled a crack out of his left shoulder, then took up his favourite place dangling lazily on the open windowsill. "I wouldn't call waiting patiently in your office for your meeting to end *appearing out of nowhere.* I only hid when you brought Charlie in with you."

"You could have meowed or something," Daniel complained, decidedly perturbed by his friend's presence. "I didn't intend to have an audience."

The faintest of smiles curled Kit's lips. "Clearly not. Things are going well, then? Am I to congratulate you on finally being honest about what you want?"

"...one might say that."

"And has your curiosity been tempered?"

"If you're asking if I know the full extent of Charlie's magic then, yes, my curiosity is satisfied." Daniel settled back into his chair as his heart rate finally began to slow to a far more regular rhythm. "I can see why you didn't want to give her magic away. Consider me sorry for having put you on the spot so many times."

But Kit merely laughed away his apology. "Come off it, Daniel. We both know you could have never rested until you knew what was going on. It's in your nature." He let out a yawn, elongated, pointed canines on full display. "Still, I'm glad you finally worked out what you were looking for from Charlie. It was infuriating watching you flounder."

"Watching me fail is one of your favourite pastimes," Daniel retorted, fishing through his desk drawer in search of a glass jar of lemon sweets that Kit was fond of. When he located them he tossed a few to the Drus, who deftly caught them in mid-flight. "Are you really my friend?"

"Your closest one." Kit popped two sweets into his mouth at the same time, savouring the sour sherbet held within their centres when he crunched straight through the hard outer shell. He glanced at Daniel. "Does that make you a bad judge of character?"

"Perhaps. Given the circumstances I don't particularly care for the notion. So now that I know what Charlie can do will you finally tell me how you know her? And is she aware you knew who she was prior to her working for me?"

A pause. Kit's entire relaxed stance suddenly looked very practised to Daniel's eyes. "I never told you that."

"Yes," Daniel replied, choosing his next words carefully, "but you never denied it, either. It's obvious you've known her for years."

"...if you say so."

When Kit did not elaborate Daniel bit back his frustration. That he was refusing to discuss the matter further meant he was hiding something. It had been the way of their relationship for decades; Kit would talk at length to Daniel about literally anything except what was truly dear to his heart.

Which meant Charlie was important to Kit.

"Just what is it you want from Charlie?" he asked. "Is she your friend? Or—"

"That's private."

In an uncharacteristically serious fashion Kit inclined his head towards Daniel and, between one blink and the next, disappeared from his office.

I'll have to push for more information later, Daniel concluded, unwrapping a lemon sweet to suck on whilst he got to work. It was clear that, so caught up as he was in his own obsession with Charlie, Daniel had ignored what was going on with his best friend.

The fact Kit was one of the Immortal Folk meant that working out his intentions was not going to be easy.

Despite his promise to the contrary Daniel ultimately found himself working very, very late, taking dinner in his office in order to try and complete everything as quickly as was physically possible.

Still, it was dark outside by the time he finished – or, at least, as dark as June got just under three weeks shy of Midsummer. He eyed the window when he was finished, wondering if Charlie had already gone to sleep.

Only to spy her outside, glamour magic in full effect, on her way to the woods.

Daniel summoned himself to her side without thinking.

"Sorry I'm late," he said, grabbing Charlie's hand and holding a finger to her lips when she cried out in surprise. Daniel had no time to waste; he'd wasted enough of it already. "Spend the night with me?"

Charlie's gaze lingered on the woods for a disconcertingly long time, wild, dark hair catching in the wind and making the young woman look, for the most fleeting of moments, like a stranger.

Then Charlie returned her attention to Daniel and the moment passed.

"I guess spending the night with you couldn't hurt," she said, smiling. Charlie squeezed his hand. "Lead the way, I guess."

"You guess?"

"I don't know where your bedroom is."

Daniel could only laugh at the realisation. Checking to ensure nobody was watching he pulled Charlie against him for a long, lingering kiss.

Then he pulled her towards his house.

Away from the woods, and back to him.

CHAPTER TWENTY-FOUR

THOUGH DANIEL COULD HAVE USED MAGIC to transport them to his bedroom he instead decided to creep through the hallways of his estate with Charlie in tow.

"Why don't you use transportation magic?" Charlie enquired in hushed tones, barely suppressing a giggle at the childishness of the both of them tiptoeing along the carpeted floor. She was struck with the image of two teenagers trying to silently return to their bedrooms after a forbidden night out.

Daniel merely squeezed her hand and shook his head. "Transport magic makes me sick," he murmured, voice low and dark as the shadows all around them.

It was something Charlie felt like she should have teased him for, and perhaps in the future – when they weren't trying to reach his bedroom unnoticed by his staff – she *would*. She certainly didn't get sick when her father used transport magic, for one. It was a weakness in Daniel that Charlie never imagined existed.

Then again, Charlie had discovered a lot of new things in the past forty-eight hours.

After a couple of minutes, during which time the only sound

to be heard was their collective soft but accelerated breathing, Daniel and Charlie came across his bedroom door. Slowly he exhaled then turned to look at her, eyes bright and feverish with barely-constrained anticipation.

"Won't you come in, Charlie Hope?" Daniel asked, opening the door with an over-the-top flourish and urging Charlie inside before him.

"You're such a showman, do you know that?" she scoffed, nonetheless making her way through the doorway ahead of Daniel. It was dark and silent inside. But before Charlie had a chance to peer into the dimness the shadows were chased away; Daniel closed the door behind him and clicked his fingers to light several sconces set into the bedroom walls. Then, with a wave of his hand, a grand fireplace on Charlie's far right erupted into dancing, flickering flames which broke the silence around her with a crackling fervour.

Charlie blinked several times, her eyes requiring a moment or two to adjust to her surroundings. On her right was an enormous four-poster bed. It was handsomely carved out of oak, with a richly-woven, deep-green cotton canopy tidily tied back to the bed posts.

The pale stone fireplace took up most of the far right wall, whilst the left wall housed an oak wardrobe and several bookshelves filled to the brim with odd, intriguing tomes Charlie did not recognise. There was also a door which led off to what Charlie could only assume was a bathroom.

But it was the wall directly facing the bed that caught Charlie's attention the most. For it was not, in fact, a wall at all.

It was perhaps the largest uninterrupted pane of glass Charlie had ever witnessed with her own two eyes.

"How have I never looked into your bedroom from the garden or the woods before?" Charlie asked, closing the distance between herself and the window in a flash of movement. Her fingers splayed across the windowpane, breath fogging the glass in front of her face as her eyes naturally located the edge of the woods, comfortingly close by.

Daniel chuckled mischievously from his position still by the door. "For an intelligent woman you truly are rather stupid sometimes, aren't you?" Charlie bristled, but before she could retort Daniel added on, "Think about it. How could I *possibly* prevent anyone from looking through such a huge window into my bedroom?"

In that precise moment Charlie realised Daniel had been right to call her stupid. The memory of the first time she came upon the exterior of Daniel's estate immediately came to mind.

"Magic," Charlie said, watching her reflection roll her eyes at how obvious the answer was. "Of course you use magic to disguise it. Uthesh forbid someone spy on you in your private chambers."

"Uthesh forbid, indeed."

There was a long, padded seat running along the length of the window at knee height; Charlie sat herself down just as Daniel walked over to the window and followed suit. His leg brushed against hers, and she became hyper-aware of the rustling of his silver robe and the way his blue eyes were limned in gold from the flames roaring in the hearth. His sudden closeness startled Charlie far more than she expected it to, and she recoiled a few inches from Daniel before she could stop herself.

She hated that her reaction made him grimace.

But Daniel was quick to school his expression. "You're nervous," he said. It wasn't a question.

"This is all..." Charlie wasn't sure what to say. She felt foolish acting like this when she'd been so bold in the meeting earlier that day and, afterwards, in Daniel's office. But Charlie had still been high from their explosive encounter in the bathhouse the night before.

Now...now Charlie was painfully aware of the throbbing of

her heart and the way her nerves twisted her stomach until she thought she might be sick. All she wanted to do was use her Influence to control the situation. *No. Don't do that. Anything but that.*

Charlie stared down at her hands, sighed softly, and admitted the awkward truth to Daniel. "This is all very, very new."

Slowly, carefully, Daniel took Charlie's hands in his own. She kept her eyes locked on his fingers intertwining with hers, large and reassuring. "It's all right to be nervous."

"I know that. I know that but still—"

"You aren't used to relinquishing even a little bit of control?" Daniel ventured.

It was true. So true, in fact, that Charlie's head shot up to stare at Daniel in surprise. A tiny smile curled his lips as if he were satisfied that he'd worked her out. Charlie was beginning to realise that – when he put his mind to it – Daniel was rarely, if ever, wrong.

"You try having Intent magic then tell me how easily you can *relinquish control,*" she muttered, breaking Daniel's gaze to glance at the woods behind the dark windowpane. In truth it wasn't all that dark once Charlie grew accustomed to it, given the time of year, and after a moment or two she could discern the shapes of individual trees and, focusing more closely, a pair of rabbits scurrying into the underbrush.

Daniel bit out a self-deprecating chuckle. "I don't think I need Intent magic to understand how difficult it is to give up control. I mean...look at my actions over the past few months. I'm not exactly a laid-back man, am I?"

At this Charlie's nervousness abruptly broke – as did her attention on the woods – and she let out a genuine laugh all her own. "No, I suppose you don't," she said, squeezing Daniel's hands. "The exact opposite, in fact. I don't think I've *ever* met someone as uptight as you."

"That's rude."

"A trait that rather represents me."

"You don't care if people regard you in such a negative fashion?"

Charlie's shoulders rose and fell in a minute shrug. "When I can Influence them to believe otherwise, why would I?"

Another soft laugh from Daniel. "Point taken," he said, letting go of Charlie's hands – she felt their absence keenly – to stand up and indicate towards a shelf laden with bottles of various-coloured liquids. "Would you like a drink?"

For a moment Charlie considered saying yes, if only to do something with her now-empty hands. But then she shook her head and stared out at the woods once more. "No," she murmured. And then, louder and more affirmative: "No. I'd rather keep a clear head. Given everything that's happened so far."

Daniel didn't move from where he stood. But Charlie was nonetheless aware of his gaze on her, intent and inscrutable. "I told you yesterday, Charlie," he said in a measured tone, "that you don't need to worry about your magic around me. About your Influence. About—"

"I know. I appreciate it. But even so..."

A moment of silence. Charlie's heart thumped uncomfortably at the idea that she might have offended Daniel. But then he said, "It's all right. I understand," and Charlie knew he meant it. With every fibre of his being Daniel meant it, which was all the reassurance Charlie could possibly need.

Within the confines of Daniel's bedroom Charlie was free to be entirely herself without judgement.

It was liberating.

She glanced towards the bed, aware that Daniel's eyes were following her gaze and understood where her thoughts had now wandered. Charlie knew what she wanted to do tonight. A coil of desire had been tightening in her all day; now it was close to unravelling entirely. All at once the heat from the fire was nothing compared to the burn that was rapidly creeping up Charlie's neck and over her ears.

But she didn't have the courage to ask for what she wanted.

She had a sneaking suspicion Daniel would do nothing *until* she asked for it.

A wicked man, truly, Charlie mused as she watched Daniel watch her. From the expression on his face to the way his posture was relaxing to the very thoughts circling his mind Charlie could tell he was growing increasingly amused with her awkward silence.

"What time do we have to be up tomorrow?" Charlie piped up, hoping Daniel would take pity on her and respond to what she *really* meant. Once more her nerves rose inside her like bile; she forced the churning back down. Then, in a move that was far too bold for her, Charlie rushed from the window and stumbled onto Daniel's bed.

She expected Daniel to laugh at her as she righted herself into a sitting position. *I am acting like a fool,* Charlie groaned, feeling altogether too young and inexperienced. She wanted to hide behind her unruly hair and run off to the safety of the woods.

But Daniel did not laugh at her.

When Charlie let out a tendril of her magic to get a sense of what was going on with him she discovered all traces of Daniel's previous amusement had disappeared. She couldn't bear to look at him, too frightened by the prospect that he'd finally come to his senses and realised that involving himself with someone such as Charlie Hope was a mistake.

And then:

"Do you regret what happened yesterday, Charlie?"

Daniel's voice was barely audible over the crackle of the flames, and it broke when he said her name. But his words echoed in Charlie's mind as if Daniel had shouted them.

Me, regret what happened? Not him?

"No!" Charlie gasped, horrified that Daniel would think such a thing. She scrunched the soft, cool sheets of his bed beneath her hands, fighting the urge to blast out her Influence to fix the situation. "No," she repeated again, trying and failing to stay calm. "Do – do you?"

"...do you honestly believe I would whisk you off to my bedroom in the middle of the night if I did?" Daniel closed the distance between them in no time at all, his expression one of utter disbelief. "I don't understand how you can ask me such a thing after everything that's happened so far."

A twinge of shame coloured Charlie's emotions. Every time she thought she'd accepted that she *did* trust Daniel she found herself doubting him once more. But Charlie knew why: she had such little self-confidence in herself that it was difficult for her to truly comprehend that Daniel wanted her.

No matter how he felt.

No matter how he looked at her.

And how Daniel looked at her now – Charlie could feel the heat of his gaze far more than the fire, or the burning of her cheeks.

I might be young and foolish, she thought, edging closer to Daniel and tilting her face towards his in the process, *but I know how I feel. And I know how he feels, too. That's enough. Of course it's enough.*

"I believe everything you said to me yesterday – and this morning," Charlie said, allowing her forehead to lean against Daniel's lips. He exhaled shakily against her skin, then gently brushed his fingers through her hair. "But it's hard for me to unlearn every defence mechanism I've put up to protect myself over the past few years. To stop from...well, from having my heart broken, I guess. If you can be patient with me then I promise I'll work on it."

Charlie could have vomited at how disgustingly honest she was. But she knew it was exactly what Daniel needed to hear.

What Charlie herself needed to hear.

Daniel's hand moved from Charlie's hair to graze his fingertips along the edge of her jaw. His touch was light. Barely there. But Daniel didn't press deeper, or venture any further, until Charlie leaned into the sensation with longing evident in her eyes.

"That feels good," she admitted, the words barely a whisper over her lips. The resultant desire Charlie felt emanate from Daniel was almost overwhelming.

"You have no idea how good it is to hear you say how you feel out loud," he said, pulling Charlie closer so he could trail the gentlest of kisses down her neck. When Charlie shivered beneath him Daniel paused to savour the sensation. "Unlike you," he continued, smiling, "I can't tell what others are thinking. You have complete and utter power over me right now...no deliberate use of Intent magic required."

"That must be frustrating for you," Charlie breathed, barely able to get the words out. Daniel's stop-and-start approach to touching her was driving her insane.

To her surprise, however, Daniel shook his head against the nape of her neck. "Now I know how you feel about me it's almost...it's liberating. You can't misconstrue what *I* genuinely feel even if I can't vocalise it properly. It means—"

"It means you can't mess up," Charlie finished for him. She hadn't thought about it that way before. To realise that her magic, which up until now had acted as an impenetrable barrier between herself and other people, could be a source of truth and freedom for a man she truly cared for, finally evaporated the last of Charlie's pointless nerves.

She prayed to Uthesh they would never return.

A mischievous smile curled Charlie's lips as she pulled away from Daniel's touch just long enough to see a look of confusion colour his beautiful face. Then Charlie splayed her hands across Daniel's chest and pushed him down onto the bed, gracefully tumbling on top of him as if it was the easiest thing in the world.

"*Charlie Hope,*" Daniel gasped, incredulous and delighted in equal measure as she began unbuttoning the delicate silver buttons of his robe. "Just what do you think you're—"

"This is a rather nice view," she cut in, because it was. Daniel's hair was in unfamiliar disarray, coming loose from the band which held it back at his neck to fan around his face. It softened the hard angles of his cheekbones, his brow, his jaw, in a way Charlie found enticing beyond words. His mouth was a wordless *o* as her fingers trailed down his chest; before Charlie was quite aware of what she was doing she had undone not just the buttons of Daniel's robe but his shirt, too.

"Take these off," she demanded, turning bolder by the moment when it became clear Daniel was responding positively to her doing so.

Very positively.

He quirked an eyebrow. "You'd have to get off me first."

"That doesn't sound very appealing to me. How about—"

A lock of Charlie's hair came loose from behind her ear and dangled in her field of vision; something about it distracted her to no end.

"Charlie?" Daniel said, uncertainty cutting through his desire. "What—"

Then Charlie worked out what was wrong. *It's odd not to have my real hair around him,* she thought, frowning for a second to drop the glamour that had held her hair in wild, dark curls. *My mother's hair belongs in the woods.* Only once it had returned to its natural state did Charlie resume trying to remove Daniel's clothes.

Daniel watched her curiously, though his hands had nonetheless begun wandering up Charlie's thighs to skim the edge of her underwear beneath her dress. "You don't have to remove your glamour if you don't want to, you know. If it makes you more comfortable."

But Charlie resolutely shook her head. "No; I'm most comfortable as *myself* around you."

That seemed to turn Daniel on even more than unbuttoning his clothes had. With nothing but a wicked glint in his eye as warning, he wrapped an arm around Charlie and bodily flipped their positions before she even had a chance to gasp.

"Whatever happened to giving up some control?" Charlie said, though she wriggled in delight beneath the weight of Daniel sitting on top of her.

He shrugged out of his shirt and robe and tossed them to the floor. "You're the one giving up control tonight, Miss Hope, not me," Daniel said, pleased with the heat that spread across Charlie's face at the way he spoke to her. He had a notion that she'd like him talking to her in an authoritative fashion in private – given their heated arguments over the past few months – and it was blatantly clear that was the case.

But that was something he could explore properly later.

Tonight was simply for the two of them to be together.

"Never be uncomfortable around me," Daniel murmured, helping Charlie shift out of her clothes before removing the rest of his own. "Promise me that and nothing else matters."

Charlie wrapped her arms around Daniel's neck, pulling his lips to hers for the barest of kisses. When she snickered the sound tickled his skin. "I think that's an order I can obey, Mr Silver."

The sun rose before either of them allowed the other to sleep.

Chapter Twenty-Five

, but beneath it everything had.

Daniel knew what Charlie could do. He was aware of her Intent magic and had not once pushed her to use it for anything she did not agree with. Not for the first time Charlie was thankful that their views on the Lopox-Eshijani conflict aligned; there was something inordinately satisfying about leaving meeting after meeting walking alongside Daniel and Crimson, knowing everything had gone exactly the way they all wanted it to go.

But, despite this, things were getting harder to control even with Charlie's Influence.

Before, when she had worked for her father, Charlie had sparsely and sensibly used her magic to Influence political decisions. The weight of her Intent carried across weeks or even months, the decisions it brought about remaining solid and certain.

Now it seemed as if, by the time Charlie settled one problem with her magic, another one appeared to take its place.

First it was the tampering of the temporary trade agreement report. Daniel had handled that himself, and well; all Charlie had to do was Influence the Alliance members into believing the false report had been an innocent mistake so they could continue to investigate who had created the false report in the first place without arousing suspicion.

Charlie thought that would be the end of the issue, but it wasn't.

The real report had gone missing. It was as if it had never existed in the first place.

Considering a better version of the Charter was being finalised it was imperative to find the report. It was the undeniable proof that making allowances for the Eshijani within the Lopox Alliance worked. Without it...

Things were bound to devolve into bitter arguments once more, or worse.

"There was another skirmish on the border," Edward said as he and Charlie wound their way through the Saturday morning market in Mt. Duega. "Two acres of forest were burned down in the process."

All around the two of them the town square was colourfully decorated for Midsummer; the very air around Edward buzzed with excitement. It was everyone's favourite event of the year.

Except for Edward, even though Midsummer often fell on Charlie's birthday, as it would this year.

He shook the thought from his head.

Today was the first time Edward and Charlie had caught up outside of work since the gala – and also the first time Edward had seen his daughter since February with her glamour up.

The wild curls surrounding Charlie's face that so reminded him of his late wife twisted Edward's heart uncomfortably. But Charlie was happy, that much was clear; it would not do to comment on her appearance.

"And a raid in Ramas on the Eshijani side," Charlie added

on, a frown of concern furrowing her brow. "They're getting more frequent. Daniel believes the incidents are all coordinated."

"Oh, is it *Daniel* now?"

"Shut up, Da."

Charlie using Mr Silver's first name gave Edward some indication as to why his daughter seemed happier – as well as the man himself. Whenever he talked to Daniel as of late he seemed far more content than Edward had ever seen him, despite the fraught political tension they were currently dealing with.

He wanted to press Charlie for details.

He resisted.

When they passed an Eshijani market stand selling a familiar apricot liqueur Charlie's eyes lit up. "Jean and Luca adore this," she said, picking up a bottle to hold its orange contents up to the sun. "It's such a lovely flavour."

"So buy some for them, then."

"It wouldn't be weird?"

Edward could only laugh in disbelief. "Why in the name of Uthesh would it be weird? They're your friends, aren't they?"

"I...yes, they are. I've never bought a gift for a friend before."

It was such an unbelievably sad, painfully honest remark for Charlie to make. But it served to show just how much she'd grown in the past few months, and Edward could not be prouder of her. Charlie looked far more comfortable in her own skin – glamour or not – than she'd ever looked before.

It could only mean good things for her.

"Are you going to continue working for Daniel after your initial year of employment is up?" he asked, genuinely curious about Charlie's answer. For lately it didn't seem as if she hated her job. Rather, considering the friends – and perhaps other relationships, too – that she'd made, Edward rather suspected that Charlie had finally found her place within Mr Silver's team.

But Charlie shook her head. "I'm not...I don't think I have an answer for that. This is the first time I've ever felt like I had a goal. A true purpose." She patiently waited for the Eshijani merchant to wrap up the bottles of liquor in brown paper before continuing. "I can see now why you've been involved with running Mt. Duega for so long. You're protecting what's important to the people; it's never been about better status or enjoying the realm of politics for you, has it?"

"You know I've never felt that way about my job."

"I know, but..." Charlie scratched her head. "I guess even though I knew you were telling the truth something still rang false about it. I never understood why people didn't simply look after their families, themselves, and the ground beneath their feet. If everyone simply lived like that then—"

"Then my job wouldn't be necessary," Edward finished for her. "Unfortunately, humans are a rather selfish species. Which is why those of us who *do* care must ensure we collectively don't destroy everything in our path."

"It feels better not to do it alone, though," Charlie murmured. A smile curled her lips which Edward was sure she had no idea was there. "Having someone in my corner who isn't my father feels quite nice."

Oh, there's definitely something going on between my daughter and Daniel Silver. Edward felt vindicated that his first instinct about pitting the two against each other had been correct. Daniel was exactly the person Charlie had needed to meet in order to grow.

Edward had a sneaking suspicion the same could be said about Daniel, too.

He patted Charlie's head as they turned from the market. "I'm glad you feel that way. But there's no rush for you to settle on one job or another; all that matters to me is that you're giving your future some serious consideration. You have all the time in the world to work out what you want to do."

"That's not true, Da," Charlie replied, waving his hand away from her head. "What if something tragic happened to me? To you? Mum was taken from us so fast. We don't have all the time in the world – not really."

It was a surprisingly insightful comment. Edward often forgot how clearly Charlie could cut straight to the heart of a matter. "All the more reason to only follow through on decisions that truly matter to us," he said. "Unless you're immortal, in which case you really do have all the time in the world."

He expected Charlie to laugh. Instead, a decidedly thoughtful expression crossed her face, and Edward realised for the first time that he had never once asked his daughter if she planned to live forever.

But he knew why that was. He knew, so Edward ignored the look on Charlie's face and swept her back to their house. It would not do to ruin the precious time he had with her thinking about such serious topics.

As with the rising conflict between Lopox and Eshijan, Edward could dwell upon it tomorrow.

CHAPTER TWENTY-SIX

Daniel Silver's bed was perhaps the most comfortable bed Charlie had ever slept in, and she couldn't imagine going back to sleeping in a bed without him in it, yet despite this unconsciousness would not take its hold of her.

She was shocked at how easy it had been to fall into a routine with him, despite the fact said routine involved sneaking around and pretending the two of them weren't together. But it was exciting and new and entirely unfamiliar to Charlie; she loved every minute she spent together with Daniel.

And yet part of her longed for the woods, and the open invitation from the Immortal Folk to dance with them.

Charlie had managed to avoid the allure of the woods during the ten days she'd spent sleeping in Daniel's bed instead of her own, but it was growing impossible to ignore the pull of the place now. Charlie wanted to feel that life beneath her feet again – to celebrate and sing and dance until she could no longer feel her body and was so exhausted she couldn't even stop.

The frenetic, surging energy of the Immortal Folk was completely at odds with the quiet that had spread through the woods in recent years. It was as if they'd spent the last decade or two in patient wait of something. Of course Charlie revelled in their new-found euphoria. The woods were the only place that had ever felt truly, genuinely alive to her.

Charlie wanted to go back. *Had* to go back.

With a fond smile she swept Daniel's hair away from his face. He was blithely naked and so soundly asleep beside her Charlie doubted even the crowing of a rooster would rouse him from his slumber. It was hard to reconcile this version of Daniel with the one who had insisted Charlie not wake him before dawn every day. Not for the first time Charlie wondered if Daniel had forced himself awake during her jaunts to the woods simply to have a reason to be annoyed at her.

To have a connection with her.

Charlie had never felt this way towards anyone before in all her life. It scared her to *know* she could feel like this; if Daniel grew tired of Charlie and tossed her feelings to the side she was reasonably certain it would break her.

Yet he would never do that, and Charlie knew it.

Even so, she had never been the kind of woman who intended to dedicate all her time and love to one man, either. Until recently Charlie believed she would never *be* with anyone the way she was with Daniel. There were other aspects of her life that were more important to her.

The woods. The woods.

As if compelled by something other than herself Charlie slipped out of bed and threw on Daniel's shirt, which lay abandoned on the floor, and checked her reflection in the full-length mirror which was set into the wall.

With a flourish of her hand Charlie threw her glamour up, watching with a strange mix of satisfaction and sadness as her soft golden hair melted away to wild brown curls.

Then she leapt out of the open window. *I won't be gone long,* Charlie promised herself and Daniel, with a final glance at his peaceful, contented face.

Just one dance, just one song, and then she'd come back.

Daniel Silver was not asleep.

For several days now he'd wanted to confirm his suspicions that something wasn't right with Charlie. She came to his bed every night – their attention on each other intense and undivided – but the moment Daniel was sure Charlie believed his blank mind and slow breathing meant he was asleep her eyes found the woods.

Now she had left his side in the middle of the night to escape through the window, and Daniel knew he would never be more important to Charlie than the home of the Immortal Folk.

It wasn't as if Daniel didn't understand her priorities, nor could he be sad about them: Daniel's work had been the most important thing in his life for years. And he had Kit, the kind of best friend Charlie's magic had prevented her from having her entire life.

He knew having more than one person, interest or cause to focus on was a good thing. And yet Daniel was disheartened, anyway. All he'd been able to think about lately was Charlie, so he couldn't help feeling a twinge of jealousy that the same could not be said of her.

Realising that Charlie had taken his shirt, Daniel rolled out of bed and browsed through his wardrobe for fresh clothes. Charlie had left the window open, the warm and inviting breeze blowing into Daniel's room full of the scent of pine needles and deep, dark earth.

He was conflicted about invading Charlie's privacy. He didn't want to follow her into the woods and in doing so have her believe he did not trust her.

But Daniel wanted to know what she was doing. He was sure that, if he could only witness for himself what was so important to Charlie she had to creep out of his bed at one in the morning, then he would understand her better. He'd understand her *need* for the woods better.

Daniel left the safety of his bedroom, jumped over the window ledge and headed for the first line of pine trees.

Beneath the trees it was always dark, even days away from Midsummer. So Daniel used the softest magic he possessed to light up the path he needed to take, focusing on the faint but unmistakable trace of Charlie's magic to find his way to her.

All around Daniel the air was so quiet he could have heard a pin drop. There were no owls hooting above him. No foxes or rabbits or mice scurrying across the undergrowth. No water running over stone or wind whistling through the leaves.

It was unsettlingly silent. Even Daniel's footsteps felt absorbed somehow.

It took him almost an hour to find Charlie, during which time Daniel questioned what he was doing in the first place. *I should have turned back,* he thought when he stopped to observe Charlie from a careful distance away. *I shouldn't have come into the woods at all.*

For Charlie was kneeling on the ground, fingers deep in the earth, a starstruck look on her face that Daniel had never witnessed before.

That look sent chills down his spine.

Daniel watched her for a while, desperately confused about what Charlie was doing. She merely sat there, Daniel's white shirt slowly falling off her right shoulder, and stared at the ground.

When he shifted his weight and broke a twig in the process Charlie jumped in surprise at the intrusion.

"Did you follow me?" she asked, displeased by the interruption when Daniel shamefully stepped forward to make himself known.

"I didn't mean to intrude," Daniel said, though of course he had. "Only, you must admit that I'm allowed to find it strange that you fled my bed in the middle of the night to come...here."

That faraway gaze again. It unsettled Daniel to no end. "Strange...yes, that's a good word for it," Charlie murmured, running her fingers through the soil beneath her. "It *is* strange. So familiar..."

"Charlie?"

"I just can't work it out."

"Work *what* out, Charlie?" Daniel knelt down beside her, lifting her chin with a hooked finger to face him. Her gaze seemed to pass through him as if she could not see Daniel at all. "What is going on, here, in the woods?"

"There's something here," Charlie said, "beneath the surface. Something *alive*. Can't you feel it? Don't you want to...join it?"

But whatever Charlie could feel – whatever held her in its thrall – Daniel could not. He had no idea what Charlie was talking about. He couldn't understand it.

Daniel waited for Charlie to elaborate but, when all that met him was silence, stood up instead. "Come back to bed with me," he said, whisper-quiet, knowing he wouldn't like Charlie's response.

Mutely she shook her head.

More than a little perplexed and incredibly concerned but with no idea of what else he could do, Daniel walked back the way he came, leaving Charlie alone with her fingers in the earth.

He knew he wouldn't sleep again until she returned.

Charlie had only just acknowledged Daniel disappearing when a pan flute began to play from the trees. The melody was sad – keening, almost – but all Charlie felt when she heard it was glee. She smiled, finally releasing her hold on the earth with every intention of dancing with the Immortal Folk until the sun came up.

"We've missed you these past few days," the flute player said, swinging down to the ground to greet Charlie for the first time. She peered through the darkness to try and see what the elusive musician looked like as he approached.

A gasp fell from her lips when she recognised him.

"You're – it's you!" Charlie exclaimed, drinking in the stark, inhuman features of the Drus she had so desperately connected with five years ago.

A small smile curled his lips. "It's me."

"Has it always been you playing? Why didn't you reveal yourself before now?"

"I have my reasons," he said, holding out his hand for Charlie to take. His venomous green eyes flashed in the dark. "Now come – you're just in time!"

Of course Charlie took his hand; her own fit so well in his.

The Drus rushed Charlie deeper into the woods, so quickly she barely had a chance to catch her breath. When finally they stopped within a meadow Charlie realised a revel of sorts was going on.

The trees had been strung up with lanterns lit with magic of every colour Charlie could imagine; in the middle of the meadow a huge, smokeless bonfire burned.

She had never seen so many Immortal creatures in her life together all at once. There were Satyrs and Nymphs and Dryads, Fauns and Sprites and Faeries, all of them laughing, eating, drinking, dancing, singing. Some were engaged in far more private activities, hidden between the ferns or in the nook of a tree, though some of them did not hide what they were doing at all.

The energy was electric. It was *focused.*

It felt as if...

"Are they worshipping something?" Charlie asked her Drus.

Hers, because he was. "Like the life I feel, beneath my feet...but I don't know what it is."

"You do not need to," the Drus laughed, before turning to face her directly. He swept into a low, elaborate bow. "The only thing of importance is this: Charlie Hope, will you stand with us? Will you protect the woods – its creatures, its land, its life – from any who would see it harmed?"

Her answer was immediate. It wasn't a question Charlie even had to consider. "Of course."

"Then let us dance. It is a long time overdue."

The Drus pulled Charlie close, planting kisses on her brow and her nose and her lips, and she gave herself over to the teeming, pulsing life beneath her feet.

CHAPTER TWENTY-SEVEN

June flew by in a flurry of meetings, stolen kisses behind closed doors, and Daniel growing increasingly concerned on Charlie's behalf. The only reason Daniel knew they had reached Midsummer's Day was from counting the nights Charlie spent with him versus the nights she crept off to the woods ever since he'd followed her beneath the dark, foreboding trees. At first she'd spent more time with him, but now...

Charlie had spent the last four nights in a row in the forest, and it was beginning to show on her face.

She was manic and driven and frenetic. If she could get something done faster by using her Influence then she did, as if she no longer cared if she were caught or not.

Daniel wasn't the only one who noticed.

"What's going on with Charlie?" Crimson demanded on the afternoon of Midsummer's Day, before the final conference with the Lopox Alliance regarding the new Charter was due to begin.

"I don't know," Daniel admitted, pretending to search the notes on his desk simply so he could avoid looking his Chief-of-Staff in the eye.

But she wasn't convinced by his answer. "Come on, Daniel.

Don't lie to me. We all know something's happened between you and Charlie. It's just that no-one other than me has the guts to ask you about it directly."

"...what's going on with Charlie has nothing to do with me. At least, I don't think it does. I hope it doesn't."

He knew it didn't. Whatever was going on with Charlie in the woods, Daniel no longer factored into the equation. His importance had faded into insignificance in the face of the *life* Charlie could feel.

Why hadn't Daniel been able to feel it?

When Crimson saw the obvious concern on his face she relented with her questioning. "I'm sure whatever is going on with her will be solved in due time," she said, though she didn't seem convinced. "And if it isn't, I guess we'll be planning an intervention."

"Oh, I can see that working flawlessly."

"Likewise. Now come or we'll be late for the conference."

As requested, the meeting was taking place at Daniel's estate due to its proximity to the border. That way, the Eshijani officials wouldn't need to use transport magic to retrieve the new Charter from the Alliance before returning home. It had grown difficult to perform such magic across the border for some reason, though nobody knew why.

A coiling tendril of dread in Daniel's stomach told him Charlie would know why, even if she wasn't entirely aware of it herself.

Daniel heard the Lopox Alliance members before he saw them. They were arguing furiously amongst themselves; only Charlie, sitting by the vacant chair saved for Daniel himself, remained quiet. A small frown of concentration on her face told him she was listening carefully to everything being said so she could work out when to exert her Influence.

Uthesh be good, she looks so tired, Daniel thought, taking in the dark shadows circling Charlie's eyes as he swept into the room to sit beside her. Beneath the table he took Charlie's hand; he was relieved when she squeezed his in return.

"Just what is going on?" he demanded, casting his gaze over the Alliance members only to realise someone was missing. "Where's Ritten?"

"Jonah has been poisoned," Crank spat out, his face ruddy with rage. "I received word this morning that he collapsed last night and shows no sign of regaining consciousness."

"He's...do you have any idea who might have done this to him?" Daniel asked, his grip tightening on Charlie's hand. Jonah Ritten had been their primary suspect for tampering with the trade agreement report on behalf of his home country, Laskey. If he had been poisoned...

"Of course it was the Eshijani," Erik Bell, who represented Ferngen in the north-east, immediately replied. "They suspected Laskey of the attacks on the border. And then there was the trade agreement – they're targeting Jonah instead of the radicals who were actually responsible! I wouldn't be surprised if the damn Eshijani tampered with the report *themselves* just so they could strike us like this!"

Daniel and Charlie exchanged a look. From the door Crimson nodded at them before exiting the room, no doubt to contact her grandfather.

"Let's not jump to conclusions," Daniel said, choosing his words carefully. "All of that is baseless speculation. If—"

"Oh come off it, Silver," Crank cut in. "We *all* know you fully support Eshijan through all this. Did you think we hadn't noticed? Not once have you put Lopox first – not even your own country."

"The last time I checked we were actively trying to prevent war, not incite it," Daniel replied, feeling his temper rising. "As an Alliance we've sat on the fence for fifteen years hoping that

Eshijan will somehow go away, thus absolving us of having to update the Charter. But it *needs* updating. You all know it!"

"But why should we? The old one works fine!"

"The old Charter wasn't fine a hundred damn years ago, let alone now!"

"Don't you dare use your *immortality* to lord over us, Silver, or so help me—"

"Why bother arguing about this when we could simply wait for the Eshijani to arrive tomorrow for the Charter and *ask* them about Mr Ritten?" Charlie finally, blessedly said, every word she spoke heavy with her Influence. She spread her hands out wide, addressing the entire table. "Call a truth-seeker from the Capital. Call three. We can get to the bottom of this in one short conversation if we only *wait* until tomorrow."

Daniel watched the reaction of the rest of the Alliance, noticing that, even with the extra magic Charlie was pushing forward – there was a faint sheen of sweat crossing her brow, and beneath the table her legs were shaking – the men in the room were proving resistant to her Influence.

But then, one by one, they fell under the sway of Charlie's magic, and all the anger that had exploded from the men simmered back beneath the surface.

For now.

"Tomorrow, then," Crank sighed. "I'm too old to head back to the Capital tonight. Bell, take Marshall and Karina – my transport assistant – and find us three truth-seekers. Daniel, prepare your guest rooms. We'll be staying here this evening."

It was all Daniel could do not to refuse. The last thing he wanted was to have to deal with a handful of politicians on Midsummer's Eve. He had wanted to ask Charlie if she was going to attend the celebrations in Mt. Duega and, if so, whether she minded if they went together.

That way, Daniel might be able to prevent her from going

into the woods.

When he stood up and regarded Charlie from above he noted just how exhausted using so much Intent had made her. *She can't go into the woods,* he thought, concerned at the sweat dripping from her brow and the pronounced sag in her posture. *Not like this. She'll collapse.*

But Daniel knew, somehow, that she would, unless he did something to stop it. Then he realised there was no reason *not* to go to Mt. Duega – as a group. A party was exactly what the rest of the Alliance needed to let off some steam, after all.

"There's a festival in Mt. Duega this evening," Daniel told the room at large as everyone got up to leave. "For Midsummer. Lots of food and alcohol and entertainment. Could I interest any of you in attending? My team and I were planning to go."

At the mere mention of food and alcohol Crank's eyes lit up. "I knew there was a reason I liked coming here. Consider me in."

Everybody else agreed; when Daniel turned to ask Charlie to pass this information onto Jean and Luca, however, he realised she was gone.

His heart fell.

She can't have gone into the woods already, Daniel mused, as he instructed a servant to prepare the guest bedrooms and settle the rest of the Alliance in the parlour room with one of his best bottles of whisky. He wanted to check Charlie's room but knew that was foolish and unreasonable of him – never mind the fact he now had to prepare an entire new agenda regarding questioning the Eshijani about Ritten's poisoning for the following day.

Charlie would have to wait.

When Daniel neared his office he was shocked to discover Kit waiting for him outside the door...in his real form.

"We need to talk," the Drus said. His posture was

uncharacteristically stiff and formal, though going by the flowers in his hair and billowing white shirt that fell to his knees Kit was on his way to the woods to celebrate Midsummer with his kin.

"Can it wait until tomorrow?" Daniel asked, feeling decidedly overwhelmed by everything he had to do. "I have to find a way to prevent the Alliance from accusing Eshijan of inciting war. Not an easy thing to do, even with Charlie's help."

He expected Kit to smile at the mere mention of Daniel relying on Charlie. To laugh. To gently chide him.

What Daniel hadn't expected was a flash of anger to ignite his best friend's inhumanly green eyes.

"I am...otherwise engaged later," Kit said, indicating towards his clothes. "As you can well see. It can't be now?"

But before Daniel could respond someone shouted for him from the parlour room.

"Tomorrow," he promised Kit, the quiet rage in the Drus' eyes unsettling Daniel to no end. "We can talk tomorrow, I swear."

Kit let out a quiet huff, then eventually nodded. "Tomorrow, then," he said, before unlatching the nearest window and leaping out of it.

But Kit did not head straight back to the woods. Charlie had been reunited with his real form – if not his name, nor the fact he was Daniel's cat – so he bounded across the courtyard until he found the window into her bedroom.

It was open wide to the hot, fragrant, early evening air. Inside Charlie was changing into one of her mother's old Midsummer dresses made of flouncy white cotton, with delicate straps and a plunging neckline.

Kit leaned against the windowsill, content to watch Charlie glamour her appearance from perfect, wavy, golden hair to unruly, rebellious curls.

The Charlie I know, Kit thought, smiling. *The Charlie I love.*

When Charlie twirled around to test the flow of her dress she gasped at the sight of Kit standing there, waiting for her.

"What are you doing out of the woods?" she asked, amazed but confused by the sight of him on Daniel's estate.

"To escort you, of course!" Kit replied, holding out a hand for Charlie to take. When she did so he sent out a wave of Immortal magic to banish her fatigue; all at once the dark shadows beneath her eyes and the slump in her shoulders disappeared.

Charlie grinned. "Thanks. I needed that."

"And you'll need more later." Kit interlaced their fingers, bringing Charlie's hand to his lips to kiss her knuckles one by one. Her breath hitched at his touch. "Are you ready for a *true* Midsummer's Eve, Charlie Hope?"

"I've been ready for it my entire life."

Kit could see it in her eyes. Gold and brown and green, the colour of the woods themselves. Charlie had been born for such an event.

"Then let's celebrate your birthday in style."

CHAPTER TWENTY-EIGHT

IT WAS BY SHEER CHANCE THAT Daniel spotted Charlie and Kit – not in the form of a cat, but in his true body – heading to the woods.

"Just what is going on...?" he murmured, fingertips splayed across the window as he watched them laugh and skip and hold hands, the epitome of a young couple in love. All traces of Charlie's previous exhaustion were gone, replaced by the glazed, enchanted expression she'd worn when she knelt in the woods and told Daniel about the life beneath her feet.

What happened to Kit's anger? Daniel thought, narrowing his eyes through the glass. The Drus spun Charlie beneath his arm like they were dancing, appearing not to have a care in the world. Rather, he seemed just as enchanted as Charlie was.

"Daniel?"

"Yes?!" Daniel exclaimed, turning to hide Charlie and Kit from Jean's eyes. The young man was decidedly shocked by his reaction, but Daniel preferred Jean being suspicious of him than catching a glimpse of Charlie running off into the woods with one of the Immortal Folk.

No. Not just *one* of the Immortal Folk.

Kit. Daniel's best friend.

"The Alliance are impatient to get to Mt. Duega," Jean said, surreptitiously trying to look around Daniel to see what he was hiding. "Are you ready to leave?"

"Ah, go on without me," Daniel said. "I have to finish the agenda for tomorrow. I'll catch up with everyone, I promise."

From the look on his face Jean knew he was lying.

"Where's Charlie?" he asked. "I haven't seen her since before the Alliance meeting."

"She looked exhausted. Perhaps she went straight to bed."

"Strange."

Strange, like whatever it was Charlie could feel. In the woods, where she is now.

"What is – what's strange about that?" Daniel forced himself to ask, knowing he was doing an awful job of sounding innocent. "Lack of sleep catches up to us all eventually."

"No, not that," Jean said, still eyeing Daniel suspiciously, "though I think everyone who works here knows fine well Charlie can run on three hours of sleep as if it were ten. It's just that today's her birthday. I thought for sure she'd be coming to Mt. Duega to see her father."

"It's her *birthday?*" Daniel spat out. And then, because he'd reacted far too violently: "She never mentioned anything of the sort to me. I'd have given her the day off."

"She didn't tell anyone. Mayor Hope told me about it at the gala in May, back when I...well, back when I was interested in her." Jean shrugged. "I guess she'll make her own way to Mt. Duega once she wakes up. Maybe the two of you could go together?"

Daniel merely stared at him, daring Jean to elaborate on why he would suggest such a thing. But he remained so expressionless that, eventually, Daniel slid a hand across his face and let out a resigned sigh.

"How long have you known?"

"That you like Charlie, that she likes you, or that you're sleeping together? Because they're three different answers."

"Then don't answer any of them. Just make sure Crank and the rest of them have a good time at the Midsummer festival for me, and I'll—"

"Check and see if Charlie's sleeping?"

The glare Daniel fired at Jean would have cowed the man if he weren't so bold. "I'm still your boss, you know," he muttered. "You shouldn't make such insinuations."

"Then give me a raise," Jean said, chuckling as he turned from Daniel to head down the corridor, "and don't be so obvious. You have an image to maintain, after all!"

For a long, awkward minute Daniel simply stood there, Jean's observations so shocking that he entirely forgot what he had only just seen through the window. *Everyone knew,* Daniel thought, when he returned to his senses and began all but running to his bedroom to change out of his formal robes. *Kit knew how I felt about Charlie before I did. And Crimson. And Edward bloody Hope. Did he know how hard I'd fall for his daughter when he forced me to hire her?*

The man had told Daniel it was worth fighting with Charlie to have her on his side. Was this what he had meant all along?

And now Jean knows and likely everyone else, too, Daniel thought, throwing on a linen shirt and trousers before heading into the woods.

Daniel was fed up of being left in the dark. Of being the last to know about Charlie's magic, about Charlie's feelings, about Charlie's damn birthday. Something was going on with her.

And something was going on with Kit.

No, it isn't just the two of them, Daniel realised, whistling in a breath through his teeth as he steeled himself to set foot beneath the trees he had once so loved. But now they had become unknown, dangerous and forbidding, all because of Charlie Hope.

Daniel couldn't describe it. It scared him. More than Charlie's creation or Intent magic the change that the woods had brought over her recently sent a wave of dread crashing through Daniel's body.

Something is going on with everything and everyone. And it all leads back to the woods.

As before, Daniel lit a tiny globe light of magic to guide his way through the dark undergrowth, though the trail of Charlie's magic did a far better job at telling him which way she'd gone. It was stronger tonight – much stronger than it had been the first time Daniel followed her through the woods.

For some reason Daniel took this as a sign that he was not going to like whatever it was that was waiting for him when he found Charlie.

When a low vibration ran through the earth and the musical lilt of a pan flute floated on the air Daniel knew he was close. Pinprick lights became visible through the trees in red and blue and green and gold and every other colour Daniel knew the name of. Then drums joined the flute, and a fiddle, and the sounds of laughing and singing and feet pounding the ground overwhelmed Daniel's senses.

All at once the trees gave way to a meadow transformed into a magical, colourful, glittering bonanza. All manner of creatures danced around a gargantuan bonfire which produced no smoke. There were long trestle tables laden with every seasonal morsel of food and drink imaginable. Musicians were scattered throughout the fray, their instruments coming together in a shockingly harmonious symphony despite their disordered placement.

There were horned Satyrs seducing blue-haired river

Nymphs. Mischievous Sprites playing tricks on the Faeries when they were too busy admiring the way the coloured lights reflected off their skin. There were Dryads and Fauns and sharp-fanged wolf-men that Daniel could not find a name for playing a game which involved a knife and several bloody fingers.

It was madness.

It was exactly what the people of Mt. Duega so palely imitated every year by stringing up lanterns, donning paper masks and goat horns, dancing around a non-magical fire and drinking from bone flutes.

This was a true Midsummer festival. If the Immortal Folk knew how to do one thing it was how to revel beneath a sky that never quite grew dark.

Once, decades and decades and decades ago when Daniel had been considering immortality, Kit had taken him to that year's Midsummer festival. The sheer energy of it – the magic of it, the mystery of it – had directly led to Daniel finally deciding to ascend.

The world held so much more beauty in it than what humans alone could create. Daniel wanted to see it all, right to the very end of time.

But even though he'd only witnessed one Immortal Folk gathering in his very long life, he knew this revel was different. Wrong.

In the shadows behind the bonfire, the silhouette of a horned figure laughed at him.

Where's Charlie? Daniel thought, stepping into the clearing despite the fact humans were not supposed to attend Immortal Folk revels unless expressly invited. But Daniel's magic was more than a match for theirs; in many cases it was stronger. If anyone put up a fight as he searched for Charlie he had no qualms about fighting right back.

Then he spied her, resplendent in a white dress with garlands of flowers in her glamoured hair, and all such thoughts of fighting vanished from Daniel's mind.

Charlie was thick in the fray of dancing creatures by the bonfire. Her eyes were closed, not a care in the world as she writhed against her inhuman friends. Beside her Kit – who had lost his shirt – played the pan flute, the melody increasingly erratic and frenetic. The dancing got more urgent as a result and Charlie let out a cry of delight at the increase in pace.

When Daniel stepped closer her Intent magic seeped into his very core, unchecked and uncontrolled. An overwhelming urge to join in the madness filled him.

He wanted to dance with Charlie. To kiss her, to touch her, to take her clothes off and then his own and—

"I knew you'd come, Daniel!" Kit burst out, throwing his pan flute to a Faerie who eagerly began playing it in his stead. Kit threaded his way through the crowd until he reached Daniel, a sheen of sweat covering his limbs from the intense heat emanating off everyone's bodies.

He grinned, cat-like and coy, before sliding Daniel's glasses off his face. "You won't be needing these," Kit said, vanishing them into thin air. "You should be careful coming this far into our territory, you know. Good thing you're more than welcome...otherwise there'd be trouble."

It was all Daniel could do to stay standing, let alone reply to his friend's almost-threat. He staggered under the weight of Charlie's Intent, and when Kit took hold of his hand to steady him Daniel did not pull away.

"What's...going on?" he struggled to ask his friend.

"Why, the Midsummer revel, of course. You must join us!"

Something about Kit's answer didn't ring true, but still Daniel allowed him to pull him through the throng towards Charlie. When she realised he was there her lovely, enchanted eyes grew clear for the briefest of moments.

"Daniel!" she cried, wrapping her arms around his neck to pull him down for a kiss. It was the easiest thing in the world to reciprocate her advances, a hand on Charlie's waist possessively keeping her too close to Daniel for anyone to get between them.

When Charlie pulled away Daniel missed the touch of her lips on his immediately. "But what are you – why are you here? What's..." Her eyes took notice of Daniel's other hand, still holding on tightly to Kit's.

Daniel had completely forgotten about it.

"You know each other?" Charlie asked, delighted by the prospect. She flashed a smile at Kit. "You know Daniel? For how long?"

"All my life," Daniel said, replying on behalf of Kit.

"I'm his cat," Kit purred, nuzzling his face against Daniel's shoulder. "And his best friend, of course."

She stared at the two of them in complete and utter disbelief. Charlie had never seen Daniel allow anyone into his personal space the way Kit just invaded it.

Anyone but her.

She was so taken aback that the hook of her Intent magic was temporarily broken. Daniel heaved in a breath as if he'd been starved of oxygen from the very moment he set foot in the revel.

It was in that moment of clarity Daniel realised, though in truth he had suspected for a while now, that Kit was the Drus Charlie slept with five years ago.

There was too much going on for him to process it.

"You're – Kit?" Charlie whispered, unsure how to cope with this new information. "The whole time?"

Kit merely laughed, then grabbed Charlie and pulled both her and Daniel to the edge of the dancing Immortal Folk, by the trees. "I didn't mean to keep it from you." A knowing glance at Daniel. "From both of you. But I had to. So let's not dwell on it!"

That was all Charlie needed to hear to be put at ease. Her Intent swept out of her again, stronger than before now that Daniel was here to celebrate alongside her, and she began dancing once more.

Daniel was helpless to join in.

This is it, Charlie thought, giggling when Kit climbed a gnarled oak tree only to swing upside-down from a low-hanging branch above her head. She pulled Daniel to her, unashamedly running her hands through his hair and down his neck, his back, his waist. His mouth found Charlie's and kissed her as if he might die if he didn't. *This is perfect. This is where I belong – and Daniel, too. He's too special for petty human politics.*

We both are.

Charlie's euphoria burst out of her, raw and untethered and dangerous. Daniel watched as her pupils dilated until her eyes were almost completely black, knowing his were in all likelihood the same.

"You're losing control," he murmured against Charlie's ear. Daniel's entire body was taut and trembling, a mere moment away from completely drowning in her Intent.

"So lose it with me," she said, a sly smile on her face. "Who is here to judge us, Daniel? Doesn't it feel good to be *free*?"

And it did. Even though that freedom was false – Daniel was a prisoner to it, in fact – Charlie's Intent made his new-found freedom exquisite and intoxicating.

Daniel pinned Charlie to the oak tree before falling to his knees, all but tearing her dress away in his haste to kiss between her thighs.

When his tongue found its way inside her Charlie let out a moan. She twisted Daniel's hair around her fingers, wanting more.

Demanding more.

A hand that did not belong to Daniel grazed her chin to tilt Charlie's face up. Kit hung above her, eyes wild with lust and only too happy to respond to Charlie's unspoken desires. When the Drus kissed her she lapped up every second of it.

It took Daniel a few minutes before he realised he could no longer hear Charlie's moans, though she writhed in pleasure beneath him. He looked up to see what was wrong.

Kit was kissing Charlie, though he was staring straight at Daniel.

"What are you doing?" Daniel gasped. He pulled Charlie to the ground, away from Kit, though his best friend merely jumped out of the tree to kneel beside him.

"Look around," Kit said, waving a hand to emphasise his point. "Look at what's going on."

He didn't want to take his eyes off Charlie for even a moment, but Daniel knew he had to see what Kit meant. He straightened up and turned his gaze to the left and then the right.

Everywhere he could see, Immortal Folk had abandoned their dancing, drinking and singing to indulge in far more carnal activities. Not a single creature cared that they were out in the open for anyone to see, skin naked and slick against each other as they gasped and cried and begged for more.

Charlie herself was so wrapped up in the pull of her own magic that she hadn't noticed what was going on.

"I don't understand," Daniel said, turning back to Kit. It hurt him to get the words out; Charlie's Influence was so strong Daniel had to physically fight it to keep talking. "You told me your kind weren't affected by human Mind magic. That your minds were too different from theirs. You *told* me—"

"That's true," Kit murmured, gently resting his forehead against Daniel's. His vibrant eyes burned right through him, daring him to work out what was going on.

But Daniel couldn't think nor process what was going on around him. Everything had gone hazy; Daniel was losing control, and he could do nothing to stop it. He gripped Kit's shoulders with trembling, desperate hands. "So then why—"

"Daniel," Kit said, so softly. So gently. "You're running on the assumption that Charlie is human."

Kit kissed him.

He kissed him, and Daniel kissed him back.

When they broke apart Kit bit Daniel's lower lip between his feral teeth and grinned wickedly, his entire being heavy with lust and manic excitement. "That's a new look on your face, my friend," he purred. "Well, aimed at me, at least."

Kit teased off Daniel's shirt just as Charlie, who had sat up to see why they weren't touching her anymore, worked out was going on. With quick hands she hoisted off her dress before removing Daniel's trousers.

He could do nothing except comply. Daniel's mind grew dark and hot, inviting him to touch his best friend the way he wanted to touch Charlie. His hands couldn't stop trembling; only when Kit and Charlie took hold of them did they grow steady.

"Daniel," Charlie begged, wishing for nothing more than for him to kiss her.

"Daniel," Kit urged, wishing for the same. On many a night throughout the years he had wished it, whenever he was a cat and Daniel, ever a clueless tease, played with his ears and stroked his back.

Daniel shuddered in a breath that didn't quite reach his lungs, and his self-control shattered into pieces. He pulled the only people he had ever truly loved into his arms.

Then there was only touch and smell and sensation, writhing pleasure and a longing for more, more, more, and Daniel lost himself to the night.

In the background, in the shadows, the horned figure grinned at the carnal mess set before them.

Chapter Twenty-Nine

Dappled light warming her skin and the sound of birdsong in her ears was what first pulled Charlie out of the fog of unconsciousness. A breeze blew over her face, smelling of grass and wildflowers, and Charlie shivered.

She cracked open her eyes and it was then Charlie realised she was not in a bed but, rather, lying beneath the bows of an oak tree, completely naked and not alone.

Daniel was sat on Charlie's left, just as naked as she was, staring at the soundly sleeping cat curled between the two of them with utter disbelief on his face.

"Dan-Daniel?" Charlie coughed, throat scratched and voice hoarse as if she'd been screaming all night. When she sat up Charlie realised her entire body felt *used*.

She stared at the tumultuous remains of the Midsummer revel all around and wondered what had become of her. Charlie could hardly remember a thing; it was as if she'd been black-out drunk, though she knew she had barely touched a single cup of wine.

When Daniel did not reply Charlie turned her attention back to him. He was still staring at his cat. At Kit.

"How are you feeling?" Daniel asked. His voice was clipped, tense. When Charlie reached out with her magic she found that he was furious and—

Humiliated?

"I feel hungover," Charlie admitted, shuffling over until her shoulder was touching Daniel's. He flinched away immediately, pulling a knee up to his chest and wrapping his arms protectively around it. "I - are you all right? Daniel...why are you even here?"

"I was worried about you. Seems I was right to be. *You*," he growled at Kit, kicking the cat with entirely too much force, "I know you're awake. Get up."

Kit slowly blinked open a single green eye. "It's rude to kick folk, Daniel," he yawned, startling Charlie. She had never witnessed a cat talk before.

"It's *rude?*" Daniel's face grew so red Charlie worried he was having a heart attack. "You have the gall to talk to me like that when - when - how could you—"

"I think you need to calm down," Kit interrupted, effortlessly calm where Daniel was furious, "then we'll discuss things." He stretched out his spine, nuzzled Charlie's hand when she instinctively held it out for him, then bounded away through the trees.

A heavy silence fell between Daniel and Charlie. For some reason she felt ashamed. *Am I responsible for Daniel and Kit acting like this towards each other?* she wondered, wanting to reach out for Daniel but worried he would flinch away again. *Just what happened last night?*

Then Daniel drooped his head against Charlie's shoulder. He was shaking. Without thinking she began to stroke his hair, desperate to reassure him. But when she sent out her Influence Daniel dug his fingernails into Charlie's thigh, stopping her in her tracks.

"Don't do that. Stay out of my head. Please."

"I...of course," Charlie said, feeling even more ashamed. Since when had it ever been acceptable for her to use her magic like this on Daniel? On anyone?

Yet she had reached for it so easily.

"Do you remember much?" Daniel mumbled against her shoulder.

She shook her head.

"Good. That's good."

For a while neither of them moved. Then, groaning as he did so, Daniel struggled to his feet before helping Charlie up. With a frown of concentration he summoned a set of clothes for both of them.

"We need to get back to deal with the Alliance," Daniel said, wincing as he pulled on a shirt. Charlie realised he was covered in bruises and bite marks.

And so was she.

"That's...Uthesh be good, is that today?" Charlie said, when the meaning of Daniel's words hit her. "It feels like weeks have passed since the last meeting."

"Only a single night."

Going by the haunted look on Daniel's face that single night had lasted years.

They passed through the woods in awkward, agonised silence. Charlie was desperate to break it but knew that she shouldn't.

Daniel was clearly processing something traumatic.

By the time they were within sight of his estate Charlie's head felt clearer, though she was no closer to recalling the night's events. But her neck began to prickle, and her skin began to itch, and when she looked back at the woods she felt a familiar urge to return.

A hand wrapped around Charlie's wrist stopped her from going back.

"Don't," Daniel pleaded. Charlie noticed his eyes were bloodshot, like he'd been crying. "Don't go back there."

"Why not?" she asked, defensive even in the face of Daniel's obvious distress.

"It's dangerous in there."

"I've never felt like I was in danger."

"No, Charlie," Daniel said, frantically shaking his head. "You don't understand. *You're* the dangerous one in there."

Charlie felt as if her heart stopped beating. Hearing Daniel talk about her like that whilst so obviously afraid was gut-wrenching.

"What do you mean?" Charlie asked, though she dreaded his answer.

"Your magic...it's strong. Too strong. Someone with your abilities losing control could be catastrophic."

Catastrophic?

"I...never felt like I wasn't in control last night," Charlie said, confused. "I—"

"You already told me you don't remember anything."

"But—"

"Don't you trust me?" Daniel cut in, his grip on Charlie's wrist tightening until she winced in pain. When he noticed the look on her face Daniel let go and averted his gaze. "Why would I lie about this? You can *tell* I'm not lying."

Of course she could. That was what made everything feel so wrong.

"Daniel," Charlie said, keeping her voice low and soothing. She held her hands up to his chest, splaying out her fingertips to feel his erratic, painful heartbeat against them. "What happened last night? What happened to *you*?"

"I just..." Daniel leaned against her, allowing Charlie to take most of his weight when she didn't buckle beneath it. "I've never been so manic or so afraid. Please don't go back into the woods. Please."

"I won't," Charlie promised, close to tears at his confession and the feelings behind them. "If you say I lost control then I lost control. I won't go anywhere."

For Daniel to have been reduced to such a state meant something truly terrible must have happened, and if it was Charlie's fault, whether intentional or not...

Then she would do as he asked. She would not enter the woods again.

Even though it beckoned desperately for her return.

"Happy birthday, by the way," Daniel murmured when they reached the front door. "I wish you'd told me about it. I would have got you something to celebrate."

He sounded so sullen about not knowing that Charlie only felt worse about whatever it was that she'd put him through the night before.

"I don't need anything," she said, giving Daniel a reassuring smile. "I only need you."

"Do you?"

Charlie didn't respond; somehow she knew whatever answer she gave would sound like a lie.

I won't go back to the woods, she thought, knowing that was a lie, too.

Chapter Thirty

For a while Kit observed Daniel through the window into his office, eyes following the man's every groan and sigh until, finally, sunlight slanted through the window at such an angle Daniel winced away from it and was forced to move in order to see the notes on his desk.

Kit deftly slid into the office in that moment. "Daniel."

Daniel jumped in fright as he always did when Kit appeared out of nowhere. But this time, especially, the appearance of his friend startled him.

Flashbacks of the night before clouded Daniel's mind. He tried desperately to wave them away but they remained there all the same.

How he got the bruise on his neck and the one on his left shoulder, which was so large it crept above the collar of his shirt. Daniel had to magic both of them away with mere moments to spare before the Alliance meeting that morning.

What he'd done to make his lips feel so swollen. His tongue hurt from overuse; it felt altogether too large in his mouth.

The ache in his hips and groin that told Daniel he had not stopped once to rest the entire night. Everything had been desperate, frenetic, non-stop.

He couldn't look Kit in the face.

"You look like you've seen better days," Kit said. He took the seat in front of Daniel's desk, which was unusual for him. He was never normally so formal.

Daniel sneaked a glance of his friend, though he avoided his eyes. Unlike him, Kit had made no attempt to magic away the physical proof of the revel. His arms, neck and shoulders were littered with teeth marks and bruises slowly blooming purple and red across his skin.

Daniel knew he was responsible for an awful lot of them.

"Whose fault do you think it is that I've seen better days, as you put it?" he demanded of Kit, still unable to look him in the eye.

"Not mine. I'm not the one with the power to pull everyone under their sway like Charlie is."

"But I – I *fucked* you!" Daniel exclaimed, the thoughts in his head forcing the words out. "And you let me! How are you so calm about all this?"

"Because I love you," Kit said simply, finally causing Daniel to look at him.

There was no sign of insincerity on the Drus' face. In fact, Kit's pointed ears were dipped low, and there was a sulkiness to his manner that suggested Daniel's reaction to their magic-induced encounter was not to his liking at all.

But how else was Daniel supposed to react? He hadn't been in control of his mind *or* his body.

"Charlie's Intent..." Daniel muttered, putting a pin in their previous topic of conversation without ever wanting to take it out again, "what you said last night. You said she wasn't human. Going by what happened I'm inclined to believe that's true."

"Half true," Kit amended. "Edward Hope is a mortal man

through and through."

"But her mother...?"

"Her mother is her mother," Kit said, as if that explained everything.

It explained nothing at all.

"Was this what you wanted to discuss with me yesterday?" Daniel asked, remembering the apparent urgency with which his friend had needed to talk to him before the revel. "About Charlie and her parentage?"

To his surprise Kit laughed whole-heartedly, though it wasn't an entirely pleasant sound. "Oh, no. I always imagined that was a conversation we would have far further down the line than this. I'm here about something much bigger than a single person."

Daniel leaned forward despite himself, curious about the uncharacteristically serious tone of Kit's voice. "And what does that mean?"

"I speak on behalf of the Immortal Folk with my concerns regarding the burning and cutting of the woods," Kit said. The words sounded rehearsed; Daniel wondered for how long Kit had prepared to have this conversation with him. "Despite your promise that you'd uncover who is responsible we still remain in the dark. It may well be that Ritten and Laskey as a whole are responsible for some attacks, and Eshijan for others, but the fact remains that the woods are getting smaller and smaller every day."

"I had hoped this would be resolved this morning during the Alliance meeting," Daniel sighed. "But the Eshijani representatives were delayed by an attack on the border. If Charlie hadn't been there to calm the Alliance down today I don't know what would have happened."

"And therein lies the problem."

He stilled. "How so?"

"You can no longer control this," Kit said simply, as if he had the final say on the matter. "My kin and I have been patient for long enough, Daniel. We will put up with these skirmishes no longer. We are, after all, the only ones who seem to be suffering from this fight."

"Don't be ridiculous," Daniel countered, not enjoying the look of displeasure on Kit's face as he so easily dismissed him. "I'm so close to having the new Charter approved. If there hadn't been the delay this morning then I'm sure it would *already* have been approved. But once it's done then everyone will benefit from it – magicians, non-magicians and Immortal Folk alike. Just a few more days and then—"

"Don't give me that, Daniel. You and I both know that – even with Charlie's help – things are spiralling out of control." Kit inhaled deeply, closed his eyes for a moment, then spoke the precise words he had come here to say. "Your precious humans want war, so it is war they will have. That has always been the way of things. But the forest is not theirs. Humans do not own a single tree nor blade of grass nor precious creature within it. They have no right to touch it."

Of course Daniel agreed with him, but he didn't like where Kit was heading. "What's your point?" he asked.

"I want you on our side; *that's* my point. Given your immortality you are far more one of the Folk now than you are human."

Kit stretched a hand across the table towards him but Daniel leaned away from his fingers. It was too soon for Kit to touch him – much too soon – though Daniel hated the way Kit's face fell when he flinched away.

"It isn't the Immortal Folk versus humans," Daniel insisted, determined to settle the matter once and for all. "But you know I don't want to see the woods destroyed. So—"

"So stand with us!" Kit shook his head in frustration. "I don't understand which part of this is so hard for you to comprehend.

You have witnessed what humans are capable of for over a hundred years, Daniel. All they've done is cut and burn and poison the earth beneath their feet with no care for what it does to the planet. To the creatures who lived here long before them and should by all accounts remain long after they have gone. But they are burning us to the ground with the trees, Daniel, and soon there won't be any of us left. Don't let that happen."

"I won't let that happen." Of course he wouldn't. "But you have to let me deal with this my way." Even though it was getting harder and harder to avoid war.

"Your way or *their* way?" Kit bit out testily. Then he clucked his tongue, rising from his seat so suddenly it clattered beneath him. "You're not like the rest of your kind. You see things through the eyes of a creature who will know forever, not just *now*. But at this rate there won't be a forever, Daniel."

"Kit—"

"How much have we been through together until now?" Kit continued passionately. He wanted Daniel to *understand*. He wanted Daniel to agree with him.

He wanted Daniel to stay by his side.

"Everyone who grew up with you is now dead," he murmured. "Everyone you loved as a mortal man has long since turned to ash. There's only me, and you, and Charlie. Don't turn your back on us now."

Daniel's heart skipped a beat. "I'm not turning my back on Charlie."

Kit merely stared at him with his vivid green eyes. "We'll see. You know where to find me if you change your mind."

"Wait, what does that mean? Don't just go!"

But it was too late. Kit and his ominous words had disappeared right before his eyes.

The woods, Daniel thought, biting his lip as he fretted over

Kit's warning. *The woods, the woods, the woods. It all leads back to the woods.*

So why was he the only one who could see this?

CHAPTER THIRTY-ONE

WHEN CHARLIE FELL INTO BED SHE could barely keep her eyes open. She knew she should go to Daniel's bedroom to discuss the night before – or, rather, find out exactly *what* happened the night before.

Now that the haze that plagued her head all day had been replaced by mere exhaustion Charlie realised her memory of the Midsummer revel was almost non-existent. But flashes of events and sensations kept crossing her mind, and they made little and less sense when she tried to process them.

Daniel in the woods.

Kit, but he was Daniel's cat as well as the Drus she'd been so intimate with five years ago.

The two of them, mouths and hands on Charlie and each other.

How is this a memory? Charlie wondered, unable to comprehend it. *How is this not some bizarre, twisted fantasy? A dream? A nightmare?*

A small *meow* from her pillow alerted Charlie that she was not, in fact, alone.

"Kit," Charlie said rather redundantly. When the cat padded across her bed towards her she frowned. "What's the point of staying in this form? Just be you."

"I thought you might have been more comfortable with me as a cat," Kit admitted, shaking himself into his real form before her very eyes. It was shocking to witness the immediacy of the transformation; Charlie knew there were shape shifters within the ranks of the Immortal Folk but in all her years of wandering the woods she'd never actually seen one.

"You look like you've been in a fight," Charlie mused, taking in the bruises on Kits exposed arms, shoulders and neck. She had looked the same earlier; pulling Daniel's cleaning spell back over her had eliminated them.

Daniel, Charlie thought, heart twinging. He had remained distant from Charlie all day, especially when she'd had to use her Influence to stop the Alliance from exploding at the fact the Eshijani representatives had not shown up for their interrogation. But if the representatives were to be believed then they had been attacked by Atralians at the border, who felled trees to barricade the road. Since transportation magic was no longer working over the border that left the Eshijani in an impossible situation.

Going by the way the Alliance members felt today, Charlie knew none of them had been responsible for the attack. So either an independent group of radicals had attacked the Eshijani...or it had been someone else entirely.

Charlie was too tired to work her way through the problem.

"Call it a sign of having a very good time," Kit said in response to Charlie's comment, a small but humourless smile curling his lips. He pulled his knees up to his chest and gently rocked back and forth. "You don't remember much of last night, do you?"

"Bits and pieces," she admitted. "None of it makes much sense."

"Probably best it remains that way...well, at least until Daniel has wrapped his head around it."

"What happened between the two of you?" Charlie asked, though the snippets of memory she did possess gave her a fairly good – if impossible to comprehend – idea.

That sad smile again. "Something long overdue. But I fear the manner in which it happened was a horrible mistake. If only Daniel wasn't so damn repressed..."

Hearing Kit talk about Daniel in such a way did odd things to Charlie. They had been best friends for all of Daniel's life; she remembered him saying that much from the night before, at least. Their relationship had spanned over a hundred years. By comparison, Charlie's relationship with both Daniel and Kit felt frightfully insubstantial.

Kit sighed, then crawled his fingers over the bed until they met Charlie's hand. She squeezed them; Kit squeezed back. "But, alas, it is clear to me now that Daniel is a lost cause. I thought he was on my side – our side – but he is too wrapped up in his arrogance that he can settle this inevitable war."

"What do you mean?" Charlie asked, not liking where the conversation was heading. "All Daniel wants to do is protect our home."

"If that were true then why did he refuse to stand with the Immortal Folk when I asked him to? To protect the woods and our *home*, as you put it, above any and everything else?"

"He didn't..." Charlie murmured, though it was clear it was true. "He must have misunderstood you. He must—"

"He means well," Kit cut in. "Of course I know that. But this war is inevitable. If you keep working with him for the Lopox Alliance then the woods and its inhabitants will surely suffer. And he *will* want you to keep working," Kit said, when it was clear Charlie was going to interrupt. "He cannot do it on his own. With every new obstacle Daniel will rely on you to fix it, and our home will always lose out. He'll control your magic – and you – even if he never set out to. But he'll do it, if he has to. And he will fail, and working for the Alliance will be for naught; you must have seen how much harder it is for even your magic to stop things from going awry recently."

Of course she had. Charlie had witnessed it mere hours earlier.

Did I really lose control at the revel? Charlie wondered. *If it is getting harder for me to control the Alliance with my Influence then how could I have possibly terrified Daniel the way I did? He is stronger than any of them. Just what did I do last night?*

It didn't make any sense. None of it did.

"Charlie?"

"So what do you want me to do?" she rushed out. In truth Charlie was struggling to process everything Kit had just said about his best friend.

"When Daniel forces you to make a choice – and he will – please stand on the side of the woods."

"Of course," Charlie agreed easily. "All I've ever wanted to do is protect my home."

The fact she'd promised Daniel only that morning not to enter the woods again felt like a distant memory.

When Kit smiled this time it was genuine and happy. He leaned forward and kissed her cheek, then rested his head on her shoulder just as Daniel had done that morning. "I knew you would. Thank you, Charlie. Thank you."

After that neither of them spoke, and eventually both Charlie and Kit fell asleep. Late in the night Kit transformed back into a cat so he could curl up in her arms; he seemed to sleep far more soundly than Charlie herself was capable of doing.

Her unconsciousness was full of nightmares. The woods in

flames. The Immortal Folk screaming. Her own father, dying.

Flashes of Charlie's mother appeared in her head: the final moments Charlie had with her before she disappeared to her doom. One moment the dark-haired woman was standing there, in front of Charlie, then the next the ground opened up and swallowed her whole.

It was the one and only time Charlie had ever been truly frightened.

When she awoke from her nightmare, she was frightened again.

CHAPTER THIRTY-TWO

CHARLIE DID NOT APPROACH DANIEL THE next day about what Kit had said, nor the next, nor the next. It was easy to avoid him: after all, Daniel could hardly bear to look at her.

But on the fourth day Charlie could no longer stand keeping the matter to herself. *All I have to do is bring the issue up and I'll know whether what Kit believes about Daniel is true. He won't even have to say anything; I'll simply know one way or the other.*

Yet the fact Daniel would not have to utter a single word in his defence was what Charlie was so afraid of. For if Kit was right and Daniel wouldn't support the woods did Charlie even want to know?

Of course I want to know. But even so...

Not for the first time Charlie almost wished that she could be fooled by a lie.

When Charlie went to knock upon Daniel Silver's bedroom door she felt awkward and nervous. Daniel had always taken her to his bedroom alongside him; Charlie never appeared there unannounced.

I should have been more forward with him from the

beginning, she realised, fist hovering over the door without knocking. *Daniel was the one who actively tried to figure me out. The one who was unafraid to act on his feelings. He knows so much about me but what do I know about him? A few days ago I didn't even know who his best friend was.*

Would he really not defend the woods if I asked him to?

Charlie was saved from having to knock when Daniel opened the door. He looked as bone-weary as Charlie felt, but did not, to her relief, appear surprised nor annoyed to find her standing there.

"I could sense your magic," he said, answering Charlie's unspoken question with a tired smile. He waved her in then promptly closed the door.

He shocked Charlie by immediately pulling her against his chest and holding her tight. "I've been awful these past few days, avoiding you," he murmured against Charlie's hair. She revelled in his warmth, wrapping her arms around Daniel's waist and squeezing as tightly as she physically could.

Of course he'll do what I ask, Charlie thought, reassured by Daniel's arms around her. *Kit was upset and clearly imagining things. Daniel won't let us down.*

"I was just as guilty of avoiding you, too," Charlie replied. "I know things have been difficult since the revel. It doesn't help that I can't remember much of it."

"That is honestly – and I mean this in all sincerity – for the best," Daniel said, chuckling softly as he pulled Charlie to sit on the bed with him.

He is in a better mood, she realised. *Clearly a bit of time to process things worked wonders for him.*

"Is there any update on Ritten's health?" Charlie asked. "I have not heard anything for days now."

Daniel grimaced. "Crank is keeping tight-lipped on the matter. It is clear he trusts no one now, not even the rest of the

Alliance. I think he believes that one of us is conspiring to deliberately incite war. Honestly I can't blame him; your father and I thought it was Ritten but the attacks on the border haven't stopped even with him in a coma."

"If that's the case..." Charlie began, twisting her hands in her lap as she considered her next words very carefully. "Then does it not feel like war is inevitable? You're only one man, Daniel, and I'm only one woman. There's a limit to what the two of us can do. Would it not be better for us at this point to focus on protecting our home and leave the war to everyone else?"

Daniel inhaled sharply. "Kit has been speaking to you, it seems."

"Is he wrong?"

"Charlie, we can't just abandon the rest of Lopox – or Eshijan. Think of the lives that will be lost if a war breaks out that we could have avoided. And we *can* avoid it, I'm sure of it. All we need to do—"

"We?" Charlie felt her heart rate begin to accelerate. *Is Kit really correct about Daniel? Will he not be on our side?* She stood up, though Daniel tried to stop her. "And if I say I'm sick of it all?" she said. "If I say I'm tired of using my magic to force people to reconsider their stupid, dangerous opinions, will that change your mind? After all, if I weren't around to Influence the Alliance then war would have broken out already. Perhaps that means it was inevitable."

But Daniel insistently shook his head and took Charlie's hands in his own. He looked up at her in earnest. "Don't say that. Please, we can do this together, Charlie. You can't give up right now. The Alliance – no, all of Lopox and Eshijan – needs you. Don't give up when we're so close. I know things keep going wrong but we can pull through. We—"

"Again with the *we*." Charlie pulled her hands away from Daniel's and ventured over to the gargantuan window. Twilight stretched across the courtyard and into the woods, dark and alluring and inviting. Charlie knew, then, that she would not be spending the night in Daniel's bedroom, and that she would break his promise to him.

He was a lost cause, just as Kit had said.

Charlie desperately didn't want this to be the case.

"Would you change your mind on the matter for me?" she said, very quietly. "If I asked you to, would you?"

She heard Daniel get up from the bed and walk towards her. "You cannot ask that of me," he said, a hand on Charlie's shoulder urging her to turn from the window. From the woods.

She didn't.

"Too many lives are at stake," Daniel continued, when Charlie did not reply. "I can't stand by and allow a preventable war to break out, however *inevitable* it may seem. I have a job to do, Charlie, and so do you. I need you to ensure our hopes for the world come true."

It was the exact thing Charlie didn't want to hear. "Kit was right," she whispered, trembling at the realisation. "You're...using me. You said you wouldn't use me!"

"How could you even suggest that, Charlie?" Daniel asked, forcing her to face him. His expression was tragic, but Charlie couldn't back down now.

"Because it's true! Was everything you said to me – everything we did together – all a ploy just to find out what I could do, then use it to your advantage? Am I just a tool to you?"

"Charlie—"

"No. Don't even answer that. I don't want to hear it. All you'll do is try to convince me to stay – to keep me away from the woods again."

Daniel shook her shoulders in his anxiety for her to understand. "It's dangerous in there! Something isn't right—"

"The woods are my home."

"*Mount Duega* is your home! Atralia is your home!"

"I couldn't care less about a country that's so eager to go to war it'll burn the very ground it stands upon to ashes!"

"I won't let that happen!"

"*You* won't, or I won't?" Charlie said, icily calm. She pulled Daniel's hands off her shoulders, turning back to the window to undo one of the latches that held it shut. "Because the last time I checked, Daniel, I was the one who was preventing conflict. You were too busy making bullets."

"Charlie—"

"Good-bye, Daniel. I truly, truly hope that you're right and war won't break out. I'll be happy to have been proven wrong. But we both know that won't happen."

She took a step over the window ledge, away from Daniel and towards the woods, then—

"Stay," Daniel pleaded. "Please stay, Charlie. I love you – you must know that. I *love* you. I won't control you or your magic. I never would. So please don't leave me."

Daniel's confession cut through the pull of the woods like an axe. All at once Charlie faltered. Nobody save her parents had ever said they loved her.

Especially not someone Charlie so ardently loved in return.

Daniel grew hopeful at the sight of her hesitation. He reached for her hand and gently pulled her back into his bedroom, twisting his other hand through Charlie's hair to turn her face towards his. "I love you," he said, so tenderly. He kissed the top of her head. "Why such a thing was so difficult to admit aloud feels foolish now. It's so easy to say. I love you. Don't you love me?"

"Of course I do," Charlie breathed. "You know I do."

"Then don't go," Daniel begged, dipping his head to graze a

kiss on her lips. "Don't go." He deepened the kiss when Charlie softened beneath him.

Charlie almost said yes.

A mewing from behind the window abruptly pulled her out of her fairytale romance with Daniel Silver.

For that was what it was: a fairytale. Their feelings for each other had been a whirlwind, sudden and violent and at times frightening. But they both had causes more important to themselves than each other.

That Daniel had such solid principles and morals was one of the reasons Charlie loved him.

Yet it would be the reason she had to be without him.

"No," Daniel bit out when he saw Kit and the resultant hardening of Charlie's expression. "You can't."

"I have to," she said, because she did. "If you change your mind you know where to—"

"Don't you dare say what he said! Don't you dare – you and Kit – you can't both do this to me!" Daniel shattered the entire window in his desperation, magic emanating from his every pore. "Why has it come to this?" he pleaded with his friend. "Why can't we work together on this? Why can't we—"

"You're the one who won't work with us," Kit said as Charlie jumped over the windowsill. "This is on you."

When Charlie turned to face Daniel she discovered she was crying. Daniel was crying, too, though he didn't seem to notice nor care.

But their tears meant nothing now. They would *change* nothing.

"Good-bye, Daniel," Charlie said once more, before fleeing into the woods closely following Kit.

She had done the right thing, she was sure. It *had* to be the right thing.

If it wasn't then Charlie Hope had just made the biggest mistake of her life, and broken both her heart and Daniel's in the process.

CHAPTER THIRTY-THREE

Kɪᴛ ᴛᴏᴏᴋ Cʜᴀʀʟɪᴇ ɪɴᴛᴏ ᴛʜᴇ ᴡᴏᴏᴅs, carving a path beneath the trees on feet which knew every branch and blade of grass set before him. It wasn't long until the pair of them came across the very place Charlie had sensed the bizarre, impossible life that was growing in the forest: the one the Immortal Folk themselves had first felt, quiet and unassuming but growing day after day, fifteen years ago.

"The Uthesh fault line runs through here," Charlie murmured, when Kit reverted to his real form, fell to his knees and pulled Charlie down to the ground with him. "I never noticed that before."

"Does that mean something to you?" Kit asked.

"Probably not," Charlie said. "Just remembering an old story. My favourite one."

And Daniel's.

"Do not be sad, Charlie Hope," Kit insisted, placing his hands over Charlie's to bury them beneath the soil. "Now is not the time to be sad. Now is the time to sing."

But Charlie didn't feel much like singing – she was hurt and angry and heartbroken. She never sang when she felt this way.

She couldn't imagine feeling happy ever again, even in the woods.

But still she sang, putting all of her emotions into every word that escaped her lips. At first Charlie's song was quiet, and the sound was absorbed by the trees around her, but slowly she found a reserve of strength within her, and her voice grew louder and more intense.

When a deep rumbling began all around Charlie, Kit quickly helped her maintain her balance so she could continue singing to the ground.

A crack appeared in the forest floor right along the fault line.

"Don't stop," Kit breathed when Charlie paused in her song, eyes locked on the rapidly expanding crack in fright. "Keep going. This is how it's meant to be."

So Charlie kept going even though she was afraid. Terribly afraid. The crack grew larger, then larger still, clods of dirt falling down, down, down into its hidden depths. As the literal break in the ground grew closer to Charlie and Kit they jumped to their feet, narrowly avoiding being swallowed by the crevasse.

When something began rising from the fault line it was all Charlie could do to stop herself from screaming. Her song danced off her tongue, instead, faster and louder and then faster still as a behemoth of a creature pulled itself from the shadows.

It was almost as large as the trees, its skin, its fur, its claws all half-rotting and black. A single horn curved off its long, angular head, and its four limbs were long and gangly. When it let out a roar Charlie spied a forked tongue and a full set of wicked, serrated teeth. She couldn't discern what kind of animal it was supposed to be; it was entirely unlike anything she had seen before.

When the monster loomed towards her Charlie recoiled on instinct.

But it didn't attack.

It crouched in front of her and obediently dipped its head. Its eyes were liquid silver.

Silver, liquid silver, moulded into the shape of many dozens of wicked creatures. Monsters with a name.

"Noben," she breathed, finishing her frantic song. "You are one of the Noben."

If Daniel could only be here. If Daniel—

Daniel would tell me to run.

But it was too late; though the creature itself seemed to pose no threat to Charlie she realised, all at once, that she had fallen into a trap.

Another song floated upon the wind to fill Charlie's ears. The Noben looked up and to the left, searching for the source of the new melody. It was a woman's voice, commanding and haunting in equal measure. A *familiar* voice; one from Charlie's memories.

A feminine figure emerged from between the trees, much smaller than the Noben, and laid a hand on the creature's snout. She was clad in a ghost of a dress, the white gauze of the skirt billowing around her legs. Upon her head of wild, dark curls was the skull of a stag with sixteen-point antlers, which lent the woman a strange and intimidating silhouette.

Yet though her ears were long and pointed, and her eyes peering through the skull were a shade of green mortal humans could never possess, Charlie recognised her.

"Mother?" Charlie whispered, unsure and afraid. She cocked her head to the side, trying desperately to wrap her mind around the otherworldly, smiling woman who stood before her. "No, it can't be. You died. You – you were swallowed by the ground and—"

The woman laughed. Serena, Charlie's mother, *laughed* at the prospect of her apparent demise. "Is that what your father told you – that I died?" she said, stroking the Noben as tenderly as one might stroke a very large dog. "I suppose the poor fool must have believed it. But you are no fool, Charlotte. I should have known you would grow into my magic. Better late than never that I find out."

"But you're not..." Charlie waved at the woman, who was not a woman in the mortal sense at all. "You're not human. So I'm —"

Serena clapped her hands together, delighted. "Clever girl. You're one of us. Or, rather, half, but the birth of an Immortal Folk babe is so rare that your pesky human father hardly matters." She took a step towards Charlie, then another, then another. "You are our blood, not theirs. And you have inherited all of my gifts. Including the most vital of them all."

Charlie stared at the Noben, then back at her rapidly-approaching mother. "This creature was dead. *Is* dead. So why—"

Serena laughed lightly; like a bell, ringing to signal Charlie's impending doom. "I am a necromancer, Charlotte. I thought that much was obvious by now. And *you* are a necromancer. And so much more! A Folk babe born on Midsummer's Eve: I should have expected huge things from you." She held out her hand. "Now come, let's return to your kin. Your *real* family."

Charlie knew she needed to run from the stranger that was her mother, in her antlered skull and airy dress. Beside her Kit looked like absolutely nothing was wrong. It was only then that Charlie realised he believed every word that came out of her mother's mouth.

He was under her Influence.

Perhaps he always had been.

"I have a family already," Charlie insisted, knowing it was a mistake to say it. She was trapped and it was all her fault.

She should have listened to Daniel Silver.

"That fool of a father whose claim to you prevented me stealing you away is not your family," her mother snapped, green eyes venomous at the thought. "Your family live here, in the woods. Now *come*."

When she spoke the words this time Charlie felt a horrible hook invade her mind, pulling her forwards with her mother even though she didn't want to move.

No. No, this is—

This is how Daniel felt under my Influence at the revel, Charlie realised in horror, reeling under the weight of her mother's Intent. She couldn't breathe. Could hardly see. All she could do was obey Serena's order, and follow her.

The Noben followed, too.

"What are you going to do?" Charlie managed to bite out as they wound their way through the woods, towards the meadow the Midsummer revel had been held in. She pointed at the dirt beneath her feet. "With your army of dead monsters, just what is it you plan to achieve?"

When Serena smiled over her shoulder at her daughter it was alarming in its beauty. "Why, I want to find my one true love, of course. Isn't everything we do for love? He's been lost and buried for so long, you see, but your war-mongering half-kin have so fortuitously made my job much, much easier."

It took Charlie far too long to work out what that meant. Her grasp over her own body was rapidly slipping.

"...they've been cutting and burning the woods," she said, gasping for air.

"Of course."

"But they're destroying our home!"

"And that shall pay for it dearly!" Serena called out just as they reached the meadow. A crowd of Immortal Folk stood there, cheering and hanging on Serena's every word.

Charlie could hardly understand what the Folk were crying... save for one word that stood out over them all.

Queen.

The Immortal Folk were cheering for their *queen.*

But when Charlie looked at the crowd properly all she could see were glazed green eyes, heavily under Serena's Influence.

When her mother turned to face her Charlie knew that whatever she was about to say next was not meant for the rest of the crowd. Serena kissed Charlie's head, a savage, gentle mockery of affection. "Yes, they'll pay dearly," she crooned, "just as soon as they're finished doing the heavy lifting for me. Until then, daughter of mine, you must stay here."

Because she demanded it, Charlie had no choice but to obey.

CHAPTER THIRTY-FOUR

Never with such urgency had Daniel Silver called upon the house of Edward Hope before.

"Edward!" Daniel hollered, banging on his front door. "Edward, open up!"

Daniel shifted on the spot when his knock was met with silence, anxious and on edge. When a full minute passed with no sign of the man he wondered if he should try the town hall instead.

Then he heard footsteps, and the door swung open.

"Daniel?" Edward wondered aloud. He rubbed his bleary eyes; clearly he had been sleeping. "Sorry. I turned in early for the evening. What's...Daniel, what's wrong?"

He had no time to waste. "Charlie is gone."

"Gone?"

"Yes. To the woods."

At this Edward relaxed and laughed easily. "She does that. I'm surprised she managed to stop herself from going until—"

"No, she's been going to the woods ever since I first took her on," Daniel cut in, impatient for Edward to understand. "This is different. She was – there's something wrong. Did you know your daughter is only half human?"

All at once the colour drained from Edward's face. "Come in and be quiet about it," Edward hushed, waving Daniel inside.

They had barely made their way into the living room when Daniel turned on Edward once more. "So you knew?"

"Of course I knew!" he bit out testily. "I'm not a fool, Daniel. I knew Serena wasn't human the moment I met her."

"...but didn't she glamour her appearance to appear so?" *Otherwise why did nobody else know?* "Did she tell you what she was?"

"Uthesh be good, no." He laughed humourlessly. "She Influenced me now and again to make me believe she was human but she was...arrogant. And I'm a good actor. So long as I kept up the appearance of believing her to be human and was completely head-over-heels for her then Serena was satisfied. She didn't bother wasting Influence on me after a while."

"But then..." Daniel didn't understand. "If you knew from the beginning, and also knew she was playing you for an idiot, why did you stay with her?"

Edward stared at him as if *Daniel* was the idiot. "I was seventeen. It was one drunk night. One single, stupid night. I knew what Serena was but she was beautiful and strange. I was hopeless against her. But that would have been it. That *would* have been it, except that she got pregnant. And Charlie..."

Ah, Daniel thought, understanding dawning on him in one fell swoop. *If it happened that quickly then Edward hardly had a chance at all to escape her. He's not the type of man to turn his back on a child.*

"Of course," Edward continued, "I knew I had to marry Serena to stop her from taking Charlie away, so I kept up the besotted act so she didn't realise what I was doing."

"She would have done that? Taken Charlie away?"

Edward sagged into a chair by the window. He ran a hand over his face. "Do you know how rare new Immortal Folk are, Daniel? I didn't, at the time, but in moments when Serena didn't pull her Influence over me I was lucid enough to find out the truth."

The bits and pieces Kit had told Daniel throughout the years about his unnatural kin began to click into place. "Yes..." Daniel murmured, frowning as he recalled what he knew. "They consider it a miracle, don't they? Since they don't ever really die but instead change form until they return to a physical body again. But Charlie...she wasn't reincarnated energy, then?"

Edward sighed deeply. "No. She was completely, naturally new. By all accounts a miracle. Serena wasn't happy when she found out she was pregnant - I don't think she ever saw herself as a mother - but her kind forbid the termination of pregnancies, so she had no choice but to give birth to her daughter. By marrying her I rightly claimed the child by their laws, too, so Charlie could never be spirited away without my consent."

"And you never gave it." It was a redundant thing to say; of course Edward Hope would never consent to his only child being torn from his arms.

"Even in the beginning, I would have never - she's my daughter." Merely thinking about her now Edward's face grew soft. "I love her. If Charlie wanted to join her half-kin when she was grown I wouldn't stop her, but while she was a child and under my care I was never going to allow it."

"And if her mother willed it?" Daniel asked, desperate to fully understand the situation so he could find a solution to it all. "Why did she agree to marry you and stay in Mt. Duega if she knew it would bind her to you through Charlie?"

"Serena...she was placed in Mt. Duega to keep watch over the goings-on of humans." A sharp chuckle. "She thought I didn't know, but I have ears and I have eyes and I have a brain. So long as she had a job to do she wouldn't leave. And, as I said, she didn't want to be a mother, and I was happy to be a father. I raised Charlie with little input from my so-called wife."

A pause. Edward's expression grew bitter and dark. "Still," he said, "Charlie followed her around like a shadow. But when I saw my wife kill our daughter's cat – Charlie called him Buttercup because his fur was as blonde as her hair – I grew fearful for her safety, and my own. When I saw Buttercup walking around the next day as if nothing had happened that fear only rose."

This hadn't been information Daniel was expecting at all. He gazed at the photos lining the walls of Edward Hope's living room and abruptly understood why he didn't possess a single photos of his 'late' wife. *She was a necromancer. A necromantic Immortal Folk who can Influence anyone she desires. And Charlie's mother. Uthesh be good, just what—*

"Truth be told," Edward added on, too lost in the memory to realise Daniel had re-entered panic mode, "when Serena left on the day of the Great Shift I was deeply, whole-heartedly grateful."

"She...left?" This was news to Daniel, though by now he shouldn't have been surprised by such a twist. "She didn't – she didn't die?"

"I'm sure she believes that's what I think, just as she thought I doted on her. Between the two of us I was the far better actor. But now...you're saying Charlie has joined the Immortal Folk? To live with them?"

And now they were back at the beginning, yet everything was so much worse than Daniel had thought when he first knocked on Edward's door.

"It isn't as simple as that," Daniel said, trying to find the words to explain his fear. "Edward, I followed her to the Midsummer revel. I shouldn't have, but I did. And I saw her...

Charlie lost control of her Intent magic. It was overwhelming. It was terrifying. It was—"

Edward held up a hand to stop him. "How long have you known what Charlie can do?"

"Since the day of the gala," Daniel said. "She sang to the plants and helped a swallow grow. I couldn't believe she possessed creation magic – it's so rare in humans – but if she's only *half* human then it makes far more sense." A pause. "I worked out her Intent magic a few days later. I...I..."

"Daniel?" Edward pressed, concerned about why he'd paused.

Bringing up the afternoon of the gala flooded Daniel's brain with the memory of Charlie singing to the swallow. A broken baby bird in her hands, not moving, deathly still and silent, and Charlie whispering words of encouragement to it until it grew and grew and got better.

Knowing what he now knew about Charlie's mother, Daniel saw the scene for what it really was.

She felt a life beneath her feet in the woods. A strange life. It didn't make any sense to her, but she felt it.

What if that 'life' was no true living thing at all? What if...

Monsters crafted by his own hand in liquid silver danced across Daniel's vision. Their bodies torn apart and separated by an ocean. A mad magician, entombed in stone, a million miles away from where Daniel had carved their likeness upon his front door.

Except there was no ocean between Atralia and Eshijan anymore, and that million miles was more like thirty.

When Daniel staggered dangerously Edward rushed to his feet to steady him, and realised something was horribly, terribly wrong.

"What is it, Daniel?"

"Did you know about Charlie?" Daniel asked in an undertone. "About your daughter?"

"I'm not sure what you mean."

"Did you know she's a necromancer like her mother?"

Now Edward was the unsteady one. "...she's...she's..." he mouthed. "She isn't—"

Daniel didn't have any time to give the man any sympathy. "I'll take that as a no. Edward, something catastrophic is coming our way. Will you help me stop it?"

"Of course!" he replied. "Of course I will. Why would you even have to ask?"

"And if it means Charlie may come to harm?" Daniel said, hating the taste of the words in his mouth. But Charlie wasn't herself right now, and Daniel couldn't get through to her. *And it isn't even just Charlie,* Daniel realised. *Kit won't listen to sense, either. Whether that means he's under the thrall of some magic or not changes nothing right now.*

Edward's lips formed a hard line. "Why are the two mutually exclusive?"

"I'm hoping they won't be," Daniel said. "I'm hoping she'll be able to see reason. But I am deeply, deathly afraid."

"Of what?"

"Of her. Of what she might do."

It was the truth, and that made it even worse.

Edward gripped Daniel's shoulder as he collected himself. Now was not the time to panic nor think in terms of worst-case scenarios. Now was the time for action.

"I would never let my daughter come to harm," Edward said, "but still, I'll help you. Of course I'll help you. The entirety of Lopox would fall apart without me."

Daniel's lips quirked into the shadow of a smile at the

comment despite the severity of their situation. *Like father, like daughter,* he mused. *I can see where Charlie gets her confidence from.*

He wished he could see her. To talk to her once more; once more was all Daniel needed to get through to Charlie. He was sure of it.

"Good," he told Edward. "Then we have no time to lose. We have to gather all the people we trust...before we lose any chance we have of saving everything we hold dear."

Chapter Thirty-Five

"You don't look very happy, Charlie."

Charlie didn't reply. She and Kit were nestled below the bows of a birch tree, the moss under them soft and spongy. It was an overcast day; beneath the shadow of the trees the air was chilly despite the time of year.

Kit curled against Charlie until she gave him her attention. "What did you say?" she asked. The situation she was in was not Kit's fault, Charlie knew. Now she knew what Influence looked like in the green eyes of the Immortal Folk it was clear Kit was under the same spell as the rest of his kin.

Her mother's spell.

He didn't listen to a word Daniel said, even though they've been friends for over a hundred years. I should have seen that something wasn't right.

Except Charlie had been too lost in the pulsing life in the woods and her mother's Influence to hear Daniel's impassioned plea, either.

It was apparent to Charlie now that she'd spent a full day in the woods that Serena's Influence lingered on Charlie far less than full-fledged Immortal Folk. She should have been grateful for this. It meant Charlie could think again, though whenever she tried to put one foot in front of the other to run away Charlie was compelled to sit down once more.

Therefore her not-quite-freedom made her so frustrated Charlie almost wished she was under the full sway of her mother's magic. That way, Charlie wouldn't have to dwell on the horrible mistake she had made.

Daniel, she cried, feeling tears sting her eyes. *Never mind his views on trying to stop the war – it was always going to be impossible – but he knew something was wrong. Something in the woods. He begged me not to come here.*

Even free of the sway of my mother's Intent I didn't listen. Even when he said he loved me.

Kit kissed her cheek. "I said you don't look very happy. Why aren't you happy? Is it Daniel?"

"Yes," Charlie said, for it was easier than lying.

"It's not too late for him to change his mind," Kit said, a hopeful smile on his face telling Charlie that he genuinely believed this. Or, at least, wanted it to be true. He rested his head in Charlie's lap, purring loudly when she stroked his hair.

Charlie wondered if Kit had taken on the animal's mannerisms before or after he became able to shift into a cat. She didn't know anything about *her* Drus, truth be told, not even for how long he'd existed or if he'd known who Charlie's mother was when they first met.

"Why do you have a scar on your back?" Charlie asked, curiosity breaking through her misery. "It's so large."

Kit stretched his spine until it cracked in several places. "Ah, that happened the first time I changed shape. It hurt so much I thought I'd die. Well, as close to dying as one of us can get."

Dying. Immortal Folk don't really die. Which means—

"I'm...not going to die, am I?" Charlie realised all at once.

"I'm not going to grow old, or suffer the aches and pains of losing my youth, or—"

"It is a gift, Charlie. If it was not then why did Daniel choose to ascend from his lowly mortal beginnings?"

"If it was truly a gift more humans would try to attain it."

But Kit merely shook his head. "There is a reason so few of your half-kin can reach such heights. It's *supposed* to be difficult, Charlie. Most people who try to ascend fail. And good riddance to them."

Charlie mulled this over. The only immortal humans she knew in person were Daniel and Grandmaster Feng. Her father didn't even want to *attempt* ascension – now that Charlie knew she would live forever the reality of this fact was beginning to sink in – and neither did Crimson. They were both good people, Charlie knew. If anyone was going to benefit the world with their wisdom it was them.

But then Charlie thought about what immortality would do to her father. Edward didn't want it; he liked getting older and changing with the world around him. Immortality would drive him mad.

It would be a curse to him.

Charlie had no choice in the matter. Did that make immortality a curse for her, too? Or was Kit correct and it was a gift?

She wished she could ask Daniel.

"Tell me how you and Daniel became friends," Charlie said, no longer able to stave off her thoughts about the man. If she couldn't talk to him then asking his best friend about him was the next best option.

Kit chuckled softly. "You would not have liked him at all. Daniel was so arrogant at your age. So young. He thought he could do anything. He had the magic to support this, though, so I suppose his arrogance was warranted."

She quirked an eyebrow. "And this made him appeal to you somehow?"

"Oh, absolutely. I was head over heels the first time I saw him twist literal nothing into beautiful, shining silver."

Charlie thought of the revel – of what little she could remember. Of what Kit and Daniel had done, and how Kit had been upset, the following day, when Daniel had not reacted the way he wanted.

"Does he know you feel this way," Charlie asked, trailing her fingertips across Kit's forehead, "or has he always believed your declarations of love to be teasing?"

"*I'm* the tease?" Kit scoffed. "He's the one who spent every waking moment with me until he met his wife. If she hadn't chosen not to ascend then—"

"Wait," Charlie bit out, "Daniel was *married?*"

Kit sprang back up to sit beside her, an animated look on his face as he recounted Daniel's mortal life for her. "For ten years, yes," he said. "Five years into his immortality they ended things. His wife was growing old and couldn't bear the fact that he was not. There is no compromise between dying and living forever; it was inevitable they would break apart."

How unbelievably sad, Charlie thought, heartbroken for both Daniel and his ghost of a wife. *That must have hurt him so.*

"Did he...ever pursue another romantic relationship?" Charlie couldn't help but ask. Now that Kit was telling her what he knew about Daniel she was unashamed to admit that she wanted to know *everything.* "Any important women – or men, I suppose – I should know about?"

Kit's answering smile was gentle and lovely. For a fleeting instant his beautiful, unearthly eyes were clear of all Influence. "Only me, and only you. It's the way it should be. The way it *will* be, I'm sure."

Charlie had believed that, too, from the scraps of memory

she possessed about the revel. Discovering who Kit was to both herself and to Daniel had made all the puzzle pieces of her life fit into place. Charlie had thought, for the first time, that everything made sense.

It was supposed to be her and Daniel and Kit.

But where was Daniel now, if this were true?

We should have stayed on his side. He so easily saw that something was wrong. We were the ones under the sway of another, not him.

"Don't forget to mention Jonathan Crank when you attack the Eshijani," Charlie heard her mother say, some distance off to her right. Serena had been barking orders at the Immortal Folk all morning, though Charlie had been so lost in her own head that she hadn't listened to a single word she uttered.

But at the mention of Jonathan Crank's name Charlie perked up.

The Nymph who'd been given the order nodded. "We will not let you down, my queen."

Serena smiled so sweetly the Nymph began grinning like she was possessed. "Of course you won't. Don't forget to burn the woods as you go. Don't leave a single tree standing."

"What are you doing, mother?" Charlie called out, careful to appear pliable and easy-going as if she was still under Serena's Influence. But her heart was hammering in abject horror at what her mother was doing to the poor Immortal Folk. Having them destroy their own home was tragic.

Serena's smile broadened; her sharp teeth glimmered in the dim light. "Why, inciting war, of course. I don't think you realise how wonderful a job you were doing of preventing it. If you and your troublesome father hadn't been interfering with my plans for so long then war would have broken out years and years ago."

I've been so stupid, Charlie blithely realised for the hundredth time. *All Da wanted was for me to keep the peace with him. And I spat it in his face. I thought his work was meaningless, when really it was the only work that mattered.*

"So you were the one behind the attacks on Eshijan?" Charlie asked her mother.

"And on Atralia," Serena added dismissively. "I need both sides of the woods searched, after all. There's a lot of ground to cover and so few Immortal Folk at my disposal. It's only natural that I have the humans do the heavy lifting."

"You—"

"Can do nothing to stop me," Serena said easily, waving a hand at Charlie and, in the process, reaffirming her Influence over her. The very air from Charlie's lungs was knocked out of her, and she sunk back into the tree hollow where Kit wrapped his arms around her, protecting her.

Imprisoning her.

Charlie couldn't move. Couldn't process her surroundings. She could do nothing now but wait and see what happened.

Daniel, Charlie thought, over and over again like a mantra. Like a song.

She would have to trust in Daniel Silver.

CHAPTER THIRTY-SIX

"Grandfather, thank you for coming over so quickly."

Grandmaster Feng had responded to Daniel's plea as soon as he received it from Crimson. They were lucky he'd already made it across the border, otherwise Daniel had a dreadful suspicion someone would have prevented the old man from reaching him in time.

"Your message was urgent," Feng replied, nodding first at his grand-daughter and then at the table at large. "Of course I arrived as soon as I could."

"So can we find out what's going on now?" Jean asked, a sentiment that was shared by Luca. Daniel and Edward had not yet informed them about what was going on when they rushed back to Daniel's estate; even Crimson knew only the bare minimum.

It was easier to tell them altogether.

"Yes," Daniel said, "but what I have to say is...complicated, so please hold off your questions until the end." He almost felt like he was beginning a lecture, though in some ways treating the matter at hand like it was a prepared speech helped Daniel collect his thoughts.

"Charlie Hope is only half human," he said, getting straight to the heart of the matter. "Her mother – Mayor Hope's supposedly late wife" – he nodded at Edward – "is one of the Immortal Folk, and a dangerous one at that. She's a necromancer."

Daniel paused, expecting interruptions, but everyone obediently remained quiet. "So is Charlie."

That was when his younger team members reacted.

"You're joking, right?" Luca exclaimed. "She isn't...don't be ridiculous."

Jean was just as incredulous. "A necromancer? I thought they belonged to myths and children's stories, not real life."

"Unfortunately not. At first I thought Charlie's magic was limited to creation and Intent—"

"Hold on, hold on." Jean held a hand to his face, processing all of this new information as quickly as possible. "Intent? As in...she can push her Influence on others? Such as, say, the Lopox Alliance?"

Daniel was impressed by the speed with which he came to the right conclusion. "You're a quick study, Jean. Remind me about that raise if we come out of this alive."

"A-alive?" Luca stuttered. "What in the name of Uthesh does that mean?"

It was Edward who answered. "It means we're all in grave danger. I'm afraid everyone has been mere puppets on strings for years now...and it might be too late to do anything about it."

Silence.

"I have reason to believe that the realignment of Atralia and Eshijan was no mere accident," Daniel explained. "And that it was planned for a very, very, very long time."

"Why?" Luca asked.

"War," Feng said, just as his grand-daughter said the same.

"The kiroji," Crimson continued. "To put them back together?"

Daniel nodded. "To wreak destruction upon Erath as an echo of the past. Someone means to dismantle everything that we know."

"And that person would be...Charlie?" Jean asked, though going by his face he didn't believe this for a second.

"Serena," Edward corrected. "My...wife. Or, at least, I suspect she's heavily involved. Going by the fact Charlie was pulled into the woods it seems the Immortal Folk need her abilities. It can't be easy work bringing all the Noben back to the surface."

"Whilst also Influencing Atralians and the Eshijani to incite conflict...and possibly also control the Immortal Folk, too," Daniel added on, thinking of Kit. He couldn't know for sure, of course, but something about the way his best friend hadn't listened to a single word Daniel said – had not attempted any sort of compromise – didn't sit right with him.

"This has to be a joke," Luca insisted. She stared at everyone sitting around the table in turn, expecting them to agree with her. "This is a fairytale. And Charlie wouldn't—"

"Charlie is not herself," Daniel said, very, very quietly. He glanced at Edward, who sadly nodded. "I suspect her mother dug her claws in some time ago. That she managed to hold out as long as she did is a miracle, really."

"But..." Jean wondered aloud, concerned, "if all the Immortal Folk are rallied behind this then how can we possibly hope to stop what's coming? And what do they hope to achieve by forcing conflict between Atralia and Eshijan?"

It was Feng who answered. "To keep us distracted, I suspect. Humans are selfish creatures. By being so focused on our own petty conflicts for the last few months – years – we could not see what's really coming until it's too late."

"So what do we do?" Crimson asked. "What *can* we do?"

Daniel and Edward had discussed this at length whilst waiting for Grandmaster Feng to arrive. Now they looked at the old man. "Intent users are more common in Eshijan, are they not?" Daniel asked. "Crimson, I seem to recall you saying something of that ilk to me in the past."

"It was the reason I knew what I was looking at when Charlie first used her magic in front of us," she nodded. "But that does not mean Eshijan is any better equipped at handling such a skill."

"But that part is simple, is it not?" Jean interjected.

They all stared at him.

He shrugged as if it were obvious. "Don't we simply make sure Charlie and her mother don't direct their magic at us? If we're not under their Influence then they can't control what we're doing."

Luca rolled her eyes. "Yes, it's as simple as that. And how do we make sure they don't direct their magic at us? Mister Silver will surely be one of their prime targets if we rally against them."

"We use illusions," Jean said, grinning at his own solution. "If they use their Influence on an illusion then we'll be free to move about as we please whilst they're distracted."

He really needs that raise, Daniel thought. *He is far more ingenious than anyone's ever given him credit for.*

Except there was just one problem.

"I've witnessed Charlie affect everyone in an area with her Influence without her knowledge," Daniel pointed out. "If she did that it would not matter what we try to do."

"But was she focusing on anything stressful? Was there anything attacking her or diverting her attention?"

Daniel shook his head.

"Then this should work," Jean insisted. "If we keep Charlie and her mother focused on singular attacks – or the *illusion* of singular attacks – the general hold in the area should waver, shouldn't it? Surely it takes a fair amount of concentration to maintain Intent magic."

"It's the best idea we have, Daniel," Edward said, chewing over Jean's proposal. "If this doesn't work then nothing else will, either."

"And if we can destroy the Noben whilst they're distracted then the threat can be tempered." Feng looked at Crimson. "We need to contact the Eshijani government. This is not something we can do alone. We need—"

A servant barged into the meeting room unannounced, their face pale and wretched and instilling a very tired kind of fear in Daniel. "The Lopox Alliance just declared war on Eshijan," they cried, brandishing a magical alert in their hands. "They set up a huge barricade at the border. The woods are in flames."

"But...I spoke to Crank an hour ago," Daniel said, stricken. He stumbled over to the window and saw dark, acrid plumes of smoke rising from the forest. "He swore he wouldn't make a move until I could tell him what I'd learnt."

"Then either he lied, or he's being Influenced, or both," Edward said, also getting to his feet to investigate the smoke. "Whatever the reason there's no more time to lose. We must get to the border."

He exchanged a look with Daniel, then addressed the room at large. "If we can – I know it might be impossible – then I want to keep Charlie out of harm's way. She doesn't know what she's doing; you know she wouldn't hurt us if she was in her right mind. So if you see her...don't engage. Run, and find Daniel."

Everyone nodded.

And what about Kit? Daniel thought, as they rushed around to gather everything they thought they might need. *If he's being Influenced and tries to attack...*

Can I save him, too? Can I save them both?

Daniel didn't want to consider the idea that Charlie and Kit were already doomed and him with them, too.

Chapter Thirty-Seven

By the time Charlie could breathe freely Kit was hauling her to her feet.

"Time to go," he said, the reflection of flames dancing in his green eyes.

Flames? Charlie wondered, shaking the fog from her head before inhaling deeply through her nose.

The air was thick with smoke.

"What's...the trees are burning!" Charlie exclaimed, allowing Kit to lead her through the woods without quite knowing where they were going. Above her head everything was on fire; not a single tree had escaped the blaze.

She tugged on Kit's hand. "We have to stop this. We can't let my mother burn the woods to the ground!"

"Your mother?" He blinked innocently at Charlie, the picture of confusion. "She didn't do this – it was the humans! We're all going to the border to deal with them."

Charlie wanted to shake him. Wanted to scream at Kit to wake up and regain control of his own body. But then she realised that, if Kit wasn't capable of overcoming Serena's

Influence, perhaps *Charlie* could overwrite it with her own.

"My mother is responsible for everything," Charlie insisted, pushing her Intent into every word. But Kit merely continued to drag her through the hot, acrid, suffocating air, deaf to Charlie's words.

Harder, she thought, struggling to concentrate against the din of burning trees and the cries of desperate woodland creatures. *You have to try harder.*

"*Kit,*" Charlie said, grabbing his arm to force him to stop. He merely stared at her, face blank, eyes empty.

"What is it?"

"*You have to listen to me. Only me. My mother is forcing your kin to burn the woods. She was the one who caused all the trouble between Eshijan and Atralia. She is not your queen. She is using you. She—*"

"Charlie?" Kit wondered aloud, cutting her off. He shook his head, then pawed at his ears as if there was something stuck in them. "What's going on? What's—"

"That's *quite* enough," Serena called out from behind Charlie, destroying her almost-hold over Kit. She closed the distance between them, a frown of displeasure darkening her eyes when she looked at her daughter. "Stop trying to resist, Charlotte. You're making this far harder than it has to be."

"You can't do this!" Charlie cried, when both Kit and Serena took hold of her arms and dragged her forward. "You're destroying everything!"

"And? We can simply sing life back into the woods together once I'm done."

"That isn't the point!"

"That's precisely the point," Serena countered. "When you can control life and death you control the world. You're young, daughter of mine, but in time you'll understand. Neither the laws of humans nor Immortal Folk apply to me, or to you."

Charlie struggled against her mother's vice-like grip. They were coming into a meadow; through the smoke she could discern the gigantic shape of the Noben Charlie herself had called up from the ground. The creature came to greet them, hellish head obediently bent low when Serena let out a whistle.

"Come," she told Charlie, and in the blink of an eye both Charlie and her mother were sitting atop the Noben. "We travel in style."

Some kind of magic was keeping Charlie firmly in place upon the creature; she couldn't move an inch. Below her Kit transformed into a cat and ran away through the trees, a flash of tawny fur against smoke and flames until Charlie could no longer make him out at all.

"I'll stop you," Charlie said through gritted teeth when the Noben began to move. Its gait was unsteady; with every lumbering footstep Charlie was sure she would fall. But her mother's magic kept her in place by her side. "I can. I will."

Serena laughed at the suggestion. "You barely reached your lovely friend for a second before I overpowered your magic. You cannot stop me, but you *will* help me."

But Charlie was prepared for the feeling of Serena's Intent hooking into her brain. She pushed out against it, testing it, fighting it, until the arrogant smile that was on her mother's face slipped away.

"Stop fighting me," she ordered. "You are simply wasting your energy – and mine. Once we reach the border and deal with the humans then we'll finally be free to find my lost love. Once you've met him you will see who *should* have been your father, and then you will be glad you're on my side."

"I don't need another father," Charlie spat out. "And I don't need you. Find your megalomaniac *lost love* and stay the hell away from me."

A steely glint lit up Serena's venomous eyes. "Watch your tongue, daughter. I have waited many thousands of years to be reunited with him. Aeons spent floating as useless energy until I was brought back into physical form. You will not insult him, nor me."

"I'll make you into a ball of useless energy again," Charlie muttered, more to herself than to her mother. For Serena had diverted her attention to the rapidly-approaching border. From their vantage point atop the Noben Charlie could see far more clearly than she could on the burning forest floor, but she did not like what she saw at all.

Dozens of Noben. Hundreds, even.

They stood still as statues, silent as the dead. Waiting to be told what to do.

Waiting for Serena.

Or...me, Charlie realised. *I raised one from the ground already. It was waiting for my orders until my mother took it over. If I can just break free of her Influence, I—*

Serena placed her hand on the top of Charlie's head, forcing her to face her. Charlie could see herself in her mother's eyes, her hair glamoured to look like the woman Charlie had once loved so much.

All she wanted now was to see gold. Gold to match her father.

Gold to counterbalance Daniel Silver.

"You will behave," Serena ordered, words dripping with Intent. "You will control the humans on my behalf, keeping them locked in place for my beautiful creatures to destroy. Do you understand?"

"I - I won't," Charlie gasped, though her mind was growing hazy once more. Serena was too strong, and Charlie was all alone.

She needed her friends.

She needed Kit.

She needed Daniel.

She needed her father to tell her everything would be all right. To fight beside Charlie as they had done all her life, together and unstoppable.

A final push of Intent from Serena and Charlie's shoulders slumped. She could no longer think for herself; the only words in her head were her mother's.

Slowly, she nodded.

"I understand."

Chapter Thirty-Eight

The air at the border was tense and electric and full of cloying, suffocating smoke. Edward could hardly see; wordlessly he and Daniel cleared the area around them with a surge of magic so they could make sense of what was going on.

He immediately wished he hadn't.

"Those are – they're really real."

"Really real," Daniel echoed back. He could hardly believe what he was seeing: towering as tall as the burning trees, with blackened skin and rotting flesh, were all manner of silver-eyed creatures.

Noben. Kiroji. Monsters no matter the name.

"They're...not moving," Jean said, his face paling at the mere sight of them. "Just what are they waiting for?"

Beside him Luca seemed like she might be sick. Daniel couldn't blame either of them for the way they'd reacted: literal monsters were their enemy.

But they weren't the enemy Daniel nor Edward most feared.

"Silver, thank Uthesh you're here!" Jonathan Crank cried out from the protection of a magic-drawn carriage. His skin was covered in sweat, his chest heaving as he struggled to breathe the hot, terrible air.

"Where are the Eshijani?" Daniel asked him, ignoring the immobile Noben for now even though they were all he could think about. "Where is the fighting?"

"Nobody got that far! By the time I got here these – creatures – had appeared all along the border. Everyone is working together to fight them off but they just don't seem to die!"

"They're *already* dead," Grandmaster Feng said, standing beside Daniel to address Crank. "They're being controlled by a necromantic Immortal Folk."

"I – you must be kidding," Crank sputtered out, incredulous. He waved at the Noben. "How could these be – an *Immortal Folk* is responsible? How could this happen? Why didn't we have any warning of this?"

"It's too long a story for now," Crimson said. "Just focus on the Kiroji – the monsters – and leave the fires to me." She glanced at Daniel. "I won't be able to concentrate on the flames *and* on illusions, so keep me out of Charlie's notice if you can."

He nodded, then Crimson fled across the border towards the flaming woods, red hair flashing in the process. She zigzagged around the Noben as if they were mere static obstacles, fearless and focused as she began pulling the flames away from the trees and snuffing them out.

"She's...wow," Edward couldn't stop himself from saying, watching Crimson get to work without a moment's doubt. "She's very impressive."

"Took you long enough to notice," Luca said, rolling her eyes. Then she walked towards Crank's carriage. "Take me to the densest population of soldiers and magicians. My healing magic is useless to them if I'm not actually around them to use it."

The man opened the door and let her in as if on reflex. "Do you have a plan, Silver?" he asked. "Please tell me you have a plan."

"Of course I have a plan," Daniel said. "Use all those silver bullets you've had me make for months now against the Noben. They won't pose a threat if they're blown to pieces."

"And the Immortal Folk?"

"Don't go near anyone who comes out of the woods. Don't give them reason to notice you. Now go destroy the damn monsters before they start destroying you!"

Crank didn't need to be told twice. The carriage pulled him and Luca away, out of the clear air Edward and Daniel had wrapped around their group and through the smoke towards the invisible Atralian and Eshijani armies.

Daniel turned to Edward, Feng and Jean. "Let's see just how many Noben we can take down together before the Immortal Folk show up."

Before Charlie shows up.

As he approached the first one Daniel was struck by how oddly beautiful the rotting monsters were. They looked like damned, fallen gods, too powerful and otherworldly for mere humans to take down.

But take them down Daniel would.

Inhaling deeply, Daniel put his hands together for a moment before spreading them out before him. The closest Noben – a gargantuan, bird-like creature whose wings were full of broken feathers – began to change from black to silver. Slowly, slowly, slowly, then faster and faster until the entire immobile monster had been transmuted into silver.

"Edward!" he called, over his shoulder. The man moved forward, grim and determined, and sent out a violent wave of magic which shattered the Noben into a thousand pieces of shining metal.

Made and unmade in silver, Daniel thought as they moved

onto the next one. *It's almost poetic.*

To their left Feng and Jean were using simple slashing magic to hack the Noben to pieces. When Daniel realised the body parts were pulling themselves back together, however, he blasted them with silver to stop them in their tracks.

"Is there anything you *can't* do with that one form of magic?" Edward asked, narrowly avoiding being hit on the head by a clawed and rotting hand when Jean cut it from a bear-like Noben.

"Apparently not," Daniel replied, thinking back to the gala when Charlie had, conversely, asked him if working with silver was all he *could* do.

Charlie, Daniel thought, heart twisting painfully as they took down another Noben, then another. In the distance Crimson had put out one portion of the burning woods and had moved on to the next section before it could ignite the blackened remains she had already saved.

"You'd think the volcanoes had erupted, it's so hot!" Jean exclaimed, pausing for a moment to take a ragged breath. He was right; beneath his robes Daniel felt like he was melting. But the volcanoes which bordered the woods were still and silent as the Noben.

What if they weren't? Daniel wondered, pulling off his robe and dumping it unceremoniously on the floor. He undid the top three buttons of his shirt for all the good it would do, then sent out a gentle wave of cooling magic across everyone. They sighed in appreciation and nodded their thanks when it hit them.

"You've given me an idea, Jean," Daniel said, eyeing the dormant volcanoes. "A foolish one, and a *hot* one, but an idea nonetheless."

Jean saw where he was looking and caught on immediately to what Daniel was insinuating. "Do you really believe you can cause a *volcano* to erupt?"

"Do you believe you can make the *illusion* of one?" Daniel countered. "To clear the area and have everyone evacuate?" *The fewer people around when the Immortal Folk – and Charlie – arrive, the better.*

"I can try," Jean said, eyes flashing at the challenge.

"Grandmaster Feng, could you lead the evacuation?"

The old man nodded, then promptly ran in the direction Crank and Luca had gone with the spryness of someone a third his age.

Daniel left Jean to it and slowly approached the woods. Once everyone was gone he *would* try and erupt the volcanoes, to melt and encase every single one of the Noben in molten rock in one fell swoop.

It was a reckless plan, but an efficient one if he could manage it. If he—

"Daniel, stop what you're doing."

The words came from the edge of the woods, awful and familiar and terrifying in their Intent.

Daniel froze, hands in front of him brimming with the magic he had been about to let loose. Through the smoke a figure came towards him, closely followed by the hulking figure of a horned Noben.

"Don't stop me, Charlie!" he shouted at her, glancing at Jean and realising, too late, that he was too busy with his volcano illusion to help Daniel evade Charlie's Influence.

As she came through the smoke Daniel was met by a wretched, blank look on Charlie's face that meant he had no hope of getting through to her. *Charlie* was being Influenced.

Daniel's words would mean nothing to her.

"Put your hands down," Charlie said, deceptively gently. She closed the distance between them, brushing her fingertips over

Daniel's until he lowered his hands. A lovely smile spread across her face. "Now kneel."

He was powerless against her magic; Daniel knelt before her, face tilted up to appeal to the woman he so dearly loved.

"Charlie, you're being controlled," he said, knowing it was useless. Pointless. But if Daniel could keep Charlie's attention then perhaps Edward still had a chance of avoiding her Influence.

Charlie's smile grew sickeningly sweet. "*You* are the one being controlled. By me. The way it should be."

"Charlie—"

Behind her the Noben roared, and all at once dozens of other blackened creatures sprung to terrible, haunted life. A willowy figure in a white dress, with antlers upon her wild hair, leapt easily from the Noben's back to land in front of—

"Edward," she said, the same sick smile that was on Charlie's face curling her lips. "You don't look pleased to see me. Haven't you missed me?"

Despite the smoke and the heat all the colour drained from Edward's face. Part of him had hoped, somehow, that his wife was truly gone. That he'd never have to see her again.

But here she was, facing him.

"Serena," Edward gasped, before an overwhelming surge of Intent forced him to his knees right beside Daniel.

They were powerless.

They had lost.

CHAPTER THIRTY-NINE

CHARLIE'S MIND WAS A MESS. One moment it was thick and heavy as mud, dragging her consciousness away from her body and rendering her unable to do anything. The next it was driven by a singular clarity: a goal which she *had* to achieve.

Destroy the humans who wished to harm her and her kin. Obliterate them from existence.

And then...

And then?

Dimly she was aware that Daniel was kneeling before her, and her father before her mother. There was a smile on Charlie's face that she didn't want to be there.

A curdled scream filled the air.

"Don't let her do this," Daniel bit out, eyes darting from Charlie to her mother and then back again. He was streaked in ash and sweat, shirt ruffled and undone to combat the heat. He was a mess; *Charlie's* mess.

"Be obedient and she won't have to hurt you," Serena said, inspecting Daniel with obvious curiosity. Her eyes roved his face and then cast downwards, lingering on the low V Daniel's unbuttoned shirt made over his chest. An outraged blush spread across his cheeks. It should have made Charlie furious to see her mother look at Daniel like that. It *did*, in fact, but she had no willpower to voice her anger.

"You have excellent taste, Charlotte," Serena purred. "Of all the human men you could have chosen you picked the best of them. And he's the immortal Daniel Silver! Even among the Folk his abilities are respected. It would be a shame to hurt him."

"Get out of my daughter's head," Edward spat out. Charlie had never seen him so furious – or afraid. But there was no confusion in his expression.

He knew what my mother was already. What she was capable of. He knew what that made me, and never told me.

Why didn't he tell me?

A roar interrupted the confrontation, followed by the sound of more screams. Human screams. Charlie breathed in through her nose and smelled blood.

Her forced grin turned manic.

"This won't take long, will it?" she asked her mother. It was taking Charlie every ounce of willpower she possessed to spread out her Influence across the Atralian and Eshijani armies, freezing them to the spot in order for the Noben to slaughter them all.

"Not long at all, my daughter," Serena crooned. She placed a slender-fingered hand beneath Edward's chin, tilting his gaze up to her own. "You did well raising her on your own, dear Edward. She really is quite talented. I couldn't have done this without her. And, by extension, without you. You have my thanks."

A low growl escaped through Edward's teeth. "Forgive me for not showing my gratitude properly."

"Oh, but you are!" she laughed. "My poor husband, having

you on your knees before me, worshipping me as you did all those years ago, is the only form of gratitude I want."

"I never worshipped you. I knew exactly what you were. If it hadn't been for Charlie I'd have run from you in a moment."

Serena's eyes glinted dangerously. "I prefer your fear to your love, foolish man. Surely you must know that."

"Do not fight her, Da," Charlie said, tightening her Influence upon him until no more words escaped his lips.

"Don't use your magic on him," Daniel begged. He was shaking from head to toe, physically resisting the hold Charlie had over him. "You told me you never would. That it was the one rule you'd never break. Just look at what that witch is making you do, Charlie! This isn't you!"

Serena hissed. "Call me a witch again and see if you escape my wrath with both of your lovely eyes intact, Mr Silver."

"I'll claw yours out with my own hands first."

A violent burst of magic sent Daniel sprawling across the ground. Charlie's heart twisted painfully at the sight of him lying in the dust, a bruise blooming across his chest like a dark and horrible flower, and her hand twitched towards him.

"Don't hurt him," Charlie warned her mother. "Touch him again and I won't forgive you."

Serena frowned at her, clearly concerned that her Influence was waning. From the ground Daniel realised that forcing Charlie's mother to hurt him was perhaps his best bet to break the hold she had over her daughter.

Above the trees plumes of acrid smoke and lashings of red began bubbling from the volcanoes.

Jean! Daniel thought, triumphant. *He must have escaped Charlie's Influence.* He exchanged the smallest glance with Edward, confirming that the man had noticed the illusion, too.

"As if you could actually hurt me," Daniel threw at Serena,

baiting her into attacking again. Charlie was wavering before his very eyes; all he had to do was use himself and the illusion of the volcano to break her free.

Break everyone free.

"I won't warn you again," Serena said, more magic bursting from her to knock the wind out of Daniel. "Don't insult me or —"

"Charlie, get out of here!" Edward cried out, eyes wide as the volcano exploded and spewed lava over the woods. All the areas Crimson had managed to remove the flames from erupted into orange and red and yellow once more.

It was closing in on them.

Or, at least, that's what it looked like to Charlie and Serena.

"The Immortal Folk," Charlie gasped, face pale, body shaking, but eyes miraculously, thankfully lucid. She turned to her mother. "We have to retreat, otherwise everyone will—"

"Let them burn," Serena said, waving a dismissive hand.

"But they'll die!"

"And be reborn in a few hundred years. What does it matter if they lose their physical forms today in the grand scheme of things?"

"You can't mean that!" Charlie panicked, gaze darting to the burning woods in obvious distress. "You can't – Kit is in there – Kit is *in there*!"

"No, he isn't," Serena pointed out, when the scurrying figure of a tawny cat careened beneath the feet of the Noben they had ridden through the woods. A few leaps and bounds later and Kit joined the group, breathing heavily.

"I have confirmation about the location of the tomb," he panted, turning from a cat to his true form. "Two hours across the border into Eshijan."

Serena clapped her hands, delighted. "Excellent work. You

can lead us there."

"But there's *lava* coming through the woods!" Charlie reminded her. "We can't—"

"There's no lava," Kit said, confused. "There's hardly any fire in the woods at all now; Crimson's put it all out."

Daniel's face fell at how easily his planned deception was ruined. Serena glared at him, then at Edward. "A clever trick, if it would have worked. Unfortunately even the best humans are stupid when compared to the Immortal Folk."

Charlie struggled with her own mind as she watched Serena once more take hold of Edward's face, kneeling down in the dirt as if she meant to embrace him. "You have long since outlived your usefulness, my husband. I might have almost loved you once, in my own way, if you hadn't been so hopelessly human."

A low chuckle, then she placed a kiss on his lips. Edward could do nothing but accept it. "But my true love – my one and only love – has now been found, and we shall soon be reunited. I hardly think it's appropriate for me to have a husband, don't you agree?"

Serena drove a dagger through his heart.

The scream that escaped Charlie's lips was far more feral and terrifying than the Noben's as she watched her father cough up blood and stare down at the hole in his chest in disbelief.

Serena stood up and turned for the woods, not in the least bit interested in watching Edward die. "Come, Charlotte," she said, waving for her to join her.

But Charlie fell to her knees beside her father and held him up with shaking hands. "*D-Daniel!*" she shrieked, desperately trying to find a song that would heal her father. But no words or sounds came to Charlie, even when Edward's eyes glazed over and he slumped against her chest.

"Daniel!" she cried again, and he realised he could move. He could move again, and he could use his magic.

Rushing to Charlie's side he placed his hands on Edward's head. It was difficult, with the smoke in his nose and adrenaline in his system and magic all around him, for Daniel to concentrate, but if he couldn't focus now then Edward Hope would die and a part of Charlie would with him, too.

From Daniel's fingertips the man's veins glittered silver, then his muscles and bones and, finally, his skin, until Edward was no longer an organic creature but one of metal, instead.

"Until we can heal him," Daniel reassured Charlie, when fat, hot tears of horror began falling in earnest from her eyes. Daniel kissed her hair, eased the heavy, metallic body of Edward Hope to the ground, then wrenched Charlie into his arms.

"Keep her out," he murmured into her ear, when Charlie began sobbing. "Keep her out of your head. You can do this. You can do this. You can—"

Both of them were forced to their feet with an overwhelming surge of Intent, and Charlie gasped. Daniel barely managed to hold her up alongside himself.

"I said *come*," Serena hissed. Beside her Kit stared at Charlie and Daniel, together again, and a flash of his old self returned. But it vanished as soon as Daniel saw it, and his friend began bounding towards the woods for them all to follow.

They had no choice but to leave Edward Hope behind, moments from death forever immobilised in pure silver.

CHAPTER FORTY

Being forced to use transport magic once they were past the border to take Serena closer to the tomb she meant to find lit a fire in Daniel that helped combat the woman's Influence.

Or that could be Charlie's doing, he reasoned, helping her climb over a smoking, fallen tree trunk as they searched for the exact location. She hadn't spoken once since Serena forced them to accompany her to the supposed tomb of her lost love: the mad magician.

Charlie hadn't spoken a word but she sobbed and wailed and cried, instead. Daniel desperately wished that he could help her. Wished that he possessed the strength to pull them both away from Serena and back to poor, ensilvered Edward Hope, so Charlie could sing his life and health back into him.

Daniel had to cling to the idea that it wasn't too late to save him. *His heart was still beating,* he thought, over and over again as Kit led their odd group deeper into the woods. The Drus kept looking back at them, his expression becoming more and more wretched as the minutes ticked by.

Kit could feel Charlie's grief. Daniel knew because he could feel it, too. Her agony and heartbreak and ice-cold fury were palpable, cutting right through Serena's Intent and thus freeing

Kit from the choke-hold she had over him.

And soon Kit will be himself through and through, then he can help us.

Daniel had to pray that this would be the case. If Kit wasn't on their side once he was no longer Influenced then Daniel didn't know what he could do.

Behind them Serena rode upon her Noben, carelessly knocking down any trees and plants and animals that were in her path. She had clearly gone mad - or had always been mad, Daniel reasoned - to possess such a lack of empathy for her home. The home of her people.

If the Immortal Folk ever broke free of Serena's Influence Daniel was fairly certain they would no longer be *her* people.

When they came upon a smooth slab of stone, scorched from the fire and recessed into the ground, Kit stopped walking. "There was a huge oak tree grown over this," he explained. "The Eshijani cut it down to make stakes so they could hide them along the border."

"You mean Serena did," Daniel corrected, not caring if the unearthly woman retaliated for his pointed remark. She no longer had a hold over Charlie's thoughts and speech, merely her actions, and had done the one thing that guaranteed Charlie would never again listen to a single word her mother Influenced into her.

In trying to murder Edward Hope all Serena had achieved was pushing Charlie closer to her humanity than she had ever been before.

Daniel almost thought he should thank her.

"Open the stone," Serena ordered, ignoring Daniel's comment in favour of sliding off the Noben to investigate Kit's find.

But Kit didn't move. His long ears twitched. "I don't possess the magic nor the strength to do so. Daniel does, though."

At first Daniel wanted to hit him for saying such a thing. He didn't want to be forced to use his magic on behalf of Serena, after all. But then he saw the look Kit gave him, and Daniel realised he *wanted* him to use his magic.

What are you up to? Daniel wondered. For Kit *did* possess the magic to break the stone; if he needed Daniel to do it for him then that meant Kit was up to something.

Scheming. Planning.

Daniel had to trust that whatever he had in mind would work.

"Do it, then," Serena said, not even bothering to Influence Daniel. She was so confident that he'd do what she wanted for fear of a dagger going through his heart that there was no point in wasting magic.

When Daniel tried to let go of Charlie's hand to break the stone she merely tightened her shaking grip on him. "Don't let go," she urged in hushed tones so that her mother wouldn't hear. "My hold over you is stronger if we maintain contact."

He brushed his lips across her ear. "Then I won't let go," Daniel murmured, reassured that, beneath her shell-shocked exterior and shattering grief, Charlie's brain was still working. Assessing the situation. Trying to find a solution.

With Kit *and* Charlie working with Daniel rather than against him he allowed himself to believe that they would make it out of their awful situation in one piece.

Right hand intertwined with Charlie's, Daniel reached out with his left and sent out a sharp, focused stab of magic towards the stone. It cracked satisfyingly in two, then four, then ten, then hundreds of tiny pieces when Daniel fired more and more magic at it.

Serena never took her eyes off the crumbling stone, impatiently waiting as Daniel pushed aside the dust and detritus to reveal a deep, gaping hole in the earth. When he risked a glance at Kit he saw that the Drus had edged towards the Noben, who remained still under Serena's command.

I have to keep her attention on the tomb, Daniel worked out.

"Let's go in there and find out what's buried," he told Charlie, who numbly nodded before allowing Daniel to first drop her into the hole and then himself.

He made a globe light to see by; it revealed a narrow room built into the earth barely twice the length of Daniel himself. In the very centre there was a bone-white tomb, untouched by dirt or water or time by a powerful magic seal.

Serena dropped herself down into the hole now that she could see what was going on. With gentle fingers she caressed the tomb, dipping her head to place a kiss at the very top of the stone.

"Open it," she ordered. "But be careful."

"What can you feel in there?" Daniel asked Charlie, when they, too, placed their hands on the stone to work on the magic that sealed the tomb.

She frowned, then pushed her hair out of her face when it obscured her eyes. Seeing that it was still glamoured to look like her mother's Charlie bit her lip then promptly removed the magic cast upon it. When lovely golden waves fell over her shoulders Daniel breathed a heavy sigh of relief.

She's putting herself back together. Good. We can do this if we lean on and trust each other.

"There's life in there," she replied, concentrating on it. "It's...faint. But it's there."

So Daniel sent out a pulse of magic, and the top of the tombstone clattered to the floor. Serena pushed him out of the way to see inside the tomb, green eyes gleaming in the dank, dark air and—

"No. *No,*" she whispered, disbelief causing her gaze to dart to and fro across the sight presented before her. "No, no, no. This can't be."

For a moment Daniel thought the tomb must be empty, but when he looked inside there was a man lying there.

Unmoving. Glazed eyes. Reduced to white hair and sunken skin but still just barely alive. His fingertips were worn down to the bone.

"Wake up," Serena insisted, stroking the man's skull-like face over and over again. But the man did nothing. He simply looked straight through her.

"He has no magic left," Charlie realised in hushed tones. "With no magic to maintain his mind, he..."

"Completely broke down," Daniel finished for her, turning over the stone lid to see scores of blackened, dried blood and ineffectual scratches upon its surface.

"This isn't *fair,*" Serena wailed. Her voice echoed around them in the living grave they stood within. "I spent thousands of years waiting to come back – to bring you back – so why are you *not there?*"

Charlie stared at her mother, hard-eyed and stony-faced. "Are you happy now? Look, here's your *lost love.* Now leave us alone."

For a while Serena did nothing but gaze at the mad magician, silent and disturbed. But then she turned her attention to Daniel. "No," she said, straightening to face them, a new agenda plain as day in her twisted expression. "No, you cannot be together when I have nothing. You have your father, Charlotte; you're free to heal him and do with him what you wish. Live your silly human life with him and grieve his loss when he dies and you must live on. But I need a replacement. A *new* love. And you..."

She smiled at Daniel, eerie and lovely in equal measure. He

could do nothing but stand there, frozen by a fresh wave of her Intent, as Serena walked around the tomb to stroke his face just as she had done her old, weary partner.

"You'll do just fine."

CHAPTER FORTY-ONE

"Don't you dare touch him."

Charlie pushed her mother away before she could wrap her hand around Daniel's collar. Serena looked as if she was torn between laughing and shouting; instead, she used her magic to force all three of them out of the tomb. Charlie held onto Daniel as tightly as she could, not wanting to risk losing him to Serena's Influence.

In the burned-out woods the Noben stood waiting for Serena but Kit was nowhere to be found. Serena began kicking stone fragments back into the tomb, a mad grin on her face. "I bury my grief here and begin again," she said. "So now, Charlotte, be a good daughter and hand over Mr Silver."

"I *told* you you're not going to touch him," Charlie growled, standing in front of Daniel to protect him. If the situation hadn't been so serious she would have found the notion funny, for Daniel towered over her and possessed far more violent magic than Charlie could ever hope to muster.

But still she stood in front of him and kept her mother back.

Daniel maintained a grip on Charlie's shoulder, reassured by the feeling of her skin beneath his fingertips. It kept him level-headed and free of the worst of Serena's Intent. But he felt useless. He wanted to burn her from existence. Eliminate her from his life, and Charlie's.

Burn, burn, burn, he thought, breathing in the lingering smell of smoke from the blackened remains of the woods. When Daniel felt a faint rumbling in the ground he turned his gaze upwards, to the volcanoes.

Their summits were beginning to glow and smoulder.

Serena laughed easily when she saw what he was looking at. "You think I can be fooled by the same illusion? You really never learn, do you? Now come stand by my side."

A hook in Daniel's brain bucked his body forward, slamming him so brutally into Charlie that they both fell over, Charlie beneath Daniel, pinned to the forest floor.

She twisted around as much as she could. "Resist her!" she exclaimed, running her hands over the bruise on Daniel's chest so he could feel her touch against his heart. It was throbbing erratically, as if Serena was trying to pull it from his chest so she could lock it up.

Daniel's eyes began to glaze over; beneath him he could see Charlie no longer but the shadow of her mother.

"Serena..." he murmured, a horrible smile on his face.

"Damn it, Daniel, don't speak her name!" Charlie cried, wringing his shirt in her fists to pull him closer to her. "Don't let me hear her name in your voice!"

Above them Serena laughed and laughed, certain of her iron grip on Daniel Silver's love and affection. Charlie knew she had to do something. Her touch was not enough. Her Influence was not enough. Her words were not enough.

Or they're not the right words.

"Daniel, I love you!" Charlie bit out, the words tumbling from her mouth. She held Daniel's face between her hands, pulling his lips to hers so she could kiss them. "I love you," she breathed. She kissed him again. Again, more insistently, then once more for good measure. "I love you, not her. You said it before, right? When you begged me not to go. You knew I loved you, yet I couldn't bring myself to let that be enough to trust you. But I'm saying it is, so *listen* to me!"

For a horrible moment Daniel didn't respond to Charlie's confession, nor her kiss. But then slowly, slowly, slowly, his hands slid through Charlie's hair and his mouth opened up against hers. Daniel kissed her back, and deeply, moulding Charlie's body to his own, because it belonged there.

"You aren't stronger than me!" Serena screamed, outraged at the atrocious sight laid out before her. "Your power is nothing compared to mine, Charlotte!"

"It's Charlie," Daniel muttered, the words vibrating against Charlie's lips. The ground rumbled beneath them, and an almighty explosion rent the air. He glared up at Serena. "Not Charlotte. It's Charlie. And she *is* stronger than you. You're nothing next to her!"

The air grew hot. Too hot; Daniel staggered to his feet, bringing Charlie with him, and he realised that lava was flooding down the sides of the volcanoes right into the woods.

Serena's expression was even hotter than the molten rock. "If you believe that then you're perhaps even stupider than Edward. Now *come to me,* or—"

The Noben, which had all but blended into the blackened woods, wrapped its gaping maw around Serena's waist and *crunched.* Only its eyes weren't silver, as they had been before.

No, they were beautiful, vibrant, mischievous green.

"Kit!" Charlie and Daniel cried in unison, triumphant, when the Drus in disguise let go of Serena. She crumpled to the ground, bleeding heavily but not quite dead.

"*You*," she breathed at Kit, disbelief overwriting her fury. "You dare defy me?"

"I dare defy you, yes," he replied, voice strangely twisted from the Noben's mouth. "I dare defend my family."

"Then you dare die, too," Serena said through gritted teeth, a sheen of sweat covering her brow as she let loose a bolt of magic straight at Kit's chest.

His Noben body melted away, leaving Kit standing there with a hole where his heart had been. He stared at it, then at his best friend.

"Dan—Daniel," he stammered. "Char—"

Daniel ran forwards and caught him before he hit the ground. "You're all right," he reassured Kit, holding a hand over his chest to surge magic through Kit's body. "Just hold on tight for a minute. We can sort this out."

Charlie stared at the two of them, not wishing to believe what she had just witnessed. *Kit can't die,* she thought. *Not like this. Not because of me.*

She turned her attention to her mother. Serena's mouth was full of blood, but she choked out a laugh. "I will heal myself and wreak my revenge," she said. "I have my creatures. I have my magic. I will defeat you."

"You will have the same fate as your *one true love*," Charlie spat out, before unceremoniously kicking Serena into the broken tomb of the mad magician. Serena let out a scream but in her heavily injured state she could do nothing to escape the hole – the prison, the grave – Charlie had thrown her into.

The trees around them began to collapse. The ground beneath them was too hot to stand on. "Daniel," Charlie bit out, rushing to kneel beside him and Kit. Kit was barely breathing; his eyes roved beneath their lids at a feverish pace. "We need to get out of here. Otherwise—"

He took Charlie's hands and placed them over Kit's chest. "Sing to him, and I'll get us out. Just...sing."

So Charlie sang, though the words were garbled and full of tears. She barely noticed when Daniel pulled his magic over the three of them to lift them out of the forest and away, away, away.

The woods beneath them turned hot, molten red. Serena's screams filled Charlie's ears, interfering with her song, so Charlie merely sang louder. *Hold on, Kit,* she thought, as his blood coated her skin and Daniel's grip on her shoulder was the only thing that kept her upright.

"Look," Daniel murmured in her ear. They were still floating above the woods; from their vantage point Charlie realised she could see the rest of the Noben melting and burning to nothing. To her relief not a single soul left on the ground was human nor Immortal Folk.

"Jean, Crimson and Feng must have got them out," Daniel said, frowning in concentration as he directed his magic towards his estate. Eventually they passed the border, and he discovered he could summon them there with a click of his fingers.

They barely touched down when he ran to the edge of the woods and pushed every ounce of his magic out of his body, sending a blast of bitter, freezing wind towards the encroaching lava. It slowed, then lost its angry glow, and eventually all that was left was smooth, glassy rock.

Daniel heaved a breath into his lungs, hardly able to stand. He had never used so much magic before. Every cell in his body ached. He wanted to lie down and sleep.

He couldn't.

"Daniel! Charlie!" a voice screamed out. Jean, Crimson and Luca came running towards them, the silver figure of Edward Hope levitating between them. By the looks of their shining, flushed faces and filthy clothes they had barely escaped the lava.

"Over here," he gasped, waving them over as he collapsed beside Kit. Charlie was still singing to him, her voice trembling but working creation magic upon the Drus nonetheless. Kit's expression had softened, no longer in pain but instead merely floating through Charlie's song.

He'll be all right, Daniel realised, overwhelmed with relief. *He's going to pull through.*

Which meant they had to turn their attention to Edward.

"Luca," Daniel said, kneeling beside the silver man with the dagger sticking out of his chest, "how good do you think you are at creating a new human heart?"

She glanced at Charlie. "If she can help me, I can do it."

"Then do it."

CHAPTER FORTY-TWO

EVERY LINE OF EDWARD HOPE'S FACE was immortalised in silver. Every smile, every frown, every cry of despair.

"Charlie," Daniel said, still breathing heavily. He didn't know if he had the strength left to ease Edward back to flesh and blood and bone.

But he had to.

"Charlie," he said again, when she didn't move from Kit. "Charlie, Luca and I need your help with this."

Her singing faltered. She stared at her bloody hands, still held over Kit's chest. "He's - he's—"

"He'll be all right," Daniel said, because Kit had to be. "I can't bring your father back without you."

"I'll keep his blood pumping," Crimson said, kneeling down beside Kit. Her red hair was scorched and blackened, and she was covered in burns, but none of that seemed to bother her. "Jean can help me."

The man dutifully complied; it was only once they gently extricated Charlie's hands that she stumbled over to her father.

Looking at his face, twisted in pain and moments away from

death, Charlie choked on a sob. But then Daniel took her hands in his and squeezed them. "Just focus. We can do this. Luca is making a new heart already. See?"

"All you have to do is help your father accept it," Luca said, smiling reassuringly. In the air she was twisting muscle fibres together, the skeleton of a heart slowly but surely beginning to materialise.

Charlie gulped, closed her eyes for a moment, then placed her bloody hands on Edward's temples. "I'm ready," she breathed.

She began singing.

She's ready, but am I? Daniel wondered, struggling to bring the magic forward that was necessary to transfigure Edward Hope from silver to man again. He couldn't fail. For Charlie to lose her father after everything that had been thrown at her...Daniel couldn't bear it.

So though he thought he might faint, Daniel pushed magic into Edward and focused, focused, focused. He had to be careful about how he brought him back. Extremities and limbs first, then his body cavity, his organs, and last of all his heart and lungs and brain.

"Luca," Daniel bit out, barely able to speak. "Now. You have to work *now.*"

Charlie's forehead was dripping with sweat as she picked up the pace with her singing, forcing life into her father even as Luca removed the dagger in his heart, cut his chest open further and removed the organ. To her credit her hands were sure and steady where Daniel and Charlie's were not.

All around them the air was tense and still. Though Crimson and Jean were focused on keeping Kit alive they were acutely tuned into Edward's literal open heart surgery upon the grass outside Daniel Silver's estate. What was being done was impossible. The chances of success were so small.

Edward pulled in a ragged breath, then another and another.

"Don't move," Luca ordered when he began shifting. "We're pulling your skin back together."

"My...what's going on?"

"Hush, Mr Hope. Just let us work for a while longer."

"Charlie," Edward croaked. With some effort he concentrated on his daughter – on the touch of her fingertips on his temples, on the sound of her voice, on the tears that filled her eyes as she watched the colour return to his face – and smiled. "You're safe."

"Of course," she gasped, voice wet with tears. "As if anything bad was going to happen to me or you. Nobody messes with the Hopes."

A garbled cough as Luca finished sealing Edward's skin. "Nobody," he agreed, struggling into a sitting position with Charlie's help. He touched his chest, then, and saw the dagger lying beside him. "What happened? I – Serena, she—"

"Daniel turned you into silver," Charlie explained, becoming more animated now that her father genuinely seemed to be okay. "Into *silver*. It was awful but it was also amazing. Then he *made all the volcanoes erupt and buried that witch who was my mother beneath the lava.*"

Edward stared at Daniel, amazed and astounded. The man was hardly conscious and swayed dangerously on the spot. "I... thank you, Daniel," Edward said, knowing there were no words to express his gratitude. "It seems I owe you a massive favour."

A delirious smile spread across Daniel's face that looked more like a grimace. "Don't have another half-Immortal child and we'll call it even."

Then Daniel staggered over to Kit and collapsed beside him. He prodded his friend's face as if he were a child. "Wake up," he said. "We have to fix you now."

"I don't think I know how to make an Immortal Folk heart," Luca admitted.

"I only need my own magic," Charlie said, ensuring her father was steady enough to sit upright on his own before coming over. "Anything that can be done, I can do alone."

Except Charlie knew nothing she did would be enough. She'd realised it as she sang to Kit to keep him alive as they escaped the forest.

But Daniel didn't know.

"Hey, sleepy-head," she murmured, sitting next to Kit's head on the opposite side to Daniel. He was holding his friend's hand, still conscious through sheer force of will and nothing else. Charlie knocked her knuckles on Kit's brow. "Come on, I know you're awake."

"Mhmm," Kit replied. "Don't you know it's rude to wake an Immortal Folk before they're ready to get up?"

"Don't you know it's rude to make me have to tell Daniel you don't *want* to wake up?"

Daniel stilled. He turned his head and found that Kit had turned to face him, too, his vibrant eyes just a little duller than they usually were.

"What does Charlie mean?" he whispered.

Kit smiled softly. "I'm tired, Daniel. I need a break for a while. And I think – no, I *know* – that you and Charlie deserve some time without me for now."

"Don't say that," Charlie scolded, inspecting the gaping hole in Kit's chest when Crimson pulled her hands away. "It's the three of us, together, remember? I can fix this, so—"

But Kit reached for her hand and pulled it away from his chest. "I know you can. Both of you are so strong; you can do anything. But I'm not so strong. I just want to sleep for a while."

Daniel refused to believe what he was hearing. "You don't

get to do this to me. You're my best friend, Kit. You're my *only* friend."

"Liar." Kit chuckled. "Just look around you. You are not as detached as I sometimes led you to believe. But I was jealous; I wanted you all to myself. Until Charlie came along."

He turned his head to face her. "When the time comes that I return, Charlie...can we laze in the sun and walk through the woods once more?"

"Of course. Of course." Charlie gripped his hand in both of her own. "I'll be right here, waiting for you."

"Daniel—"

"*No*," Daniel cut in. He leaned into Kit, resting his forehead against his shoulder. "You're not dying. Who was the one who convinced me to become immortal?"

"You silly creature." Kit stuck out his tongue. "I'm not dying, not really. I'll be back."

"In hundreds of years. You expect me to live hundreds of years without you?"

With difficulty Kit pulled Daniel and Charlie's hands together, across his stomach. They exchanged a hopeless glance before both looking at Kit.

The green of his eyes was fading.

"It'll pass in a heartbeat," Kit said. "Ah, no cruel joke intended. But you have each other, and that's all that matters. You have to make a million memories, then share them with me in the future! Do you promise?"

"I promise," Charlie whispered. "I'll see the whole world then tell you about all my favourite places."

The smallest of smiles. Kit's ears drooped. "Good. I'll look forward to it. Daniel—"

"You love me. I know." Daniel ruffled Kit's hair, scratching him behind his ear one final time.

For now.

"And you love me, too," Kit replied, nuzzling into the touch. "Take good care of each other."

Then, just like that, Kit was gone.

Daniel and Charlie didn't say a word. They kept their hands entwined over Kit, hardly able to process what had happened. Even when Edward, Crimson, Luca and Jean slowly eased them to their feet they didn't let go of each other.

"Come on," Edward said softly, slinging an arm around his daughter to pull her towards Daniel's house. "You need to sleep. We *all* need to sleep."

Charlie knew he was right, but still it felt wrong. There was so much to do. Atralia and Eshijan and the woods were a mess, their collective peoples damaged and confused. Charlie had to fix it.

One look at Daniel Silver and his lost, heartbroken face was all it took to change her mind.

"Sleep," Charlie agreed, allowing everyone to help her and Daniel to his bedroom. It was a struggle – everyone was exhausted and injured, and Daniel was taller than everyone else – but, eventually, Charlie and Daniel were dropped gently upon his bed.

Only once the door was closed and they had lain together in stunned silence for several long minutes, too tired and upset to clean the filth that covered their skin, did Daniel finally move of his own accord.

"Don't leave me, Charlie," he cried, voice cracking on her name, burying his head against her chest when she pulled him into her arms. "D-don't leave me, and I won't leave you."

It was the most vulnerable Charlie had ever heard him be. Had heard *anyone* be.

"I don't ever want to be without you," Charlie reassured him, kissing the crown of Daniel's head. Then, because all she could think to do in such a dire situation was to lighten the mood: "Although you might get sick of me once my year of employment is up."

Daniel let out a strangled laugh at the ridiculous comment. "Oh, Uthesh be good, you're fired. You missed too many days of work."

"That's fair. I think there's a job I'd be better at, anyway."

Daniel stilled in her arms. When he looked up at Charlie there was a determined glint in her eyes he hadn't expected to see. "And what...what would that job be?" he asked, either too numb or too stupid to work it out for himself.

Charlie grinned, though after everything that had happened it felt altogether too forced. Still, she held it in place. She and Daniel – and everyone else – had to move forward. They *had* to.

"Mayor of Mt. Duega," she said, laughing at the look on Daniel's bemused face. "I like the prospect of protecting that one little corner of the world from harm, the woods and Immortal Folk included. Think my da will hand the position over?"

"For you? He'd give you the world if you asked for it."

"Would you still love me if I lived in a little house by the woods instead of in your massive estate?"

Daniel pretended to mull over his answer. In truth it had been something he'd been considering ever since he fully accepted his feelings for Charlie Hope. "How about I live there with you, instead? It's high time I took a break from politics and enjoyed my immortality...and if your father is so cruelly out of a job perhaps I can convince him to take over my spot on the Lopox Alliance. What do you think?"

When Charlie dipped her face Daniel eagerly tilted his upwards to kiss her. "I think," she breathed against his lips, "that's the best idea you've had since the day I met you."

"Oh, it's the second, for sure."

"What was the first?"

Daniel stared at her, utterly incredulous at Charlie not immediately knowing. Her hazel eyes grew soft when he stroked her cheek. "Taking you on to repay the massive favour I owed Edward Hope, of course."

For a moment Charlie froze. It shocked her – even now – to know that Daniel truly loved her. A blush spread across her ashen face, bringing her deliciously back to life in his eyes.

"...it's a good thing you have forever, then," she murmured, smile bashful in the face of Daniel's affection. "Repaying such a massive favour is no easy task."

"Do you think my debt will be paid by the time Kit decides to wake up from his overly long nap?"

Charlie squeezed her arms around Daniel. It would take a very long time indeed for either of them to stop hurting whenever they thought of or spoke about Kit.

But it would get better. Time, after all, was what they needed to recover, and time was exactly what they had.

"Maybe," Charlie said, finally allowing herself to fall into a heavy slumber alongside Daniel Silver, "or maybe it will simply take forever."

Epilogue

"Could you help me with this, Crimson? I can't quite get to grips with your quantity spell."

"I told you to call me Wei, Edward. My hair isn't even red anymore."

"You spent so long correcting me before that it's hard to stop!" Edward said, shifting over when the woman took hold of the spell that was still cultivating between his hands.

She laughed softly. "I suppose you're right. But we've been working together for two months now; it's high time you got the name of your own employees correct."

"I'd hardly call you my *employee,* Crim...Wei."

"And what else would you call the Chief-of-Staff to the newest Lopox Alliance member?" Wei quirked an eyebrow. "Because last time I checked that made me your employee."

"All right, you got me there," Edward chuckled. "Even so: equals. You're not my subordinate."

Wei's eyes flashed at the comment. "Equals. But then, as your equal, I feel that it's important to tell you that you're late."

"Late? Whatever for?"

She merely stared at Edward expectantly, though an amused smile curled her lips when the realisation of what she meant dawned on his face.

"Daniel!" Edward gasped, pushing the rest of the quantity spell towards Wei before rushing for the door. "I told him I'd help with his garden this afternoon. Thanks for reminding me, Crim – Wei!"

"Say hello to Charlie for me," Wei called out from behind his back, chuckling good-naturedly. Having worked with Edward for two months now she had come to discover that the man could not be more different than Silver. He was hectic, quick to laugh, sociable and loud, and Wei adored him for it. She never imagined that she'd be given the opportunity to work with Edward Hope in such close quarters; now Wei realised it was all she'd wanted for years.

Equals, she mused. *And friends. Maybe, in time, more than that.*

Neither of them wanted to ascend to immortality but, still, it felt like they had all the time the world.

Edward chose to risk transportation magic to get to Daniel and Charlie's new house on the very edge of the woods, though it was a kind of magic which always left him feeling out of breath for several minutes after he used it. But perhaps because he was in such a rush, or because he hadn't seen his daughter for two weeks now, or because the heart Luca had made him was fitter than his previous heart had ever been, Edward's magic worked flawlessly. By the time he rushed around the back of his daughter's newly built, modestly-sized red brick house and into the garden Edward felt barely fazed by his magic.

Daniel Silver was kneeling in front of a large clay pot full of soil, dirt smeared across his forearms and up his white shirt. Edward wondered if the man was aware of the fact he no longer had to dress so formally or if Daniel simply preferred to dress well even when in the comfort of his own home and garden.

At the sound of his approach Daniel straightened up to regard Edward with a stony expression. "You're *late*."

Edward shrugged. "I lost track of the time."

"Like daughter, like father," Daniel replied, his previously unamused mood instantly dissolving into an easy smile at the observation.

"You shouldn't put on such an authoritarian tone of voice outside of work," Edward scolded, sitting down upon an upturned wooden box by Daniel's side. "You're retired now. You should be enjoying the easy life, not giving out lectures."

"I would...if I could get these tomatoes to grow."

"Isn't Charlie helping you?"

"I want to do it on my own. Without magic."

"A noble pursuit, to be sure," Edward said, bending over to inspect the soil in the pot, "but it's already September. A bit of magic to help the plants out before winter creeps up on them wouldn't hurt."

Daniel tutted loudly. "That's what Charlie said, too."

"Where is she, anyway?"

"Where do you think?"

"*Ah.*"

Edward didn't need any further elaboration; of course his daughter was in the woods, in her favourite meadow. Or, rather, where Charlie's favourite meadow had once stood, for the woods were currently a mess of cooled volcanic rock and charred tree trunks.

Charlie and the Immortal Folk had been working around the clock for two months solid to repair the damage wrought upon their home by Serena, the Noben, the Atralians and the Eshijani. But everyone knew it would be a very long time indeed before the forest was as vibrant and teeming with life as it had been before Daniel set the volcanoes to erupt.

Daniel tapped the clay pot somewhat morosely with fingers covered in dirt, at a loss for what to do in the face of his non-growing plants.

"Add peat moss to the soil," Edward finally said, taking pity on him. "You need to make the soil more acidic. Do that and you should see some growth in the next week or so."

"Why didn't you lead with that?" Daniel demanded, a frown creasing his brow.

"I wanted to see if you would take the easy route out first. But if you're serious about gardening then it's time you picked up a book or two and learnt how to do it the old-fashioned way... just like I did."

A pause. Daniel stared off to the west, in the direction of Edward Hope's house. "You were responsible for the garden? Not Charlie?"

He could only laugh. "Of course it was me. Charlie spent too much time running off to the woods to maintain the garden. And besides, whenever she *did* help me the garden grew out of control. Eventually I had to ban her from singing to the plants."

"That sounds like her." Daniel expression softened as he thought of Charlie. His eyes flickered to the woods, then to Edward, then back to the tomato plant. "Perhaps you could go and see her before helping me here," Daniel said. "She misses you, though she hasn't said anything of the sort aloud."

"She's been trying far too hard to be independent lately." Edward chuckled, a little sadly. "I don't want her to ever not rely on me."

"That's the nature of children growing up, Edward."

"I know. But even so...if she is to live on forever then I want to spoil her for every moment I have left with her."

Neither of them said anything about this. Charlie herself had barely made mention of how she was adapting to knowing she would live forever, and her father had not dared broach the subject with her. But not talking about important matters had nearly cost them their lives two months ago; Edward knew he had to be more honest with his daughter.

He stood up, slapping his thighs as he did so. "Right, I'll go and see what my idiot daughter is up to. Will you be all right on your own?"

Daniel rolled his eyes. "It's only gardening. I'll manage."

So Edward picked his way through the garden around fledging vegetable patches, a small apple tree and a wild, twisting rose bush which looked suspiciously like Charlie had gotten to it. The woods began right on the edge of Daniel and Charlie's property; the trees were tall and strong, the edges of their leaves turning yellow with the promise of autumn very nearly on their doorstep.

It was clear Charlie had been using her magic to regrow the woods directly from her house inwards. As Edward made his way further into the forest fewer and fewer trees stood undamaged, and underfoot the ground was smooth with volcanic rock rather than covered in ferns and moss.

One step at a time, Edward thought. *She is fixing the woods one step at a time. It is all she can do.*

Edward could not be prouder of his daughter for understanding she could not fix everything in one fell swoop. If there was one vitally important lesson Charlie had learnt over the past year it had been patience...a lesson Edward himself had never been able to teach her.

It did not take long for Edward to find Charlie. She had worked her magic upon the meadow with the help of the Immortal Folk, who were focused on regrowing the woods starting from the Uthesh fault line, so the clearing acted like something of an oasis within the husk of the woods. But she wasn't singing further growth into the meadow, as Edward expected.

Instead Charlie was sitting beneath the boughs of an oak tree, its trunk and heavy branches towering over the rest of the forest. The monstrous tree was far larger than it had any right to be.

Edward knew why.

It was a memorial for Kit.

"What nonsense are you telling your friend today?" Edward asked, startling Charlie from her position kneeling beneath the tree.

Her posture relaxed when she realised it was her father, and she smiled for him. There were dark circles under her eyes – proof that Charlie's day had begun very early indeed and that she'd likely worked late the night before. "Da," she murmured. "I thought you were supposed to be helping Daniel with the garden?"

"Knowing you, you would have stayed in the forest until the middle of the night and I wouldn't see you," Edward replied, ruffling Charlie's already dishevelled hair as he came to stand beside her. "Does Daniel not miss you when you spend all your time in the woods?"

"He comes here a lot, too," Charlie replied. "And besides, he knows he couldn't stop me from staying in the woods even if he wanted to."

"Try not to make things *too* hard on the poor man."

When Charlie rolled her eyes Edward stifled a laugh. "I don't think he'd have it any other way," she said, wincing when she dragged her fingers through her tangled hair to tie it back. "Does Daniel strike you as someone who demands his partner submit to everything he wants?"

Edward considered this for a moment. Charlie was right, of course. "You don't want him to be lonely, though," he eventually relented. "Especially given..." He waved towards the oak tree.

Mutely Charlie nodded, and returned her attention to the

tree. At its base, etched into the bark, was a beautiful depiction of a cat relaxing in the sun. Daniel had carved the drawing in private one day, once Charlie had exhausted her energy growing the oak tree from a mere acorn and they'd finished burying Kit's corporeal form beneath its roots.

He came out here to talk to his best friend even more often than Charlie did, though Daniel had tried to keep his excursions secret. That didn't stop Charlie from knowing exactly when he traversed into the forest simply to murmur nonsense about his day to the oak tree.

But that was Daniel's grief, not Charlie's. It wasn't something for her to relay to her father.

"Do you want to come round for dinner at the weekend?" Charlie eventually said, choosing not to respond to Edward's previous comment. "I've been learning to cook."

"I thought cooking was beneath you?" Edward teased, though he was happy for Charlie. "That it was for servants and—"

"Make fun of me all you want but I'm getting quite good at it. You'd be surprised."

"Then consider me delighted to attend."

"Bring Wei."

"Now it feels like you have an ulterior motive."

Charlie wrinkled her nose mischievously. "Perhaps. Even so, bring her."

"Fine, fine," Edward relented, not displeased in the slightest with Charlie's ulterior motive. "Do you want me to leave you be for now, then?"

"If you don't mind." Charlie indicated towards the base of the oak tree. "I was in the middle of telling Kit about Daniel trying and failing to grow tomatoes."

"He might be able to grow them yet. Give him the chance to learn."

Charlie snickered. "Oh, I have no doubt he'll work it out... eventually. Love you, Da. See you at the weekend."

"Love you, too. Don't stay out too late."

She didn't reply, which meant Edward knew Charlie was likely to fall asleep precisely where she was currently sitting.

He made sure to tell Daniel when he returned to retrieve his feral daughter before she caught a cold.

Daniel waited until the sun had dipped beneath the horizon and Edward was well on his way home before wandering through the woods to find Charlie. When he came across her, curled up fast asleep beneath the inhumanly large oak tree she had grown just for Kit, his heart swelled with affection.

The two of them had made a habit of talking to the tree almost every day, though neither of them admitted to the other quite how often they really did it. Daniel had never been a man of faith – and indeed didn't feel like starting now – but he couldn't deny that there was something comforting about sitting beneath the branches of the oak tree to talk to his best friend. Daniel couldn't feel his friend's presence any more there than he could in his own garden, or in the market of Mt. Duega, or in the Capital, but the ritual of bringing a bottle of Eshijani apricot liqueur and toasting a drink to the tree almost felt like Kit *was* there, drinking with him.

Almost.

For he wasn't gone, not really. Kit would be back. Whether in five years or five hundred he would return.

It was up to Daniel and Charlie to live the best version of their lives until then.

Quietly, Daniel crept towards Charlie's sleeping figure and knelt by her head, smoothing back tangled locks of golden hair from her face. He shook his head in knowing bemusement at how cold Charlie's skin was against his fingertips.

"You know better than to sleep out here come nightfall now

it's September," Daniel murmured into her ear, easing Charlie back into consciousness. "You'll catch a cold."

"The Immortal Folk would never..." Charlie yawned, struggling to open her eyes. "They would never let me get sick."

Daniel helped her into a sitting position. "Maybe so. But I miss you when you don't come to bed with me. Is that a good enough reason not to sleep in the woods at night?"

Charlie smiled softly at him. Despite the shadows under her eyes, the dirt across her cheeks and the riotous mess of her hair, the smile illuminated Charlie's face like an angel. "How can I refuse such a request?" she said, easing herself onto her knees to stand up. "Lead the way back home, Mr Silver. Ah – *Daniel*."

Without a word Daniel easily swept Charlie into his arms, holding her close against his chest as he began walking through the woods towards their home.

"I can walk, you know," Charlie complained, half-heartedly thumping Daniel's chest with a fist. "I don't need you to carry me."

"But what if I want to? I'm allowed to take care of you, am I not?"

Daniel bent his head to kiss Charlie's hair but his glasses began to slip in the process. She reached out a hand and pushed them back up the bridge of his nose. "Just so long as I can take care of you, too. Da said you're having trouble with the tomatoes."

A thoughtful look crossed Daniel's handsome face. "I think I might be all right now. I've ordered some books from the Capital to help me with the garden."

"You truly *are* an old man."

"I don't care," Daniel said, shrugging as much as he could manage with Charlie in his arms. "I like what I like."

"Now you sound like me."

"Is that a bad thing?"

"Maybe," Charlie giggled, "though I like to think I've been improving as a person over the last few months."

Daniel didn't reply. He merely held Charlie closer to his chest, and whispered a kiss into her hair. He knew Charlie was trying incredibly hard to fix what she perceived to have been an incident she could have – should have – prevented. It would take some time for Daniel to convince Charlie that nothing Serena did had been her fault.

A long stretch of silence fell between them as Daniel resolutely trekked through the mess of the woods. Perhaps, by the time the forest was back to its original state, some of the wounds Charlie and Daniel had both sustained would heal. For the burned husks of trees and smooth, shining trails of volcanic rock underfoot only served to remind Daniel about what they'd lost two months ago – and how close they'd come to losing even more.

Daniel shivered, thinking of the tomb of the mad magician reuniting the man with his immortal paramour, forever encased in cooled magma.

But that wouldn't prevent either of them from *returning* forever. The lava had killed them both, returning their life energy from whence it came: Daniel knew fine well both the mad magician and Serena would come back in one form or another over the next few hundreds or thousands of years.

He hoped thousands.

When Charlie looked up at him in concern Daniel realised she must have caught onto his thoughts. After all, there was no use hiding anything from Charlie Hope and her magic.

"You shouldn't be alone out here for so long," Daniel said, to redirect her attention.

Charlie snickered at the concept. "I can handle myself."

"I don't doubt it. But what if you meet a handsome and

mysterious man who steals your heart?"

"Isn't that man holding me right now?"

"Damn right he is."

Wriggling in his arms, Charlie reached up and kissed Daniel's chin, murmuring in pleasure when he tilted his face down so she could kiss him properly instead.

When she pulled away from the kiss, face flushed and breathless, Charlie joked, "The only other handsome and mysterious man I have space for in my heart is Kit, and he isn't even a man."

"I have no doubt he can hear you from wherever he is, so don't give his ego any further reason to inflate."

"Maybe he'd return faster if we showered him in compliments. How about you actually tell him you love him?"

Daniel had, privately, countless times over the last two months.

"The bastard can come back if he wants to hear me say that," Daniel said, turning his head in the direction of the giant oak tree as if to make sure Kit heard every word.

It was Charlie's turn not to say anything. She merely nuzzled against Daniel's chest, revelling in the warmth and presence of him. She still couldn't quite believe that they were together like this – that they had found their way to each other.

She knew everything else in her very, very long life was bound to change at some point or another, and Charlie was fine with that. It was the inevitable way of things.

Being together with Daniel Silver, however, was the one thing Charlie intended to remain permanent.

No magic required.

PRINCE OF FOXES SAMPLE

Lachlan

TODAY WAS THE QUEEN'S FUNERAL AND LACHLAN, her only child and heir to the throne, was deliberately avoiding the ceremony.

His mother would understand, he was sure. He'd never been one for mournful occasions; most of the Seelie folk weren't. Their lives were long enough to be considered immortal by the humans who largely lived, unknowing and unseeing, beside them. If Lachlan allowed himself to be truly sad he'd spend centuries feeling that way.

It was the last thing he wanted.

So Lachlan was currently whiling away his morning following a human girl who was collecting early autumn brambles on the outskirts of the forest. She lived in Darach, the closest human settlement to the central realm of the Scots fair folk. The people who lived there were, in general, respectful and wary of Lachlan and his kind. They saw what members of the Seelie Court could do fairly regularly, after all. The rest of the British Isles was another story entirely, though it hadn't always been that way.

Everybody in the forest knew things were changing.

The advancements made in human medicine, and human

technology, and human ingenuity, meant that humans were beginning to forget what it felt like to fear 'otherness'. They believed themselves above tales of faeries, and magic in general, though Lachlan knew there were humans capable of magic, too.

Not here, though, he thought, creeping from one tall bow of an oak tree to another to trail silently after the girl. She was happily eating one bramble for every two she placed in her basket, seemingly without a care in the world. *Not on this island. Not for centuries.* Lachlan knew this was largely because his mother, Queen Evanna – as well as King Eirian of the Unseelie Court far down south, in England – spirited all such magically-inclined British children away to the faerie realm, to live for all intents and purposes as faeries themselves.

That's certainly better than being an ordinary human, especially now, when they've forgotten about us.

A stiff breeze tearing through the oak tree caused Lachlan's solitary earring to jingle like a bell. Adorned with delicate chains and tiny sapphires, and spanning the entire length of his long, pointed ear as a cuff of beaten silver, the beautiful piece of jewellery had been a gift from his mother from a time long since passed. Back then Lachlan had been enamoured with the blue-eyed faerie, Ailith, and had been convinced the two of them would marry. The earring was ultimately meant as a gift for Ailith, he'd decided. His mother would never be so direct as to give it to Lachlan's beloved herself. It wasn't in her nature.

But then Queen Evanna had married the half-Unseelie faerie, Innis, who was the Unseelie king's brother. He had himself a grown son, Fergus, who came with his father to live in the Seelie realm. The two were silver where Lachlan and his mother were gold, and Ailith had become betrothed to his new-found stepbrother instead of him.

So Lachlan lost his love and, now, he'd lost his mother. The earring was all he had left of both.

I should go to the funeral, he decided, turning from the girl as he did so. *I am to be king, after all. I should –*

Lachlan paused. He could hear something. More chime-like than his earring in the wind, and clearer than the sound of the nearby stream flowing over centuries-smooth stone.

The human girl was singing.

"The winds were laid, the air was still,

The stars they shot alang the sky;

The fox was howling on the hill,

And the distant echoing glens reply."

Lachlan was enamoured with the sound of her voice. The words were Burns; the melody unfamiliar. He thought perhaps she'd invented the tune herself and, if so, she was a talented girl indeed. He peered through the yellowing leaves of the oak tree, intent on seeing what the human with the lovely voice truly looked like.

She was not so much a girl as a young woman – perhaps not quite twenty – though since Lachlan himself had lived for almost five times that long she was, for all intents and purposes, still simply a girl. Her skin was pale and lightly freckled, though her cheeks held onto some colour from the fast-fading summer. Her hair was a little darker than the oak trunk Lachlan was currently leaning against. It flashed like deep copper when it caught the sunlight and hung long and wild down her back, which was a sight rarely seen on a young, human woman.

A cream dress fell to her ankles and sat low on her shoulders. Small leather boots, made for wandering through forests and across meadows, were laced across her feet. A cloak of pine-coloured fabric was slung over the handle of her almost-full wicker basket. *Well-made clothes,* he concluded, *but nothing elaborate or expensive. Just an ordinary girl.* She dithered over the correct words of the next verse of her Burns poem as Lachlan merrily watched on. *Fair to look at, for a human. But it is her voice that is special. Special enough to ask her name.*

He delighted over thinking how his stepfather and stepbrother would react when he brought back a human girl, enchanted to sing for him until the end of time. *I wonder what Ailith would think. Would she be jealous? Would she mourn for the loss of my attention?*

Lachlan was excited to find out.

He stretched his arms above his head, causing his earring to jingle once more. Below him the girl stilled. She stopped singing, dark brows knitted together in confusion.

"Is somebody there?" she asked, carefully placing her basket down by her feet as she spoke.

"You have a lovely voice," Lachlan announced. He was satisfied to see the girl jump in fright, eyes swinging wildly around before she realised the voice she'd heard came from above. When she spied Lachlan standing high up on the boughs of the oak tree she gasped.

"You are – it is early to see one of your kind so far out of the forest," she said. She struggled to maintain a blank face, to appear as if she wasn't surprised in the slightest to see a faerie standing in a tree.

Lachlan laughed. "I suppose it is. Today is a special occasion; we are all very much wide awake."

The girl seemed to hesitate before responding. Lachlan figured she was trying to decide if it was wise to continue such a conversation with him. "What occasion would be so special to have you all awake before noon?"

"The funeral of the queen. My mother."

"Oh."

That was all she said. Lachan had to wonder what kind of reaction he'd expected. Certainly not sympathy; he had no use for such a thing.

"You are not at the funeral?" the girl asked after a moment of silence. "If you are her son—"

"I shall get there eventually," Lachlan replied. He sat down upon the branch he'd been standing on. "Tell me your name, lass. Your voice is too beautiful to not have a name attached to it."

To his surprise, she smiled. "I do not think so, Prince of Faeries."

Clever girl.

"You wound me," he said, holding a hand over his heart in mock dismay. "An admirer asks only for a name and you will not oblige his lowly request? How cruel you are."

"How about a name for a name, then?" she suggested. "That seems fair."

Lachlan nodded in agreement. The girl could do nothing with his name. She was only human.

"Lachlan," he replied, with a flourish of his hand in place of a bow. "And you?"

"Clara."

"A pretty name for a pretty girl. Is there a family name to go with—"

"I am not so much a fool as to give you my family name," Clara said, "and I think you know that."

He found himself grinning. "Maybe so. Come closer, Clara. You stand so far away."

He was somewhat surprised when she boldly took a step forwards, half expecting her to decide enough was enough and run away.

Even careful humans give in to the allure of faeries, he thought, altogether rather smug. *It won't be long until I have Clara's full name.*

When Clara took another step towards him Lachlan noticed

that her eyes were green.

No, blue, he decided. *No, they're –*

"Your eyes," he said, deftly swinging backwards until he was hanging upside down from the branch. Lachlan's face was now level with Clara's, though the wrong way round. She took a shocked half-step backwards at their new-found proximity. "They are strange."

"I do not think my eyes are as strange as yours, Lachlan of the forest," she replied. "Yours are gold."

"Not so uncommon a colour for a Seelie around these parts. Yours, on the other hand...we do not see mismatched eyes often."

Clara shrugged. "One blue, one green. They are not so odd. Most folk hardly notice a difference unless they stand close to me."

"Do many human boys get as close to you as I am now?" Lachlan asked, a smile playing across his lips at the blush that crossed Clara's cheeks.

She looked away. "I cannot say they have."

"Finish your song for me, Clara. I'll give you something in return."

"And what would that be?" she asked, glancing back at Lachlan. Her suspicion over the sudden change of subject was written plainly on her face.

He swung himself forwards just a little until their lips were almost touching. "A kiss, of course."

"That's...and what if I do not want that?"

"Then I guess I leave with a broken heart."

Clara's eyebrow quirked.

"You do not believe me," he complained.

"With good reason."

"You really are a cruel girl."

The two stared at each other for a while, though Lachlan was beginning to grow dizzy from his upside down view. But just as he was about to right himself, Clara took a deep breath and began to sing once more.

There were four verses left of her Burns poem, about a ghost who appeared in front of the poet to lament over what happened to him in the final years of his life, and it was both haunting and splendid to hear. Lachlan mourned for the spirit as if it had been real, and wished there was more to the poem for Clara to sing.

But eventually she sang her last, keening note, leaving only the sound of the wind to break their silence. When Lachlan crept a hand behind her neck and urged her lips to his Clara fluttered her eyes closed. The kiss was soft and chaste – hardly a kiss at all – but just as it ended Lachlan bit her lip.

The promise of something more, if Clara wanted it.

The girl was breathless and rosy-cheeked when Lachlan pulled away. A rush ran through him at the sight of her.

"Tell me your last name," he breathed, the order barely audible over the breeze ruffling Clara's hair around her face.

She opened her eyes, parting her lips as if to speak and –

The sound of bells clamoured through the air.

Clara took a step away from Lachlan immediately, eyes bright and wide and entirely lucid once more.

"I have to go," she said, stumbling backwards to pick up her forgotten basket and cloak before darting away from the forest.

No matter, Lachlan thought, as he dropped from the branch to the forest floor. *I shall see her again. I will have her name next time.*

But he was disappointed.

Now he had to go to his mother's funeral alone, with no

entertainment to distract him from his grief when evening came.

Acknowledgements

Is this my first magical fantasy *not* based on a classic fairy tale? Oh my!

The first few chapters of this were hell to write, even with an extensive outline. It took ages for me to find the right voice and style. I blame the pandemic.

I've always wanted to write an original fantasy as opposed to one based on an existing fairy tale, myth or legend. I hope you enjoyed it! It was fun to have both a father and his daughter as main characters; the relationship between Edward and Charlie was super interesting for me to include (and, of course, their relationship with Serena). Exploring family as a theme (both blood-related and found family) is something I always enjoy doing.

Who was your favourite character? As I wrote Intended my favourite kept shifting between Charlie, Daniel, Kit and Edward, though it returned to Daniel most often. He's hopeless and I love him.

I'm awful at flowery writing but I wanted my writing about *flowers* in Intended to be pretty. My editors loved my floral descriptions so I hope everyone else did, too.

The ending of Intended was bittersweet but I couldn't have written it any other way. Although I feel bad for poor Kit...at least he'll be reunited with Daniel and Charlie at some point in the future! And then he'll bother them until the end of time ahahaha.

As with every book I'd like to thank my editor and best

friend, Kirsty, my partner, Jake, my lovely bunnies and of course everyone reading this. It's been a difficult ride but it was worth it.

Here's to the next one!

Hayley

ABOUT THE AUTHOR

Hayley Louise Macfarlane hails from the very tiny hamlet of Balmaha on the shores of Loch Lomond in Scotland. After graduating with a PhD in molecular genetics she did a complete 180 and moved into writing fiction. Though she loves writing multiple genres (fantasy, romance, sci-fi, psychological fiction and horror so far!) she is most widely known for her Gothic, Scottish fairy tale, Prince of Foxes – book one of the Bright Spear trilogy.

You can follow her on Twitter at @HLMacfarlane.

ALSO BY H. L. MACFARLANE

FAIRY TALE SHARED UNIVERSE:
BRIGHT SPEAR TRILOGY
PRINCE OF FOXES
LORD OF HORSES
KING OF FOREVER

DARK SPEAR DUOLOGY
SON OF SILVER (COMING 2023)
HEIR OF GOLD (COMING 2023)

ALL I WANT FOR CHRISTMAS IS A FAERIE ASSASSIN?!

CHRONICLES OF CURSES
BIG, BAD MISTER WOLFE
SNOWSTORM KING
THE TOWER WITHOUT A DOOR

OTHER BOOKS:
GOLD AND SILVER DUOLOGY
INTENDED
REVIVAL (RELEASE DATE TBC)

MONSTERS TRILOGY
INVISIBLE MONSTERS
INSATIABLE MONSTERS (COMING OCTOBER 2022)
INVINCIBLE MONSTERS (COMING 2023)

Thrillers
The Boy from the Sea

Rom-coms
The Unbalanced Equation
Courtney Can't Decide (release date TBC)

Short Stories
The Snowdrop (part of Once Upon a Winter: A Folk and
Fairy Tale Anthology)
The Goat
The Boy Who Did Not Fit